Frances P.

Neon Hemlock Press
www.neonhemlock.com
@neonhemlock

Collection Copyright © 2021

Unfettered Hexes:
Queer Tales of Insatiable Darkness
Edited by dave ring

Cover Illustration by Robin Ha
Interior Color Illustrations by Frances P
Interior B&W Illustrations by Matthew Spencer
Cover Design by dave ring
Interior Design by dave ring

Paperback ISBN-13: 978-1-952086-30-4
Ebook ISBN-13: 978-1-952086-31-1

UNFETTERED HEXES:
QUEER TALES OF
INSATIABLE DARKNESS

Neon Hemlock Press

UNFETTERED HEXES

queer tales of insatiable darkness

edited by dave ring

A Note From the Editor

THERE ARE INNUMERABLE reasons that readers and writers, queer and otherwise, might be drawn to witches and witchery. Among them, perhaps, are power and stigma, craft and community. I have always found it intoxicating how witches so often seize their otherness as a strength. I courted that feeling with this anthology. And yet, throughout the process of curating these tales, it quickly became apparent that I should stay wary of my own expectations, whether it be of those writers invited to take part, or of those whose stories were tendered for my consideration. More often than not, I discovered how seemingly familiar incantations might veer into strange cadences or take on unexpected syllables, and either way, I found myself chanting along. That was the most profound gift I found within these pages as an editor: being led by the hand to traverse unforeseen realities.

Just as witches have many faces, so too does the darkness. The darkness here cocoons as often as it constricts as often as it conceals as often as it consorts—regardless of its temper, it may be best to sinply give in to it. I suspect you, like me, will be the better for its ritual.

dave ring
July 2021
Washington, DC
On unceded Nacotchtank & Piscataway land

TALES

The Underworld as a Heart Meditation

IMANI SIMS

Dive into dark
discover what wraps
wrists a haloed

thread of tether
tucked neatly twixt
ventricles, vested vein:

unbroken exchange.

I swallow. Sweat
gathers in pits,
signals my discomfort

not ready to
admit this closeness,
this want, this

tension pool—gentle
swell of egress—

I always leave.

I always leave.

I

Always

Leave .

THE PASSING OF SINCLAIR MANOR, OR, THE HOUSE OF MAGICAL NEGROES

DANNY LORE

HONESTY IS IMPORTANT in these stories, so let me start with this: I missed the funeral of the last member of the Sinclair Manor coven. I could have made it; I'd already taken all my bereavement time from work, came back to (right outside of) town. It wouldn't have taken but twenty minutes to get dressed and driven up the hill to old Negro Manor, but you know what?

I couldn't be bothered to put on the suit.

Got the slacks on, and the white shirt, but didn't get to the point where I tucked it in. Thought about the shoes, shined up the way Auntie would have expected them to be, placed them up on the hotel room nightstand so I could examine them under the light.

They stayed on the nightstand when I left wearing a pair of Timbs (they were, at least, gray, which was almost appropriate). Got in my car, sat back, and it took more time to start the thing up. Nothing was wrong, long as you didn't consider my inability to process reality. On the seat next to me was a folder of paperwork that had been priority shipped to me back in New York.

I'd read it, unnerved by the legality of the language, the way my aunt had signed pieces of paper written in language she'd never use.Like most people in the Sinclair family tree, even from my offshoot, she'd never been fond of classic legal bullshit. That's not how Sinclairs, Graves, or any of the others made promises. But she had to, for this.

I was already late when I started driving to my aunt's funeral. The last member of the Sinclair manor coven.

Last one besides me.

"**C**ARTER?"
Walt's voice isn't gentle, hadn't ever been. There's a rough dustiness to it, a rasp that fades in and out of a familiar baritone. I'd left years ago, and only got to rock with Walt for a few years after our voices had settled into adulthood, but it was still alarmingly familiar.

I didn't turn around immediately, inhaling the way that Walt still said my name, just *like that*, even now. I exhaled nostalgia, imagined it dispersing around me, lingering around the gravestone at my feet. Pretended this was a form of magic to steady my nerves, even though magic hadn't been my bag for a hot minute.

"Fuck me, it is, isn't it?" Even in the dirt and grass, I heard Walt's steps as if across creaking, untended wood. "Why weren't you—"

"Traffic," I lied.

He knew my lie and didn't call me on it. "It's good to have you back."

"Oh, I ain't—" came out too fast, too awkward. I regretted it. In penance I finally faced him, bearing witness to the flinching that flashed across Walt's smooth, slender, dark features.

Unlike me, he'd dressed properly for the cemetery. Walt had grown from a slender wisp of a teenager up into a slender wisp of a man, the kind a well-placed gust could whip up and toss away. He swallowed. My eyes traced the space from his throat to his lips—fuck if those lips hadn't aged beautifully like the rest of him.

Except…except for something watery and weak in his brown eyes that I'd never seen before. Guess hurt did terrible things to a man's features.

"This is, uh, temporary," I explained. "Gotta settle some things, and then I'm gone."

Into the silence he offered, I said, "The house. Can't sell anything without…"

Walt swallowed, ashamed for having hope. I didn't tell him I understood, because I wasn't *that* thoughtless. "'Course. Figure you would've called. Or wrote." Walt made a face. "Guess you would have needed my address for that."

"Wait. Are you not staying…" I gestured up the road, where Sinclair Manor slept like a gothic Olympus.

"I've got a place. In town." I didn't believe it. "No one stays up at Sinclair since your aunt went into the nursing home." Walt never called it the manor, like everyone else who'd stayed inside of it. Never called it Negro Manor either, like everyone who feared it. "She was the last one to leave me."

He didn't mean to say it like that, and I allowed him the mistake without calling it out. After all, who and what Walt was aside from…whatever we were…wasn't something that we'd ever talked about as kids, or as teenagers. Besides, he was right— I had left him. Everyone else though?

Walt moved to stand next to me, staring down at Auntie's grave, positioned next to her sister Birdie's. My mother's. Someone had tried to clean them both, but they were covered in rude knife defacings and acidic paint, using *Witch* like it was a derogatory term, or *Black Magic Bitch* like she wouldn't have laughed.

The other headstones were the same. "No way all of y'all left the place empty."

Walt snorted, pushing at an errant weed with the toe of his shoe. "Who's all of y'all? No one in the bloodline around, so couldn't really stay up there."

"Reggie would have—"

"Reggie sold his family house two years ago. Said it was

getting too easy to die here. Something about the quiet."

It was that quiet that descended over us, as I felt the back of his hand near mine. I closed my eyes for a moment, because that was the one thing that almost summoned tears, the first ones I would have shed in or near town since I left. A finger of mine hooked around a finger of his and I didn't know who initiated the action.

"You sure it was the quiet…and not the Haywoods?"

"No, I'm not sure." Walt's voice *did* go soft and quiet at that, the way the breeze from up the hill stilled. Which one of us was responsible for *that,* I wondered? "Wouldn't be surprised though. They're trying to get their hands on everything in town."

"They *have* everything in town." The bitterness in my throat was everything the touch of his fingertips wasn't.

Walt looked me dead in the eyes. "Not Sinclair. That's all yours."

Was it, I almost asked but, just like sulfur announces the devil, the crinkling of dead leaves brought another voice behind us. A summoning, but one no one in Sinclair would ever wish on this world.

"Is that a goddamn *Graves?*" My name sounded so much fucking worse in Thomas Haywood's mouth. "Carter Owens Graves, in *my* town?"

The most aggravating thing about the man was *still* that put-on bullshit drawl of his. Now it was worse, damn near making me feel self-conscious about the way NYC had messed with my accent. Tommy's accent was *Southern*, because we were born and raised in Upstate New York, but this white boy's *drawl* was the affectation of a rich family bitter they were Northern rich. Bitter that it was Sinclair Manor looking down on the town, rather than the Haywood Plantation.

Nothing else had changed about that fraudulent piece of shit in the past decade, save his age, if that cocky tone of voice meant anything. He didn't even have the decency to show up in a suit; casual brown slacks, a beige polo shirt…looked more ready for the golf course than paying respects. I wasn't too sure if he could spell respect.

I stared down at my mother's gravestone. It was the second time I'd ever seen it, because me and Pops left right after she was put in the ground—hours afterwards, with my father driving while I asked some dumb bratty question about why we left her books behind, that I bet some spell in there could have teleported us to NewYork instead of the highway.

I tilted my neck, cracking a crick in it before turning. Walt shot me a look, butI couldn't avert my gaze in supplication to the town bully. I let my shoulders stay loose, I didn't shrink away.

Haywood noticed same time as Walt froze up beside me. It must have been a long-ass time since someone acted like a Graves in front of a Haywood.

The jackoff leaned into my personal space, his pasty ass mug squarely in step-the-fuck-off range. My fingers itched with an arcane heat I'd forgotten but came naturally standing with the family plots.Walt grabbed me, entangling his fingers in mine, as I started to curl my hands into fists. His palms cooled the heat for now.

Haywood guffawed. "Duke and Birdie's boy just rolling into town, huh?" Say it, I dared him internally. Give me a reason to…

I sucked my teeth, refocusing on Walt. "I should…get back."

"To Sinclair?" Walt asked carefully.

"Nah, he's staying at the highway motel, aren't you, Graves?" Haywood kept chuckling.

"I was talking to Walt." I barely kept from glaring at him. "I'm not staying at the manor. I'll, uh…see you."

I don't know which one of us caused the friction as I pulled my hand away, whether I hesitated, or he resisted, but I shoved that hand—hot with magic and cool with comfort—back into my pants pocket. "Peace, Haywood," I muttered.

He waited until I was a couple of feet away. "It's *Officer* Haywood, nowadays."

Shit.

"Expecting it to become Sheriff next election."

Double shit. He'd win too, with everyone he'd driven out. It didn't matter. I wouldn't be here. Maybe that was why my response was so sarcastic and hurried. "Congrats Officer."

"Birdie teach you to be that rude?" Haywood wasn't following me yet, but he raised his voice. I gritted my teeth, and didn't stumble at all until he continued, "Or was it Dea—"

"Watch yourself, homie," I warned. Didn't need him to start going off about my folks.

That got a big chortle. "Why?" Haywood mimicked something between my accent and a minstrel show parody, "You gonna try some of that black magic?" He dropped the accent, presumably because it was hard enough to maintain his own bullshit. "Way Wally tells it, the whole source of your power's gone and run off, or died in a fire. Shame about that."

My head snapped up and I stared back at Walt. "That right?"

Walt shook his head fast, pleading, explaining. "That's not what I, that's not—"

"Something like that." Haywood stretched every word, glad to have burrowed his way under my skin. "Anyway, you and I both know that without your people, you're nothing but some fake city boy passing through." There was a pause. "You *are* passing through, right?"

Haywood probably thought that came out as a threat, rather than a hesitation. I lifted my chin again. "If I was *nothing*, you wouldn't have come over to see me. You wouldn't have checked where I was standing. Fuck, if I was nothing, the manor would have mysteriously burned down years ago. Or, I don't know, maybe you would've moved in."

That did it; Haywood flinched.

That flinch got me acting real bold again. I chuckled. "That got you all fucked up, doesn't it? What, *did* you try to move in?" The bass in my voice wasn't intentional. "You try to ram your way in there and the house don't want your ass?"

Stupid, stupid, stupid, but it stunned Haywood into silence long enough for me to walk off towards my car. I tried not to think about having left Walt back there.

I WAS AT the door to my car before I saw Haywood's fucking department vehicle was parked near by. Since I didn't see the car, I didn't notice that his buddies were waiting in it.

I recognized each of them though, and even though they didn't speak much, I remembered what it sounded when each of them said "Negro Manor."

Perry wouldn't been in the year below me. His brother Jeremy, two years older. Old man Fuller's kid...Mason? Marco, something like that...he came out next and he'd grown up *big*, hadn't he?

And of course, coming down the road, Haywood and his laugh.

I didn't have back-up. See, Haywood was right: they *had* all "run off or died in a fire," or were frozen in fear further down the road because *Walt couldn't call anyone either could he*? There was no one left in Sinclair doing dark and solemn and joyous magics to call on, because those that survived had been left so scarred, like my father, that they'd died miles away with nothing to show for years of coven life.

There was no one left here but me and the sound of my folks' voices in my memory, telling me how important Negro Manor was, how it was gonna need me now that there was no one left to watch over it.

No one on my side, and four on theirs. Nothing that happened next qualified as a fight.

I wondered how long, exactly, Negro Manor had been emptied.

I tasted blood.

S INCLAIR MANOR LOOMED over me as I dragged myself out of the car. There was blood on my pants, and more of it on my shirt. Underneath, my torso ached as if my ribs were attempting to rise up, challenge those fuckers to another round—a round the rest of me wasn't ready for. My feet didn't want to move either, but I ignored the pulsating soreness of my left ankle in

order to get to the one place Tommy Haywood and his gang of
chucklefucks wouldn't follow.

I wasn't planning to go in my first day back, but it was far
closer than my hotel room. I'd wanted to be able to ease my
way in—into the area, into the town, into the manor...and then
grab Auntie's important papers so I could get out of this ghastly
fucking place.

But Haywoods loved to snatch away your options, so here I
was.

I spat blood on the grass—not the entrance, my mama taught
me better than to just give houses my blood—and dragged my
jacked-up ass into Sinclair for the first time in over a decade.

The cobwebs and furniture battered about me at first,
followed by a wave of dust that fell when I closed the heavy front
door. I coughed, choking on dust ghosts and silvery webbing.
The foyer's silence lacked stillness: a cold, sharp breeze did its
best to push me back where I'd come from. I felt the pressure of
palms in the chill.

Down the hall, silhouettes of a man and woman, the shapes
of a suit and top hat, a dress and bun, but little else. The lack
of features didn't mean they weren't staring me down. Had I
interrupted a memory? A party? A funeral? A philosophical
discussion? A stolen dalliance between lovers or a hushed
disagreement between siblings?

I swayed on my feet, accidentally shifting my weight to the
wrong one. I tumbled as the pain shot upwards, hitting my
side on a piece of furniture that was either for hanging coats or
offerings, and collapsing. I screamed, and it echoed, then once
more, this time more muffled than the last.

Had I spooked them? Were they disgusted by me? Either way,
they were whipped up in dust dancing in the distance hallway.
The remaining shadows belonged to furniture and dark corners,
not the remembered dead.

Besides, none of them were the right shape.

One of the house's many voices laughed through whistling
wind and colliding chimes. Bitterness played out through the
groan of oan out-of-tune pianos. I clenched my teeth and shook

my head.

"I know you're as interested in me showing up as I am about being here." The proposal left me in wheezes, rattling like the chimes. I brought up the image in my mind of the manor's dead, as they lived and as they died. I knew I should show them respect, but venom and copper tinged my voice. "But you *knew* this was gonna happen one day."

Something thumped and my bag—had I brought that with me?—slipped from my shoulder and smeared a dust-free spot into the floor. It pissed me off. "Look, those white folk out there? You know the ones, the live ones—they hate me, but they're *scared* of you. Give me a break, I ran out of other options."

The house answered with a scraping sound that didn't amount to words—but the chill stopped pushing at me.

I wanted to say thank you, but I couldn't. "You were nicer...at the graveyard...Walt..."

The manor, I think, caught my head as it all faded to black.

I FORGOT THAT when you're still, you can feel Sinclair Manor breathe.

No, not you. *I* can. I don't even think my whole family could do this; I'd asked cousins, even some of them who had the Sinclair name, and some of them looked at me like I was absolutely wild for suggesting it.

The magic of the house, you see, came from what the coven put in it. Our spells and parties built up all the energy in its walls. The house couldn't breathe. The house wasn't alive.

But my Auntie, the one whose gravestone hadn't yet been fucked over by some Haywood the Thirds or whatever? She shushed the cousins who told me I was wrong. She told me to ignore them when they made me cry, because she knew exactly what I meant.

When I wasstill, in a chair, or laying on the floor, and I closed my eyes, I felt the house inhale and exhale. I was a young teenager then, and imagined it was what waking up next to a man would feel like. When I was older, laying next to Walt, we breathed the same. It was the same rhythm, whether we were in the manor or in town, or laying in the grass—that was when I understood what he was, for the first time.

Sinclair Manor breathed, Auntie told me. The manor breathed, its heart beat, and, my Auntie assured me, it cried.

I WOKE in an overstuffed leather chair, sneezing as a cloud of dust imploded near me. My head rung and my chest felt like someone had carved out the insides of it like a gourd. Bright sunlight flooded the room.

I blinked, groaning as I sat up. This was one of the Manor's many studies, and while it didn't look the same without family coming in and out of it...I remembered it. Remembered how much bigger this chair seemed when my mother and her siblings sat in it.

When a silhouette appeared in the light, I thought it was the house's memory ghosts until the glare cleared.

No point in asking why Walt was there; I didn't make a habit of asking doors how they opened. "How long was I...?"

"Just overnight," Walt said. He tied the wall-long curtain off so it wouldn't fall back into place. His footsteps on the creaking, untended floor beat in time with my head. "I cleaned you up. Found a t-shirt in your bag."

I looked down and saw I was wearing a worn dark gray shirt. I touched my chest, and felt the bruising underneath the fabric. Fuck me. "Fuck off," I groaned, loud enough to make it clear that I wasn't, technically, talking to Walt or the manor.

Neither took it personally. "Thought you weren't coming here tonight." Was he mocking me? Walt had never been one for that. "Didn't like thinking about you alone in here."

I'd never been alone in the manor, and was fairly certain that Walt was the only one who ever had. Even now, dusty volumes tilted out of the shelves as if they were reaching out. The house did things like this when it felt neglected, and if I were to grab at the book, the house would fling it away. Strange, seeing it happen while Walt was in front of me.

Petty ass shit. That was all that was left here.

Walt was talking, but I missed it. "What'd you say, babe?"

I didn't realize I used the nickname until Walt cleared his throat awkwardly. "I was asking what you needed from me."

"I didn't say I did, unless I started talking in my sleep."

The tilted books dropped from the shelf in response.

I dragged myself up out of the chair. Fine, if Walt was going to be a brat about it, I wouldn't argue. Instead, I went to clean up the fresh mess.

"You said you needed something in here, right?" Walt pointed out.

"I didn't ask for your help." I didn't mean to have all these sharp edges, but it was the same kind of idiocy that got me in trouble with Haywood. Except taking that tone with Walt meant I couldn't look him in the eye anymore. "I just need some of Auntie's paperwork connected to the deed, and then I can get out of your space." That was louder than I intended, and echoed against the walls of my audience.

I ignored the names of the books I grabbed as I put them back on the shelves. Grimoires and clan histories, annotated tomes of family spells. I smeared the dust on one cover and realized I'd mimicked my father's handwriting that was within.

It's not the house that provides our power, read the near illegible scrawl, *but like Sinclair's foundation, it supports us.*

For all the good that support had done me. Done Birdie and Deacon Graves.

"You know he's coming back to the house, right?"

I shoved the book back on the shelf, letting the other covers smear what I'd scribbled. "Dead doesn't come back, you know that. The 'ghosts' are impressions, memories and emotions."

"I meant Tommy."

"Tom—Haywood?" I turned back to face Walt. "I don't wanna think about Haywood anymore than my ribs are forcing me to."

"I'm trying to help you clear out of here before he shows back up and does something even worse."

I leaned my forehead on the books on the shelves. I took deep breaths, both because I needed to and because if I paid close attention to my breathing I didn't have to feel the house's. "The Haywoods tried to burn this place *down*, remember Walt? He can't do worse." What could be worse than killing most of my family?

"Sure he could. Folks like him can always make it worse." Walt moved in close. I felt his shadow, the way the inches between both of us felt full of pressure begging to break. "And I know you well enough to know you talk a lot of shit, but you won't do anything about it."

I focused on the pressure of the spines against my skin. "Why weren't you here?"

"You know why."

"No, Walt, I don't," I snapped. I talked a lot of shit, but I had a lot of questions to ask as well. "If anyone should have been in this house, it was you. Not me, not Reggie, but *you*." A canyon's worth of emptiness opened between us as Walt jumped back. "Did you run off and leave Auntie alone in here, or did you wait until she was brought to the nursing home?"

One of us shuddered, or maybe it was the bookshelves, the rustling of the books on the shelves and the curtains. The latched windows snapped open, latches tinkling to the floor.

I breathed heavy, in time with the house, with Walt. It took a moment before I could see the tears in his eyes, because too many clouded mine.

"I stayed until I couldn't protect her anymore." Walt's voice was hoarse, rougher than before, hitching at times that felt unnatural. "And then she was gone, and the manor was empty. I can't even stand in here without one of you connected to the manor. Inside of it."

I knew it was true, even though no one had ever said as much. "So what happens if I sell?" When he didn't answer, I pivoted, slightly. "Where's the rest of the paperwork I need, Walt?" I was done pretending he didn't know where everything was in the manor.

He sucked his teeth. "Downstairs, in Birdie's old study."

I walked past him, each step agonizing for more reasons than bruised ribs.

"You won't be able to get in there."

"Why the fuck not?"

"I can't open the door."

"Bull*shit*, Walt!" I spun around at him. "There's not a single part of this house you can't—'

"I've been trying this whole time."

Walt was how a black ghost would really look, I thought. Pale brown skin, ashen and ancient. Had I not noticed, thrown by the sight of him after all these years, or had he felt like he had to use all of his energy to hide this from me? Which one made me the bigger monster?

He looked down at his palms. "I don't know if it's because your Aunt died, or because I've been away from here for months. Or maybe it's because of you wanting to be rid of this place, of me…" For a moment, I swore I saw the outline of the window and the bookshelves *through* him. "I haven't been the same since the fire, Carter. It keeps getting worse. I can't…move in here like I used to. I can't open the doors or feel the furniture on my skin." He laughed, mournfully. "I was able to get in last night because you left the door unlocked, and as much as the manor…as much as I missed you…this place can't lock up without your say-so."

I blamed the Haywood beating on why I needed to lean against the wall. I shook my head no, wanted to start a million arguments. None of them came to a head. I gestured to the shelves. "And that's why this keeps happening? The fits?"

"I can't stop them. Or start them. I don't even know if it's me anymore." Walt looked me in the eye. "It happened once or twice when your Aunt was here. She fixed it with some Sinclair magic." He shrugged. "I don't have that."

Neither did I, I wanted to say, but then I heard a big *slam* from down the hall. "The fuck was that?" Walt looked as bewildered as I was—of course, he just explained why he couldn't tell me anything—as it happened a second and a third time.

Running hurt like a bitch, but I was moving before I realized.

WALT AND I were teenagers making out in my bedroom
when we smelled the smoke. Downstairs, the music was
still playing loud enough to come up through the floor, old jazz
with the static of a vinyl record, my mom's favorite magical focus.

There was a party that night. *That* yearly party, where the
whole family tree, every ragged limb and grafted-on subset came
to the Sinclair Manor looking their best, with their best trunk
of magical tools in the backs of their minivans. The younger
generations cooing at the house they barely remembered, the
elder cousins smugly recounting their half-true memories of
running through the halls.

Before we'd gone upstairs, Walt had stood beside me,
repeating whispered truths and falsehoods as I tried not to
laugh. Both of us were shuffled around the room for a few hours,
being introduced to everyone as 'Birdie and Deacon's boy' and
'Oh, yes, he's the *house*, yes, I know he's not Gertrude, but a new
face means the bloodline is going strong." Occasionally my
Auntie would have to sharply add "Yes, his last name is Graves,
not Sinclair. I've got no problem with his mother's married
name and neither does the house," to some jealous relative who
squinted at me.

I didn't know I was considered important, and I'd never heard
of anyone named Gertrude. I asked Walt about it, and that was
when he led me upstairs.

He wasn't the first time the manor had been a person, he said,
and probably wouldn't be the last. Before Gertrude, there'd been
Rufus. It happened sometimes, when the Sinclair magic sank
deep in the ground and the framework. Rufus had even married
into the family (how that worked, I didn't ask, and didn't care).

Why now?

Walt told me the first thing he remembered, in his whole
existence, was the sound of me, five years old, running and
laughing in the halls, my father chasing after me. He heard
me tell my father I loved the manor more than anything in the

world, and my father said that was good. We should love our roots, our home.

Walt told me he became alive when he heard I loved him. So I kissed him. It wasn't my first kiss, but it was the best one, the most important one, and in the seconds we separated for breath, the whole house gasped in time with us. The music downstairs was louder, the laughter and magic my folks were trying to weave—I didn't remember what, couldn't care what—felt stronger, buzzed through my veins just like Walt did.

And that was when the smoke hit.

HAYWOOD AND HIS ILK were standing on the expanse of land in front of the manor. I opened the door, nearly tumbling out onto Perry and Jeremy. The two of them moved back, barely in time, and I caught myself on the outer wall.

I locked eyes with Haywood. He'd brought a mob to bang on my door, but didn't have enough of a spine to stand in the doorway. I felt bile as my head spun and my fingers warmed.

"Figured out why you're here, Graves!"

My eyes stung from a dozen bright things: torches, in the hands of all of Haywood's supporters. It lit their skin a sickly orange, never getting close enough to singe it black. Haywood's face was framed by the light of several torches, or maybe my gaze was so drawn to him that it just felt that way. I grimaced. "Did you now?"

"Can't have your type moving back into Negro Manor, Graves."

My lips parted wordlessly for a moment, my mouth dry and tasting of smoke. I didn't know which of his words were more offensive to me.

"Nobody's moving back into Sinclair manor, Tommy." Walt's voice was at my ear before I felt him behind me, his hand at the small of my back. "So why don't y'all just turn and head back to town."

It wasn't a brave declaration, but Haywood flinched in surprise as if it were. "I know you're not telling me what to do, Wally.

You're lucky you haven't been run out of town yet."

He scowled, taking a few more steps forward. I laughed, and I don't know if stepped back, but I felt the pressure of Walt's palm increase.

I laughed, but suddenly I remembered that there had been a Gertrude and a Rufus before him, whose names I had to learn and my heart skipped a beat: Could Walt defend against that? If they came at him with punches and torches, at his flesh and blood and beautiful lips, and he wasn't in the house, what would happen? Would he feel it, would the house feel it? Would he vanish?

"You don't get to laugh at me, you witch freak," Haywood growled, closer than he had been.

The windows on the second floor of the manor burst open at the same time, each and every one of them.. The mob lurched back. Haywood hesitated and Walt's fingers curled into a claw or a fist on my back before flattening back out.

"Witch freak?" I choked out. "What, black magic bitch too many syllables for you today?"

Again, Walt tried to save the moment. "Carter wants to sell, Tommy. He wants it to be over." Walt almost made it through those sentences without a stutter. "So if you all," he raised his voice a little, talking more to the mob than to its increasingly mortified leader, "head home, give this a couple of weeks, it's *all* over. You won't have to worry us up here ever again."

The mob muttered, angry and confused. I don't know if I cared what their actual opinions were, except in that I wanted Walt and I to walk away from this. Whether it was Walt's pleas or fear of what the house was capable of, it didn't matter to me. I wanted it to be done, just like Walt had said.

But Haywood was recovering. "You think we trust a word that comes out of your mouth? *Over?* Your kind has been running roughshod over my town from before my daddy's time. With your curses, and parties, all smug up on this hill. We were doing just fine with you gone, and you don't get to come back."

"You're right," I said softly.

THE FAMILY who could work with incantations tried to throw up shields, block the burning of the house and the children. And as the fire raged on, the manor did what it could. It flung open doors and windows, burst its own pipes to rescue those that it could.

The house could push and prod us all it wanted, but it couldn't force us to move in any direction, not without shutting doors and making things worse. The house couldn't stop smoke inhalation as people clawed their way out of the building, as they shouted for each other.

Walt was speechless, breathless, gasping and struggling to keep up with me as we made our way down stairs. I didn't know if he was in pain, if he felt the heat, didn't know if the bubbled burn on an arm was from a flame or a reflection of the house itself. But I knew that if we couldn't find my folks we'd be dead. So I grabbed him by the hand and ran, shouting for my mom, my pops. Switched to their names—Birdie and Deacon, Deacon and Birdie.

The front door had been barricaded from outside—later on, I'd find out the angry mob had used rocks from the quarry to hold it shut, things the house couldn't control.

I needed to do *something*, because I wasn't going to die, or get killed by whoever it was outside.

There was a voice I didn't recognize—no, I recognized it, but it didn't *belong* here. A bullshit faux-drawl from down a hall. Walt must have heard it or registered my reaction to it because he gripped my hand hard.

I stopped shouting my parents' names. I let go of Walt's hand. I ran down the hall.

"Tommy *fucking* Haywood."

Another open window, except Tommy had taken a tumble trying to get in the house. Trying to *get in*. Fear and rage collided, and when I should have been trying to use that window to get out I came at him, shoving him against the wall. My hands ached with a heat that wasn't from the fire, a heat that I'd never known before.

I had him by the collar, a collar whose threads curled and scorched when my fingers touched them. He winced as my knuckles touched his chest. I raised my fist. "The *fuck* are you doing?"

I knew, somehow, that it was him and his folks at the lead here. His family that still managed to look at every branch of the Sinclair family as if they were better than us. As if we didn't deserve the manor, or the magic, or even to exist.

For the first time, though, I saw more fear than derision in Tommy Haywood's eyes, the kind of fear the rest of the white folk in town had learned to have. And it wasn't the house or a Sinclair that it was directed at, but a teenaged Graves. I let him go, not because I didn't want to hit him, but because I heard my name in the crackling of wood, in the low scratch of Walt's voice, in the way that the doors opened and slammed shut suddenly in harmony.

The house needed to save as many of us as it could. We could take revenge for what was done to it later.

But as I climbed through the window, as I ran, I heard Haywood's words: "I needed to see you witches burn myself."

HAYWOOD LOOKED SHOCKED. "Excuse me?"

Walt's hand suddenly jerked from my back, and I heard the crying creak of the windows slowly swaying above my head. The rustle of vines and ivy on the walls as the very foundation shuddered.

"You're. Right." I stretched the words deliberately. "We've been running roughshod over this town for a long, long time. Before you." I stood straighter. "Before your daddy."

I glanced over my shoulder at Walt, who was confused for a moment, before I nodded. He put his hand on the archway of the door. I'd always felt the house under my feet, under my palm. I could feel it breathe and react to me, but I'd never realized before how much I could feel Walt in the house, how Walt's pulse flowed through the heat of my hands.

It warmed my bruises. My family's magic wasn't because of the house, my dad had written, but it fed the house. And the house, in turn, supported us, down to its very foundation.

"So if we've been here so long, and the house has been here… what makes you think that you'll outlast it?"

Haywood's eyes went wide, and the torch flames *flared*. Some of the mob dropped theirs, but the grass didn't burn.

No. I didn't *let* the grass burn. I was too young during the first fire, didn't know what it felt like to have spent a *decade* burning with this, with this seething ember of hatred, but I knew it now. And maybe it wasn't the magic that my Aunt or my parents would have wanted, necessarily, but it was a magic that the house and I *knew* instinctively.

The house, I realized, had been angry because I broke my word. Because I never came back to support it. To get revenge. But now that I was here…

The flames grew larger now, not burning the mob but merging, taking shape. Silhouettes that triggered a memory—of a pair of ghostly shadows in the hallways. Not ghosts, not mere memories like I'd thought but…

"Gertrude…" Walt gasped behind me, and I knew the other was Rufus. Fiery giants towering, making the mob run. "What's happening?"

"I've got an idea," I admitted. "But I'm gonna need your help, Walt. You trust me?"

I felt Walt's sudden absence and for a moment I panicked; had that been too much to ask of him?? In front of the house, the flaming giants moved towards each other, twisting like dancers, spinning like a tornado, until there stood only one. One slender sharp flame. Who Haywood knew all too well from the way he turned, stared, and stumbled back even closer to me.

I grinned at Haywood, and hoped the fire lit me like an onyx skull. "You wanted to watch burning witches, right?"

His face was frozen in fear, his hand reaching up to his chest. But Haywood wouldn't die here.

The ignited giant Walt looked back at me with eyeless flames for a face, tilting his head and waiting for my instructions.

There were so many I could give. I could burn the whole town. That would be a fitting revenge, a patch of nothingness where empty cowards once slept. My fingers ached to do it. Or I could have them walk the streets, stride past the graveyard to protect the resting places.

But I had a better revenge.

The fiery giant collapsed, a sudden flood of heat, pouring back into the ground. No longer the shape of a person, but rather a river, a moat of flame encircling the house. I watched the mob all run, let them find patches of air without fire to leave. It didn't matter, as long as Haywood stayed watching.

I crouched down beside him as a flame wall rose. "You and *your* kind are never going to take this house from me, you hear? You'll have to get them through all that," I gestured as the flame burned blue, "and *then* I'll be waiting for you. The house'll be waiting for you. So have your Sheriff-hood or whatever. Go running back to your office. But know that it doesn't matter anymore because you'll never be the big man in town ever again."

When I stood, I marveled at the way nothing hurt. I turned my back on Haywood's whimpering form—if he didn't move soon, the flames would hasten his exit.

I went back inside. I took a deep breath as the door closed behind me. I felt the heartbeat of the house thunder, as it exhaled in sync with me.

"I think...for now," I finally said, and I don't know if it was minutes or hours later, "it's over."

Walt's arms were cool as he came up behind me, wrapping them around my waist and dropping his chin on my shoulder. We looked out over the town, the manor looking on behind us, and for the first time in a long while, I knew what a homecoming was supposed to be.

LOVE AND LIGHT

H.A. CLARKE

THE HOUSE WAS TERRIBLE. It wheezed at the end of a block in a sooty city neighborhood, the worst and most crumbling corpse-colored brownstone in a row of remarkably bad lots. It looked hewn from a chunk of moonrock. Lichen bloomed in the façade's chipped crevices and greasy smoke peeled from a gooseneck chimney at odd hours. The gate latch had been bashed in and the barred door couldn't shut right, hung open and creaked with the breeze. It was a vile, peaky structure and it was not built to last. The mortar flaked in veins, obscured the boundary between the outside and the in. Pink light and snare oozed through the cracks.

Witches lived inside the house. Lovers, three of them—his name Lola, hers Vivian, theirs Saltpeter, each a quarter century old under different names on their legal papers. They worked constantly with scant documentation to show for it. Prickly gruesome dykes the lot of them, or persistently lovely in Lola's case, each more horrible than the dyke preceding. Together they were sometimes seen venturing out to have picnics by the city's obsidian superfund river, to shoplift hosiery to rip in warehouses after midnight, to trespass, demonstrate, blaspheme, brawl, and play, and to commune with others of their kind, hold mass in grassy underpasses, conduct their work. They were known for their work and were rarely without it. They seldom went outside.

Vivian had left the house for the sake of consensually robbing a liquor store, which is to say the women who worked the counter had smoked with Vivian at some point and gave her the bottle for free. She carried it in her arms like a baby. Vivian wore a faux leopard coat to her knees and ruched tulle gloves, slunk rather than strolled, kept rolling her bony left shoulder as she kicked wide the broken gate. She'd slept on it funny the night previous and it felt sour and over obvious now. She whittled the paper of a sucker's stick between her stained blue teeth, and the stick dipped in her lips as she craned her neck, peered at the house's shifting roof top. It was crowned with dappled pigeons, hundreds of them, and something else. A long, living shape. She thought what she saw was the suggestion of Lola's body, his movement against the sunlight, slow and easy. Vivian considered wolf whistling but thought vaguely he might fall if she did, and she couldn't have that. Feeding pigeons trail mix was one of Lola's most sacred loves, and she couldn't kill him during something so abjectly adorable. She couldn't kill him ever, probably, even when he left his dishes by the sink and wore his boots in the bedroom. He was too precious. Even Vivian had lines.

She tucked the bottle under her arm and took off her earring, on which dangled her ring of keys. She pinched them between thumb and forefinger and approached the door.

A note hung there. It read: INSPECTION TERRIBLE TRESPASSERS MUST BE GONE ASAP OR WILL CALL COPS WILL BE IN TOUCH YOURS TK.

Vivian blinked. She glanced up in Lola's direction, his solid dark silhouette cut against heaven, and sliced the note into ribbons with the key's teeth. The confetti shreds fell, and she stomped across them as she unlocked the door and shouldered it wide. It banged against the opposing wall. She seethed in the threshold a moment, ribs working in the void inside her jacket. The crash sound of door on wall echoed in her head.

Dust sparkled in the air. Music shifted from the unleased apartment that she and her girlfriends had furnished for the sake of whomever needed it being able to use it, the familiar honeyed kick and swell of doom metal, and swirled with a low roar of layered human speech. Spiderweb fishnets clung to the crown molding, the walls gleamed a lurid bottle green. Breath came in thick, clung to her small palate, smelled spiced and like copper.

She'd dimpled a little hole in the wall with the doorknob.

Vivian tossed her keys in the air and caught them, squeezed them. The tricky edge bit the heel of her hand. She curled her lip, and the pain came in quick, bright, tommy gun bursts, like fairy lights being crushed deep in the wells of her eye sockets. Light and color clapped. She hissed an exhale. Her grip slackened. She swaggered across the foyer, keyring now dangling from a crooked fingertip, and pressed her broken hand to the hole she'd made in the wall.

"In lux Luciferis," she said.

Something turned. Hearing this the wall drank of her, the dimple rippled, and the surface smoothed and was unblemished once more, content with its drop of her body. A shimmer unfurled in space around her head. Her skull gave off light that bled through the part of her pomade-slick pin curls, cast shadows through the bannister bars that fell on the opposing wall. The pain ebbed, and the wound was gone. She rubbed her hand against her jacket, stroked the splotched teddy bear fur there, and she and her oil slick aura traipsed up the stairs to her apartment and kicked the door.

Stillness, silence. The door was a door and stayed that way, didn't move or instantaneously become sentient and helpful.

She leaned her forehead against the wood. It smelled like Lola. Lola must have fixed it at last. This house was more bodily cosmic superglue than building material at this point. She glanced down at the keys in her hand, tried to gather the will to make her hand move. Exhaustion clouded her, made her grip clammy, her fingers chill and boxy stiff. She cleared her throat, called, "Babe?"

A beat.

The knob jittered, and the door pulled in. Vivian staggered forward, gravity catching up with her, and fell into Saltpeter's waiting arms.

Saltpeter was naked, the horn-rimmed glasses aside, and covered in swirls of red paint. They put a hand between her shoulder blades and patted her absently, frowning, said, "Oh, you got more wine. Thank goodness."

"Were you mid-beholding?" Vivian shuffled them both inside, skimming her tongue over her teeth. It was warm within the apartment's boundaries, the space seething with acid-bright houseplants and a mist of churning frankincense and weed. Candles grew like mushrooms on every flat surface. A half-finished Jenga game sat beside a clamshell ashtray. Mirrored walls, mirrored ceiling, rugs more string than woven surface. Vivian thrust down the wine bottle on a beaten leather chaise and threw herself across a duct-taped wingback armchair, keys discarded somewhere on the floor between hither and thither, and scrubbed her hands over her face. Her makeup clung to her heartlines. It'd be thoroughly fucked up by the time she was done, more so than it'd been when she'd initially put it on. She cleared her throat. "If the cosmos is frothing inside you right now this very moment, I can wait to ruin things until after you're done."

"You didn't interrupt anything. I was waiting in the wings," they said dryly. They plucked the bottle up and brought it close to their face, examined the label. "Hm. This is three steps to the left of being syrup. I am unsure if the contents of this bottle legally constitute wine, Viv. This is candy."

"The Devil loves candy," she hissed.

They answered with a thin throaty sound like, *fair enough.* They glanced up at her. "How do you plan on ruining things?"

"Grim tidings. Dispensing knowledge."

Their brows shot up and they laughed, a single fluttery kick of their diaphragm. They folded their thumb over the cork. "Irony's delicious. Alright, let's go. Bestow upon me facts and ruination."

"Tim Kilpatrick found out about the commons. He's pissed."

The smile that had been lingering on Saltpeter's face
dropped. They blinked, adjusted their glasses. Swigged their
words around their mouth for a moment before they asked, "Was
it an eviction notice?"

"Nothing so formal or spine-having, no. He said he'll be in
touch. Like he's the fucking Godfather." Vivian folded her hands
over her stomach, eyed a dartboard on the side of a bookshelf.
She was terrible at darts. "What are we going to do?"

"Contact housing advocates and brush up on squatters'
rights," they said vaguely, eyes unfocused. They rubbed circles
on the cork with their thumb. "Tell people who stay in the
commons. See if clients can spread it around fast. I don't know.
I've got no fucking idea."

"A question for your beholding." She covered her eyes with
her hands.

There was a thump, then the whine of a window closing.
From behind her, to the right: "Want me to just call him?"

"I don't know if this is a man with whom rational negotiation
can occur. He's a grifter. Categorically landlords care fuck all
about ethics and compassionate rationality, and I don't know if a
phone call would be enough to sufficiently bamboozle him into
relative decency," Saltpeter said. A pause. "Lola, why like this?
Why not the door? Why?"

"Hello Vivian," Lola said, breezing right past his girlfriend's
chiding in favor of flashing his girlfriend a winning smile.
Vivian could *hear* him smiling, could hear it curling the edges
of his voice. She split her fingers and peered in the window's
direction, and there Lola sat on the sill, lace curtains billowing
in at either side of him. It gave him the look of having wings.
He wore torn denim and a pale shirt unbuttoned to his sternum,
the sleeves cuffed, or rather smooshed, above his elbows.
Rough boots, snowy piercings in his brows, through his bridge,
in infinite notches up his ears. He looked between the two of
them and nodded, folded his hands in his lap. "I tried to fix the
showerhead, but it would've taken more blood than I can give
right now, so I guess we'll be sponge bathing 'til our next client
comes round. Anyway, Saltpeter's going to perform a grand

beholding soon. I did their glyphs. That's why they look so nice."

"I noticed," she said. "Exquisite. Top of the line tiddy glyphs, love. Must say, though, I'm backing Saltpeter up, here—I don't know what calling the fucking landlord would accomplish."

"Communication," Lola said. He slid off the sill, shook a hand through his sickle curls. "Always good. I would like to at least attempt working shit out man to man before anything else, and besides that, I want to see if he's got a worker hired for the shower situation."

"This is far more fucking dire than the shower situation," Saltpeter said.

"I know." Lola shrugged. He reached down his shirt, produced his phone from his cleavage, and was texting before Vivian could think of a more compelling argument than, *this is stupid and life is torture.* His thumbs flew, knuckle tattoos dancing, then glanced up and smiled with teeth. "Well, look at that. He's in his office. I'll run over and talk to him now."

Saltpeter and Vivian glanced at each other. They both glanced back at Lola.

He was on his feet. He crossed the room, ducked under veiny green fronds, ran his finger along the record player's edge as he passed it. He buttoned his shirt up, rolled the wrinkly sleeves down, thrust his phone in his back pocket and put his hands on his hips. The keys jangled on his carabiner. He nodded at Vivian, then at Saltpeter, and folded his collar down. "Happy beholding, tell him I say hello, I love you, I love you, I'll be back home soon."

He left without another backwards glance and Vivian and Saltpeter were left staring in his wake.

A moment passed. Downstairs someone laughed hard enough for the sound to bubble up through the floorboards, along with the rumble of a baseline. Saltpeter took their glasses off. They folded them gingerly, placed them in an ashtray. They massaged the bridge of their nose, kneaded the dents the cushions had left, and lifted the bottle of wine. "The beholding," they said. "Would you like to come with me?"

Vivian felt grimy. Spent frustration caked in her pores and

she wanted to scour herself down with steel wool, wanted to be drenched in something brutally astringent. She did not feel her ritual best, but when she'd first beheld him she'd been on the brink of crossing irreversible lines, she'd been worse then, and still light fell over her. Light came unto her when she was tangled and matted and vile. Still, it felt weird, now. Disrespectful to herself as much as him. She preferred his illumination when she looked less like a bruised piece of fruit.

"It's alright if you'd rather not. I can go alone. That was the plan," they offered. "You can get some rest. Whatever bullshit Tim's about to put us through, it won't happen in the next half hour."

"No," she sighed. She peeled off her false lashes and stuck them above her top lip, groaned, stretched, and nearly spilled off the armchair. She pulled herself upright, pushed the coat from her shoulders. She was gooseflesh in her bustier but that was fine, felt less constricting. She wrinkled her nose. "Wallowing won't do me any good. I'd rather see, I think."

Saltpeter tried a smile. It faltered but the thought was nice.

She stood and drew the curtains, snuffed out the afternoon. It was dark, their lamps gave off odd hues, and her reflection in the walls looked ghastly. She leaned into that, reveled in it. Contorted her face to look more haggish. She imagined herself a harpy, belly and thighs wrecked with slippery feathers, vicious pink raptor claws erupting from her ankles, nails splintering the hardwood, bag wing fingers stretching ligaments and filling the room with translucent vein-laced skin, breasts and neck and human mouth excruciating to behold. Still pierced, still painted, unfamiliar and defiant of comfort. She held this in her heart as she struck a match. She lit the candles while Saltpeter rolled back the rugs.

The sigil beneath had long been cut into the floor. Saltpeter uncorked the bottle, the air twinged with cloying sweet tannins, and they poured wine onto the winding shallow grooves. The sigil filled. By candlelight flicker it looked like something that had come from Saltpeter's body, thinner than blood but as vital. Saltpeter plucked a snuff box from a side table, lifted it to their forehead, then leveled it by their sternum. They walked into the sigil, waited at its core with the box shut.

Vivian joined them there. She did not peel her clothing off, stayed clasped and zipped, felt prouder that way. She stood toe to toe with Saltpeter. She looked at them, plunged into world-consuming eye contact, and their reflections flew backwards, the room expanded, the structure ballooned around their shoulders and rushed past perception. The room clung close to her shoulders, was everywhere and nowhere. She saw Saltpeter, saw herself reflected in them. They saw her with their eyes half shut. They didn't blink. Candlelight and the anemic din of lamp bulbs cast shadows along their browbone. Between them the box pulsed.

Her hands moved, and she opened it.

There was fruit inside, and the glint of an instrument.

She plucked up the fruit and Saltpeter's lips parted. Their tongue was impossibly red and impossibly long, she could've tied back her hair with it. She offered the fruit, small and beaded for them, and they received it without dropping their gaze. Her throat prickled. Something stirred in her gut. She brought the fruit to her own lips after and at once it became fuller, richer, filled her palm with noticeable weight and gave off a dark and tart perfume. She broke its skin between her teeth. The flavor cut through her. It zinged in her occipital bone, seeped electric sourness along her jaw and down the seams of her throat. She swallowed the meat, and as it descended, Saltpeter wet their lips and spoke.

"We are within ourselves, we are ourselves, we are bodies inside of a room. We are one another's bodies, our bodies share particulates, we share matter between our bodies and with the substance of a room. We are a room inside a room. A room is a room inside a room. We contain each other. We are within and without each other. I am Saltpeter and she is Vivian, we interlock and are inextricable, we are ourselves and each other, we stand within this room and are this room. We are this structure. We are stitches of thread enmeshed. We each are multiple. We spill and shuffle endlessly. We are independent and autonomous, reliant and distinct. I look at Vivian and I see myself. In the spiral current of our looking, without hierarchy or polarity, is you. We call upon you and draw you to this room. We call the beast incarcerated, the being on fire, he who reviles human as servant-enforcer of god and languishes for having glorified human the beholder, knowing, unkneeling, without fetters of innocence and submission. We call you who is an amalgam of every infinite sex, whose prismatic gender is more elastic than can be quantified with speech. You of the body, you of the room, you who is me, who is Vivian. I conjure you serpent of the flow. Come between us that we might look upon your brightness and learn of you. Sit lux mihi dux."

The Devil in the likeness of an alchemical journal sketch came between Vivian and Saltpeter. His eyes were enormous, scalding pink with pill-shaped pupils turned clockwise, parallel with the lash line of his rounded bruisy eyelids. His fur had crow feather iridescence. It looked silky, compelled stroking. Wicked red twists of horn jutted from his crown, and below stretched a body with human glow and fat, a scaled belly, long feathered thighs. A barbed tail stirred the air between Vivian's ankles. His breath came soft. His tattoos rustled, warped across his skin and reformed. When he spoke, light spilled from the back of his throat. He said, his voice gentle, "What would you like to know?"

"I am proud to stand beside you, I am grateful for your light. Our landlord found out that we've broken the locks on the downstairs unit. He learned that we've made that space a common one. He wants the people boarding there gone, and he might want us gone with them. I seek to protect this space and the people inside it. You've taught us how to make another body of this building, how to upkeep it with the material of our flesh, and my pulse is inside these halls because of this. Vivian's blood, Lola's blood, the blood of our clients who contribute their blood to the keeping of this house in exchange for services performed. Landlords have power. I am unsure of myself in the face of it. I worry about how things might unfold," Saltpeter said.

"As above, so below," Vivian said, more for punctuation than clarification. She thrust her chin out. "Our peril is an echo of yours, if not smaller and meaner."

"Lend me the box," the Devil said.

Saltpeter lifted it, and the Devil took it from them. Its lid yawned open.

Vivian reached inside.

"For Saltpeter," the Devil said.

It was an albino peacock feather, longer than could feasibly fit inside the box unbroken. Vivian withdrew it in one smooth motion, but she had to stretch her arm to its fullest before she glimpsed the feather's moony head. It was an odd trick, identifying objects only with periphery vision. She had to keep her eyes on Saltpeter. She furrowed her brow and they nodded, so she ran the feather up the seam of their sternum. Its tendrils tripped the caked paint there. Saltpeter squirmed, their face twitched, but they kept their composure. "I feel," they said. "I am."

"For Vivian," the Devil said.

She twisted the feather around and the plume shrank, spiked like starlight, pinwheeled in space. Saltpeter took the Wartenberg wheel from her. They held it delicately, lifted it high enough to examine it without pulling their attention fully from Vivian's face. They frowned, sucked their cheeks in.

Vivian squared her shoulders.

They brought the wheel from the spoon of her clavicle down her breastbone, made a red dotted line on her skin. The pain crackled. It sparkled like tinsel, and her body brightened, she was seething and ecstatic with herself, inside herself. She caught her breath, said, "I feel and I am."

"In the box I will provide a tool for you to wield against lords and tyrants. Its use will reveal itself." The Devil extended the box, and Saltpeter returned the instrument to it. The box closed, light frothing under its lip, and the Devil lifted his head. Steam rose from his pink nostrils. He said, "There is someone at the door."

Vivian's attention snapped up. The door opened, the Devil became vaporous and vanished from sight, and Saltpeter caught the box just before it smashed to glitter against the floor.

Lola careened inside. He lurched when he stepped, shoulders heaving, the color gone from his face. He had one hand pinned between the meat of his opposing upper arm and his ribcage, and as he pitched nearer Vivian saw the wetness on his sleeve, the splotches. His hand was open, bleeding. He sweat like a candle drips wax.

Vivian moved first. She darted out of the sigil and got her hands on Lola's shoulders, fought for his gaze. Her head was on fire, still zinging from ritual, and her eyes were stretched so wide they could've sprang forth and taken orbit. "Lola, baby," she breathed. "Hey, what's—"

"Saltpeter, get dressed," Lola said. He shook under Vivian's hands. "He's coming up, he'll be here any second."

"What?" Vivian rubbed her thumbs into his shoulders, bounced on the balls of her feet. "Who's coming up? Slow down, sweetheart. You're bleeding, what happened?"

"Tim Kilpatrick slammed my hand in the door," he said.

Vivian's tongue flopped dead in her mouth. She stared at him. Something atavistic and pre-moral eeled around her gut. "Beg pardon?"

"I tried to explain and he," Lola said, "he started yelling, he got up from his desk and howled in my face, I stood up, I tried to calm him down, I backed up and he pursued me, I bolted for the door and he drove his shoulder into it, I don't know what I said, I was explaining the commons, I was explaining how the house was crumbling and how we did the upkeep ourselves, I tried, he kept screaming and screaming and I loped all the way here, it's bleeding a lot I think but I can't bring myself to look at it. He followed after me. He followed me."

The front door slammed downstairs.

Saltpeter had shrugged on Vivian's leopard coat, buttoned it. It fell to the back of their knees. "That's assault," they said as they opened the snuff box. "Lola, I am so sorry, and I will do my damndest to make sure he's—"

"What's in the box?" Lola leaned into Vivian and she put her arms around him, cradled the back of his neck. His pale shirt was a gradient of pink and vile maroon. None of them had insurance. There was a syncopated *BAMBAMBAM*, the battering of oxfords on a rickety staircase.

"A faucet," Saltpeter said.

"What?"

Saltpeter held the faucet, as might be attached to a bathtub, in their hands. They rolled it in their palms, bewilderment plain on their face. They must've retrieved their glasses at some point. They sat crooked on their nose. They looked over the silver snakehead faucet, then at Vivian, at Lola, at Tim Kilpatrick twitching in their doorway.

The dykes held still.

Tim Kilpatrick shuffled inside. He was a thin sallow man, youngish, unremarkable to the point of uncanniness. His suit jacket hung off his frame, obscured the shape of his body. It was too light to be navy. His eyes were too light to be blue. His mouth opened and shut, chewing his curses before he spoke them, and he scanned the room's perimeter, huffed in all the textures and florid lush colors in one gasp. He trampled the sigil's edge. His nose wrinkled. He looked down, saw the outline he'd crossed, and looked up at the tenants with a rage indescribable. Language escaped him. He sputtered a moment, bristling, and then managed with great spray: "You fucked up the fucking floor."

Vivian blinked. A smile broke over her, and a great rush of knowing. She looked at the faucet in the hands of her lover, at the bloodied beloved tucked against her neck, then back at her landlord. "Are you here to fix the shower?"

"I'm here to call the cops. You'll be on the street in a week, you'll be charged for the damage you've done to my property, I'll," he panted, "I'll seek compensation for the damage to my reputation done by your little party suite downstairs, I swear to fucking God."

"You haven't called the cops yet," Saltpeter said. "To be clear."

Lola sucked in a hard breath.

Tim swayed for a moment. He bashed his hands up and down

his chest, then over his thighs and the flat of his ass, searching for a phone with which to kill them.

Saltpeter locked eyes with Vivian.

She smiled wider.

They dove forward and cracked the faucet against Tim Kilpatrick's jaw.

The metal struck the biochemical apparatus of his mouth and stuck there. Momentum carried him, his head twisted around and teeth scattered like pearls off a necklace, clattering across the floor, dissolving in the sigil's wine grooves, but the faucet didn't make a full arc, couldn't. The cylinder bled into him. It folded into the muscle tissue, distended his jaw hinge. His cheek warped, rippled around it. The eye jumped wild in its socket.

"Oh," Saltpeter said.

"Lola," Vivian said. "Do you want to sit down awhile?"

"Mm." He peeled himself from her, took his bad hand and squeezed hers with it. The pain made his face blotch green. He kissed her forehead and took a few steps away from her, heaved himself down on the leather chaise. He looked at the faucet man, then looked at his girlfriends, then at his own reflection on the ceiling. "Ave."

Vivian lunged. She struck a hand against Tim's stomach, Lola's blood on her hand Maraschino bright against his blue blazer, and she drove his rind inward, flattened him, bowled him out, pressed until the skin of his belly kissed the skin of his back. His organs maybe reformed with mercurial flexibility, or perhaps inside of him was a slushy mess of jam. Vivian did not give a fuck. Inspiration sang in her. Light made a sculptor of her and she moved her hands, made a crater of him. Saltpeter moved across from her, seized his arms and shoved them inwards, turtled them in on themselves. Vivian pulled his flat torso wide, beat him like clay, kneaded him. Saltpeter crunched his shins into his thighs, displaced the spare weight into the basin. She and they brought the head down together. She bit her tongue, spat at him, and his features foamed and then smoothed, subsided, became a wash of marbled cornflower blue. His ears crystalized, made knobs at either side of the faucet. The claw feet looked human only via abstraction. A luster brimmed in Vivian, and she looked across the bathtub and saw it in her lover's face, saw it hovering auralike around the crown of their head.

Vivian looked at Lola, panting.

Lola peered at the bathtub. His hand glistened, looked terrible by candlelight. He tucked it between his thighs. He cleared his throat.

Saltpeter hugged their arms around their chest, squeezed fistfuls of faux fur. "Yes?"

"Does it have a heartbeat?"

Vivian tested her hand against it. Her fingertips throbbed. She withdrew and eyed Lola, gave a sharp nod. "He's alive."

"It's not hooked up to anything," Lola said. He gnawed his bottom lip. "Does it work?"

Saltpeter gave an ear knob an experimental twist.

Hot water poured from the faucet in a column clear as glass. It smelled crisp and fragrant, as though welled from a stream untouched and running deep underground, and as the bath filled the mirrors fogged, the plants luxuriated, the prickles of candleflame twisted on their wicks. Light rose from the bath, rippled through the water. The familiarity made Vivian want to cry.

Lola stood up. He peeled off his ruined shirt, cast it away from him, and Vivian and Saltpeter were at his side at once, unbuckling and unbuttoning him, stripping him of the clothing that bound his body. He walked naked over the rolled lip where the rugs ended, stepped over the sigil's boundary, approached the bathtub's edge. He peered down at his reflection in the water for a moment, the horns briefly visible beside him. He'd been crying at some point and had the stripes to show for it. He stepped into the bath. The water rose to his kneecaps and a sound escaped his lips, and the house made the sound with him and around him, a windy, ragged sigh. He lowered himself into the water. He submerged his purple hand, winced on initial contact, then swallowed, lolled his head back. His neck stretched for a thousand years. His curls tumbled, and Saltpeter sank to their knees beside the tub, dipped their hands in the water to wash them.

Vivian sat on the edge of the tub. She got her hands on the open wine bottle, drank generously, then rested the bottle's base against her hipbone. It tasted like cough syrup. She breathed in the steam and felt full.

"Lola," she said eventually. "How were your birds today?"

Saltpeter's fingertips worked his scalp, and he only rolled his eyes to look at her, his lashes long as a fawn's. He grinned a little, wary, still brilliant. "They feasted. Pure bird bliss."

THIS DEVIANT FLESH

DIANA HURLBURT

TODAY 11:05PM

lol you want to hear something fucked up
last night I dreamed we were at Aspenwall again
that fucking place

TODAY 11:32PM

know what else is fucked up
well, of course you know
what the fuck am I doing texting you?
at least you won't tell me to shut up.
but this dream, seriously. it was like we never left. like we were trapped,
when only one of us was trapped.
you know how in dreams sometimes it's like, the person you're looking at
looks like someone you know, but at the same time you know it's actually
someone else?
I saw her, and knew it was really you.
the house hadn't changed either. gothic fuckshit. rich people have too much
fucking money.
we should've known better.

Today 11:40PM

you always knew better. how come not that time? at Aspenwall.
Aspenwall. even the name. the moss-eaten brick, those trees like toy soldiers,
the little hill and the brick walls and the garden and the brick walkway.
brick brick brick, brick everywhere.
even the one in her hand.
Shae says I need to get over it.
that rich bitches never get what they deserve.

Today 11:57PM

Shae says I need to stop texting you too.
but she never wants to hear about it. Aspenwall.
and I sure as hell can't afford therapy on retail hours.
so who the fuck am I supposed to talk to?
she's right tho
bitch is always right.

Today 11:59PM

I wish they'd just unlist your goddamn number or however it works for
phones now.
then at least I couldn't be tempted.
then I'd be alone for real.

Today 12:00AM

. . .

THE HOUSE hasn't changed.

Brick walk—delicate herringbone—lichen-kissed, a gap in the pattern to be skipped when nearing the front door. Plush lawn of green velvet below raw, sun-shot skies silhouetted with twin gables, and the line of quaking aspens at the street's edge signalling elegant spite. Quaking aspens, white as Shaker lips, and whose house, after all—whose lineage?

Aspenwall, storied and studied, locally famous or infamous. Those Shaker girls who'd claimed their foremother's spirit thrived in them, spoke with their tongues, those young women driven out and despised for what was lauded in men…they were no older than you when you died. They lived.

I live. And so does she.

By the look of it, she's living well.

"I honestly cannot believe you came," she says. "Really, it's so fucking good to see you."

Fucking. It's glib, the casual cussing endemic to all of us—all of us except girls like her, not good girls but weird girls, awkward, religious without the god—you'd scream if you could hear her. But maybe you can.

It's like she's been re-skinned: sewn into a new persona: written over with droll, quirking lips, blunt-cut red hair, and is that a *tattoo* slinking from beneath her sleeve? Something sinuous nestled into the crook of her elbow, the spot you always said you'd get inked first. We were going to go for your eighteenth birthday. I was too much of a coward to do it alone.

The rite of memorial is *mine.* Not hers.

"Do you mind if we stop into the library first? Then I'll worry about dinner, I promise." She's not waiting for an answer; she sweeps along like an heiress should. Luxe rugs and polished tile, gobbled underfoot. "I've just got to show you that book. God, can you believe we're about to graduate?"

"Maybe you are," I say. "I dropped out."

"No! Really? God, how come?"

The repeated *God.* What god? *Religiouswithoutthegod* is a particular brand of girl-weird. Why would anyone homeschool their kid if Jesus wasn't making them? She was *so* homeschooled, back in the day. Homeschool kids, they got to the public high school and it was like that reality show about the Amish on rumspringa. How much damage can someone get up to in a town like ours? Enough. Why get drunk when you can call up spirits, perform mystic rites, commit a little lite ritual sacrifice?

The house's main corridor, curving down to cradle, to embrace, smother.

Like I could've made it through college without you. I promise I tried.

She'd said we'd eat, not that I'm hungry, but no food is waiting in the library. There's only the books I craved back then, so furious so heart-deep—nah, be real, that feeling resided in my cunt—there's the towering wall-to-ceiling cherry-glow shelving, spine-stuffed, provocative. Each title ready to be cracked, marrow drip, red leather and creamy-yellow leaves. There's books, and then there's a book.

Open and lascivious, sprawled on the table, a velvet ribbon nestled in its central pages like a finger drawn down flesh.

I can't pretend I don't want it. Can't pretend I abandoned it—all of it—books, ink-scribbled spikes we called sigils and stones marked with period blood for burial on property lines—can't pretend after you died I didn't crave it anymore.

Today 2:12PM

I know what I saw, I don't care what Shae says
I saw you typing
saw your number composing a message. whatever. so all I can figure is she
has it
and she's fucking with me.
lol coming here was a mistake.

THAT DRONE.

"Of *course* when I discovered it, I contacted the university library. Special collections." Her voice, endless, hypnotic. "They've been out to examine it—in context, they said," modest yet self-important, "and they're interested in adding it to the collection. They've got an incredible selection of local history and ephemera—you'd love it. I can't believe you dropped out! You were always just *made* for college, you and—"

Me and.

"—so smart and *so* well-read, like, totally ahead of everyone else. Do you remember that time you argued with Ms. Payne about *L'Etranger*?"

Of course she would use the French title.

"Or when we hacked the guidance counselor's email and forwarded all that stuff he was sending Erica Johansen to the principal?"

Is it really *hacking* if teachers leave their computers logged on all the time?

So she's still living in high school. Cheap insult. I am too, maybe. You definitely are, because you never got a chance to leave. Eternally seventeen, trapped inside a first-generation iPhone with a homemade Paramore case, a grainy newspaper photo, a Not Pictured yearbook entry.

"Come on," I say at last, snapping her off mid-stream just as she starts eddying toward *the time you and—wrote RAPIST on Justin Fairmount's locker.* "Just be honest. Do you have the phone?"

Today 3:01PM

she says she doesn't have it, doesn't know what I'm talking about
says why would you say something like that
says let's mend the past, I'd love to be friends again—like we were friends
then
like friends do what she did.

Today 3:04PM

Is it bad that it's comforting in a way
to be here
to talk with her.
it's like... after so long, after what happened, we still speak the same
language.
Shae's the closest friend I've got but all she remembers is you.
not you at Aspenwall.
do you know how lonely that is? for the one other person in the world who
speaks your language to be
her?

I<small>T'S LIKE</small>, weirdly casual.

Just make yourself at home, she says, *I've got a video conference for an hour or so but please,* please *love the library like it's your own.*

Rich people's voices turn certain phrases into precious gems.

We'll look at this beautiful little bitch later, right? Together. I'd love *to know what you think—but the special collections people were so persnickety about it. They gave me these white gloves to wear while handling it.*

A giggle, a flip of that dyed-red hair over her shoulder, like carefully-deployed vulgarity knits us together, makes us co-conspirators.

We're already that.

We hold an ugly truth between us; we've been raising it all this time like a foundling: your vital warmth stolen away for a twig-corpse buried in the rural cemetery, your voice bound into a silent forever-scream. We're in lockstep, matched—the truth I've been drowning in all these years versus the lack of evidence that buoys her above the waves—we're, now, nothing more than a sleepover club. Two girls where once there were three, huddled over our books and candles, worshiping our own belief, our own power.

There's coffee on if you want some, feel free. There's charcuterie in the fridge, help yourself. There's Perrier, there's ibuprofen, there's a meditation room second floor third door on the right there's the wifi password there's AppleTV so totally connect your Bluetooth there's...

On and on, a litany of abundance. Such beneficence. Such smug assurance, her belief that everything in her home is hers to be proffered, that nothing freely given may be stolen, that the humble are never anything but grateful, that four years later I'm still nothing but your shadow, that I have no motive save that of earnest, bookish, dweeby interest.

I put my hands on everything.

Corruptor.

A thrill moves through me, glacial and luxurious, like an ice cube eased between my legs. I imagine rot and ruin coursing out from my fingers as they slip in between book covers and finger crystal drawer-pulls and probe fleshy succulent leaves. I imagine tearing this house down brick by brick, pissing on history, sowing new life in your ashes. White gloves indeed—the special collections librarian's skin would crawl off their bones if they knew the spiritual decay I'd like to bring into this house and its treasures. I imagine nothing more complex than revenge.

The lion's share of magic, after all, is intent.

TODAY 7:32PM

she ordered a pizza. you know, like normal people do! like we really are having a sleepover. like we'll paint each other's nails and play truth or dare next.

like the last 4 years haven't been one long game.

TODAY 7:33PM

who are you texting, she's all giggly. right, of course, now it's time to whisper about boys.

it was never time to whisper about boys
I told her I was texting my girlfriend
almost true.

TODAY 7:40PM

of course you can't know what it was like after you died.
you can't know that loneliness, which I have to believe is different from the loneliness of death.
you didn't see your own obituary. what people said about you. how suddenly the weapons they liked to stab us with when you were alive became blessings on your gravesite.
how your face was an icon, glowing.
not even the shitty black-and-white photo in the paper killed that glow.

TODAY 7:58PM

I want to see you typing.
and I don't.
I want it to be you, not her.
real, not fake.
true, the way I've known the truth all this time.

THE BOOK is the book is the book. It's not like I've been idle all this time. Not like I totally wasted my year-and-change of higher education—I'm not too cynical to admit that yeah, the university library is impressive and there's stuff in there our wildest teen selves could never have dreamed of. But a book is just that: text on paper, calf-skin binding, engraved title faded gold. It's an artifact, dead flesh. This book is a good one by any metric collectors care about—rare, beautifully made, in near-mint condition, hiding outrageous suppositions and assurances inside its covers—but the urge I felt at first sight subsides once we look at it together.

A book can be a well, poisoned by proximity. The book, spread open in her hands, appears obscene.

"Can you imagine what it must've been like for those girls?" she asks. People who use *can you imagine* as their starting point never believe you can. "Can you imagine being our age"—she means *our age* back then, *our age* the last time we were truly a plural— "and receiving visions? Speaking with the voice of the dead. Or of God. Being possessed, totally possessed."

I remember what it felt like. I remember being taken, utterly: taken over inside out, taken by wind and water, transported, enslaved and freed in one motion. Oh, we were possessed by those girls, our forebears, those young women from whose hands spilled bright paint and from whose mouths spilled truths their community found difficult to chew. Malleability is what adults prize in girls…but only be malleable to certain hands, only be pliant for certain creeds, only be spoiled by certain rods.

You believed, then, that we could be those girls born again. Overwrite our code, rewire our cortexes. To be made available, to be open-pored and aching.

"Here." She taps a page gently, forefinger encased in white. "After the Era of Manifestations was declared at its end, the girls who kept speaking…well, you know, they were eventually quieted, right? Of course! Like always. But girls are hard to shut up."

She laughs and there's something beneath it, inside it, a husk instead of a sound, a chrysalis peeling away to reveal—

My phone rattles in my pocket. There's no message on the screen when I take it out.

She says, "Your girlfriend can't get enough of you, huh?"

TODAY **10:39PM**
I'm aching for midnight.
I know I'll see it again. you typing. and then I'll see the words.
whatever it is you have to tell me.

TODAY **10:43PM**
she said she's tired and I can go to bed whenever I want.
guest room—it's dope, of course. queen-size bed, velvet comforter. the
bathroom's bigger than my bedroom at home.
it was strange, looking at that book with her.
it's a Shaker commonplace book like so many they wrote, but weird. wrong,
maybe
maybe fake
maybe it's just that she was like 'if you think about it, a commonplace book
is just another type of grimoire'
and all I could imagine was you saying that instead.

TODAY **10:44PM**
you saying anything at all.

WHEN I WAKE up I swear your face is on the pillow next to mine. Bloody hair in its fat braid, coiled around your throat like a ritual snake; a slash of black lipstick; glimmering mismatched earrings shoplifted from Claire's. Then I see it's not your face but hers and I recoil, struck starkly awake by baffled revulsion that I could ever mistake you—or wonderment, because how is it that her face is so close to mine and yet out of reach, hovering and bobbing, a mirage that moves from the pillowcase to the far wall to play amid the moonlight?

I'm awake and not. Alive and not. When I blink one more time, my eyes open to quiet dark, no fata morgana on the wall and the bed empty, not even warm where my body has lain.

Awake, then. Maybe not alive.

I need to piss and I'm starving, so hungry, every biological demand my body possesses ringing at once in a five-alarm cavalcade of strident bells. Somehow, beneath the clamor and beyond shame, there's desire. For what—for who—no point.

Aspenwall lies wrapped in the night-soft quiet of deep space, muffled and cloaked against the wider world of the university, the town, the interstate's hum and the river's murmur. My feet make no sound on the staircase runner. No light leads me, only the sense of a towrope rooted beneath my ribs, pulling me out to sea down the stairs through the kitchen, depositing me at a door I didn't notice earlier in the evening in my penetrations, roamings. I don't recall it from the last time I was here either, four years and a lifetime ago. It's out of place with the house's carefully-maintained Dutch Colonial interior, a rough-hewn and rounded door of plain pine planks set almost behind the fridge.

It has no knob or latch, but falls open under my palm without a creak.

A basement turned cavern of light, illuminated by dozens of candles and further magnified by mirrors—some frames ornate and antique, others tiny cheap IKEA cubes, a full-length lipped in bronze and a half-shattered hunk of bare glass, garbage-picked—their surfaces beaming back not just carnelian flickers but a lithe motion, pale-flashing skin and red hair deepened by the surrounding light.

I hate what she's become, this shell she's pulled over herself. I hate the insipid shadow of you peering out of her eyes, the weak-tea mimicry of her arms as she raises them in that stance only you ever claimed: I'd be cross-legged and she'd be kneeling and there you were between us, upright and proud, arms stretching in a V toward the heavens. There was no one like you then, and when you left the Earth you left a void, a singular outline, the vacuum of God.

That tattoo I've only glimpsed so far burns on her arm like a brand. How did she know what you'd planned, the spell-crossed mark you designed yourself, the sigil you drew over and over until it was carved into your brain, seared into the ether—a notebook's worth of twinning inky lines before you even texted me a picture.

To remain unseen, you told me. *To be seen only by those who matter. To be seen and not seen.* Your face, hungry and open as a wound. *Imagine really being seen.*

Not a question, *can you imagine.* A command.

How would she know what your dream looked like, unless she has your phone?

Of course she has your phone.

"I couldn't give it up," she says over one bare shoulder. "My parents were furious after that night—God, did you know they sent me to a sort of Jesus camp that summer? Like spiritual rehab. So I'd be ready for college after that sort of *trauma.* But I couldn't let it go. Those girls, back in the days of the Shakers. They'd spoken to us. They were my ancestresses and they wanted something from me. They were still speaking and I couldn't just stop listening, right? It'd be the *worst* kind of betrayal, especially after—"

She turns. Her nakedness isn't shocking, barely registers. She holds not the Shakers' commonplace book, their inverted log of days recipes prayers hopes lists refusals pleas, but a phone. iPhone, first gen, silver; black rubber case ModPodged with a print-out photo of Hayley Williams; spiderwebbed screen, cold black. We'd stood in line for three hours on the day the first generation dropped, skipped school to drive two hours to the Apple Store in the Syracuse mall, spent the remaining two hours of the school day marveling over the gut-pleasing click of the touchscreen buttons.

It's a brick now, archaic as its half-brother, the OG iPod. There's no way it works, no way she has a cable to charge it, no way no way no way.

"I couldn't give it up," she says again. "When God speaks, you listen."

I say, "That isn't God."

I say, "You've never had God's ear."

"You're a murderer," I say, "or at the absolute fucking best you lied, you kept the truth from the authorities, even if you didn't do it yourself and even if it was an accident you prevented justice. You kept her from peace. You used her memory. You're living in her shape like a fucking vampire. You're a grave-robber, you're—"

Because I want to make her angry. I want her to come at me. I want her within my reach.

I want to do what you attempted, what those Shaker girls never managed. Let this be what you'd want, all that's left for me to offer.

Today 12:13AM
this is the last time I'll message you.
lol this is the last missive out of Aspenwall.
remember when we talked like fucking… I don't know, Lord of the Rings characters, all elaborate, for a month or so in middle school? missive. a Mr. Prentiss vocabulary quiz word.
this last time, before I destroy it
this last time just for me, not because i think you can see it.
this last time, and then you'll be free.

THE BRIDE

SUZAN PALUMBO

I STAYED LATE at the family bridal shop that night to help my sister Sharlene complete alterations on a wedding dress the bride demanded we finish by the next morning.

"Alice, I don't know why you don't sell Mama's old broken down house and come live in town near we," Shar said. Haranguing me was part of *her* cherished locking up ritual. She filed the day's receipts as I wiped and oiled my shears like Mama had taught me when I was a girl. "Yuh can't wok seamstry magic wit blunt scissors," she used to say. Shar came to stand in front of my work desk, her hands on her hips, after she'd finished her paperwork.

"Yuh not frighten? Alone in dee bush, nobody to call if yuh leg break or some wajang come to rob and kill yuh?"

"Dee wajang and dem don't have anybody to call for help from me either." I winked. "I taking a few days off." I grabbed my purse from behind the counter and headed for the door.

"God, yuh see dis woman?" Shar kissed her teeth. " Come back by Tuesday. We have to get dee Williams dress done," she called before the door shut behind me.

I got in my car and headed north. By the time I'd turned onto the long road that would lead home, the moon was a swollen pearl in the petrol black sky. There were few oncoming cars—*A lonely road for a lonely life in we dead mother's house*, I could imagine Shar saying whenever friends and cousins asked how I was. *Jackasses*.

Ma's house had become my sanctuary against the daily battery of *How come yuh not married, Alice? Yuh not ugly. Yuh want to meet dis boy meh cousin know?*

Ma had known my heart wasn't tailored for men and marriage, so when she died she left me independent, willing me the house along with a share in the business she'd built. This life suited me, so much so that the commute back and forth to the family bridal shop was pleated into the fiber of my muscle memory, my spine flexing in sympathy with the asphalt that would deliver me home.

I slowed that evening, easing into an upcoming bend, when a person appeared at the periphery of my headlights. I swerved to avoid hitting them. Mashing the breaks, the car spun to a stop.

I glanced in the rear view mirror. My heart pounded like a hot tassa drum. A woman, bathed in moonlight, stood by the roadside. I got out of the car and faced her. A wide brimmed hat hid her face. Her dress streamed iridescent over the hollows and swells of her figure. She was luminous, like no flesh and blood woman I'd encountered before. I lingered on the whirl of fabric over her hips. *No. No.* I strangled the quiver blossoming in my abdomen. She could have killed herself, and me, darting in front of the car.

"What dee hell yuh doing in the middle of de road?" I yelled. She didn't respond.

Was she hurt? Lost? My anger unraveled. "Y-yuh okay?" I stepped towards her.

Her palm shot up. A wall of heat slammed into my chest, barring me from coming closer. The night went quiet. She cocked her head and stood still for a long moment, then she turned and with an uneven gait walked into the bush.

I ran to where she'd vanished. Hoof prints pressed in the dirt were all that marked where she'd stood. The clouds churned, devouring the moonlight, plunging me in darkness. The air grew sharp against my skin. I went back to my car and sped home, a dull ache throbbing in my chest, as if her hand had clutched my heart and seared it.

THREE DAYS later, a new bride-to-be was in the change room trying on her eighth dress. Her mother, sister and aunt sat on the couch in front of the change room waiting for her to appear. I sat behind the glass counter that held our tiara selection, ready to greet anyone who might come in, a sketch pad on my lap to pass the time. They'd been here hours but finding the right dress wasn't about fit or a trend. The right dress chose the woman. It would transform her from within; it would light up her eyes. I'd seen that look on this bride's face earlier but I couldn't force the choice. She had to embrace it herself.

"All yuh hear dee news? Dey find a man dead in a ditch up by Verdant Vale yesterday. He neck was break in two place," the aunt said, shaking her head.

I glanced up. Shar was watching me while she stood by the change room door.

"Is Radika son-in-law, Sanjeev," the mother of the bride said. "Radika say dey find he wit he clothes on inside out and a cow hoof print crushed in dee center of he chest." She placed her hand below her collar bone and pressed down. "Good he dead. Radika say Sanjeev did beat she daughter Chandani black and blue." The hoof prints by the side of the road surfaced in my memory. I kept my mouth shut.

"A la Jablesse have one cow foot and one human foot." The aunt clapped her hands. "Is she who kill Sanjeev for he beating he wife."

The bride's sister rolled her eyes. "I can't believe all yuh still believe dat devil woman foolishness."

"Gyal, listen, dese tings is tru—" The bride strutted out of the change room and the three shifted their commentary to everything terrible about the eighth dress.

When they'd paid the deposit on the second dress she'd tried on and left, Shar came to the tiara counter.

"Did you see anybody on dee road that night, Alice? Did you pass where dey find Sanjeev?"

"No." I shrugged, keeping my eyes on my sketch.

Shar hovered over me, a bloodhound on the scent of the truth I hadn't told."Dat a new design?" She pulled the sketchpad towards her. Her eyes widened as she took in the form, the drape of the cloth, the vanishing face. She kissed her teeth and chucked it back at me. "Yuh *did* see dee la Jablesse."

My face burned. Silence anchored itself between us.

"Go home early, I don't want you driving in dee dark," she said, when I did not relent. "Let we get ready for dee next appointment."

S HAR CHASED ME from the shop before three pm in the following weeks. I'd drive home, eat, and troll the unlit back roads in the lonely evenings, hoping to encounter the woman in white. The ache she'd planted that night burrowed deep in my chest. For the first time the house provided no solace—the rooms slackened around me like over stretched elastic where they'd held and comforted me before. Twice, I drove to town and back at midnight, searching for her.

She haunted me in the starlight spilling across the road, on the crests of the Maracas waves, in the whispering edges of my dreams. My hands longed to caress the warp and weft of her, to feel the soft fabric of her dress slip between my palms and the heat of her chest. She'd seen me that night and let me be. It was more than anyone, other than Ma, had ever given me.

I caught the syncopated sway of her hips again in Port of Spain, amidst an afternoon crowd walking East on Ariapita road while I was traveling West back to the bridal shop. Her dress flowed as if it were an extension of her commanding poise. Men on the street stop to stare and look back at her. I was trapped in the flow of traffic and couldn't turn around to catch her.

An American tourist was found dead two days later near
Avocat Falls. His wallet, flushed with cash, still in his pocket.

MISADVENTURE the coroner had ruled the fatality, the
papers said.

"Misadventure, my foot," Shar said when a customer
mentioned the death at the shop.

IF I COULDN'T have the woman in white, I'd have her dress.
We'd never had one like it in the shop before. I researched
patterns and contacted the fabric shops to locate the perfect
cloth, settling on a special order white charmeuse.

"Should I charge dee shop account?" The clerk at the fabric
store asked when I placed the order.

"No. No. This isn't for a customer. It's for me. I'll pay for it
myself when I pick it up."

"This is wedding dress material, Alice. Yuh getting married?"
The smile in her voice was palpable.

I pretended not to hear her and hung up.

I SAT AT Mama's pedal sewing machine, the manual one her
mother had bought her when she was a young woman, the one
she'd taught me and Shar to sew on at home, and set to work.

"Did yuh know yuh mothah does wok spells wit cloth?" she
asked me once when I was little.

I'd raised my eyebrows at her, thinking she was fooling.

"Yuh don't believe me?" She went to one of her drawers and
pulled out a yard of white silk.

"What is dis?"

"Cloth?" I said matter of factly.

She faced me in front of her full length mirror and wound the
silk around my waist.

"What is it now? And who are you?"

I giggled. "It's a ball gown and I am a Queen."

She laughed with me and crossed it around my chest."Now?"

"I'm a soldier and it's a bandolier."

She saluted me, her expression stoic. With a flick of her wrists she uncrossed the silk and dropped it over my head, covering my face so I could no longer see myself. "And?"

"It's a veil. I am a bride but my groom is dead."

She tugged at the cloth; let it fall on the floor. Her eyes shone, as if she was trying not to cry.

"Why yuh say that, Alice?" Her voice had become a whisper. I could hardly hear her.

"I don't know. It was in my mouth," I remember saying, twirling in front of the mirror.

She pursed her lips and put the cloth away.

I BEGAN SPENDING more time away from the shop to focus on the dress. My body fell into the rhythm of the foot pedal and the guiding push of the material. Mama's seamstress magic, revived, pulsed through me. Some nights I found myself asleep at the sewing table, the dress put aside and my feet still rocking. Those nights I'd dream of the woman in white, the taste of her mouth and the warmth between her thighs.

As the garment formed beneath my hands, the headlines mounted:

MAN DROWNED.
DEHYDRATED HIKER BITTEN TO DEATH BY FIRE ANTS.
BUSINESS MAN'S SKULL CRUSHED IN FALL FROM CLIFF.

"Police believe a serial killer is targeting men in the Northern regions of the island," the somber evening news anchor reported. "Men are urged not to stop for strangers, to avoid walking along back roads alone, and if they have been out drinking, to travel in groups."

No one was immune. Grey haired grandfathers, university students, and men with wives and young children at home, were all pictured among the missing and dead.

The news cut to a live reporter interviewing a bar
patron. "Are you concerned about the recent deaths of men in
the area?"

"Is not no serial killa, gyal. Is a la Jablesse. Yuh think I 'fraid
some woman, a jaggabat? Give me five minutes with she. I have
dee ting she need." He leered at the camera before it switched
back to the news anchors.

I rolled my eyes.

"Witnesses have reported seeing a red sedan leaving the
vicinity of where some of the men were last seen." The anchor
resumed. "Police have labelled the driver a person of interest.
Anyone with information is encouraged to contact them through
their tip line."

I shut the TV off and continued sewing. I hadn't been out at
night with the car since I started the dress. It didn't matter. I'd
be done tonight.

A CAR PULLED UP to the house at seven am the next morning.
"Alice!" Shar yelled, her voice crackling with urgency.
She never drove up to visit me much less at seven am on a
weekday. Worried, I ran to the front door.

"Everything okay? I was coming in today."

She glared at me, her hands on her hips. "Your car is red."
She pointed at it.

"You drive up here to give me a heart attack and tell me dis? I
thought somebody get sick or have ah accident."

I went back to my room. She followed me.

"People dead and is you who dee police want to question."
Shar stood in the bedroom doorway. I brushed my hair. "Yuh
think people go want to come to dee shop if dey hear police
question you? Yuh go ruin everything Mama and I wok for."

"I wok for it, too. Shar. If it wasn't for me doing dee sewing
yuh woulda gone broke long ago. Yuh can't sew a pillowcase for
yuh life."

She kissed her teeth. "Don't play, Alice. You know Mama's give yuh piece of dee shop because yuh would ah never make nothing of yuh life. Yuh wasn't even going to get married because yuh—"

Shar stopped and stared at the dress hanging on the hook on my closet door. She took it down, her forehead gathering creases like the fabric in her hands as she twisted and turned it. There was no denying my power with thread.

"What dee hell is dis?" She shook it at me.

"It's a dress, Shar. A damn dre—"

Something banged the front door. I gasped. A human fist couldn't make such a noise. Shar opened her mouth to speak but again the knocking erupted, hard and sharp, pummelling the door and burying her voice. It grew heavier, the door frame shuddering, and the galvanized gallery roof reverberated like a death knell.

Shar screamed. A prickly shot of fear plunged straight through my abdomen to my toes. The entire house shook as if buffeted by a malevolent gale and we strained to stand our ground. Whatever was demolishing the front door would be upon us soon. There was nowhere to run. Shar flung the dress at me and crouched into a ball, covering her head.

The banging stopped.

We didn't move. We hardly breathed; ears ringing, insides trembling. After twenty minutes we tiptoed to the front door and opened it. There was no one there.

The door had been battered from top to bottom. The splintered double tear drop indent of a cow's hoof covered its surface.

Shar swallowed audibly as she crossed herself. Her voice wavered when she'd gathered the nerve to speak. "Alice, I go say a prayers for yuh. Don't come to dee shop. Stay away from meh children until you cut dis blight from yuh life." She walked to her car.

"Shar!" I called. She waved me off without looking back and left.

I turned to the door.

"You were here with me," I whispered. I touched my forehead to the wood and kissed the center of the hoof print closest to me.

I went to the spare room where I kept the trunks of Mama's clothes. The ones I couldn't bring myself to give away or burn. She'd been a stylish woman, sewing most of her own dresses until arthritis had robbed her fingers of flexibility. At the bottom of one of the chests I found the hat boxes I'd been looking for. I opened the largest and took the lace veil out.

Something borrowed, I thought, holding it out in front of me.

I SLIPPED THE DRESS on and pulled the veil over my face. Cut on a bias, it hung perfectly on my frame.

Who yuh is now, Alice? I imagined Mama asking.

I left the battered front door agape behind me and headed out into the night. Moonlight coursed along the road ahead of me. The guttural cry of howler monkeys grated my ears. At one point an oncoming car passed, the drunken passenger leaned out his window and yelled. His voice melded with the grim chorus of nocturnal animals. I squared my shoulders and continued. I was meant to travel this road.

I saw the vehicle well before I heard its engine. It was pulled over on the shoulder. The la Jablesse stood by the driver's side window. I froze, not wanting to intrude on the privacy of her conversation. She stepped back from the car. The back seat door shot open - a command not an invitation.

She shook her head. I must have caught the corner of her eye in the distance because she stepped back further and turned to me.

"Whore!" A deep voice yelled before the door slammed and the car peeled off. We stood across from each other like that first night. Moonlight, again, the connecting thread between us. I took a step forward. She did not put her palm out; did not forbid me coming closer.

I walked towards her, lingering on each step. She was dazzling, magnetic. Every stride I'd ever taken had been along this path towards her. The night went silent and the air filled with the scent of puli, oleander and the repugnant trace of cow dung. The flutter I'd quashed months ago bloomed.

Her head moved up and down, slowly taking me in, my dress a pale mirror of the bewitching one she wore. She offered me her hand. I accepted it. It was warm, yielding, like it had been molded to fit mine. Ambling on her hoof she led me into the jungle. The trees bent before us, creating a bower. She brought me to the edge of a precipice. A stream trickled far below, tinkling an ancient wedding march. She reached for my other hand and we faced each other. Until she let go and tossed her hat into the abyss below us.

The ache in my chest throbbed. My knees verged on buckling. Her face. That face. Her eyes were kind and unforgiving; her mouth supple and severe. She was gorgeous and repulsive. My body strained against the dual urges to flee and draw nearer.

"Kiss me now," she said in a tumbled gravel voice. Were these the last words men over the centuries had heard? The ones who'd followed her and, when she'd revealed her truth to them, chosen death and pain over her? I saw myself in her face. I saw every girl I'd ever known: Mama and Shar and each woman who'd ever entered our shop.

I lifted my veil and kissed her, with all of the loneliness and sorrow of a lifetime. We stumbled closer to the cliff's edge. She pulled me against her and kissed me back, her urgency deepening and tasting of over ripened fruit. She trembled, the relief of her want too overwhelming to contain.

I pressed myself into her to quell her shaking. I wanted to hold her here forever but how? How could we stay together? And then, as if she'd heard my thoughts, she shoved me hard. Her rebuff was a pin pushed into the center of my chest. She'd never wanted me after all. I tripped over the edge of the cliff, like countless men before me, plummeting to the river below. Except, I wasn't alone. The woman in white jumped after me and held me fast.

We hit the ground together.

She helped me stand and regain my balance when I'd caught

my breath. My right foot remained flesh and bone but the left was now made of hard keratin, like hers. She braced me as I learned to walk again beside her. She hadn't scorned me.

We would be together forever, for better or worse, brides of dead men, joined.

BLOOD FOR BLOOD

CHELSEA OBODOECHINA

I.

THE YOUNG GIRL'S HANDS shake as she brings the bowl to her lips. Evelyn watches her eat for what seems like the first time in days. She dreads to turn her out onto the street again.

Evelyn is not good at keeping company. She is isolationist, crude, and secretive. She was lucky enough to find a partner that could suffer through her stress headaches and the long bouts of silence that bitter the domestic tenderness of the everyday. Others can only stand her for so long.

This child—teenager, really—came to Evelyn's door, unbidden. Earth knows how the girl found Evelyn's shed in the thick of the Guyanese bush off to the remote west, where few people roam. Most children have been cautioned against approaching strangers, and the *obeah* woman is an especially horrible stranger. She is the woman who will steal your shadow, infest your home with cockroaches, and plague your crops with nothing but a rotten fish and ill intent. The paradox of disgust and reverence is so dizzying to outsiders that boys from a nearby village will throw stones at her house, only to run off screaming bloody murder the moment she steps out of her house brandishing a machete.

Evelyn's partner Sammi does not have to ask what she is thinking. She only has to take a look at Evelyn and say, "We should keep her for the night, at least."

"She is a child," says Evelyn. "Her parents will be looking for her. I have yet to dispel rumours that I have eaten that boy that got lost in the woods some time ago. They will think I'm ready to cook this one up, too."

"Isn't she too old to be eaten?" Sammi's eyes glitter with barely contained mirth.

Evelyn huffs. They gaze at the child from the other side of the shed, where they pretend to wash the laundry over a tin bucket. The girl fidgets now, probably fully aware of the eyes that cling to her like the sweat on her broad forehead. She wipes it away with the sleeve of her tattered school shirt, flicks her eyes over the clay jars that dot the floor, the paintings Sammi stored in the corners of their home, the towers of books that threaten to topple off the rickety shelves, and the carved masks of faceless ancestors made of timber wood. Then her eyes retreat to the bowl, her soup unfinished.

Sammi waves a hand in front of Evelyn's face, angles her chin towards the girl. "Talk to her. You know she came to see you."

That is the problem. It is not the first time that people have wandered to Evelyn's shed in the hopes of learning the intricacies of the craft. Her reputation a powerful witch attracted many people to her door, but she has always turned them away. None were as scrawny and young as this one.

Despite something in Evelyn telling her to hold back, she sighs and rises to her full height. The girl's eyes dart over to Evelyn, no longer holding the illusion that she did not notice the staring. Her eyes are wide, showing a vulnerability that strikes at Evelyn's heart.

She takes a couple of strides towards the young girl and seats herself in the chair across the table. They hold each other's stare, the girl's visibly terrified, but otherwise steady in their conviction.

"What is your name, girl?"

"Mackenzie, ma'am."

"What do you want?"

The girl blinks and sits up in her chair, her thin shoulders squaring a little.

"I want to study *obeah*," says Mackenzie. "I made a promise ten years ago. I want to get back at the person who killed my parents."

Evelyn bites her lip, takes pause, then scratches the side of her neck. She looks over to Sammi who responds by vigorously cleaning Evelyn's shirt with a metal scrubber.

"Where do you live?" asks Evelyn. "I'm taking you home."

"With all due respect, I can't leave," says Mackenzie. "I'll only come back."

"Then I'll just turn you into a toad!"

The shed goes quiet. Sammi no longer scrubs, opting to watch for a potential unfolding of a disaster. Mackenzie shakes with nerves, but she doesn't look away from Evelyn.

Evelyn's skin itches, as if she herself was cursed. Her barbed words are still sharp on her tongue, but she swallows them back. Instead, she sighs and says, "One night. Then you're gone. You hear me?"

The switch from grave determination to a bright smile is a jarring one. Mackenzie nods excitedly.

"Thank you," she says. "You won't regret it."

II.

EVELYN REGRETS IT. It's not in the way she thought she would, though.

Mackenzie is an excellent student. She reads diligently when she is not out among the trees, listening to the earth, taking note of the chittering of monkeys and the crowing of red and yellow birds that flicker across the interlocked branches overhead. Her cooking is precise, patient; never once has the meat in her

pepperpot been tough or chewy and her chow mein is rich
with colour and flavour. She makes rounds to the nearest town
market, which is half a day's walk away, all without complaint.
Sammi is already enamoured with her work ethic. Frankly,
Evelyn often thinks of kicking Mackenzie out, but the moment
she opens her mouth, the words flee her tongue and leave her
empty.

"When can I learn how to turn people into toads?"
Mackenzie asks. She hauls large palm leaves over her shoulder as
they make their way back to the shed with ingredients for a basic
medicine to ward off stomach worms.

Evelyn grunts and adjusts the chopped stalks of palm trees
over her broad shoulder. "You can't actually do that, girl."

"But you said…"

"I know what I said," says Evelyn.

Mackenzie huffs. She has lived with Evelyn and Sammi for
over a year and has taken on some of their mannerisms. Evelyn's
annoyed sigh, Sammi's gesticulations when she talks about
something that she has read.

"All I've been learning is how to make medicine," says
Mackenzie. "You know why I'm here, ma'am."

"As long as you're here," Evelyn says, "you will do as you are
told. I'm the teacher, not you."

It takes Evelyn a moment to realize that Mackenzie has
stopped walking alongside her. She turns in time to see
Mackenzie throw the leaves for the medicine onto the forest floor
and cross her arms. Despite the discipline she has learned in
Evelyn's house, she still falls back on teenage tantrums that got
her what she wanted in the orphanage.

"I came here to learn *obeah*," says Mackenzie. "I will learn
how to cast hexes, with or without you."

Despite herself, Evelyn releases a crooning laugh that speaks
of disbelief.

Mackenzie does not shake or flinch. She has become far
too comfortable with her. Evelyn isn't sure how or when this
happened, but it is abundantly clear to her now.

"Go on, then," says Evelyn with a careless wave of her hand.

"Get from here and find a new teacher! You know how long I've been meaning to be rid of you?"

This seems to shake Mackenzie out of whatever rash of rebellion she was afflicted with. She starts to shake her head and mutters something, but Evelyn does not hear.

"What?" Sammi is not here to pick the razors from Evelyn's tone this times. "Speak up!"

"I'm—I'm sorry." Mackenzie's eyes glisten with a wall of unshed tears.

Evelyn feels her heart drop into her belly. She sucks on her teeth, agitated. "Stupid girl." She motions to the leaves on the ground and says, "Pick those up. You don't speak to your elders in such a way. Y'understand?"

"Yes, ma'am." Mackenzie squats down to pick up the leaves. "Sorry, ma'am."

The rest of the walk is done in silence.

The next morning, Mackenzie is gone.

III.

"YOU DID SOMETHING."
"I did nothing."

"What," Sammi asks, for the fifth time, "did you do?"

"I did *no-thing*," Evelyn says, clapping for emphasis. It seems Sammi is not moved by her clapping because she scowls at her like she cursed her in tongues.

"Mackenzie has been nothing but a sweetheart since she got here," says Sammi. "She had no reason to just run off. You said something to her, I know you did. Don't lie, now."

Evelyn scratches the back of her neck, her eyes trained on the tabletop. Her gaze gravitates to a small engraving near the edge that reads, "MACK '67". Her neck feels as if there are bugs crawling under her skin and she scratches harder.

"Don't do that, Eve," says Sammi. She gently removes the fingers from Evelyn's neck and places a cool palm on the burning skin. Her voice is quiet. "She asked about black magic again, didn't she?"

Evelyn doesn't reply.

"Mack has been through a lot," says Sammi, tone contemplative. "Already, she's lost her parents. She is trying to find peace in what she knows."

"I don't want to contribute to violence," says Evelyn, her voice just as low. She feels she is made of glass without a frame, that she will shatter if she speaks too loudly. "Not anymore."

"Your reputation precedes you," says Sammi.

"It does." Evelyn glares at the little inscription on the table. "I've been down that road once before, too. I don't.want anyone else to go through what I did. It festers inside me."

"I know."

Evelyn sighs, unfolds from her chair, and rises to her feet. Wordlessly, she slips away from Sammi's soothing touch and packs a waterskin, a packet of arsenic beans, a machete, and a handful of conch shells before stepping outside.

IV.

WITHIN THE THRUMMING crowd of the marketplace, where merchants call out to potential customers and argue with hagglers, a ripple of quiet swims through them when they see the *obeah* woman. The crowd parts and stares, clutching their purses and hats as she walks along on bare feet. A woman dares spit in her direction and another heckles, "Devil's seed!" They are but a number in a crowd. The *obeah* woman does not see them and she does not care to.

She does hear when the jovial chatter lapses into hushed, hurried whispers. "She killed Ezra's boy, didn't she?"

"I hear she ate him right up."

"Ah-ah! And she dare show 'er face 'ere?"

The rumour still persists, apparently. She must contain a sigh of exasperation. While Mackenzie did market runs for Evelyn

and Sammi, Evelyndidn't have to suffer through the stupid talk.
Or, at least, she did not have to hear them.

She promised Sammi that she would not curse anyone on
this trip. If worse comes to worse, she will run them off with her
machete.

The fruit merchant gasps and skitters a couple of steps back
when Evelyn's eyes fall upon him. She approaches his booth and
bows her head.

"Pleasant good afternoon," she says in her most level voice.
"Would you happen to know anything about an orphanage
around here?"

"No, I don't know anything," he says. His eyes are wide and
his forehead shimmers with sweat. "Nothing at all. So, if you
have no business here——"

"Evelyn?"

At the sound of her name, Evelyn turns and sees Mackenzie
standing just behind her, among the crowd. A frown mars her
face. They are only a couple of feet apart, but Evelyn is aware of
the rift between them.

Whatever apology she finely crafted on the way to the market
is but a slip of a memory now. Evelyn opens her mouth, closes it.
Mackenzie waits for her to speak. A group gathers round them.
The lack of privacy makes Evelyn's skin feel like it's about to
break out in hives.

"We should talk." Evelyn meaningfully casts a cursory glance
at the strangers surrounding them. Mackenzie, arms crossed and
hand wrapped in torn cloth, only nods in response. Her face is
stiff as stone.

V.

T HEY PULL AWAY from the market and Evelyn breathes a
little easier, although it is not by a lot. Just a quarter mile
east, there is a plain full of tall grass, dotted with bundles of
palm trees that stand like slender fingers against the setting sun.

Mackenzie pauses on the dirt path that leads to home and stares at Evelyn, expectant.

Evelyn opens her mouth.

"It was you, wasn't it?" Mackenzie asks.

Evelyn lets her mouth hang ajar for a moment before she lets it fall shut. A sigh escapes her nose in a quick gust. She shuts her eyes. "I think so."

"You think so."

"It's been ten years," says Evelyn. "Those years of my life are a blur—"

"Look me in the eye," says Mackenzie, "and tell me what you did. "

More than anything in her life, Evelyn thinks that this is the hardest task that she has to undertake. However, Mackenzie was right in pulling back the curtain and wishing to face this horror that has haunted her—them—all her life. In a way, it would do Evelyn some good to remind herself of where she was, how far she has come. Where the road must end.

So, she looks at Mackenzie and fights to keep eye contact, much like Mackenzie did a year ago. Or ten years ago.

"I used to live in a nearby village with my mother," says Evelyn. "She was already a widow then. My father fell sick and died before I was born. No one wanted to help her, especially when people began to call her an *obeah*. They told her she was cursed. We had to eat boiled bark to survive."

The gnawing, painful hunger. Sicknesses that her mother could only barely heal with soothing songs in her ear and salves that she had to craft herself. Evelyn pushes away the ghostly feelings, reminds herself that it was a long time ago.

"The villagers hated us," says Evelyn. "As we slept, men bust into our house and took my mother. They hauled her away into the field, past the trees. I never saw her again."

Mackenzie's expression does not change. She waits for Evelyn to continue.

"I was your age when it happened." Evelyn nods to Mackenzie. "Despite my hunger, I was spry. I ran off before they caught me. But their faces were burned into my mind."

Evelyn can feel her heart stuttering in her chest when she calls to mind the fire that burned in her veins, the honed edge of her hatred towards the men, the entire village, as she ran into the forest for shelter. "The trees, the earth, and the water spoke to me while I hid in the forestg," says Evelyn. "It was there that I learned their secrets. The villagers were not wrong about there being an *obeah* woman in their village, but it was not my mother."

Evelyn's eyes slide away for a moment, into the palm trees that sway gently in the sea breeze. "I took a year to myself and waited. I came back to the village, armed with knowledge. I took the earth upon which they and their wives walked, mixed it with salt, and nailed it to the trees. And, in nine days' time, they became violently ill and perished."

The breeze picks up into a violent wind. The smell of rain rides on its waves and buffets the loose robes round Evelyn's figure. She spares a look at Mackenzie who holds herself like she is cracked clay, her palm pressed against her mouth, eyes tightly shut. Evelyn bites her lip and looks away.

"I remember going to one of the men's house," Evelyn says. "To check to see if the job was done. There were three bodies in their bed when I walked in. I pulled back the covers and found—"

"Me." Mackenzie's voice is raw, harsh. It does not sound like her. Evelyn nods, gravely, despite knowing Mackenzie could not see her.

Evelyn clears her throat and spits before she can help herself.

VI.

HERE IS THE TRUTH: Evelyn released a sputtering gasp upon seeing the child between the corpses and stumbled back. The child sprang into a seated position, her face streaked with sweat and tears and snot. Beside her were a man and a woman, their bodies emaciated and covered in boils and sores. They reeked of death. Evelyn could hardly stomach the stench and pressed her hand to her mouth and nose to keep out the miasmic breath of the fresh dead.

They stood in silence, the girl and the not-woman, and could only stare at one another in mute horror.

The child was first to open her mouth.

"O…" She raised a shaking hand and pointed directly at Evelyn. "*Obeah* woman."

A witch. Evelyn felt bile rush up her throat, but she swallowed a couple of times to keep it at bay.

"Did you…?" The girl looked lost, disoriented. How long had she been lying there, with the rotting corpses of her parents as her macabre cushions? Evelyn felt too sick to respond.

The girl clambered over her mother's body, careful not to touch her, and stood to face Evelyn. She only reached Evelyn's waist though Evelyn was only on the cusp of womanhood back then.

"I—I didn't know they had a—a child." The excuse sounded dead to her own ears. "I'm…I'm so…"

She would not apologize. Not for this. Not when she had just lost her own mother a year ago and continued to bleed and ache and blubber for the gaping wound of her loss. Nothing would ever replace that emptiness.

But. Evelyn could not just leave either.

She removed her hand from her mouth, took in a deep breath of the putrid air, and strode to the young girl. The girl did not flinch, but her eyes widened when Evelyn sunk to one knee so they were eye-to-eye.

"I was the cause of this," said Evelyn. Her eyes drifted to the bodies for a moment, then snapped back to the young girl. She steeled herself with the same resolve it took to wander into the village to witness her handiwork. "When you come of age, child, find me and take your vengeance. It is only fair. I promise I will not fight you when you do."

The girl stared and Evelyn grew impatient.

"Y'understand?"

Another beat. Then a hesitant, timid nod. The girl understood.

Evelyn rose to her feet, pivoted on her heel, and marched out of the house without another glance or word.

VII.

"LORD IN HEAVEN," whispers Mackenzie, her tears clogging her throat and choking her. "Jesus Christ."

The grey clouds above parted slightly to reveal the starry night sky as Evelyn told the story. The moon beamed on the empty field. Each of Evelyn's breaths feels like thorns tumbling around in her lungs. Her hand finds the centre of her chest and scratches.

There are no words that can rectify this. Only action.

"You said you promised, right?" asks Evelyn. "To kill me."

Mackenzie's sobs become muffled whines as she collapses to one knee and openly weeps. It is pain to Evelyn's ears.

"I did not teach you evil *obeah*," says Evelyn, her voice loud enough to be heard over Mackenzie's crying, loud enough to hide her own wobble of grief. "But I am mortal, like any other. Anything that can fell a mortal can kill me."

She lowers the bag by her hip to the ground and unzips it to remove the machete. She cautiously lays it on the dirt road between her and Mackenzie, its edge gleaming.

"I will not fight it, child." Evelyn offers her a small, wary smile. "As promised."

Mackenzie's bloodshot eyes linger on Evelyn, then sink to the machete that lays between them.

She sniffs and says, "You stupid hag. You stupid *fucking* hag."

Evelyn listens, patient.

"This is how—" Mackenzie hiccups and swallows, her eyes turning skyward, as if to seek divine intervention that she knows will never come. She sucks on her teeth and levels a poison, ugly glare against Evelyn. "This is how we got here in the first place. You know that."

"I do."

"You foolish woman," Mackenzie mutters. After a moment, she reaches for the hilt of the machete, grabs it tightly. The bandages have fallen away, revealing bloody knuckles.

Mackenzie ascends from her kneeling position, her eyes a torrent of fury. Deep, deeper within, there is a quiet. Mackenzie raises the blade, its crest twinkling like a moonlit tear. Evelyn takes in a deep breath that fills her lungs and closes her eyes.

Only. There is a muted clatter and a shaky sigh. Evelyn keeps her eyes closed, but she feels weakness enter her body. She waits another while. Opens her eyes.

Mackenzie is gone. Evelyn is numb from her toes to the crown of her head. The machete lays on the road, facing east.

FOR CLOSURE

TANIA CHEN

HERS ARE THE break-ankle style heels you see in movies. The pencil-skirt, a sensible shade of grey that outlines her silhouette against the chipped oak door of the entrance. She's smiling, a row of perfect white teeth behind red. The kind of woman men always make comments about and then grin at each other. Even now, the boy's father winking at him, motioning with his head at the lady and smiling.

His hand feels small and sticky, wrapped inside his father's own and stinking like chamoy. The boy does not understand but he knows to nod, to make the motions to pass and satisfy his father. Great-grandmother was the same way, vacant nods to particular questions—unspoken tests that could have catastrophic consequences when failed. There is a none too gentle tug for him to follow, nearly tripping on the uneven payment leading to the entrance of the house.

"Welcome, welcome—"

"—I apologise for the late hour, traffic was beastly."

"It is no matter." She turns the knob and gives a quick tug. The door yawns open, a gust of cold air and dust greeting the three of them. "This is the best time to visit, the light is simply divine."

The boy feels again the impatient tug of the hand, his father brushing by the woman to enter the house, ignoring the buzzing by the door's entrance. A wasp nest in winter, the boy squints to make out the yellow and black shapes, huddled and trying to escape the chill emanating from inside the house.

From the entrance foyer, a set of cement stairs are decorated with lush green plants. The boy marvels at how they can survive the dark and cold of this place until he reaches out to find their leaves to be waxy and very much dead—plastic.

The Realtor—that is what his father calls her, because her name is unimportant in the grand scheme of things, in the business side of things—heads up the stairs.

She has no shadow.

The boy raises one pudgy finger to trace the place her shadow ought to be, except his father is looking at the ceiling's dust coated chandelier, and complaining as they walk past the first door.

This room looked small from the outside, the ceiling beams high and, along the left side, built-in shelves from top to bottom that have now been emptied. He drifts over, touching the bottom shelf with sticky fingers, leaving behind a trail.

His father has long ago let go of his hand. The boy barely noticed this happen, drawn in by the faded ocean green of the carpet, the scorched dark circles that stain it. He thinks he smells herbs: albahaca, ruda, romero, lavanda—all meant to ward evil and provide protection, according to the abuelitas at the mercado stalls with their incense and loteria cards.

"This was the library." The Realtor launches into an explanation that the boy does not care for. As if the material of the chimney and shelves makes a difference to an eight-year-old who is more interested in stepping inside each circle on the carpet.

He counts ten jumps from left to right and stops next to the window. It has been left open by the Realtor on her way out ("Oh, come this way, you'll just love the garden."), his father on her heels as she continues the tour.

The boy stops at the threshold between inside and out.

There is a man here. An old man who sits by the window when the light hits it just right, and if the boy blinks and squints and narrows his eyes just enough, there is a flicker of him there still.

(He heard it said by his great-grandmother as she got ready for Sunday's sermon at San Jacinto, "*algunas casas son brujas.*"

Though what she meant by that, he had been too young to understand. When the boy asked his mother, she had simply shaken her head. "*Mijo, es así como son las cosas. Hay casas que son brujas.*"

As if *that* cleared anything up.)

He turns back inside towards the indentations left behind by furniture and squats down. There had once been a mahogany table here used to prop up old books and rows of knives—he could see a flicker of it in his mind's eye.

From the dining room he can hear the echo of voices, the Realtor ever so slightly higher than his father's as they discuss—money? He thinks they might be haggling but the words are both distant and indistinct.

There is a man here. An old man with paper-thin skin and a mouth with more gaps than teeth. If he looks close enough, the boy can see they have the same shaped nose, the same coloured eyes, and closer still: yellow spotted sclera, olive green sweater, rancid breath.

There are flecks of red on his sweater that make the boy think of sour-sweets, the taste so vivid his teeth shudder.

He wonders if the old man is hiding some in the closet of his room. If that is why the stains are so deep and violently bright against the translucent shape he inhabits. He wonders if those thread-bare pockets are weighed down with the promise of hidden chamoy-flavoured treasures.

The boy reaches out, shameless in his quest—

But the smell is all wrong and it is not just the promise of decayed teeth in an old mouth. There is something acrid and metallic in the air, unwelcome—

The man grabs the boy by the shoulders and begins violently

shaking him.

*(it feels a little like falling, a little like choking on thick, dry mangoes
left on the shelves for too long and he wants to run, to run, to run but it still
feels a little like falling*
   *a little like choking, raking his nails and tearing them open and he sees
that realtor's red lips, bright and smiling become wider and teeth becoming
gaps and now he is falling*
   falling and the floor rushes up—)

The boy grabs the man by the hand and digs his nails in,
yowling like a tlacuache in a hunter's trap. He pulls away until
the scent of mangoes no longer clogs his nose, and the absence of
it is oppressive in its arrival.

He crawls into the closet, knees scraping against the navy blue
carpet and leaves behind the scorched circles of the library.

There is a man here—

Algunas casas son brujas. The boy closes his eyes and
remembers: some houses are witches. Older than even his great
grandmother, who sat down by the window and waved.

There is a man here who wears *his face*. With more wrinkles
and less teeth, but it is still undoubtedly the boy's face.

He crawls until his knees go numb, and the smell of blood
and rancid breath gives way again to something sickly sweet
and spicy. The carpet becomes stone, then stairs, and finally the
cobbled, uneven stones of the street.

The boy finds himself standing alone before the wooden door,
well polished under the rays of the afternoon sun. The doorknob
of indistinct shape is now clearly bull-shaped and shiny.

The sign in the same crimson red of her lips by the window:
FORECLOSURE.

He blinks and it's gone.

The sun has gone cold and there is an old man sitting at the
window, waving.

Excerpts From Various Periodicals Found Within The Foundation of 246B Apex Rd. South

JORDAN SHIVELEY

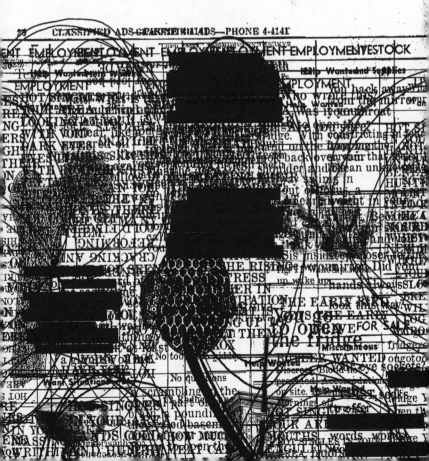

HOT SINGLES IN YOUR AREA, HARVESTING THE CORNERS OF THE NIGHT, WEAVING THEIR ROBES UPON THE LOOM OF EXULTANT SORROWS, DROPPING CROONING PRAYERS INTO THE WELL OF CARRION DELIGHTS, VOID SIGILS OF POSSESSION BLOOMING ON EVERY CHEEK, MONDAYS AMIRITE

THERE ARE MORE BONES NOW THAN THERE WERE BEFORE. You hear this as you stand looking at your reflection in the mirror. THERE ARE MORE BONES AWAKENING SOON THEY WILL BE HERE. What the fuck? You swear you just saw your lips move in the mirror but that's not possible.

Wait. What is that figure behind your reflection? It is unclear, like a smeared oil painting, like smog swirling against glass to billow in on itself. CAN YOU FEEL THE BONES. THERE ARE SO MANY OF THEM.

HAVE YOU SEEN me? Reward offered for seeing me. Have you? I have seen you. Yes, YOU. Such tears and wailing. You would thing you had caught at least a glimpse of me. HAVE YOU?

HOT SINGLES IN YOUR AREA, HANDS COLD AND HUNGRY, GRASPING THE GIFTS LEFT BY THE THING THAT KNOWS EVERY WORD, MOUTHS DISTENDING, JAWS UNLOCKING AS THEY SWALLOW THE WRITHING GIFTS, HOWLING IN UNHOLY FERVOR AS THEY BEGIN TO CHANGE, SOMETHING DARK AND ANCIENT GROWING DEEP WITHIN

HOT SINGLES IN YOUR AREA, HOLDING DARK OFFERINGS BENEATH UNQUIET WATERS, LETTING THEIR CANTS DRIFT DOWN TO WHAT SLEEPS IN THE DEPTHS, RAISING THEIR DARKLY SHINING EYES TO THE RISING HUNTRESS MOTHER IN ANTICIPATION OF WHAT IS RISING UP TO MEET THEM, XOXOX

You back away from the mirror, your throat constricting, fear trapping the scream that feels like an unknowa

weight in your throat

Because no your skin is

itching and

you step closer to the mirror. Did your hands always look this way?

TYPIST seeks to offer services for the words words words words wordswords wordswords words word wordswords

RETIRED HAUSENJAEG R SEERS GAINFUL EMPLOYME NT Has own hand lathes and wardin, aprons need only be give the location of any feral hearths to start full Construction Efforts. Wood Grain Speaker, ha worker.

Did you kno

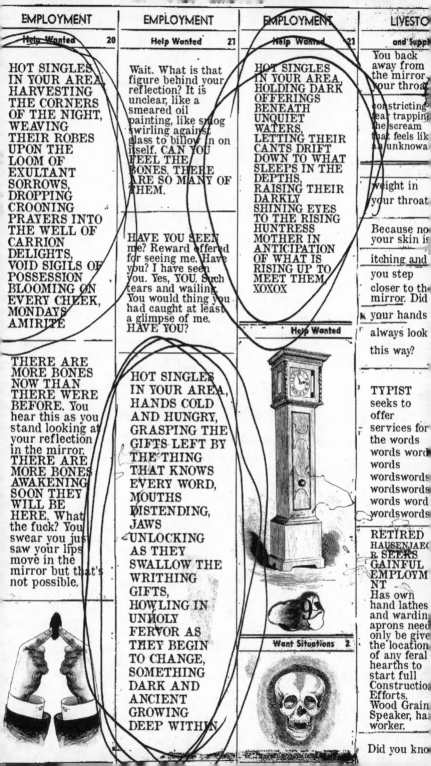

EMPLOYMENT

Help Wanted 20

OT SINGLES
YOUR AREA,
OOKING AT
OU WITH VOID
ARK EYES,
YES LINED
ITH ROWS OF
EETH EVER
PIRALING
NWARD, EYES
OU COULD GET
OST IN

Want Situations 26

OMETHING TO FILL
ng if you know what
need 349-2198

EETH teeth teeth
teeth teeth your-
teeth teeth
teeth teeth teeth
n TEETH your-
teethteethteeth
TEETH your-
teethteeth teeth
th TEETH your-
teeth teeth teeth
teethteethteeth
n TEETH your
teeth teeth teeth
teeth TEETH your
teethteethteeth
TEETH teeth
teethteethteeth

teeth.

EMPLOYMENT

Help Wanted 21

**AGING COUPLE
SEEKS YOUNG
COMPANION**
Must provide
evidence of strong
teeth and warm
but not too warm
blood. Must be
deep sleeper.
Preferrably no
living relatives. A
large supply of
crimson robes is a
bonus. No need to
call. We will call
you...

TOOTH
DIVINERS

No jaw too small

No tooth too hidden

No questions

12 Redber Lane

**HOW MUCH
MEAT CAN
YOUR BODY
HOLD?**

Call for the
surprising
answer

209-918267353

**HOT SINGLES
IN YOUR AREA,
JOGGING PAST
YOUR HOUSE,
AGAIN AND
AGAIN,
SMILING,
WAVING, EACH
TIME LOOKING
MORE LIKE
YOU, EXCEPT
FOR THOSE
TEETH**

EMPLOYMENT

Help Wanted 21

**THE EARLY BIRD
GETS THE EARLY
GRAVE**

Who wrote this?
Was it you?
Are you sure?

fig. 11 Wake up...wake
up...wake up...

**BUTLER
WANTED**
Discreet. Blood
not provided.
Accomodations on
site. Late nights.
Mornings off.

Help Wanted 22

HOT SINGLES IN YOUR
AREA, DIGGING
TIRELESSLY THROUGH
THE NIGHT, PACKING
EACH OTHER'S MOUTHS
WITH DEEP COLD
EARTH, UNCEASINGLY
WHISPERING DOWN
INTO THE WET LOAM,
PROMISING THAT
WHICH LIES WAITING
THAT SOON SOON THEY
WILL BE REUNITED,
THIS COULD BE
EVERYONE AND THEY
ARE NOT PLAYING

fig. 9 a dream forgotten

lost.

LIVESTOCK

and Supplies

Whatever is beneath
your floorboards. We
want it.

**HOT SINGLES
IN YOUR AREA,
STANDING
EVER SO
STILL,
LISTENING SO
SO CLOSELY,
HEARING THE
SOUND OF THE
DEVOURER
THAT HIDES
JUST AT THE
EDGES OF
YOUR SIGHT, A
SLOW HUNGRY
BREATHING, IT
WILL NEVER
LOG OFF THEY
CROON**

FOR SALE

Miscellaneous

A dream you
thought you had
forgotten

A dream you wish
you had
87-594-32

What was written
here is lost

remember what
remains...

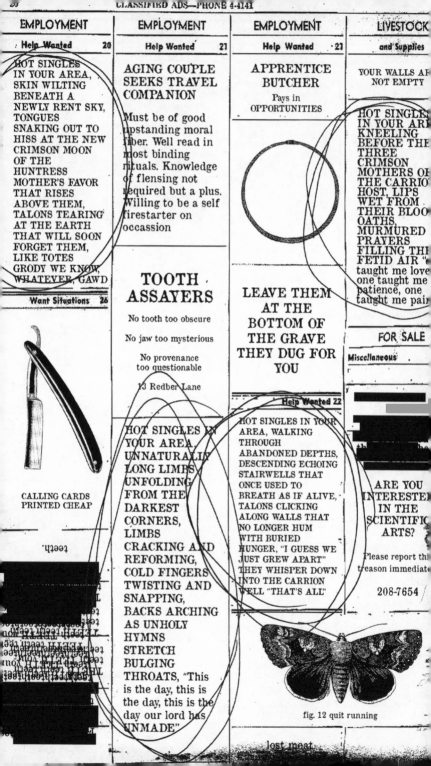

EMPLOYMENT

OT SINGLES
 YOUR AREA,
ASSING IN A
RITHING
OUND OF
INATURALLY
NG LIMBS
D LUMINOUS
ESH,
ANDIBLES
CKING IN
HOLY
MMUNION,
ENING THE
RGOTTEN
NT BACK
D FORTH, IT
E IT ME IT ME
ME IT ME IT
E IT ME IT ME
E IT ME IT ME
E IT ME IT ME
ME

EMPLOYMENT

You go to open the
fridge but what is
inside is not what
you remember.
Later you go back
to open the fridge
again. Something
stops you, .

a scrambling in the
animal part of the
brain, a pounding
at the sealed
basement door of
your memory. You
go to open the
fridge..

You go to open the
fridge. You don't
remember the door
being so dirty. Rust
dried smears
flaking in patches
the same color as
your your hands.
Your hands, your
hands shake as you
grasp the fridge
handle, the veins in
your forearm
bulging. What is
inside is not what
you remember.

You go to open the
fridge. You lean
your forehead
against the
humming door of
the freezer. Your
skin feels flushed
and the door is
deliciously cool.
Your teeth ache and
when you run your
tongue over them
they wiggle loosely
and your mouth
fills with the
familiar taste of
iron.

EMPLOYMENT

You go to open the
fridge. With your
hand on the door
you look back over
your shoulder and
the hallway swims
in and out of
focus, a lens
smeared with
vaseline, a pulsing
liminal canal.
The fridge hums
waiting. You think
you know what is
inside ...you're
wrong.

You go to open the fridge

HOT SINGLES
IN YOUR AREA,
MOUTHS
ENGULFING A
SWELLING TIDE
OF SHADOWS,
LONG FINGERS
SEEKING THE
SEAMS
OFCREATION,
REPLACING
WHAT THEY
FIND INSIDE
WITH SOMETHING
OH SO HUNGRY,
UPVOTING THE
CHARNEL HOST

You go to open
the fridge You
go to open the
fridgeyougotto
openthefridget
hefridgethefrid
geyougoto
open You go to
open the
fridge You go to
open the
fridge

LIVESTOCK

HOT SINGLES
IN YOUR AREA,
HANDS
UNEARTHLY
BENEATH THE
HUNTRESS
MOON,
PEERING INTO
ECHOING VOID,
COLD MOUTHS
WHISPERING,
NEW PHONE
WHO DIS?

FOR SALE

You go to
open the
fridgeyougoto
openyougotoo
penopenopenI
T IS OPEN
open You go
to open the
fridge You go
to open the
fridgeYou go
to open the
fridge You go
to open the
fridgeyougott
oopenthefridg

ridgeyougoto
open You go
to open the
fridge You go
to open the
fridgeyougoto
too
penopenopenI
T IS OPEN
open You go
to open the
fridge

Did you know?

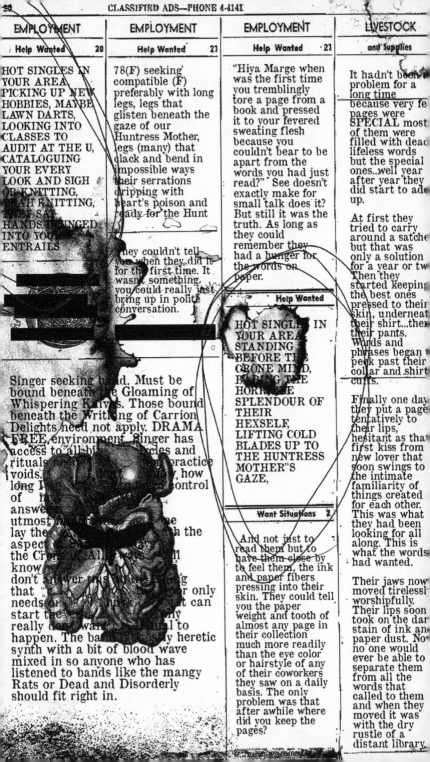

EMPLOYMENT
Help Wanted 20

HOT SINGLES IN YOUR AREA PICKING UP NEW HOBBIES, MAYBE LAWN DARTS, LOOKING INTO CLASSES TO AUDIT AT THE U, CATALOGUING YOUR EVERY LOOK AND SIGH OR KNITTING, AH KNITTING, HER SAD HANDS PLUNGED INTO YOUR ENTRAILS

They couldn't tell you when they did it for the first time. It wasn't something you could really just bring up in polite conversation.

Singer seeking band. Must be bound beneath the Gloaming of Whispering Knives. Those bound beneath the Writhing of Carrion Delights need not apply. DRAMA FREE, environment. Singer has access to all blood circles and rituals needed, just needs practice voids. I don't know how long I... control of answe... utmost... lay the... th the aspect of... the Cron... All... don't answer this... that "...or only needs... it can start the... really don't want it all to happen. The band is mostly heretic synth with a bit of blood wave mixed in so anyone who has listened to bands like the mangy Rats or Dead and Disorderly should fit right in.

EMPLOYMENT
Help Wanted 21

78(F) seeking compatible (F) preferably with long legs, legs that glisten beneath the gaze of our Huntress Mother, legs (many) that clack and bend in impossible ways their serrations dripping with heart's poison and ready for the Hunt

EMPLOYMENT
Help Wanted 21

"Hiya Marge when was the first time you tremblingly tore a page from a book and pressed it to your fevered sweating flesh because you couldn't bear to be apart from the words you had just read?" See doesn't exactly make for small talk does it? But still it was the truth. As long as they could remember they had a hunger for the words on paper.

Help Wanted

HOT SINGLES IN YOUR AREA STANDING BEFORE THE CRONE MIND, BARING THE HORRIBLE SPLENDOUR OF THEIR HEXSELF, LIFTING COLD BLADES UP TO THE HUNTRESS MOTHER''S GAZE,

Want Situations 2

And not just to read them but to have them close by to feel them, the ink and paper fibers pressing into their skin. They could tell you the paper weight and tooth of almost any page in their collection much more readily than the eye color or hairstyle of any of their coworkers they saw on a daily basis. The only problem was that after awhile where did you keep the pages?

LIVESTOCK
and Supplies

It hadn't been a problem for a long time because very fe pages were SPECIAL most of them were filled with dead lifeless words but the special ones...well year after year they did start to add up.

At first they tried to carry around a satche but that was only a solution for a year or tw Then they started keeping the best ones pressed to their skin, underneat their shirt...then their pants. Words and phrases began t peek past their collar and shirt cuffs.

Finally one day they put a page tentatively to their lips, hesitant as tha first kiss from new lover that soon swings to the intimate familiarity of things created for each other. This was what they had been looking for all along. This is what the words had wanted.

Their jaws now moved tirelessl worshipfully. Their lips soon took on the dar stain of ink an paper dust. No no one would ever be able to separate them from all the words that called to them and when they moved it was with the dry rustle of a distant library.

TO HELL, WITH HOPE

DIE BOOTH

[Proposal]

NOTHING HAPPENS.

It's spring, but still cold. Maybe it's the time of night, or the concrete walls holding in damp and chill, funnelling the breeze through either open end of whatever this is—an underpass, Junior guesses. A drainage ditch? The candlelight flutters, scattering shadows across the chalk lines on the floor. Underneath, where they brush the rain-watered floor dry enough to draw on, the sweeping arcs in the muck look like some kind of urban zen-garden.

"Kabkalios, reveal yourself." Junior repeats. If they're honest, the concrete walls are comforting; an anchor. It's the unknown greenness, pressing in from the darkness at either side of the tunnel, which is unnerving. If anything is going to appear, it's going to be from there. Junior gazes out into it, until their eyes lose focus and the different shades of dark form images, writhing and multiplying like cells under a microscope. They see faces, and wings. They see yawning maws and curving teeth. They see—

"Hello."

The voice behind them prompts a startled noise they didn't mean to make, and they almost fall over, spinning around to see a figure standing there, in the candle-carved shadows. "Hey. I'm just—" Junior trips on their words. Stumbles into silence as they realise that they don't actually have to explain suspicious, but ultimately harmless and not-illegal, activity to a stranger who is also prowling around in fields in the deep of night. "Going," they finish.

The stranger tilts their head. Their arms are held very straight at their sides, clad in a white, short-sleeved shirt despite the night-chill. "Going? Then why did you call me?"

A feeling suffuses Junior's limbs, like anaesthetic in reverse, spreading. Their hands shake with it, an adrenaline break, prickling sweat along their hairline, parching their mouth. "Are you the devil?"

"I'm *a* devil."

The stranger just looks like a man. A short man, with cropped, greying hair and wire-rim glasses.

"Kabkalios?"

"At your service."

Junior doesn't miss the amused up-tilt of one corner of the stranger's smile. They were expecting... not this. Not a man. But it doesn't matter. "Do you take souls?"

Kabkalios raises one eyebrow, an almost imperceptible flicker. "You want to sell your soul?"

"No! Not that," Junior says. The cool crowds around them, the wrong side of midnight. "I don't want anything for it. I want to give it to you. It's yours, just take it. Can you?"

"You want to *give* me your soul?" Kabkalios repeats, slowly.

"Yes. Take it."

Brown eyes regard Junior incredulously. "Get lost, kid."

"Please," Junior says, but by the time the words are out, they're already speaking to empty darkness.

[1]

T HE DEVIL COMES as a swarm of moths, the scandal scent of May blossom, a single piece of thistledown.

"Kabkalios, reveal yourself."

The thistle seed drifts idly on its parachute of white floss. Junior catches it on the tip of their finger, seed-point balanced.

"Stop summoning me." The voice seems to come from all around, from within and without.

Junior tilts their head. Addresses the little puff of fluff. "I'll stop summoning you when you take my soul."

Around them, the trappings of the Eleventh Rite are laid out, on the bare concrete of the underpass. The whispering hiss of the devil rushes around the walls. "Take it where? To Hell?"

A shrug. "To wherever, I guess."

"What's your name?"

Junior brings their finger closer to their face, eye level with the tiny seed. "Junior."

A wind whips up, plucking the scraps of paper with their inked sigils from the floor, extinguishing the candles. "Go home, Junior." They try to catch it, but the thistledown takes flight, twisting up on the breeze and out of sight in the darkness.

[2]

T HE DEVIL COMES as a vast maggot made of burning blood, with quartz bones and skin like geodes.

"You're not going to put me off," Junior says.

The maggot sighs, its rippled sides heaving, luminous. The light of it glows on the concrete, reflects red off the rain water running down the tunnel's walls.

Junior says, "You look kinda cool, anyway. Can I come home with you?"

"No."

It's Junior who sighs now. They kick at a fringe of grass

growing through a crack in the underpass pavement. "But why not?"

"Why would you want to give your soul away?"

"I don't want it anymore."

"Why not?" The grating voice of the blood maggot becomes Junior's own voice, mimicked back at them.

Junior rolls their eyes. "Personal reasons."

"You wouldn't like me owning your soul." Its voice becomes stone scraping stone. The light is getting brighter, intensifying. The creature glitters and rolls, lucent bones blazing like rock in lava.

"How can I tell if you don't let me give it a go?"

The creature glows. Junior squints, raising a hand to shade their eyes. Brighter. Junior can't; covers their face with an arm. When they lower it, Kabkalios is gone.

[3]

THE DEVIL COMES as temperature drop, the prickle of hairs on neck, the chill of cheek-skin in earache winds.

Junior shivers, even though they're indoors this time. Wraps their arms around their ribs and watches their breath steam away.

"Is this your bedroom?"

The answer's broken by chattering teeth. "Uh—huh. I want—wanted to. Show it. To you."

"I like your curtains." The voice whines like wind carving ice.

"Thank you. You can ha-have them. If you take. Take my soul."

The Arctic wind sighs. "You *can't* just give away your soul."

"I want to."

"Why?"

Junior looks around them. They can hear it, crying. Can feel its frigid clutch, their skin chilling, starting to numb. The windows are icing over. The mirror too, unfurling delicate thorns of frost. But the curtains don't stir, the inked papers strewn around are still. "Because if I give you my soul, then I'll belong to you. I won't be alone anymore."

The room is quiet. Cool. Junior says, "Kabkalios?" It comes out white. Disperses. They rub their arms, clench and unclench their toes. Breathe, invisibly, as the room begins to warm.

[4]

THE DEVIL COMES as wet heat, dripping green leaves, salt licking the creases of the backs of knees.

"Hey Kabkalios. How's tricks?" Wiping a hand across their brow, Junior leans back against the wall behind their bed.

"Have you not listened to anything I've told you?" Kabkalios's voice babbles like trickling sap.

"I know." They shift, their shirt already starting to stick with sweat. "You don't just take souls. But hear me out. I'm not like other people." The still air seems to ripple, so humid it has weight. "I'm not afraid of you. I don't care what you look like. I understand you."

"You're just as guilty as they are. No matter what form I take, you're already convinced of my nature."

Junior bites their lip, their eyelashes damp. "So, what are you, really?"

The air breathes. "This voice," they hear. "I'm you."

"You're me?"

"We're all me. Us. All of us are each other."

Junior wipes their eyes, blinking. This time, the absence of the devil feels like a hand removed from their throat. Like an arm unslung from around their shoulders.

[5]

THE DEVIL COMES in a rain of sparks that turn to ice and melt when they touch fingers.

Junior twists their hand, admiring the flicker and glitz. "Hey Kabkalios."

This time the voice spits, fifth of November firecrackers, the split of roasting nutshells. It sounds impatient. "Sell your soul? It's a fallacy. A con. You can't give away what doesn't belong to you. How will you pass it on? What *is* your soul?" Its voice crinkles in tinfoil rips. "Energy. We are all made of each other and we will return to everything, infinitely."

Junior cups their hands. Watches the sparks melt into their open palms, merging. "Then if I give you my soul, it doesn't matter. You'll only be taking back part of yourself. Something that's already yours. Already *you*." They don't sound quite pleading. Not yet.

"I think you're missing the point, kid," Kabkalios crackles.

"Wait! Don't go!" The room is already quiet. Junior looks down at their hands. The light is gone. All that's left is a slight dampness, like drying tears.

[6]

THE DEVIL COMES as a single singing note, tilting ear-balance floor-wards with carousel lilt.

It makes Junior sit down heavily on their bed, but they don't cover their ears.

"Hello Junior." The note bends to the words, like silver wire.

Junior stares at their feet. "I just called you to say goodbye."

"At last." The air rings, clear and pleased. "I'm glad you've finally abandoned that terrible idea."

"Yeah. Whatever. Anyway, bye." The sound can't be seen, but Junior isn't looking anyway. "You can go now. I promise I won't summon you again."

A tinnitus thrumming, so intense it's nauseating. "Junior. Is something wrong?"

Junior shakes their head, but the look in their eyes disagrees. "Nothing we've not talked about before. You made it plain, right from the start, but I asked and asked. Now I've given up hope. It's what you wanted."

The note intensifies. It's almost a vibration, raising all the hairs on Junior's arms like static electricity. "You have to have hope, though. *Dum spiro spero*, and all that."

"To Hell with hope." Junior frowns. The sound is starting to rise in pitch, to get inside their head, making their ears ache.

"You missed something." Kabkalios says. The chime of its voice vibrates faster, frantic. "A pause. A comma. The tiniest thing can make all the difference. To Hell," The sudden second of silence swallows every sound in the world, "with hope."

"Kabkalios, I dismiss you."

"What are you doing?" Feedback whines as the pure note starts to warp, to crackle as it breaks down. The circle of candle flames flicker; their wild light makes the gold-inked sigils writhe on their paper.

"Kabkalios, I dismiss you." Junior says.

The quiet wraps around them, like a shroud.

[Conclusion]

IT'S NEARLY AUTUMN when Junior goes back to the fields. A slow, warm day, droning with flies. The *other* flickers through: distance warping like heat haze, stretching the grass and sky.

The underpass draws them like homesickness. It's different in the daytime. Less mysterious and more dingy, the concrete walls streaked green with algae water. It looks smaller, somehow. Overgrown with nettles and that long, feathery grass that Junior always thought was wheat as a child.

They amble towards it, anyway. Desire paths through life, through the bracken and nettles. It's almost unsurprising when a patch of shadow moves. When what they took for graffiti on the wall gains mass and detaches, steps out into the middle of the path.

"Hi."

"Hello Junior."

The short man with the cropped hair and the wire-rim glasses looks different in daylight, too. Diminished, somehow. Junior tilts their head and squints, at the devil silhouetted in the tunnel's mouth. "What are you doing here?"

"I came to see you."

They hadn't even realised that Kabkalios could manifest outside of alloted hours. Stepping out into the sunlight, the figure before them looks even more unremarkable. Just, like a man. "I didn't summon you."

"I know."

The breeze swishes the knee-high grass. Birds choir. "I was lonely. When I kept summoning you, I mean."

"Why did you stop?"

Junior stretches out a hand, to catch a drifting puff of dandelion clock. Instead of slipping through their grasp, it settles in their palm. "Because...I just wanted a friend. After a while, seeing you all the time, it felt like I had one. I didn't feel alone anymore." They pinch the burst of white fluff carefully between thumb and finger, studying it. "Then it was like you said. We're all made of each other. I'm my own best friend." Junior looks up. "Why did you come back?"

"Nobody's ever just wanted to hang out before," Kabkalios says.

Junior nods. They hold out their hand, cradling the seed carefully.

Kabkalios takes it.

TRANSGRESSIONS IN PAST TENSE

ELIZABETH TWIST

E VERY TIME WE TRAVEL backward in time, we die, but we need to keep going until we don't. The Construct has weaknesses, that much we know. There were times—points in history—however brief, where the truth shone through it like a dark diamond, rich and full, and we could see ourselves as ourselves.

Those moments are rare, and rarer still, where I come from. When I come from. By our reckoning, mine was the furthest-flung of our futures, and the bleakest of our timelines.

Picture me there, in a world where the rhythms of life are optimised by benevolent AI, and made easy by automata. There's nothing difficult but what humanity chooses to take on for itself, no conflict but what it creates for its own amusement. I know only that I feel what others don't: a yearning for bodies of all kinds, not the sanitised, bubble-gum inertness a girl is supposed to feel, until a boy puts her name in his mouth.

There was (there is? there will be? there would be? would have been?) no name for what I am, no one like me. So I yearned, and I kept my silence.

Picture me finding my way to my own magic, squeezing through a grate, tracing my way down the concrete river that ran (would have run?) under our city, finding black cables on the ground, unlike anything I'd ever seen, walking along them until they twisted and squirmed, while I chanted *take me, take me there*, and the world writhed around me, no idea what would happen next.

Picture me climbing through a frame of living black rope into a room filled with glowing screens, to find Johnna and Trace, Rachel and Switch, each in their four corners, and Baphomet, sitting cross-legged in the middle of the room, swaying back and forth, with her hair fashioned into horns. (Her joke, for Baphomet is no goat woman, just another one of us, albeit the oldest by far). A thousand faces looking in; a thousand of us casting a spell.

"Oh my God," Johnna said, opening her eyes to look at me. She was like no one I'd ever seen: solid and plain and short-haired and tough and wonderful. "It worked. Check it out. We conjured a whole entire person."

It took the rest of the night for me to understand where they'd conjured me to. The year was 2042, and the world was bleak in the way it had been for a great long while, and the Concept ruled, letting those who loved it accrue outrageous wealth and eat the Earth. The circle of those who found me—Johnna and Trace, Switch and Rachel and the not-goat lady Baphomet—had been working their magic, calling in their sisters and brothers and siblings who understood them, asking for help, wherever they could find it.

They'd gone far, before I reached them. Johnna had set up the dark networks, and Trace had written a manifesto, and Rachel had researched the deep, uncanny metaphysics of the world underlying the physics, and Switch had dropped a ton of acid one night and followed black lines on the floor as they turned into snakes, followed them far, far back, all the way into a cave where a not-goat woman danced.

When Switch had woken up the next day, Baphomet had been sitting on the corner of their bed, poking them with a flute the size of a didgeridoo, carved from a mammoth's femur.

"You came to me. You. In a dream. Twenty-four thousand

years ago."

Baphomet claimed she was immortal. Naturally, she'd joined the cause as well. She'd refused to die, in the name of living long enough to do so.

My yearning and their ritual had brought me to them. As far as we could tell, I came from the year 2300 or so. It was hotter then, even as far North as I was, and timekeeping had become a thing of the past. No one marked years and no one marked decades and no one complained, not aloud, not unless they wanted to disappear, or have their brains scrubbed by benevolent AI.

It was because of me they figured out things would only get worse. The Concept was steadily gaining power. That was its purpose, to take more and more for itself. Sometimes money specifically, sometimes ideas, mostly, human will. It strangled difference because those who were different had reason to keep their will for themselves.

The Concept hid in plain sight. It said things were getting better. It spoke of boundless progress, endless growth. And it did grow, while humanity served it.

"It's exactly like we've said." Trace spoke somberly into a camera, her ruby red lips pressed close to a microphone. "Things seem to get better, but the bar always shifts. We gain a little; somewhere else in the world, we lose. We win victories in name, but we're still hated, we're still misunderstood. It's a net loss, one we fear we'll keep losing. Now, thanks to our visitor, we have proof."

She brushed her hair back from her face with manicured nails like razors, then waved me over. "Tell us where you're from, sweetheart," she'd said. Bit by bit, I told my story into the mic, awed by her beauty, which was mesmerising.

"We know the future, and we know that waiting for it to arrive isn't our best shot," she told her audience of thousands. Word of the success of the ritual had spread. "We know how this is going to go if we don't take action. We need to do more, but now isn't the time. Theoretically, we aren't limited to now, where we have a disadvantage, and the Concept is strong. We know the past. We think we can travel back, together, find a better opportunity. We need to try again. We need to try earlier."

We stayed up all night answering questions, debating, discussing. In the end, we had a consensus: we would look back, go back. We had no mechanism to go forward, but I'd come back and survived, and Switch had travelled back in a hallucination, long enough to contact Baphomet.

First, we tried 2020. Maybe you remember that year. A plague year. The Concept was transparent then, or, that was how we perceived it. Power strolled arm in arm with control, then, the pair of them hurling bullets. More people than ever sickened under their rule, and wanted to push back.

Travel was a problem; the ritual, a disaster. Many of our thousands couldn't break through the hard shell of rationality that coated that reality, so they were left behind in the present, or injured coming through. The rest, well, many died, many tried to raise the Concept so we could isolate it, and the effort pushed them from their safe places. They ended up in the streets, fighting and exposed, maskless and infected.

We retreated a little further back, to 2014, when things were calmer, although the undercurrent of the Concept was still there, still heavy, just sublimated under the belief many people had back then, that things were going to be okay, because they'd appeared to be improving. There was no camouflage like contentment.

We rested then, and planned. We found houses and apartments, we found jobs. I, who had been coddled by the metallic arms of automata, who had never had to do much for myself except metabolise the food that appeared before me, delighted in filling my time. I went to work: the grocery store, a funeral parlour, a 24-hour laundromat.

At home, the others taught me about food: how it grew, how harvest worked, and how to cook it. I burned everything, including my fingers. One night Switch and Rachel lost patience with me, and shooed me out of the kitchen. I sat in the corner of the dining room with Baphomet, and fed her apple slices, and listened to her.

She spoke in a constant murmur, her eyes sharp and steady, her voice like something that came from a dream. She told me I was dreaming now, that everything we thought while we were awake was a dream, and that was how the Concept snuck in, that was how it colonized us.

"See it from the corner of your eye. Turn your head very fast to look: it's gone," she said. "That's where it hides. That's where it lives. In you. In your ideas." She tapped my head. "In the thoughts that you think without knowing it."

Words issued from her hard-toothed mouth like a prayer, like a mantra.

"I've seen a place, I've been to a place, where light shoots up from the ground, between the roots of a tree like fingers trying to cup the earth, trying to clasp it back down. As bright as the sun, but wrong, false. A fountain, they call it, a well of life. There's a price to pay for bathing in it. I saw him there."

"Him?" I brushed her hair. It was thick and coarse, piled high on her head.

"Him. The one you seek."

"The Concept?" Johnna had come up with the term. Once we could name it, we could destroy it, she'd said.

Baphomet had a bony ridge on her forehead. Her face protruded, her large nose sticking far out, her chin small and delicate, like no person's face I'd ever seen. Her skull, under the horns of her hair, was flat on top.

"Before he was an idea, he was just a man," she said. "He stood on a broken road, and told me not to follow, so naturally I did. I followed him to the fountain. I watched him go into the light, his bones showing through his skin, his intentions showing through his eyes. To take us all into his belly. When he came out, he greeted me, and told me he would make me safe, told me he would make everyone safe. I threw rocks at him. His head split, the blood poured down over his eyes and blinded him. I followed him until he died, to make sure the evil left the world, but it spread out to the far horizon. It went everywhere."

I closed my eyes and pictured a man dissolving into a red syrup lake, the fluid transforming into the motor oil drips from the servitors that brought my food, in the time from which I came. One change became the next, and then the next; one vile intention binding all.

We talked about it as we ate the dinner Switch and Rachel had made: the man who was no longer a man. We called others in, and asked what they knew. Switch tranced, went in search of more information.

Ludovic came to us the next day, knocking on the door of the house where we lived, a tidy man in an old-fashioned suit. Like Baphomet, he was immortal, from one of the lands conquered by Rome. He'd been taken as a slave, rewarded for his hard work with a position in a rich man's house.

He smiled at Switch. "You and I met. Do you remember?"

"I think so," they said. "You were dressed differently."

"Two thousand years ago. You told me to come here, now, and report what I saw."

We all watched Switch in awe. They smiled sheepishly. "I wrote our address and the year on my hand. Apparently I could still read it, in trance. After the trouble Baphomet had, I wanted to make sure we were easier to find."

Ludovic told us what he'd seen: an ambitious man, a Roman sorcerer, who had patrons behind him, Caesars, and the bankers, and dark cabals, the ones who use certain paths and ways to gain power.

"I saw what they did," Ludovic said. "I saw him turn to dust and disperse in the air, a glittering darkness that spread over the gathering. I saw them inhale it. I saw them glow with light. I was nothing, I was a slave, but I saw, and I washed their feet after, and I had to let them wipe their fingers in my hair, I had to let them do many other things beside."

Some time later, Ludovic told me he had no taste for the intimate touch of others, and never had. He held my hand, and curled against me at night, and we called it love. He showed me his scars, the many places where he'd tried to let his life out. He told me he was glad he'd lived so long, to find us, to find that there was more than one type of secret cabal, and that some of us were interested in liberation.

We welcomed him, but we despaired, for we understood that the break in the world hadn't only happened once, but repeatedly, and perhaps often. Perhaps it happened all the time.

It was too late, some of the thousands argued. We'd failed already: after all, according to our best information, which was my report from the future, the world would become a place where no argument was to be had, where no differences would be permitted. We were doomed: the Concept refreshed itself whenever it wished, and it wished a lot, whenever a new avatar saw an opportunity to feed. We had no way to best it.

I wondered. Switch had followed the writhing black lines backward, as I had done. Could they be traced forward? The future hadn't happened yet. Could we read it again?

We went questing then, Ludovic and I. We wandered the great vast interior of the continent. I looked for cables on the ground, black cables where no power lines should be. I saw them, running across the empty landscape, running through the woods, but always they went backward, into the past.

Finally, in an abandoned hotel in what was once a great city, I found more than I'd ever seen, snaking across the floor: in an old ballroom they split, and turned, and went not just to one future, but many different ways. I didn't wish to travel, for I feared what it would do to me, and I couldn't leave Ludovic, but I laid my hand upon them and I felt my way along their tracks, and I knew we could change our fate, that there were choices. What was more, the splitting points weren't just the in present. They had happened in the past. We had complicated the future, or we would. We had always complicated it.

The thousands worked a long while, after Ludovic and I returned. Our little family thought and we planned, along with the others across the world. We gathered our most lively ideas, when we were awake and aware. We pressed and moulded our formulas and understandings and came to this: if the Concept was once a man, and again once a man, and he became something more, again and again, then there were many times when we too might be something more. Not once, not only once, but repeatedly, and perhaps often. If not now, then earlier; if not then, then perhaps earlier still.

Together, we listened to the stories of the past, heard the music and watched the movies. We read the books, we read the plays. We combed through the old song lyrics, through the histories, looking for rifts, for the times when the weaknesses in the Concept's architecture opened, and our dark showed through.

Baphomet whispered that the deep past was a place of freedom, and if we could, we should go there. Some agreed with her, and made a case for Ancient Greece; others wanted to go to Asia, anytime before the influence of the Concept infiltrated it, which had happened later than in the rest of the world.

Forget the future, they argued. We should use our power to save ourselves, as many of us as we could.

The debates carried on, and many left before we made the attempt, claiming that our cause was tainted by our inclusivity. They said I didn't belong, because I liked, potentially, anyone. That Ludovic didn't belong, because he didn't want anything to do with sex. That Trace didn't belong, because she liked men. That Johnna didn't belong, because she had decided we did.

"It's him," Baphomet croaked from the corner, seeing more clearly than any of us could. "He draws these lines. He separates one thing from another. That's why they think that cutting some of us out is the answer. That's the curse working through them. Divide and conquer, isn't that what they say?" Baphomet had a fondness for aphorisms. "Not the oldest trick, but one of the most popular."

Among the seven of us, we agreed she was right. We would try to stop it ourselves, to battle our enemy like we always should have, in a fight on our own terms. We couldn't go back to his beginning. Baphomet couldn't remember exactly when she'd known him, or where; if the fountain of light that came up from the ground were a real thing, it had long since vanished, or hidden itself away, and in any case, we had no proof that the man she saw was really the first. We looked instead to the recent past, a year in the latter part of the twentieth century, but not too late.

The thing that draws us is a song. You know the one. Or if you don't, you've heard it, and haven't noticed, and that's okay. It's playing on the radio when we follow the black cables back along the floor, all of us going together into the past once more.

Baphomet is still in her corner, shining like a high priestess, and Trace and Switch and Johnna are each in theirs. Ludovic and Rachel and I take the centre. We're in some room: the cables chose it, since they took us here, or maybe we picked it together, or maybe the one or the force that wrote the song helped us find it. It doesn't matter: we're here and we're safe, we're unnoted and all-important, both at the same time.

Together we amplify. Ludovic and Rachel and I hold hands. Johnna and Trace and Switch and Baphomet hold the outside. We're a speaker. We're a satellite dish. We're a perfect hollow orb made of the human need to find beauty in difference, and we sing that difference and that beauty out into the world.

I'd like to say the Concept shatters. I'd like to say it breaks all at once, but we don't see it in our lifetimes, not for ourselves.

Instead, I write an instruction manual for following the black cables, hoping that it makes it into the future, so people can trace us back and join us. Switch giggles as they stand at a photocopier in the small public library in our small town, making a hundred copies of it by hand, and stapling them to bind them. They look up the addresses of the people we knew in the future, the ones who joined the cause when they were older, and they mail them out.

In a few years, at the first dawning of the internet, Switch will type the instructions into a computer and find a way to post them, with an introduction about the manual's spooky and mysterious origins. It will become an urban legend, and, later, a point of nostalgia. It will spread.

We wonder about the shape our revolution will take, but we don't have to wait for long. Soon, our sisters and brothers come, from several futures, telling us the news of how it will play out. In some versions, there is turmoil. There's a fight. Those who cling to the Concept don't want it to dissipate, they have guns, they have harsher weapons than ours. We lose.

In other futures, there's promise. There is peace, and gentle anarchy. There are gift economies. There's an interest in many people's stories, in the specificities of who each of us is, and how we want to live. There is room for difference.

There is room.

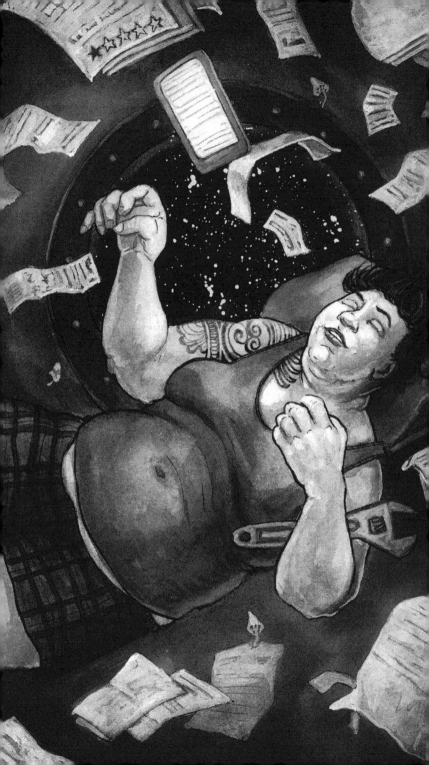

Effects of Altitude on the Blood Elevations of Love

MARIANNE KIRBY

Most Helpful 1-Star Review of Maison de Champignons
Username: rightround

Um, ew. I didn't know until I got there so just in case you don't know, this restaurant serves mushroom dishes but the mushrooms are from witch blood. The Trifecta witches running this place are serving us their blood and that's just gross. Only eat here if you want to eat blood mushrooms!

Reply to rightround from Maison de Champignons
Our station directory entry clearly states that we serve mushrooms dishes that include ingredients cultured from the deepest mystery of the Trifecta. Your meal was comped when your misunderstanding was explained. Brightness be yours.

Excerpt from *Metaphysical Monographs on the Theories and Praxis of Lunar Theurgy in Interterrestrial Orbits*

Of course, not all practitioners are so forthcoming with the secrets of their ritual. The witches of the *Lunar Refusal* space station, in an orbit closely aligned with that of Jupiter, guard their systemic framework with particular fervor, going so far as to impose restrictions on the oxygen levels of their designated sector within the space station itself to prevent casual visitation.

Scholars have posited that the process by which initiates to the mysteries of the Trifecta must then be acclimated to a demanding new physical environment functions as a powerful ritual for community inclusion, marking them with the status of the Other and thus removing them from the everyday workings of the space station.

The *Lunar Refusal*'s practices have inspired imitation within more than one of the Inner Ring population subcultures, perhaps as a mark of differentiation from the imposed normative status enforced by the safety protocols put in place by the station's administration. To that effect, some youths spend time in artificially oxygen-poor environments as a form of both recreation and rebellion. The examination of these youths has demonstrated a change in the formation of their red blood cells and the capacity of those blood cells to retain and carry oxygen. The change is not viewed as deleterious; however, long-term side effects are not yet known.

Excerpt from Repair Manual - Airlocks

An airlock is a rotary valve. For the valve to seal properly, the vanes of the rotary value must fit closely to each other and the housing. The vanes must be adequately lubricated in order to both maintain static pressure on the valve's inlet side and a differential pressure or vacuum on the valve's discharge side.

PERSON INVOLVED IN THE INCIDENT

Full Name: Theodorsia Martina Lexing III

Home Address: Inner Ring, Bay 7, Berth 12

Contact Numbers: 47121903

☐ Student   ☒ Employee   ☐ Visitor   ☐ Vendor

INCIDENT INFORMATION

Date: 36254.7   Time: 800   Police Notified ☐ Yes ☒ No

Location of Incident: Airlock Gate 4

Incident Description: Engineer Lexing III was repairing seal on Airlock Gate 4, temporarily increasing oxygen levels in that quadrant of the Outer Ring. Unknown Trifecta witch appeared and lodged a complaint with Engineer Lexing III. Witch appeared confused but euphoric, possibly due to unanticipated elevations of blood oxygen saturation. Engineer Lexing III offered medical assistance but was refused. Engineer Lexing III ceased work on repair to report incident. Repair on Airlock Gate 4 is incomplete.

Were there witnesses to the incident? ☒ Yes ☐ No   *If yes, please attach a separate sheet with the names, addresses, and phone numbers of the witnesses*

Was the individual injured? ☐ Yes ☒ No

Describe the injury or the body part injured and other important information

Was medical treatment provided? ☐ Yes ☐ No ☒ Refused treatment

Where was the treatment provided? ☐ On site ☐ Emergency room ☐ Other

REPORTER INFORMATION

Name of Individual submitting the report:

Theo Lexing III

[signature]

Date completed:

FOR OFFICIAL USE ONLY

Report received by: Dani Version

Date: 36254.8

INCIDENT INFORMATION

Date	Action Taken	Name
36254.8	email sent to official Trifecta distro list - email bounced	D.V.
36254.9	rep sent to conference B-42 - no witches present to confer	D.V.
36258.2	email received from Trifecta Maven Lopez. Incident closed.	D.V.

Excerpt from Observation Report - Theo Lexing III

For this project, as is customary and required to ensure the consent of all initiates, I observed my sister's initiation class for three hours, via view screen and special permission provided by the Trifecta Maven overseeing the class. As a condition of their approval, the Trifecta mandated that all observation would be visual only, so I was not privy to any audio/audible communications that took place. There were five initiates in attendance along with two lower mavens and a higher maven who led the group. Two of the initiates were twins, which caused some perceived excitement from the two lower mavens.

For the sake of transparency, I did recognize one of the lower mavens from an encounter I had while working repairs of an airlock at the Outer Ring. She appeared to recognize me in return and we traded a nonverbal greeting at the beginning and ending of the initiation session.

When the viewing began, the initiates seemed very shy and wary of the camera; they had been informed of my observation (and signed the appropriate release forms) but the reality of being observed was, of course, different in practice than in theory. However, half an hour into the gathering, the initiates seemed to lose awareness of the cameras and return to normal, uninhibited behavior under the guidance of the attending mavens.

After a period of apparently casual conversation, accompanied by some receptive laughter on the part of the initiates, the initiates were led to cots, where they laid down under their own power and were covered with blankets mapping the constellations. The lower mavens then used autoinjectors to dose the initiates with an unidentified substance.

One of the initiates objected. The lower maven (the one with whom I am familiar) attending to her did not force the initiate to receive the injection. Instead, she calmed the initiate's upset with what seemed to be soft words and reassuring touch to her back and shoulders. The initiate was allowed to observe the reactions of the other initiates to the shot: deep slumber with active dreaming indicated by rapid eye movements apparent due to twitching of the eyelids. Upon this visual confirmation no harm was being experienced, the initiate consented to her own injection and shortly succumbed to similar unconscious visions.

The supervising mavens monitored the initiates closely and I at no point doubted the safety of the initiates undergoing the ritual.

At the two-hour-forty-five-minute mark, the first initiate woke, sitting up suddenly and throwing her hands above her head as though to ward something off.

Both lower mavens attended to her; one provided access to food and water while the other offered reassurance in the form of physical contact, which seemed very effective. My sister was the next initiate to wake and she also sat up abruptly but did not appear to be in any distress.

The other initiates all woke peacefully, including the initiate who was initially reluctant. The lower maven with whom I am familiar spoke with the higher maven, though I could not hear the exchange.

INVITATION FROM TRIFECTA MAVEN LOPEZ TO THEO LEXING III

You are hereby invited to witness the secondary phase of the current initiation class inclusive of your sister, known at this time as Maven Presumptive Isadore. Please present yourself at the appointed time at Airlock Gate #3, with the previously negotiated safety equipment to assure your own breathing capability is supported.

MOON WITCH TEA RECIPE

Ingredients:

- 2 cups lunar water
- 3.5g of dried mushrooms, preferred varietal
- 2g of decaf black tea in a sachet
- Ginger and honey to taste

Instructions:

1. Filter 2 cups lunar water and then heat to between 366.5 and 373.15 degrees K.
2. Roughly crush 3.5g of preferred mushroom varietal in a stone mortar with a wooden pestle.
3. Place ground mushrooms into ceramic vessel.
4. Remove water from heat source and let sit for 10 exhalation cycles.
5. Pour half of the water into the ceramic vessel over the crushed mushrooms.
6. Add sachet of tea to ceramic vessel and steep for 6 minutes.
7. Remove tea bag and strain liquid through a filter into a clean drinking vessel.
8. Add ginger and honey to taste.
9. Repeat process for second serving.

SAFETY VIOLATION REPORT - THEO LEXING III

Description and location of unsafe event:
Engineer Lexing III was observed by her supervisor to be reducing the oxygenation of her tank for external station repair work. When questioned, Engineer Lexing III responded that she didn't think the decreased oxygen level would cause any

harm. She indicated that the Trifecta witches of the Outer Ring
exist in an atmosphere of lower oxygen saturation at all times
and believed that the mix would allow Engineer Lexing III to
complete a longer shift of external station repair.

When reprimanded by her supervisor, Engineer Lexing III
corrected the oxygen mix of her tank and returned to work
without incident.

No disciplinary action is recommended.

RULE #57 - INTER-RING FRATERNIZATION

Rule Title: *Guidelines for Inter-Ring Fraternization to Insure Positive
Relations*

Rule Summary: In an effort to reinforce good relationships
between the demographics occupying the Inner and Outer
Rings of the *Lunar Refusal*, and to instill general harmony across
diverse populations, be advised that contact with the Trifecta
witch colony occupying the Outer Ring of the Lunar Refusal
Space Station by those who have not been inducted into their
mysteries is prohibited unless initiated by a member of said
colony. While casual interactions taking place in the main
areas of the Inner Ring of the Lunar Refusal Space Station
are not subject to this rule within reason, in order to allow for
the normative expectations of etiquette and commerce, any
denizen of the Inner Ring of the Lunar Refusal Space Station
shall be advised they may not privately comm a Trifecta witch
of the Outer Ring of the Lunar Refusal Space Station without
a pre-existing relationship in which permission to communicate
has been granted. Trifecta witches may initiate contact via such
forms as: personal text, email, dreams, coded missives in station
publications. Coded sigils and covert messages from second
parties will not function as permission to communicate with
Trifecta witches.

It's Classified #23

MISSED ⚲NNECTION - I THINK YOU RE⚲GNIZED ME AS I RE⚲GNIZED YOU, A VIEW SCREEN BETWEEN US AND THE WORK, ALWAYS THE WORK THAT MUST BE DONE THOUGH SOMETHING IN ME REBELS AT IT EVEN AS THE REST OF ME THRILLS TO IT. D1D YOU☽◖●⊕⌒ 5EE ME ○○ , WILL YOU ● ⚲ME TO ME ⚥⚲⇔⊕, CAN YOU●☽◖ TELL ME ⚶ <u>YOUR N4ME</u> 1N THE D4RKNE55 OF THE NEW M☾N WH1LE <u>WE RE5T</u> FROM THE PULL OF THE T1DE ⌣◌●◖THAT TUG5 AND TUG5 4T <u>OUR HE4RT5</u> 4ND <u>OUR L1VER5</u> 4ND THE 5WEETME4T5 OF <u>OUR PRECIOU5 BOD1E⌣</u>? MEET ME WHERE FIRST I GLIMPSED YOU AFTER THE JOB THAT BRINGS YOU TO ME IS DONE IF THE HEART OF YOU CRIES OUT IN HARMONY WITH MINE.

Excerpt from Trifecta Manifesto

Where there is one of us, you will find two more. We will travel in threes, will always witness the birth-life-death cycle that governs us, teaches us, nurtures us. We will embrace the natural world, especially the parts of it that bear witness across time and space, that demonstrate the way of being that leads to Collective. We will resist assimilation. We will resist being understood. We will resist contempt—both for us and from us. We will follow the way that leads to Collective. We will be three until we are all.

Observation Report, Part 2, Incomplete - Theo Lexing III

My previous observation was via silent remote viewing; in a continuation of my observation of the first phase of initiation ritual, I observed my sister's second initiation class for two and one half hours in person by special permission of Trifecta Maven overseeing the class and at the invitation of one of the lower mavens also present and governing the ritual, introduced as Neoma, after an old earth name for the new moon.

Neoma confirmed that initiated witches take new names within their community and that my sister will also follow in this tradition. The higher maven, introduced to me as Mona, then interrupted us and recalled Neoma to her post. I apologized for offering disruption but Mona stated that it is well for us to learn about each other. I felt very welcome as an observer.

This time there were only four initiates; I later learned that one of the twins I observed in my first session (Maven Presumptive Dianne) declined to return. The initiate who originally balked at the injection during the first ritual *did* return and appeared to have no reservations about participating in further ritual.

The initiates did not demonstrate the same reservations as when I was viewing via view screen, indicating a higher level of comfort with in-person observation, perhaps based on their previous experiences being monitored by the Trifecta witches involved in the ritual.

My in-person observation allowed me to hear the chant the three Trifecta witches and four initiates participated in after a brief period of socializing. I have agreed not to speak of the details of the chant in order to preserve the privacy of the Trifecta witches and the sanctity of their practices. This chant was followed by a similar injection procedure.

EMPLOYMENT PACKAGE, MEDICAL RECORDS RELEASE FORM: TRIFECTA MAVEN NEOMÁ (FORMERLY DIANNE BIRNDER II OF II)

You may use or disclose the following health care information:
☑ All my health information, including but not limited to: Communicable Disease Information, Behavioral Health Care/

Psychiatric Care, Alcohol and/or Drug Abuse Treatment, if any.
☑ Medical records created and maintained by the supervising medical coordinators of the Trifecta after my initiation into the Trifecta wonders.
☑ Blood status, including but not limited to: oxygen saturation levels and bloodborne concentrations of the relevant fungal growth.

You may disclose this information to:
Maison de Champignons

It's Classified #73

°CNNECTION NO LONGER MISSING, ONLY DELAYED AS WE WERE FORCED TO PART, TWO BEINGS ●)(● ACCLIMATED TO DIFFERENT ATMOSPHERES, DIFFERENT WORLDS WHOLE AND ENTIRE YET OVERLAPPING ENOUGH FOR US TO TOUCH HAND TO HAND ACROSS AN OPEN AIRLOCK, OUR MISMATCHED CALLUSES GREETING EACH OTHER IN PASSING AND HOPING FOR MORE TIME, ALWAYS MORE TIME TO °CMMUNE. RETURN TO ME WHEN YOU 4RE ABLE, WHENEVER THE DES1RE RISES 1N YOU 45 THE W4X1NG MⓍN GROW5. FIND ME UNDER THE FULL MⓍN WHERE THOSE WHO WOULD HAVE BEEN MY SISTERS HAVE WORKED THEIR SMALL BLⓍD MAGIC—I'LL RESERVE A SPECIAL TABLE JUST FOR TWO.

Maison de Champignons Menu - Specials of the Night

Specials!

Crispy Mushrooms with Creamy White Beans and Kale:

Maitake mushrooms, pan crisped, accompanied by a white bean puree and wilted greens, feta, and toasted pepitas.

Brothy Farro with Eggs and Mushrooms: House Mushroom broth with sautéed House Mushrooms and a raw egg yolk stirred into each bowl.

Grilled Porcini-Rubbed Rack of Veal: The name says it all!

SAFETY VIOLATION REPORT 2 - THEO LEXING III

Description and location of unsafe event:

Engineer Lexing III was observed by her supervisor to once again be reducing the oxygenation of her tank for external station repair work. When questioned, Engineer Lexing III responded that she needed to acclimate herself so that she could join her lover in the low-oxygen conditions of the Outer Ring. Engineer Lexing III commented that the moon exerts forces on her and at the full moon we will see that she "is not full of shit about her having a girlfriend." Engineer Lexing III, when questioned, confirmed she has not experienced harassment regarding her orientation, merely that her coworkers seem skeptical about the existence of her relationship.

When reprimanded, Engineer Lexing III corrected the oxygen mix of her tank and returned to work without incident.

A verbal warning was recorded. No disciplinary action is recommended.

APPLICATION FOR TRANSFER OF HABITATION
DECISION: DENIED

Theodorsia Martina Lexing III's application for habitation access to the Outer Ring. was missing the following:

> An invitation from the Trifecta governing body.

Invitation by a lower maven does not suffice for the cause of granting habitation access. Should Lexing III receive such an invitation, she shall be required to submit a new Application for Transfer of Habitation and pay a new processing fee.

CASE ID: 458435R6RX

Border Violation Report - Theo Lexing III

Description and location of border violation:
Violator Lexing III claims invitation was received via coded message from one of the lower mavens. However, no higher maven could be found at the time to verify this claim.

Help Wanted Ad #39

Seeking assistance altering the airflow of a single personal berth. Reply to Box 3174529 if available for this work. Compensation negotiable.

Security Footage 1 - Theo Lexing III

00:00:00 Subject enters berth, carrying a take-out bag from Maison de Champignons.
00:00:15 Subject places take-out bag on nightstand and removes a to-go cup.
00:00:30 Subject removes lid of to-go cup, which is seen to contain a viscous red fluid.
00:00:45 Subject removes a small box from the take-out bag,

opens it, and retrieves an autoinjector.

00:00:60 Subject fills autoinjector with viscous red fluid from the to-go cup.

00:00:75 Subject checks classified section of *Lunar Refusal* common publication.

00:01:05 Subject exhales and injects self in leg with viscous red fluid contained in the autoinjector.

00:01:15 Subject exhibits signs of rapid onset sleep.

00:02:05 Subject exhibits signs of dreaming

Security Footage 2 - Theo Lexing III

00:00:00 Subject enters berth, carrying a take-out bag from Maison de Champignons.

00:00:15 Subject places take-out bag on nightstand and removes a to-go cup.

00:00:30 Subject removes lid of to-go cup, which is seen to contain a viscous red fluid.

00:00:45 Subject removes a small box from the take-out bag, opens it, and retrieves an autoinjector.

00:00:60 Subject fills autoinjector with viscous red fluid from the to-go cup.

00:00:75 Subject exhales and injects self in leg with viscous red fluid contained in the autoinjector.

00:00:85 Subject exhibits signs of rapid onset sleep.

00:01:05 Subject exhibits signs of dreaming

Safety Violation Report 3 - Theo Lexing III

Description and location of unsafe event:

Engineer Lexing III was observed by her berthmates to be reducing the oxygenation of her sleeping area. When her berthmates inquired as to the purpose, Engineer Lexing III was withdrawn and exhibited signs of depression. In the morning, Engineer Lexing III appeared to be lethargic and exhibiting signs of disorientation. She reported auditory hallucinations of "her girlfriend's voice" instructing her to enter the Outer Ring.

Engineer Lexing III was taken to the medical wing and placed in a high oxygen environment to encourage recovery.

A copy of this written warning shall be amended to Engineer Lexing III's file. No disciplinary action is recommended at this time. Continued oxygen therapy is recommended.

It's Classified #147

WE KEEP SHARING MOON RISES THE SAME WAY WE SHARE DINNERS, ALL DREAMS AND OUR BLOOD HUMMING TOGETHER IN MY VEINS. THEY WON'T LET ME JOIN YOU; I'VE MADE MY ROOM READY FOR YOU IF YOU CAN SLIP OUT THROUGH THE PLACE WE FIRST MET.

Border Violation Report - Trifecta Maven Neoma

Description and location of border violation:
Violator Trifecta Maven Neoma was found in the common space adjacent to Airlock Gate 4, euphoric from oxygen exposure. Two other Trifecta Mavens were alerted and Trifecta Maven Neoma was returned to the Outer Ring. Trifecta Maven Neoma declined to explain her presence in the Inner Ring.

Security Footage 3 - Theo Lexing III

00:00:00 Subject enters berth, carrying a take-out bag from Maison de Champignons.

00:00:15 Subject places take-out bag on nightstand and removes a to-go cup.

00:00:30 Subject removes lid of to-go cup, which is seen to contain a viscous red fluid.

00:00:45 Subject removes a small box from the take-out bag, opens it, and retrieves an autoinjector.

00:00:60 Subject fills autoinjector with viscous red fluid from the to-go cup.

00:00:75 Subject exhales and injects self in leg with viscous red fluid contained in the autoinjector.

00:00:85 Subject exhibits signs of rapid onset sleep.

00:01:05 Subject exhibits signs of dreaming.

00:75:05 Subject exhibits signs of distress while sleeping; subject cries out for the new moon.

00:75:25 Subject goes still and life support alarms initiate.

OFFICIAL MEDICAL COMPLAINT - FILED BY THEO LEXING III

Description of complaint:
The moon—the new moon—chose me for her and that means there are three of us now: she and me and the moon make three. We will be three until we are all. I hear her. I dream her. My blood is prepared for her and for the moon.

Application for Transfer of Habitation
DECISION: APPROVED

Theodorsia Martina Lexing III's application for habitation access to the Outer Ring was granted for the following reasons:
> By medical exception

Lexing III will be treated by the governing medical body of the Trifecta due to bloodborne contamination facilitated by a maven of the Trifecta. The applicable Processing Fee has been waived at the request of the governing medical body of the Trifecta.

CASE ID: 458435R6RX-2

7.0 Final Summary:

7.1 It is the final finding of this safety task force that the Trifecta witches of the Lunar Refusal Space Station acted in accordance with their own bylaws and procedures and did not violate the accords agreed upon by the Trifecta governing body with the administrators of the Lunar Refusal Space Station.

7.1.1 The individual formerly known as Engineer Theodorsia Martina Lexing III shall be escorted to the Outer Ring and placed under the supervisory capacity of the Trifecta governing medical body and in the care of Trifecta Maven Neoma.

7.1.2 Her records and affiliated identity papers shall be amended to support her occupation as designated and permitted spaces within the Outer Ring without loss of privilege of movement within the public and private spaces of the Inner Ring as commonly and reasonably permitted.

7.2 It is the final finding of this safety task force that the restaurant known as Maison de Champignons, located within the Inner Ring and serving the denizens thereof, shall cease offering menu items featuring the psychoactive ingredient commonly referred to as "blood shrooms."

7.2.1 All fungal ingredients shall be procured via the hydroponics labs of the Inner Ring and certified as safe for consumption by hydroponics lab personnel.

7.2.2 Menu descriptions shall be edited to include the source of any fungal ingredients and their anticipated impact on denizens of the Inner Ring.

It's Classified #275

LET'S REVIVE AN OLD FAVORITE! UNDERGROUND SUPPER CLUB FOR THE ADVENTUROUS MINDED AND THOSE OF BOLD PALATE OFFERS ONCE-IN-A-LIFETIME OPPORTUNITY TO SAMPLE DISHES FORBIDDEN BY THE SAFETY TASK FORCE. TAKE A DEEP BREATH (IT MIGHT BE YOUR LAST!) AND REPLY TO BOX 3174529 ☾ FOR MORE 1NFORM4T1ON.

Most Helpful 5-Star Review of Maison de Champignons
Username: JessaPeek2173

Honestly, when I saw Mushroom House—that's what me and my bunkmates call it — was open again after being closed for blood contamination violations, I wasn't sure what to think. But we got our reservations in before the rush and, wow, was it ever worth it. I don't know what those witches are doing but the Trifecta-trained chefs really know their stuff. The risotto was toothsome yet tender, which is not a sentence I ever expected to write. I hear the service was better before the shutdown but you can't have everything, especially when they were still obviously sorting out a new procedure. To be clear, the witches are no longer allowed to use the hallucinogenic mushrooms cultivated from their blood samples, but I don't see anything wrong with regular mushrooms from the hydroponics lab anyway. Five stars for one of the most delicious and romantic meals I've ever had!

BEFORE, AFTER, AND THE SPACE BETWEEN

KEL COLEMAN

A NECROMANCER'S MAGIC is strongest on the anniversary of their death.

This bit of Izaani lore cannot be twisted to benefit the lightless scrawlers and is thus unproven by their standards. So, it surprises me to find you, after a childhood of rejecting your heritage, preparing for a spell this frigid evening.

It has been nine years to the day since my soul and body were parted.

You are born with a headful of brownish-red wisps. It is the most remarkable thing about you, so we name you Sanguine. This obvious likeness to your father seems to encourage you to regard me, more often than not, as an uninvited guest. I suspect you wean yourself at eight months just to spend more time with him.

The little fish who swam inside me all those months is becoming her own, separate person…it tastes of unripe winter berries, this feeling.

Y OU ARE IN a night-cloaked meadow, wearing my old ritual dress. Another Izaani tradition I never thought to see you embrace. Though you have your father's dusty-brown skin and his striking hair, I am reminded of myself at your age: tall—too tall some said—wide hips and soft belly shaping the shift dress, small, high breasts, dark nipples apparent through the sheer white fabric.

Spine stiff, feet planted, red curls exploding in all directions, you stand in the center of a circle formed by the linked hands of eight other Izaani. They wear sheer dresses like yours or shorts with chests bared, open to Moon's energy. If any of you are cold, you don't show it.

You drag the plain dagger across one cheek. You wince but do not hesitate before opening a second line across the other. You place the dagger on a square of leather and pick up a clay pot.

I buy you a charm bracelet when you turn five. I add a charm on special occasions. As you grow, I have to add links as well. Even when you aren't speaking to me, the tinkling of that bracelet as you move around the house says enough.

W HILE YOU rub an herbal paste into your wounds, I look around at your circle.

The two necromancers bear dozens of white dermal piercings from ring-finger to elbow, the beads of bone forming roiling patterns. It's a shortcut for solid spellwork, but at least they're proud to wear their heritage. The rest don't display their affinities, but I can sense them. One is a conjurer, another a diviner. Three are animancers and whatever you have planned, Little Fish, I hope it's got nothing to do with combining your affinity with *theirs*—I've been gone too long to be reanimated. To be sure, I reach for any dead nearby and am relieved to find only small animals like insects and rodents.

The last of your circle is Eerie. Her frizzy afro puffs have transformed into back-length braids twined with thin copper wire. I ripple with amusement. She is still following you everywhere.

Suddenly, you fling your arms wide and your circle hums, a melody of struck ore and summer heat.

The scrawlers chant. They need words and pictographs and our very souls to make their magic. We need only our inner light, our voices, and our connection to Universe, Sky, Earth, and—especially for necromantic purposes—Moon.

You close your eyes and sway back and forth. Your circle hums louder. Eerie brings her hands together, bridging two of the animancers' hands, careful not to let go until they are joined. She steps into the unbroken circle and reaches for the dagger at your feet. When she has cut her own cheeks and sealed the wounds with the herbs, she takes your hand.

I am wrenched into the space between planes.

You are seven—"and-a-half," as you are fond of adding—when you come home from school, crying, and lock yourself in your room. You won't talk to me, so I send in your father and go to the kitchen to chop vegetables. He finds me putting a tray of rainbow squash and carromatoes into the woodstove.

Your father gently rubs my back while I am still bent over. "Some kids found out she's taking remedial spellworking. They've been picking on her for weeks."

I straighten and wait. I can tell from his crossed arms and tight lips that there is more.

"They tease her about her clothes and her accent. And one of them hexed her desk to jumble her pictographs during a practical—the teacher put it down to her shoddy work and failed her."

I have to consciously unclench my teeth to speak. "Which teacher?"

Which kids?"

"She won't tell me."

I slam the stove shut and turn to my quick-bread batter. "We should never have left."

He sighs. This isn't a new argument.

"She deserves a normal childhood," I say, stirring too vigorously. The bread will be tough.

"There were no jobs back home, the opportunities here—"

"Aren't worth it if they teach her there's something wrong with her, with her magic, if she becomes just another scrawler, if—"

"They're called scribes," says your stony voice from the hallway.

I don't look up from my batter. "It's not real magic."

"It works just like yours does," you say. Yours. Not ours.

I point my wooden spoon at you. "Because they use the souls of our people to power their little scribbles."

"They aren't souls, Mama. They are excess mystical energy." You articulate each word carefully, as if they have been drilled into you.

I am horrified into silence. What have they been teaching you at that school?

THE SPACE BETWEEN is darkness and silence so dense, so suffocating, it makes me wish I could die again. The trip is usually swift, as it was when I was initially drawn to you this evening, because only one or two of my senses are engaged in your stratum of reality. This time, though, I am to become something close to flesh, so I am suspended in darkness for eternity.

Then—

BRIGHT GRINDING SEARING

I squeeze my eyes shut and slam my hands over my ears to adjust to—

The feeling of grass between my toes, the evening breeze tickling the flyaways at my neck, the pepper scent of your herbal mixture. I lower my hands, drawing in a shuddering breath, and open my eyes. You are close enough to touch.

The magic you have worked is strong. I know, without looking, that I appear not as I was when I was sick or when I was put on the pyre, but as you remember me.

Half of your circle forgets themselves in surprise at my apparition and there is a break in the humming. The deep-sea calls me across mountains and valleys, a twinge in my chest, but the humming resumes and I am grounded.

Your eyes fly open. Your swaying stops. You stare.

"Mama?"

"Sanguine," I say, almost too quietly to be heard over your circle's steady humming. I press my hand to your cheek. It's like brushing silk. "You've gotten so…you're so grown up."

When Eerie lets go of your hand and steps to the side, you barely notice and say, "Everybody says I look like you."

I hold my breath—*I can breathe*—waiting for the denial, the distancing.

But a wry smile quirks your lips. "I can see it."

Not only can I breathe, I can cry, apparently.

"When Papa couldn't locate your soul," you say, brushing away a red curl that strays near your eye, "he thought something must have happened. He'd hoped you'd found a way to Life After. I didn't have the heart to tell him I'd sensed you over the years."

Even with those visits, I know I've missed so much. I want to ask you about your life. Who are these friends of yours? Did you land that warding job or has your father convinced you to join the family business? How did your necromancy get so good? What made you decide it wasn't beneath you? Is Eerie your girlfriend? Finally? Is roast lamb and root soup still your favorite? Did your father give you my recipe? Did you ask for it?

But I don't voice any of this. Your light cannot burn all night.

On your ninth birthday, I decide it's time you receive your first serious lesson. We sit out in the garden, legs crossed, hands joined. The evening grass is chill beneath us, but the air is warm and thick with magic.

"Can you feel them?" I ask, already brushing the souls in the nearby rose bushes with tendrils of my necromancy.

You fidget, shaking your head, no doubt wondering how soon you can get back to your new toys.

"Try," I say. "Close your eyes."

"I could probably do it with a conduit. I've practiced with the ones at school and—"

"You...What? Why? You have your own magic!"

You tear your hands free of mine. "It's just practice! And it's easier—"

"Because you're manipulating the power and control those souls earned over a lifetime. Give me your hands."

There are tears in your eyes now. You glance longingly back at the house.

I repeat, "Give me your hands," in the tone that tells you the only choice is obedience.

You obey, but refuse to look at me.

I rebuild the magic while I speak.

"Herbs, song, willing souls like the ones in our garden, even blood... all of those have their uses, depending on the spell. But conduits are for scrawlers—"

"Scribes."

I reach out to the souls flitting around the green roses and ask their permission to borrow energy and commune. "Call them whatever you like, their power is stolen."

"That's just superstitious—"

I jerk your hand to get your attention. "They are souls, Sanguine." We have let this go on too long. "I know because our work sometimes involves conduits. We come across them or people bring them to us, and if the soul within wishes it, we free them."

I funnel my magic into yours, linking you to the spell I am working. Your eyes widen when you feel the touch of the Izaani in our garden. They are transformed but undiminished by death. "Some of them make a home here because they were trapped for so long, they are barred from Life After."

You yank your hands away and get to your feet. You stare down at me, jaw tight, tears streaming. Your expression reminds me of the time you were five or six, back from a trip to your grandparents, and I broke the news to you that your turtle had died. Disbelief, blame, even a touch of hope that I could fix it somehow.

Now, as then, you run to your father, who is better at reassuring you with hugs than sharing terrible knowledge.

ILET GO of your cheek. "Why am I here?" Disapproval bleeds into my tone. You have removed me from my reality so wholly that it will be a long time, perhaps longer than I would have risked, before I will see you again.

You huff, hands on hips.

Before you can snip at me, I say, "I want to spend hours, days with you, but you know it will bind me tighter if I don't return on my own. And even Lace family magic has its limits."

Sometime around eleven or twelve, you stop volunteering to tend the garden and I stop asking. The last few times, you fouled the magic so badly it took me hours to clean the taint. We finally lost the dinzen bushes. The souls that had fertilized the touchy plant fled for roots with less concentrated resentment.

"IHAVE IT under control," you say, but you drop your arms. "I brought you here because...I want to release you if you'll let me."

Oh. Those bitter winter berries again.

"What if I don't want to be released?"

"Mama," you say, "you can't stay forever."

"What if I want to?"

You sigh. "I don't want you to."

I press a palm to my chest, as if it can suppress the ache. I manage to ask, "Can you even do this?" It is difficult magic.

"I wouldn't offer if I couldn't," you snap.

"I hate you!"

The bracelet I gave you almost a decade ago flies across the hearth room, marking the wall with a tiny indent.

You stomp down the hall to your room and I sigh, too tired to follow you. Instead, I walk over and scoop the bracelet from the floor. Later, I wait for you to ask after the crowded piece of jewelry, but you never do.

"L ook, can we not?" you say. "I wish you could stay. I wish—" You swallow. "You were always trying to get me to accept our way of doing magic, but I'd thought that was just you being you, you know?

"Then I joined this Izaani group at school and I started to realize maybe you were right. About some of it. The stuff they could do without scribing, without sacrifice, was *beyond*. Better than what I was learning in most of my classes. So I asked some of them for lessons, I studied the family archives and your journals, and Papa even showed me how to release two souls from conduits." You frown. "One had to stay in the garden."

"What changed? All those years I tried to—" I shake my head in dismissal. I don't want to ruin this.

But you know what I was going to say. "I wanted to help you." You look down and when you meet my eyes, yours are shimmering. "And I missed you and it was a way for me to feel close to you, for the first time really. I'm sorry for being so condescending, sorry I wasted all those years, sorry I didn't come sooner, I—" Your voice breaks.

My arms are around you before the first tear falls.

"Please?" you ask. "Just a few things?"

"What's wrong with the clothes you have?"

"I just want to look normal. Please, *it's my last year."*

I start to tell you that 'normal' is overrated and expensive, but these days, you're as remote as any sixteen-year-old and this is the first time you've wanted to do anything with me in months…so, we head into town.

Tucked in my satchel is the money I've been saving for my new ritual dress, the one I will need when I hand my old one down to you.

When we get home, my leg aches strangely. From all the walking, I suppose. I ask your father to handle the day's gardening and you offer to help him. Before the familiar jealousy can flare in my heart, you hug me so hard I lose my balance.

"Thanks for today," you say, steadying me, and leave a kiss on my cheek.

I sit in bed that afternoon, an ice bundle on my leg. The swelling is going down, but the pain is bone-deep.

Through the open window, I listen to you two work, chatting all the while. The envy creeps up on me again, but I swat it away and open my satchel. I take out the charm I bought while you were in the changing room and add it to the bracelet I carry with me everywhere.

"**I** SHOULD HAVE…come sooner," you repeat, speaking between sobs. "I was just so…scared."

"Scared?"

"That one of us would…say the wrong thing and…we would fight and then…then that would be the last time we spoke."

I pet your hair. "Shh, it's okay."

I don't know how long we stand there, embracing, your tears a whisper against my neck, but I become increasingly aware of the summons from my resting place: a bracelet tangled in seaweed, charms shifting with the currents.

You must sense it too because you pull away, eyes wide and frantic.

Every first-born Lace for four generations has donned this ritual dress for important spellwork, for momentous occasions.

But no, you have to wear the school tunic for your graduation practicum. A thick, high-collared affair paired with long pants. You might as well erect a ward between yourself and your true power.

I am still simmering over the lost argument as your father pushes my wheelchair close to the patch of grass you've been assigned for your test. I notice that most of the Izaani students, including your friend, Eerie, wear light robes or dresses—proper *ritual attire.*

You kneel on a large, wooden platform and dip a pen into a mixture of goat's blood and rare thorned tulips to draw a circle. You fill the circle with inscrutable letters and symbols.

While you and the other Izaani power spells with your own magic, your lightless classmates use pocket-watches, broaches, coins, and other trinkets, shunting the trapped souls' magic into their circles. Cords of my necromancy escape, drawn to the conduits, tempted to crack them open like seeds and release the spirits.

Your father threads his hand in mine. "She's doing very well."

I clamp down on my instincts. "You understand what she's doing?"

"A little."

I know he's been helping you with homework. I hadn't considered some of that might involve scrawling. I shake his hand loose, disgusted, but I watch you closer and wonder how much I've missed.

"**P**LEASE LET ME do this for you," you say. "You always talked about Life After as a right, because everyone deserves respite, but you've been stuck here all these years."

I swallow a bitter laugh. We're finally seeing things with the same eyes and now it's time for me to go?

"I'm okay," you say, reassuringly. "I have a great partner"— you glance back at Eerie—"and good friends. I help Papa with the garden and the business is doing better."

I try—fail—to fight the waves of rightness. My chin quivers. "Will you promise me something?"

"What?" You sound suspicious.

"Promise you'll do what makes you happy. I caused us both so much grief—"

You shake your head. "No, Mama, I should have—"·

"*I* should have appreciated who you were. Yes, I wish you would have found your magic sooner; yes, it hurt seeing you embrace the scrawlers and their conduits. But you would have come around sooner if I had been less stubborn and more patient."

You laugh. "Maybe, maybe not. I'm just as stubborn."

You are wrapped up in your float year, a carefree eighteen-year-old traveling with friends, sampling local food and local magic, living rough and loving it.

I know your father has begged you, more than once, to come visit.

You promise you will, then extend your trip a few days. Those few days pass and you make another promise.

When I reassure him I don't blame you, I can't admit it is because I blame myself. For pushing you all these years. Pushing you too hard. Pushing you away.

Meanwhile, I'm too sick to tend the plants let alone the spirits that enhance them, too weak to even bottle the tonics. At this rate, we can't afford the next phase of your education. Though I can't envision any child of mine in such a stuffy institution, you deserve the same opportunities as your classmates.

I put a plan into motion to secure your future. It goes against my deepest beliefs, but it is my last chance to apologize and to tell you, I love you.

"Just promise me you'll find your own path."

"Okay, okay. I promise." Your smile fades. "You trust me? You're not scared?"

"Of the spell?"

You nod.

"I trust you. But I am scared of leaving you." I look up to Moon, amused, helpless, supplicating. "I can't help it. I'm your mother."

The conduit gives a sharp tug and I gasp.

Your poor father. I'm snippy, even for me. Constantly asking after the post, trying to get out of bed at each knock on our door, being short with family and friends who come to say goodbye. Part of it is pain, the other part is worry. If they don't show soon, it'll be too late and you and your father will only receive the deposit.

But the scrawlers, the ones who make conduits, turn up eventually. I know it's them at the door because I can hear the shouting from our bedroom. Your father demands they leave with a vibrant assemblage of curses.

When they show him the contract—my "mystical energy" in exchange for more money than we've seen in six harvests put together—your father storms into our room. He glares at me, wound up with rage I didn't think he possessed. I stare back, serenely. We have traded roles at the edge of my death.

YOU GRIT YOUR TEETH, tears flowing silently over the stiff blood and herbs, awakening them like rainfall on desert soil. Your circle hums louder, the notes morph, each Izaani finding a new melody that complements the whole. A forest of music, as distinct and harmonious as the joining of birdsong, wind whistling through trees, mammals scurrying, insects chittering.

Still, the conduit pulls and soon, I will be essence again, trapped in the sea until the bindings slacken enough for me to break loose. I take you in for the last time in this world. You aren't singing with your circle.

"It's now, or wait until the next ebb," I tell you.

Your father can't change my mind, but he insists on doing the transfer himself. The conduit makers allow it, happy to cut costs and escape his rage.

Y OU WIPE AWAY your tears and straighten. Eerie steps up and
puts a steadying hand on your shoulder.

You lift your gaze and trill, tremulous at first then resolute.
Your voice is the ceaseless chord the forest was missing, a
waterfall cascading over a timeworn outcropping. My heart
aches for all the magic I never taught you, all the music we never
made.

*Your father carries me, naked and shivering, out to the garden under
Moon and his children's light and lays me on my favorite patch of grass,
near the green roses. He places the piece of jewelry over my heart. Before
I can protest, he splits the air with the wordless melody of a song about
the changing colors of autumn leaves, how they drift to the ground and are
trodden to mulch.*

*He is supposed to shackle me to the silver necklace provided by the
scrawlers. Instead, he tethers my soul to your charm bracelet. He hopes it
will give me solace in the lifetime to come.*

I CRY OUT in fresh agony. Tiny rips appear along the seam joining
the luminescence of your magic to my soul, my soul to the
conduit. I focus my energy and interweave it with yours, fighting
the pull. Through the pain, I say, "Tell your father I love him."

You rush to raise your dagger and I grab your wrist. "Stay
calm."

When I let go, there's a phantom sheen of water on your skin
that smells faintly of brine.

With a shaking hand, you pull the blade along your arm. In
the dim light, the rivulets of blood are black.

"Stay calm," I repeat. But my words are whispers and you
aren't listening.

You drag the blade up your other arm. Your singing falters.
Blood surges from the wound, flowing too fast.

The strands of magic connecting us begin to unravel. The
night darkens.

Despite the seriousness of your injury, you resume your
singing. I try to shake you, to tell you to stop and let someone
heal you, but I'm barely here anymore.

You sway and drop to your knees.

*Your father delays the conduit makers, making excuses and dodging their
visits.*

*The bracelet doesn't fit around his wrist, so he carries me from room to
room, task to task, setting me down only when he needs both hands. I'm not
inside the bracelet so much as leashed to it. Your father can't see me, but he
can feel me and talks to me throughout the day. Occasionally he voices the
possibility of not fulfilling the contract, of releasing me. I cannot speak to
him with words, but I make my feelings known with a churning of energy
that makes the conduit too hot to hold.*

*At night, when he lies awake in our quiet home, I send pulsing waves of
warmth through the bracelet, timing the rhythm with his heartbeat until he
falls asleep.*

*The third day after my transfer, you finally come home, too late to say
goodbye face to face. You find out what I've done and, despite my silence,
you and I have our worst fight yet.*

ONE OF the Izaani breaks your circle, rushing toward you. I
am hauled, hair's breadth by hair's breadth, into the space
between.

I lose the salt taste of my tears.

I lose the metallic smell of your blood.

I lose the feeling of grass between my toes.

I lose the murmur of worried voices.

When I am greeted by familiar, suffocating black, I can still see the afterimage of you, blood-soaked and unconscious in Eerie's arms.

The little girl who receives my soul complains that it isn't the necklace she picked out, but her parents insist she make do; she needs a conduit for school and the mistake has gotten them a steep discount. Besides, "the bracelet isn't THAT ugly."

On a family sailing trip, the bracelet 'slips' off her wrist and into the water, dragging me down with it.

A SWIRL OF rainbow shatters the darkness. It reminds me of colorful motes behind closed eyelids.

For a change, I have form here, a body not of flesh but so conceptually similar as to make little difference. The motes brush against me, lamb's ear soft. They turn my attention toward a line of light. It's nearly impossible to see, so thin that if I look away I'm sure it will vanish like an illusion.

The path to Life After.

You did it. Your spell worked. I'm free of the conduit and—

My gaze snaps toward you.

You are here, in the space between, and that can only mean...

The first time I manage to break away from my underwater prison, I am overwhelmed with gratitude, though you obviously don't know I'm here.

It has been a year since my death. If I couldn't sense this, I would know because you are scattering my ashes under the green rose bush in our garden.

Your father kneels down next to you, with some effort, and invokes Moon with a short prayer. When the invocation is finished, neither of you moves. You stay on your knees until I am impatient—you shouldn't be outside for so long without coats.

You glance my way, as if you sense me and my irritation. But you close your eyes again and put an arm around your father.

I watch the tears crystallize on your cheeks until the conduit reasserts itself.

I CANNOT GIVE VOICE to my grief and horror in this void. They expand to fill me, then the black nothingness until they reach you, until *I* reach you. Our bodies, only as real as we need them to be, disintegrate until we are only magic and souls.

Stripped of our barriers, there is no beginning and no end to either of us. I am you and you are me. We wonder at the miracle of knowing one another, drowning in our euphoria, our fear, our heartbreak, our love.

We sense its magic before the glowing ember net descends and trawls the plane. My experience with animancers prepares you such that you are not shocked when the spell takes hold and begins disentangling our essences.

I am able to visit you from time to time—often in moments of pensiveness or when you are doing something I believe reminds you of me, like cooking or gardening with your father.

The time between each visit lengthens, like the conduit is getting stronger. Or you're forgetting me. For an endless stretch, my anchor holds firm against all my attempts to leave and I try to accept that I will never see you again.

Then one evening, across mountains and valleys, from a night-cloaked meadow, you reach out to me.

THE LAST THING we share as you are dragged back to the living world is relief. There is also regret, but it is yours alone.

When I am by myself again, the cloud of dust nudges me toward the glowing border, dancing sapphire and gold, teal and coral. I know I shouldn't want you to miss me, but I clutch your regret like a talisman. No, like a charm. Like that small, bronze fish I gave you when you were a little girl, when I longed to be close to you in any way you would allow. I slip into my next life, secure in knowing it meant as much to you as it did to me.

UNDERCITY SPELLWORK

C.B. BLANCHARD

Feral's first client of the day was a suit. A suit, all the way down here in the undercity. Driven in by his expensive self-driving car, gleaming silver and sleek outside Feral's boarded window.

The local kids would have it stripped to the skeleton in five minutes.

He sat in front of Feral, gave xer an obviously fake name. He looked around the room, nose wrinkled in a sneer. Xe knew what he was seeing, how the shelves of found things would look to a man from his spare and barren shiny world. Weeds from the cracks, bones from the terrifying feral pigeons that folklore always held would eat a whole person, if you let them. Broken plastic from the streetlights, bricks and concrete and metal. Jars that looked empty, but that contained moments, words, emotions. Each one whispering to Feral with life, with magic.

He, of course, couldn't see any of that. Just junk, piled on cheap shelves.

"This is not how I expected it to look."

Xe leaned back and smiled. "Times have changed, witchcraft changed with it." And why are you here, xe thought, down where there's no sky at all. Why me, when you have the money for almost anything. When your sort normally deny that mine have any power or truth at all.

"Let me get to the point." He brushed some imaginary filth off his jacket. "I would like a love spell."

He wasn't the first to ask, of course. Feral took a deep breath and started to rattle off xer usual Love Spell refusal and explanation. Which was that anyone who needed to be spelled into loving you wasn't worth having, that shouldn't you want someone who chose you of their own free will, and that at the heart of it a love spell was, well, evil. Ready to offer the thing xe normally did, which was a ritual to ready you and open you for the right love to come your way.

He cut xer off at 'free will'.

"I don't care about any of that. I want a love spell, and I'll pay." He named a price that seriously tested xer sense of ethics and morals. Enough to pay rent for months.

"Love spells are evil," xe said, instead. "They're magical rape."

He huffed, rolled his eyes, and Feral knew exactly what he was.

"Can you do it or not?"

"I can," xe said. "But I won't."

He closed his eyes, as if Feral were an incompetent underling testing his patience. While he did, Feral let xerself see. Opened xer inner eyes to his real Self. Tracked the broken bits in him, the damaged places. Found an emptiness that puzzled xer, a whole streak of nothingness. Even the worst people didn't have pure void running through their Self like that. A hollow place or two, sure, but utter absence?

"I am asking politely," he said. His real Self coloured ugly in a complicated mix—anger, all red streaks and the tinny reek of blood. Lust, longing, pining, twisted around each other in knots. Confusion. A touch of loneliness, almost worth pitying. But most of all the sour yellow and petrol tang of entitlement.

And the void, sucking, hungry, wrong.

"No," xe said.

His eyes narrowed. "People don't say no to me."

Feral could believe that. Clean good looks, money, and a manipulator. Xe pulled away from the truth of him. "I think it would do you good if more people did." That, at least, was the truth. That at least was help, of a sort. Feral had once promised xerself xe'd help everyone through their door, even if it wasn't in the way they expected.

He stood up, gave a last disgusted look around Feral's shop. "I'll find someone else."

Probably. There were enough who'd use the comfort of the money to override any ethics they had. But he'd struggle to find them, without the contacts Feral had.

A faint shape followed him as he left, but many people had ghosts like that. Feral had a few xerself.

Xe locked the door behind him. Then laughed at the muffled swearing as the suit discovered half of his fancy car missing.

THE THING ABOUT MAGIC was that it found its way through. Not necessarily in the way people expected. In this, the world-city, the city forever, the one and only city—it forced through. Burst through in the brief gleam of real sunlight and not red smog. Crept in via silent alleyways. Screamed out from bloodstains and the corpses pulled out of the rivers. Lived stronger and weirder down here in the undercity than up where the rich lived. Sung out in love, wailed in terror, simmered under the rage and exhaustion that hummed, barely audible under the shine and gleam of the skyscrapers. Once there had been stars to cling to, but no one living had ever seen them.

If there had ever been any other way to do magic xe hadn't known it. Some of the older witches xe knew talked of a *feeling*, that once there had been something else. As far as Feral knew, the city was eternal, and that was what xe had to work with.

Xe went to the river, mask on against the reek of it. Thick and sludgy, a toxic mud rather than a water source. Thin children skimmed metal mesh through it, catching the discards of those

much richer than them. When they got something good, an
excited cry would go up.

There was a small shrine there, for the woman brought up
a month ago. Nameless, dead three days when Feral found her.
Obviously murdered. One of them. Feral left a glowstick by it. A
light, a light to come home by.

The corp nagged at xer. That void space inside. Xe'd never
seen anything like it before, not once. Like something had
been ripped out of them, only the edges had been clean, almost
surgical. He was dangerous.

And whoever he was trying to love spell needed warning.

Lucky that Feral was a witch, then.

SO THAT'S WHY Feral was at the crossroads of an abandoned
underground, unfinished. Scrap of fine fabric in one hand
and a tarnished coin in the other. A perfect place, built as a way
for a rich asshole to hide the money he didn't need, pay it back
to himself with interest, and abandon as soon as he was bored. A
no-place, a never place.

Xe thought of the suit as much as xe could. His face, yes,
but faces changed in the city all the time. Faces didn't matter.
Xe thought of the tangled yearning cruel thing inside of him.
Thought of his suit, fine thing, aggressively expensive and just as
aggressively conservative. Thought of his voice. Fixed on him,
with xer real eyes, with xer mind. At the crossroads, xe spoke
the name he'd given—false as anything no doubt, but even false
names carve out paths. The things people called themselves
made shapes, even if their true name was secret.

It made xer sweat. Made muscles tense and heart pound.
Magic cost, and this one was hard work. Xe cut the back of xer
arm. A new scar would be there, with some others—a payment
in blood. Blood always was the most effective key. Xe wrapped
the fancy fabric around the wound and let the blood soak in.
The empty crossroads, the road stopping dead, the rain dripping
through concrete making stalactites. Close as a cave as xe'd ever

get. The wind picked up, stirred through xer hair.

Lights that had never been hooked up or even installed flickered on. For the briefest of microseconds, the crossroads that could have been *was*, the shadows of cars and people thronging, making distant whispering echoes. The lights burned brighter in one direction, and as the ghost of never-was faded, marked a path in the air.

And then it was gone. Feral knew where he was. He was marked, and would be until the wound was a scar.

XE GLAMOURED XERSELF. He didn't seem the sort to remember a face, and makeup and different hair could do a little, but a touch of glamour didn't hurt. Just enough that xe didn't quite look like xerself. If he noticed xer at all, it would be in the vague way of thinking he must have seen xer walking down the street once, and he would forget again.

He'd be at a party that night. Getting in wasn't hard, not when xe went through the back dressed in black and picked up a tray. People never looked at those who served them. Inside xe quietly deposited the tray and slipped into the edges of the party. Hold a drink, smile like you know a secret. Witches learned these things from each other. A witch who couldn't slide into any place was no witch at all.

All these people, wearing expensive clothes and talking about money, sex, and power. Which, for them, means all the conversations were about power. How much they had, how much they could get, how scared they were of not having it any more.

Feral could tell them something about not having power, about having to grasp for whatever you could get just to survive. All xer old selves were with xer, every day, and anyone who looked properly would see a hungry, dirty, angry child, fists clenched tight around rusting metal.

The plan was loose, but involved sticking near the suit—there he was, drinking champagne and smiling, all handsome—until his potential victim became clear. Then warn them, if they would listen. Even if they wouldn't, Feral would have done xer duty. Weakened him, protected his victim. Even if his target was a suit too, didn't mean she deserved what he planned to do to her. That hijack of her personality, desire, choice. Wrong in the bone-deep way. The world was full of so much wrongness, but if Feral could stop this one—

A few hours in, and he showed no signs of moving. He didn't even seem to be getting drunk and xe wondered—was he chipped, or just a heavy drinker?

That's when She came in. And he stopped. His eyes honed in on her, in her simple high-necked red dress. And Feral—well, xe understood it. Beautiful, yes, in the way a lot of well-off women are beautiful. Glossy well-styled hair and smooth clear skin. Not quite inhuman in her perfection, because that was a statement now. I'm rich enough to afford surgery so good it mimics natural human asymmetry. Feral preferred honest imperfection, not something made by a surgeon. Interesting, rough-edged, wonky-nosed and missing-toothed and stretchmarked.

All that said, the woman was a beauty of a sort that would definitely appeal to the suit. But what struck Feral was the energy around her. A fire, an ocean, a storm. Magic, and a lot of it, glowing so bright xe was surprised it didn't blind the world. Feral was marked by magic, and any witch would say xe shone in the night, but this woman gleamed like the stars no one saw any more.

Then Feral looked away, and the woman's face slipped out of memory, leaving only a recollection of beauty. Strange.

He went up to her, nervous and boastful. She smiled like he was nothing. He *was* nothing. Feral watched him, watched for anything in her drink, any gesture, anything. No. He'd not found anyone else yet, apparently. Xe waited til he left, fury and rejection boiling in him, poisoning him.

And then xe approached.

The woman's eyes locked on xer and Feral felt dizzy. This was very strange, very powerful. A mystery here. Or maybe it was just desire, despite how this woman was not Feral's type.

The woman eased herself out of the flock of people around her to stand alone by a table. She held a glass near her mouth but didn't drink. Her hair was the crackle of electricity through wires. Her eyes were the night.

"I thought I knew most of the witches in the city. I sure would have heard of someone like you," Feral said.

"Well, anything can slip under notice, even of your eyes. Very clear. Very sharp." The woman cocked her head. "You can call me Astra."

"I'm known as Feral."

"Feral." She laughed. "But you're practically domesticated. Stray, at best."

Feral bristled. "I name myself, I declare myself. I make my own shapes. Astra, is it? Like the heavens, the stars? Who are you to claim that power?" And not share it, xe didn't say.

Astra took a drink, and her throat worked. Feral stared. "You can see exactly why I claim it." And after a pause. "Would you like to see the stars, one day?"

"No one has in years. Not even the richest here."

Astra made eye contact. "I have."

This was an impossible lie. "I came—I came here to warn you. I wonder if you need it."

"A warning is a kindness, even if I don't."

"Your admirer there." Feral nodded at the leaving suit. "He came to me asking for a love spell. I refused, of course, but there are those who won't. Now you know."

"Now I know." Her face held secrets. Her real Self was vast, immense, impossible to see all of it and read it true, lit up by the magic she held. Astra. "He'd go that far."

"He would. And even a woman like you could be overwhelmed by the right push."

"It'd have to empty me out to work."

Yes. It would. "He'd like that, I think. He seems the sort to like an empty vessel that exists to fuck him and say words it can't mean any more."

"He is." Astra put the glass of champagne down. "Have you seen the empty space?"

"Yes. I've never seen that before."

"Find out what caused it. Don't worry, I'll watch my back. I have defenses."

"Find out—wait, I normally charge for witchworkings, I have bills—"

Astra tossed her hair. "Oh, you'll be rewarded."

Then, she took every expensive bit of her away.

What the fuck?

FERAL SPENT the next week almost contacting every witch she knew and several she didn't, asking about this woman who blinded like the sun and who had a strength no one should be capable of having. Not with magic in scraps and tatters, not with steel and plastic cutting through the shapes and lines of the world, not with so many having their Selves cut apart to fund the empty wealth of others.

Not one person had heard of Astra.

One man, very old, got back to her with a theory, a rumour.

"There used to be...something else," he said. "The level of power you're talking about...it could be that?"

Feral pushed.

"There was a goddess. We ate her," he said. "They laid her on an altar and we ate her." He paused. "Metaphorically, I think. But possibly not."

"Everything has a cost," another said, the woman who had taught Feral. "And I wonder about the city. What that costs. There is something missing, but the thing is that missing things are mainly notable by not being there."

"What about Astra," Feral asked, frustrated. Xe could almost hear xer mentor shrug.

"It's magic, Feral. Who knows?"

Feral leaned out of xer window, into the smog-choke and always loud streets. Listened idly to an argument between a drunk couple, took a little of their outrage and anger to keep in a jar. Looked up to the city above, where they got a smog-choked diluted sun. Down here, only electric lights in a misted darkness. The only world Feral had ever known. The city, stretching from border to border, across seas themselves. How could such a thing be born, be maintained, even as parts decayed and were forgotten and unfinished. As children scavenged abandoned neighbourhoods, as the skyscrapers rose higher and brighter, as people died choking under the weight of the air. How could such a thing continue, if not for—-

Sacrifice?

Questions regarding the suit were more productive. His name was Peter Fanshaw, quite high up in one of the major corporations. Feral had seen all kind of damage to the Self, scars and wounds bleeding neon and hollow spaces where something had died, but never anything so clean and sharp as that broad void in Peter Fanshaw.

The wound on xer arm was barely scabbing over. He was still marked. Find out about the void, Astra had said. Sure.

The time for merely seeing was past.

XE DID THE obvious thing. Xe called him. On his personal number.

"How did you find this number?" was his first question after he'd heard xer voice.

"I am a witch." In fact, xe'd paid a hacker of their acquaintance for the information. Anything could be had for a price.

"Why—"

"I've reconsidered. On the love potion. I could use the money."

His voice, oozing smug satisfaction. "I thought you'd come round. But I'm offering less now, as I've had to look for others."

"Less? You came to me because I'm the best."

"I came to you because you were the first I heard of."

"Tell me. Is this woman you want—has she a very strong personality?"

Silence on the line. Feral could picture Peter, in his suit, at his bleakly shiny desk, thinking things through. No doubt he had the mind of a predator. But then, so did Feral.

"Yes. She's—" he sighed. "She's astonishing."

Xe felt a queasy sympathy.

"I want her. I love her. I need her, I—I can't stop thinking about her. And she won't look twice at me. I've offered her everything I have. So she's given me no choice, you see."

"I'll come to you," Feral said. "But you have to be alone. I'll bring everything I need."

"To me, but—"

"Oh no. I'm not doing something like this in my shop. I have a reputation."

Peter laughed. "The amount I'll pay you you'll never need to work again."

"Yours. Or I don't do it."

It was a risk. A breath, a heartbeat.

He gave xer an address.

Men who were only out for themselves were easy to lie to, because they thought everyone else was like them.

XE DREAMED OF Astra, and Astra was the sky, full of stars. Xe cried, because xe had never seen the stars and they were beautiful.

Astra was beautiful.

Feral woke up, face wet.

PETER FANSHAW lived far above the undercity. He never even had to look at it if he didn't want to. Greenery grew outside his broad clear windows, carefully engineered to survive smog and low light and still be beautiful. Feral stood in his living room looking out at a tree, at grass, at flowers bright facing up at the smothered sun.

Feral noticed something strange here. A sense of walking two steps behind an echo, a person not here but still present in anything. A woman, xe thought, unhappiness and fury trailing behind her like expensive perfume. Not here now, but not so long ago.

On xer way out of the undercity, through the mid, to this upper layer—out of xer home, Feral had seen a child missing both their eyes rummaging through garbage, stuffing anything even half edible in their mouth.

Peter Fanshaw had fruit on display. Real fruit. Xe looked at the orange a while, the way the sunlight-identical brightness reflected off the dimpled skin.

Peter waved xer to one of his painful and painfully expensive sofas.

"Have you—did you—how does this work?"

His nerves were obvious. Feral would have felt sorry for him if what he was asking for wasn't so obscene. Xe touched him gently on his covered arm.

"Sit on the floor and close your eyes," xe said.

He frowned at Feral, but did it, removing his jacket first. Feral didn't trust people who wore suits at home. Or at all, really. Eyes closed he looked almost like a person. Feral repressed that. Xe was about to do something pretty bad, in order to prevent something worse.

Feral pulled out a bottle of oil. It had sleep and rest and trust in it, and the essence of an open door that xe'd found some months ago, that opened into secret places. Powerful things. Xe ran some over xer thumb and pressed it to Peter's forehead, his closed eyes, his mouth.

"Shh. This is how I know how to make the right spell," xe said, as he opened that mouth. "Close your eyes, and think of something that relaxes you."

As he slipped, drifted, as he opened, Feral dipped xer inner toe in, and then xer whole inner Self, leaving the body kneeling on the real wood floors. Kept that dull discomfort in a corner, a place to grab at. Xe went deeper than a casual sight. Always a risk. You could get lost in someone else, sometimes. Could forget who you were, the paths that led you home.

H E WAS...well. The tangles and sourness that Feral found before were very loud. The roots deep, as such things so often were, but maintained by self-justification and lies. The pain real, and beating, but vicious and unkind. *No love, nothing for me, mockery and cruelty every day I know. Make myself untouchable, unstoppable, take the brutality and wrap it so deep into myself there's no getting it out. And why shouldn't I, why shouldn't I take whatever I want, how dare people say no, no makes me want to kill—*

That. That, Feral followed. *Kill.* Feral'd known he was a rapist, in mind if not action, the second he waved away xer explanation of what love spells actually were. Most corps were killers, even if it was just in the abstract, but to do it yourself, hands wet with blood, watching another person die...something you learned, going into people like this, was the way that people made themselves forget. But Feral had never seen it done so well. He'd done the cutting himself. In another life, he'd have been a skilled witch.

People don't say no to me. Spat at an ex-wife. But she wasn't dead, only hated. Feral laid her aside, her distorted memory smiling false.

He'd gone down into the undercity. Some weeks before he'd ever met or heard of Feral. He'd gone down the way the rich do, to make tourism out of the lives of others, to have something authentic. He met a woman, with tattoos, wild and loud and obviously willing—

No. Not so. She made fun of him.

Feral knew those tattoos, had seen them over the skin of a dead woman—

People didn't stand in his way. Didn't say no. He was swimming on drugs, high on his own entitlement, and she pulled her hand away from him, hit him when he tried to kiss her, and he—

No matter how much you might forget, what you did is still there, in the architecture. He forgot it, but he still did it.

Hungry desperate woman, name unknown. She said no. She laughed at him. She didn't want him, when he was lowering himself to even ask.

Feral *knew that face.*

Cold, very cold, Feral remembered the corpse in the stagnant river not far from xer own shop, just three weeks before Peter Fanshaw walked through her door. Not uncommon, common in fact, corpses more frequent than sunsets. But the face, the face was the same. The tattoos.

This was the echo, following him everywhere. That he'd tried to cut out. Not just of her own life and his, but out of memory, out of existence entirely.

Gasping, Feral pulled back. Xer hands shook. From the sofa the echo of the woman looked at her with silent, burning eyes.

Feral produced a bottle from xer bag. It was coloured water. Xe scratched nonsense symbols on the plastic cap, making sure he heard. It would do nothing. Xe waited for his eyes to open.

"Here," xe said, thinking; I know what you are. I know what you did. "Put this in something she eats or drinks. She'll see what's worth loving in you."

He looked at it, hungry.

"Yes," he said.

Xe left him there, staring at a bottle of coloured water like it was salvation.

Iᴛ ᴡᴀsɴ'ᴛ a surprise to find Astra in xer bedroom when xe got home.

"You know," Feral said. "When I look away from your face I forget what it looks like?"

"That's because it's not my face," Astra said.

"I think I've got an idea who—what—you are."

Astra stretched up. Her face shifted, her hair spilled over the pillows. She lay back on Feral's bed.

"Will be, maybe. I'm not there yet."

Feral sat beside her, let xer fingers touch a warm, bare arm.

"Normally I prefer my lovers to wear their own faces."

"We'll be lovers, will we?" She was grinning, sharp. Predatory.

Feral reached for her.

LATER, AFTER, naked in the neon glow, Feral kissed her. Mouths loose and damp, bodies sweat-slicked together. "I gave him a fake love spell."

"He'll come to me, then."

Feral propped xerself up on one elbow. "Why did you need me? Why not you? Would any other witch have done?"

"He wants to spell me," Astra said "How could I have gotten close on my own? "

Feral twisted Astra's hair through xer fingers. Now black, now red, now blonde. Curly, kinky, straight. A thousand women, a million women, in one.

"Let me tell you a story," Astra said.

ONCE THINGS were different, which is the same thing as saying things were. It's always true. But once there were gods, and demi gods, and all kinds of things, and they walked among the people. Forests were wild. Magic was wild, it had its own paths. Feral, the kind of workings you do would be considered the work of children.

Some decided they didn't want it that way any more. Great changes require great sacrifices. They tricked the gods, and they took them to the altars. They cut the gods open on their sharp knives. They fed people the pieces, and the world changed. The city became all there is, all there ever was, and people forgot.

Now, blood and life keep the city—this city— running. A permanent sacrifice machine. How else could it exist, with no farms to feed it and none of the things real cities need, which is places that aren't cities and people who live in those places?

Instead, the city eats lives, the lives of the undercity, and uses them to sustain itself.

All the same, magic found its way through the cracks, and the open doors, and the forgotten places, and rooted in people, their hearts. Where things were most... needed. The city made its own gods. None of them lived—a god can be still-born—but maybe, the time is right now. Maybe not. It's always a mortal who decides. It has to be.

"IS THAT true?"

Astra shrugged. "It's a story for children. It's simplified, but the heart is true enough."

"Am I the one who decides?"

Astra looked at xer. "She chose you at the moment of her death," she said. "His victim. Blood spilled and an empty space. It made the right paths. The right shapes. It has to be you."

ASTRA LIVED in a hotel room—"lived," Feral supposed. Words have started appearing in xer head since they fucked, words which were never there before. Xe lets them slip around each other, not ready to be spoken yet. Words that would transform, bring forth, turn Astra into something old and new all at once. Words that would shape all that power so it could fit into the empty god space. A new Goddess, and Feral her Priestex.

It's up to xer to decide. Feral had never had so much freedom, not in the world city, the undercity. Xer only real choices had all been choosing between different kinds of bad, for all xey'd carved out something that looked a little like a life.

Feral waited. Astra waited. The power in her blinding.

Peter would be here soon.

A knife waited on the table.

A knock on the door, a sick, excited taste in Feral's mouth. Could xe do this?

"Do you want more than scraps?" Astra shone beside xer.

Feral nodded. So much more than scraps. A life with stars in it.

Astra opened the door. Peter stood, handsome, smiling, carrying a bottle of adulterated wine.

"Wait." His face changed when he saw Feral. "Wait, what?"

Between them they held him. Feral brought silence out of one of its bottles. Powerful and rare, silence. Feral took the knife in one hand. Paused. Xe looked at Astra.

"A change requires a sacrifice," she said.

Feral thought of xer rent, of the stinking river, of the shacks, of starving children, of the waste in his expensive house, of the woman he killed and denied even memory. Xe thought of the stars.

"Goddess of the Undercity," Feral said, and brought the knife down.

WHERE THE LIGHT HAD BEEN

PRIYA CHAND

THE WITCH-QUEEN wore a cloak of selfish desire, her second shadow. Its gentlest sigh absorbed the most powerful attacks of her enemies, for their hate was about her and so belonged to that part of her bound in the cloak. Against those squirming tendrils, not one of them could touch her.

Nor I, her consort.

One late night—more precious than sleep, when a country steals your days—I ran my fingers across her side, over the pockmark where a soldier, finding he had struck a rib, also found himself removed from his body. His soul lingered in some dark corner of her workshop, a dusty bottle among other dusty bottles. I do not think souls care what holds them if it is not flesh, and I have cleaned enough for a lifetime.

My eyes drooped. I did not know when my hand slid off the witch-queen's skin and onto the cloak. I only felt my fingers fade, and screamed.

She sat up and wrenched my wrist. "Careful, Adia!"

I whimpered.

The witch-queen lifted my injured arm to her lips, moving upwards in gentle strokes, pulling me onto her body. I knew she was distracting me, but I wanted to be distracted.

WE ATE BREAKFAST in an inner chamber lit by long scented
    tapers, a gift from one of the many artisans I had invited
to our capital. Guards stood outside the heavy door, doubly
sealed with spell and key.

"I wish you would remove that thing when we're alone," I
said, watching the cloak twist in the flickering light. My voice
echoed off magical walls and physical stone. If anything were
impenetrable...I smoothed my face. There would be time for
fighting after we had heirs.

She frowned, toying with her fruit. "You know I cannot. You
have seen me."

I had. With my eyes and fingers and tongue, the constellation
of pink indents, ignoring the envy that fought her lust when she
saw my unmarked flesh. No one hunted a consort who organized
merchants as she'd once organized maids, not even to hurt the
witch-queen. Able to go where she could not, I had walked every
inch of our castle, sent workers in pursuit of gaps and cracks until
the walls were smooth as her face against my palms. When she
said that was not enough, I doubled the guards and hired foreign
witches, whose magic her enemies would not know to counter.
There was nothing else I could do but tell her I loved her and
would love every inch of her as long as our bodies drew breath.

"Your bedroom is safe," I protested. "This is safe." I moved to
touch her hand, drawing back when I saw darkness nudging the
table.

She frowned and shook her head. "Are the rents in Watergirl's
District lowered?"

I did not want to be distracted, but the question was too
important to ignore.

S OMETIMES I WOKE to her bending over me, cloak spilling
across her body, blending scars into shadows invisible against
her body. Perhaps that gave me the idea.

That day, I lifted my head and kissed her—I loved even her
morning breath—she pecked my cheek and withdrew.

"The Ilastrians are clearing the North Wilds." Her face was
uncarved onyx. The cloak enveloped her body. Unable to hold
her, I sat up and fretted with the sheets. The witch-queen was
Ilastrian-born. She would not say more, never had. She had cast
aside her name. Even she could no longer speak it.

The North Wilds guarded the river marking our shared
border. We both knew the Ilastrians were fearful of our success,
as our impoverished city bloomed into a nation in its own right,
but neither I nor she would ruin her country for them. Never.
She would not even allow me to levy troops, that we might at last
silence the Ilastrians. She would herself defend the land she had
claimed, and no more.

I lay back and watched her dress. Boots, tunic, leather greaves
and gauntlets appeared as the cloak shifted back and forth.
An ida bounced against her leg, too dull to cut grass, instead a
channel for her spells. She learned battle magic long before I
knew her.

"I am going," she said. The cloak blotted out the golden edges
of dawn that made it past our shuttered windows.

"Goodbye," I said to the place where the light had been.

I MADE PROVISIONS for the incoming caravan routes and long-
suffering renters. The witch-queen had advisors, cowed
by whatever she had done to conquer this land. They would
neither betray her to the Ilastrians nor think creatively. But with
guidance, they would keep her country prospering.

Conscience clear, I extricated a rough shirt from a chest,
diving underneath my old innkeeper's apron, tucked breeches
into scuffed boots, and once provisioned, slipped out a side gate
before sunrise.

There is a certain humility in which all quests must be
approached.

I followed the road until it bent east, when I turned to enter
the West Wilds, following the banks of a widening stream.
My stomach growled. I munched cheese from my bag and
picked berries, bright red and delicately sour. A relief after rich
castle food, though not something a person could survive on
indefinitely. I reflexively considered our grain stockpiles. Winters
were lean, but no one would hunger this year. We had done
well, and would continue to do well, as long as the witch-queen
remained safe, and our borders were free of Ilastrians.

The stream became a broad shallow river which, nearer
my destination, flooded the sunken earth. The twigs crackling
underfoot were replaced by leaves glistening under a thin coat
of water that chilled my ankles through the worn leather of my
boots.

The witch who ruled this swamp did not cast spells. He
merely knew things: how to make a net to catch one's heart's
desire, and more importantly, how to make her forget the net
was there.

As the water reached my calves, I saw him. He sat cross-
legged outside his hut. Unmoving, unmoved, he watched me
drag myself through the muck. He could have extended his dry
land to me, and the both of us knew it.

"What brings you here?" he said.

I reached the shore and stood facing him, a trail of black mud
behind me. "A cloak of healing for my beloved. For her past
injuries, and those she fears to come."

"How will you pay me for this?"

"A pregnant goat," I said promptly.

Glancing towards his meager, lonely kitchen, the witch
nodded. He knew the worth of my word. "Use a cedar shuttle
on your loom. Weave these herbs into a cloak of cloud-silk"—a
rapid-fire list. Between the merchants and the witch-queen's
workshop, it was not daunting—until he finished with silphium.

"The plant of love does not grow here," I said, baring my
teeth.

He tilted his head. "Are you sure?"

I knew his price for this knowledge. I considered what—who—brought me here, and why. I could not be unfaithful, not when she would never betray me again.

"I will find it myself," I said. "Expect the goat soon."

I continued west, removing my boots when the squelching became unbearable. Past the swamp, the river widened into a delta, air redolent with the oily tang where sea- and river-fish met. One flitted by me, a green log with a nubbled back.

Silphium is a coastal plant. With the silt washed out, our coast barely deserved the name. Little grew here. It would be easy to spot that green stalk, leaves extended in permanent formal dance.

As I searched, waist-deep in water, clothes cold on goosebumped flesh, holding heavy boots, I saw nothing but flat swirls of dirt and the occasional fish on the tide.

Nothing.

Every morning began with mud on my nose, funneled there no matter how carefully I placed the oilcloth over my bed the night before. Less unpleasant than my dreams: always I returned to discover our advisors betrayed us to Ilastria. Always the witch-queen arrived as I cowered, clutching the withering silphium, and always she called for my execution in Ilastri-ken, a language I barely understood, until I awoke. And remembered I was here for her and not her country.

I spent longer looking than I should have.

My back hurt, needles pricking my spine as they had not since fourteen-hour days at the inn. I tried not to scream as I foraged, hunger burbling through my gut. I became weaker, slower, foggier. One morning I crossed the same rotted log twice and tripped. I sunk into the mud and howled.

And then I saw it, a thin pale shoot, green brilliance obscured by muck. Heart shaped leaves. I did not wish to pull the whole thing, not when the plant was so rare, but it was for my witch-queen. I reached for its base and lifted, roots and all.

Prize tucked away, I returned home, mud drying on my body, careful to avoid the witch in his swamp.

As I slipped through the side gate, the shadow of my
nightmares lifted immediately. Life had continued in my
absence, the witch-queen's advisors still dutiful, her presence
still distant. I summoned the seneschal to the bathing pools and,
scrubbing myself, told them where to send the goat.

Once dressed, I descended to the witch-queen's workshop.
I swept old cobwebs and insect carcasses off the precise labels,
only to discover the jars were tight beyond my strength. The
witch had not specified fresh herbs, so I held a flame to the lids
until my arms ached and mixed them all together, the silphium
actinic green and soft among the crumbling bits of the rest.

An innkeeper's child does not spend much time learning to
weave. I wanted the best for the witch-queen, and the swamp
witch had not specified the work must come from my hands.
I scoured my closet, holding each cloud-silk garment until I
found one that rested like breath on my fingers. I summoned
the artisan, and for a handsome payment she set up a loom
and asked no questions. I watched her when I was not occupied
by the scryers' frequent updates on the North Wilds, and the
caravans, and the landlords, and so on.

The guards showed me Ilastrian arrows retrieved from
hallways where they had long since blocked the arrow slits.
"They are using magic to penetrate the walls," they said.

"I will be careful," I promised. "Watch out for yourselves." I
thrilled in the Ilastrians' desperation—the magical expenditure
to do such a thing was enormous, even without our wards—
though it was no substitute for the witch-queen's warmth, from
her callused feet through the nape of her spine, to the head with
its beloved flowing curls. My fingers spread across her half of the
bed, and every morning I awoke buried in her pillow.

I did not dwell on the Ilastrians. Once the cloak was finished,
they would not matter.

The cedar shuttles kept breaking. The soft wood gave way
right as the artisan would settle into her rhythm, frustrating her,
but here the witch had given explicit instructions. A fortnight
passed before she finished, the slowest she ever worked. Her deft
touch produced a garment that could have been a sigh kissing

my fingertips, scented with the fresh sharpness of medicinal herbs. I paid her double our agreed fee.

Folded, the cloak lay against my skin like a piece of cloud, freedom incarnate. Exactly what my witch-queen needed. I wished to keep it with me always, ready for her return, but even a mere consort cannot hold court with perpetually full hands. I rested the cloak on the armchair in our bedroom, and through the lonely nights and busy days I awaited my witch-queen.

Inevitably, the Ilastrian army retreated, the North Wilds disheveled but intact. Our scryers showed me birds returning to the spindly trees dotting our border.

Soon.

NOT ANNOUNCED, not befitting a ruler or even a country's most powerful servant, but a shadow pressing a hot palm against my cheek.

My witch-queen had returned.

I opened my eyes but did not move. "You're home," I said, twisted in my sheets.

By witchlight she was haggard, grey newly spread near her temples. I rose to embrace her and she put out a hand.

"The cloak," she said. Outside the castle, she abjured it to shade every inch of her flesh. It had not yet retreated to its usual size.

All my arguments, the careful ground I had planned to tread—persuasion by day, a slow nighttime smoldering—were flooded by those words. I could not touch my lover because of—what, the Ilastrians? The ones she forced back to their border alone, though she could have sent a legion and saved some of herself for me?

The Ilastrians already had her name. It would never pass my lips, or those of our future offspring.

My frustration erupted in tears.

I am not proud. Even as a child, I hated the sound and drip and salty tang.

I hated that my witch-queen would pity me.

But she let go the cloak and stepped past its puddling shadow to wrap her arms around me, body tight against mine, thinner but still beloved. Always, always beloved.

She gasped and slid down my body, limp as yesterday's eels.

I grabbed at her, doing nothing.

There had been no time. Her eyes were wide, the Ilastrian arrowhead peered from her chest, glimmering with the force of the magic on it.

Directly through the heart.

There was still warmth on the O of her lips and I kissed them. That nightmarish second shadow had dissipated, but it meant nothing without her soft response.

I felt something slide from me, bigger though not deeper than my grief.

My witch-queen had protected me. She gave everything she possessed to protect me, her luck and the way she was dismissed in a world where witches were usually servants. She even gave me the brief innocence of her childhood, a safety she barely remembered. I had not known poison berries or crocodiles or assassins, and they had not known me.

The cloak of selfishness she kept only because it could not, by nature, be given away.

That depth of love was too much. I had not meant to require that from her.

I whimpered—if I were killed, the advisors would surrender to the Ilastrians—and, reminded of the swamp witch, scrambled towards the armchair. Unthinking, I draped myself in the cloud-silk, my aborted gift.

I breathed and the breathing was easy.

The swamp witch had told me to include silphium, an odd choice for healing. But without it, I would have done something rash and ultimately harmful to myself, and therefore the—my—country. I stood and let the cloud-silk drift around me.

The corpse on the floor must be dealt with. Its sight should have broken me, the rushing memories of touch and taste and smell, every conversation and aspiration we had shared. Now I remembered loving it as one remembers an old grave, the hole filled in, though there is a difference in that texture from the rest of your soul. But from a distance it is unnoticeable, no more than a slight bump in the grass.

Cloak light on my shoulders, I opened the bedroom door and called my guards. "Take her to her workshop," I said. "Place her on the table against the eastern wall." It was where she had ensured those battle-sundered souls could never return to their bodies. Someone would know how its runes might instead be used to restore. Meanwhile, the workshop's spell of preservation would keep her whole.

As they cleared the body I dressed for a late-night council session. The cloak ensured my grief did not fester anew, and as my advisors bickered, I considered our coffers, all the citizens crowded in Watergirl's District.

We would need an army.

Sutekh: A Breath of Spring

SHARANG BISWAS

RESURRECTION was never comfortable.

Os's lungs had been perfectly content in their laziness, with nothing to do but decay peacefully. Now, they wanted air again. But there was no air: just thick, clinging fluid and a bitter, metallic taste.

Heave—gasp—choke.

Now his lungs were on fire. It took a minute for his brain to start up again before he could claw at the sides of the tub and haul himself up.

His face broke free of the surface. Blessed air.

Gurgle—splutter—BREATHE.

No matter how many times he died, his body never seemed to remember the particulars of resurrection.

Fresh blood clogged his throat. He coughed, forcing the last of it out of his lungs, before launching into one of his usual lines. "Isn't a tub of blood a little theatrical?"

"I don't make the rules of magic," a voice replied.

Os froze. The voice was different. Deeper. Sharper. Masculine.

He scrubbed blood out of his eyes.

A stranger stood before him, regarding him skeptically. A slim, young man with skin the colour of the desert sands and scalp-tattoos so dense they could be mistaken for hair.

"Os, hurry up out of the tub, or it'll congeal," the stranger said, his tone bored. He bent over and began gathering the snuffed-out candles that ringed Os's tub.

Os hesitated. They were in the familiar, rectangular ritual chamber at the back of Isis's cave, with the tub in the centre. Oil lamps on hooks lit the stone walls and their painted reliefs. Shelves were directly carved into the southern wall, filled with papyrus scrolls and stone tablets. Sculpted into the eastern wall was the false door his soul had entered through, lured by the— he glanced down and yes, it was there—plate of fresh fruit on the stone floor next to the tub.

The plate had gained a new offering. Nestled among the berries, dates and figs, there appeared to sit a raw hunk of meat. No, not just meat: a bloody heart. Os wrinkled his nose at it. But the chamber smelled of incense, which, while cloying, was also familiar.

Os realized he'd been dumbly gazing around the room.

"Where's Isis?" he ventured.

"Who?" The man looked up. His eyes were blue-green chips of faience, much like Isis'. "Isis? The witch? Are you her brother or...?"

The man stood up, hands still full of candle. He was dressed like her: white linen skirt, gold bracelets, nails varnished a deep red. He wore no tunic though, and his bare chest was lightly muscled.

"Os, I'm pretty sure you were mauled by a Sacred Hippo on your last delve in the Pyramid. So why are you acting as though you bumped your head on a rock and went nuts?"

His voice turned gentle, patient—condescending, even—as though he were speaking to a five-year-old.

He continued, "I'm Amu-Aa, the witch who drags your sorry ass back to life every time you die. Now will you please get out of the tub? It's very hard to clean congealed blood."

GURGLE—splutter—BREATHE.

This time, as soon as he caught his breath, Os leaped out of the tub, narrowly avoiding the food offerings.

"You're back!" he said, eyeing the witch.

Amu-Aa scowled.

Os shivered, naked and drenched in rapidly-cooling blood as he was.

"Os, seriously, are you playing some kind of idiot prank?" Amu-Aa asked, handing Os a towel. "Or did Ammit the Devourer chew up your brain as well as your heart?"

The towel wrapped snugly around Os's waist. Its warm softness seemed almost alien to Os, who had grown used to the hard edges and blistering heat the Pyramid offered. And it was certainly more comfortable than anything Isis had ever given him.

"I thought..." Os tried, but didn't know how to finish the sentence. Amu-Aa clearly had no idea who Isis was. Must be a witch thing. Maybe Isis had bespelled the man, at the behest of the Gods, or something.

The pause stretched awkwardly between them.

"Congratulations on your first thought?" Amu-Aa finally said, though he sounded more confused than mean-spirited.

"Never mind," Os muttered, blushing. "Could you pass me my armour?"

Amu-Aa lifted the leather-and-bronze affair off its shelf in the southern wall.

"I polished it for you," he said.

"Yeah?"

It showed. The bronze glowed a comforting red, as though lit from within. Os could smell fresh wax. "You didn't have to."

Amu-Aa shrugged.

"You're the only one idiot enough to repeatedly venture into the Pyramid. Not many other mythic heroes for me to care for, and the villagers like to leave me alone. You're the most exciting thing around here."

Os considered this as he donned his armor. He'd never really thought about Isis growing bored, or how she spent her free time. Well, he'd actually thought about how he'd have *liked* her to spend her free time, specifically with him—

"Os, you're blushing again."

"What? No, I'm not!"

"You have green skin, Os. A blush shows up pretty well."

"Just give me my sword!"

—*SPLUTTER*—*BREATHE.*

"How do you keep getting new armor?"

"What d'you mean?" Os asked as he toweled the blood out from under his arms. It had the unfortunate habit of clinging to his hair.

"You always have new armor," Amu-Aa said, holding a breastplate up to his face. "See? This one has carvings of Lord Anubis in it. And more straps. More straps than metal, really; don't know how that's supposed to protect you against anything..."

"I—err—" Os stammered, unused to answering questions about himself. Isis had never seemed interested. She had been all smoky-eyes, lingering looks, and husky comments about his battle prowess or the size of his muscles. Though he was sure there was at least one time it wasn't his *muscles* she had been referring to—

"You'd never find something of this quality in town," Amu-Aa continued. "And I can't believe the Pyramid just *happens* to be stocked with fresh armaments for any self-important jock trotting inside!"

"I mean, I slew Ammit the Devourer this time..."

"This is *Ammit the Devourer's* armor?" Amu-Aa spluttered. "What, you just thought, 'Oh here's the fresh corpse of a demon-god I just killed! Why don't I strip off its armor and don it myself!'?"

"She wasn't *in* it!" Os snapped. "She doesn't wear armour!

She's not even human! More like a crocodile...lioness...thing..."
he finished lamely, gesturing vaguely in the air. "Can I have it,
please?"

"Not really an excuse," Amu-Aa muttered, but brought it over
anyway. He cleared his throat noisily. "Turn around."

"Huh?"

"I need to help you get into this, you himbo! You're never
getting into all these straps and buckles by yourself!"

—BREATHE.

"Don't you get tired of it?" Amu-Aa asked as Os scrubbed
his chest with another impossibly luxurious towel. He sat cross-
legged on the floor, popping figs from Os's offering plate into his
mouth. Os noticed that Amu-Aa didn't seem to mind the flecks
of blood that had dripped down from the heart and onto the
fruit. Where did he find all these fresh hearts, anyway?

"What d'you mean?" Os asked absently.

"Dying all the time? Isn't it—I don't know—tiresome? I
mean, you just got pecked to death by a Dire Heron! How
embarrassing is that? And I know the resurrection process isn't
pleasant."

Os dropped the towel and regarded Amu-Aa. His expression
was puzzled, even as he daintily placed a ripe fig between his
lips. Dried blood stained his skirt, no doubt from preparing the
tub for Os's inevitable arrival. And he'd forgotten to snuff out the
candles.

"Amu-Aa, have you just been watching me all this time?"

"What?"

"You haven't even begun to clean up like you normally do..."

Amu-Aa scowled and scurried over to the candles, snatching
at one before he had even blown it out. As he touched it, the
flame grew white hot, stretched upwards, and hissed, sending
sparks fizzing. Amu-Aa yelped, dropping the candle onto the
stone floor and hastily sticking his fingers in his mouth.

Os reacted without thinking. Reflexes honed for dodging

plague-mummies and jewelled death-crocodiles surged into action. Like a scorpion sting, he leaped towards Amu-Aa and stamped out the offending candle.

The witch, unprepared for the violence of Os's reaction, yelped again and stumbled backwards into a stone shelf, sending papyrus scrolls flying.

"Are you alright?" Os asked.

Amu-Aa's eyes were wide. He merely nodded.

"Show me your hand!"

"I'm fine, Os. No, really! It's a minor burn! And besides, I'm the one who's supposed takes care of you!" He smiled to show Os that, yes, he really was fine, picked himself up, and began to retrieve his scattered papers. It was somewhat of a weak smile.

"What was that?" Os demanded.

Amu-Aa shook his head. "Nothing! I forgot to discharge the candle, that's all."

Os hesitated, then nodded. Amu-Aa was a witch. He knew what he was talking about, didn't he? "Just...be careful," Os said. "If something were to happen you...I'm not the one who knows resurrection magic..."

Amu-Aa did not respond, seemingly busy with his cleanup. His sandals *clack-clacked* against the floor as he continued to tidy the chamber. Presently, he made his way to Os's equipment. The sword had been replaced by a crescent-shaped battle-axe.

"I do, yeah," Os said suddenly.

"Hmm?"

"Get tired of it. But that doesn't mean I don't have a duty to do. I need to vanquish Set. And if that means I die a thousand deaths, to be pulled back from the Duat a thousand times, so be it!"

Amu-Aa made a funny noise in his throat as he retrieved a breastplate from the shelves.

Os nearly winced. Even to his own ears, the words sounded trite and rehearsed.

Isis' conversation had never been deeper than, "Have you sufficiently recovered for your next venture, Lord Osiris?". More than once, he'd wanted to say "No, I'd like to rest for a bit!", or "Would you care to join me?" but he had never felt brave enough to actually speak the words.

He was supposed to be brave.

Os stood there, naked and helpless, a peculiar new feeling rising in him like the waters of the Nile during the flood season.

Amu-Aa, armour and axe in hand, froze when he caught Os's expression. He stood perfectly framed by the false doorway behind him, a vision of magic and mystery.

"Os, what's wrong?"

Os bit his lip. Murderous two-headed jackals he could dispatch with ease. Flesh-burrowing beetles were old hat. This... this was new territory.

"Amu-Aa, can I—could I rest here for a bit? Before venturing back into the Pyramid?"

"Oh...sure? I need to clean up, anyway..."

"No, I mean—" Os floundered, "—I mean would you like to...talk? For a little while?"

"Talk?"

"Yeah."

"You want to delay your epic, tomb-delving quest for a chat?"

"...yeah?"

Flickering lamplight glittered off of Amu-Aa's polished scalp, almost animating the tattoos. His brow creased as though he wrestled with some internal dilemma. Finally, he nodded.

"All I can offer you is goat's milk," he mumbled.

oslover616 | Dec 20, 2020, 2:28 AM
GENDER-SWAPPED ISIS MOD

Hey Folks! It's finally here, V1.0.0 of my mod! It was inspired by @osisboss's fan-fiction about a gender-swapped Isis. Let me know what you think? Special thanks to @PyramidPenny for her amazing 3D rendering and animation work!

I haven't touched the actual game mechanics. You should be able to plug this mod in even if you're in the middle of a run.

(I tested it with all three difficulty levels just to be sure).

NOTE: The original developers wrote a MASSIVE amount of text for this game, so there might be a few plot-continuity errors here and there. File a bug report here if you spot anything weird!

XOXOXO

"WHAT DO you mean, lava?"

"I mean the floor is literally made of lava."

Amu-Aa looked up from whatever mysterious animal he'd been busy dissecting. He looked skeptical.

He'd added a table and two stools to the Ritual Chamber a few resurrections ago, modest, wood-and-leather affairs. He would work while Os talked.

Os had begun to learn something about himself: he liked talking. He didn't really have much of an opportunity within the Pyramid: monsters tended to be more "eat first, ask questions later," and the Gods left behind only short messages to accompany the blessings they bestowed.

And Isis had been...beautiful, yes. Intriguing, yes. But an interesting conversation partner? Well...

Amu-Aa was easy to talk to. In fact, when the fangs of an Acid Asp sank into Os's flesh, a plume of flame from a Trumpeting Camel spiraled towards his head, or whenever a mortal blow reared up from somewhere in the Pyramid, he found that he was looking forward to his death. He was looking forward to the impatient orders of "Hurry out of the tub, you himbo!" Looking forward to relaxing on a leather stool while Amu-Aa pretended not to pay him any attention.

"Why did Lord Set decide that lava was appropriate construction material for *any* part of the Pyramid?" Amu-Aa asked, his left eyebrow quirked so high it disappeared into his scalp tattoos.

"I don't know, Amu! Why does Lord Khepri push the sun around every day? Why does Lady Sakhmet only drink beer when it's dyed red and poured into pools in front of her? Why do the Gods do anything?"

Os brought his hand down on the table, but only lightly, not wishing to disturb the carcass that constituted Amu-Aa's work.

Amu-Aa's mouth quirked. "Himbo," he muttered, turning back to the dead creature. Bone-tweezers whirred as he expertly removed the corpse's vital organs and placed them in a precise pattern on an inked papyrus sheet. Os noticed feathers. It might have once been a bird.

"What are you working on, anyway?" Os asked, fully expecting a sarcastic joke about his own intelligence. Amu-Aa was always fiddling with something bizarre. With Isis, apart from the tub of blood, it had always been lotus flowers, chrysanthemums, and honeyed potions. Amu-Aa favoured things like beetle dung, baboon intestines, and on one memorable occasion, the half-digested remnants of a man regurgitated by a pregnant lioness. ("A very potent ingredient," Amu-Aa had solemnly intoned.)

"A present for you," Amu-Aa replied, without looking up. He was doing something extremely delicate and extremely disgusting with the bird's eye.

Os paused. He had never seen Amu-Aa blush; his skin was always the colour of the swirling sands. But he tended to clear his throat noisily when embarrassed. Like he was doing just now.

"A present for me, Amu?" Os said softly.

Amu-Aa grimaced. "Shut up, Os. It's a prophecy to help you in your next delve. So you don't die as quickly. And so you stop bothering me by letting bathtubs of blood congeal."

He wouldn't meet Os's eyes. The sounds he was making from his throat might have suggested that he'd swallowed a whole frog.

"Err, thanks?"

A small smile curled on Amu-Aa's face as he placed a dismembered beak onto his papyrus diagram. "And you have my permission to continue," Amu-Aa added.

"Continue what?"

"Continue calling me Amu. Since you've done it twice already without asking."

Os, on the other hand, could blush deeply and profusely.

ActionKilla212 | Dec 24, 2020, 10:23 PM
PANDERING?

So I love Amu-Aa as a character. He's WAY more fleshed out than Isis. But is the flirting between him and Os a bit much? There's never a hint that Os is into dudes. He's always been (if I read between the lines) kinda into Isis, or even Bastet. Forcing this gay element onto Os seems to be pandering to the LGBT?

I'm not homophobic or anything, but is this the representation gays really want? Isn't this kinda like bullshit tokenism?

Or AITA?

GirlPhreak | Dec 24, 2020, 10:31 PM
RE: PANDERING?

@ActionKilla212 Yes, you are the asshole.

"**O**s?"
          "Yeah...?" Os opened one eye. Arms crossed behind his head, he had been happily dozing against the eastern wall, next to an image of Lady Bastet painted in greens and yellows.

Amu cleared his throat. "Come help me with something?"

Os opened his other eye. "You want *my* help? With witchcraft?"

Amu shot him a withering look. "It's about the Pyramid, himbo. You're the only one I know who's been inside it."

"Really?" Os asked, picking himself up. "No-one from town has ever been curious?" He stretched lazily, feeling his muscles pop. It was good to spend time outside his armor and clothing. He thought Amu might be watching him but when Os turned to look, Amu was bent over a sheaf of papyrus, swallowing audibly.

"Well, the only one I know who's still alive," Amu mumbled. "Are you coming?"

Os sauntered over. "I'm only alive thanks to you, Amu," he said, leaning over the witch.

Amu kept his workspace neat. A single sheaf of parchment, a few reed pens nestled in a case, and an inkwell. The leather surface of the table shone, as though oiled recently. Os braced himself with one arm near the edge.

Amu's eyes flickered up at Os looming over him before returning to his hieroglyphs. "Yes, well..." he murmured, gesturing dismissively with a hand. "Have you seen these glyphs anywhere in the Pyramid?" he asked, stabbing at a string of symbols with his pen. "In one of your lava-rooms or something?"

Hovering above the witch, Os smelled...lilies and cinnamon, with a touch of honest sweat. Smiling, he allowed his eyes to rove the papyrus scroll. He was hardly a scholar, but he'd seen some unusual stuff in the Pyramid. This however, escaped him completely. It started familiar enough, but then grew strange, as though a different language altogether, letterforms spiky and ominous.

ERROR 504
UNDEFINED VARIABLE:
"AMU-AA"

"The hieroglyphs refer to Set," Os said, frowning. "But I don't know whatever that is after it."

Amu nodded thoughtfully, while his fingers traced the strange writing. "I recognized Lord Set. Which is why I wanted to ask you. Due to your, err, *connection* to that particular deity..."

"You mean my blood-sealed oath of vengeance?"

"You took the words right out of my mouth."

Os shook his head. "Honestly, it looks a bit like Greek? Or maybe Latin?"

Amu's head snapped upwards so fast Os had to jerk back to prevent being struck on the chin.

"What?" Os asked, excited. "Did you figure something out? Did I help?"

Amu's eyes were wide. "Himbo, you read Latin and Greek?"

A twinge of hurt wriggled up from Os' belly. It must have shown on his face because Amu's expression instantly changed from surprise to dismay.

"No—Os, I didn't mean—just—I wasn't saying that you're stupid or anything."

Os turned away from the table. It was about time to head back anyway.

"Os, I—that was—"

"Don't worry about it," Os muttered, reaching for his breastplate.

"Os, please don't go!"

Something new in Amu's voice tugged at Os, yanked his head around to look back at him. The witch had stood up, hands balled at his sides. He looked upset.

"Os, please stay?" Amu pleaded, no trace of acid or barbs in his voice. "I'm sorry."

Os smiled, his ill-feeling melting away under the brightness of Amu's obvious consternation. He trotted over and placed a conciliatory hand on Amu's shoulder.

"Well, if you insist," he began, "But only because it's really fun to bother this one witch I know while he tries to work..."

"Please don't make me regret my decision."

Os's laugh was luminous and rosy, like the dawning sun.

AN EXCERPT FROM *FAGS, FANDOMS, & THE FUTURE: HOW LGBTQIA MODDERS & AMATEUR GAME DESIGNERS IMAGINE A QUEERER VIDEOGAME MULTIVERSE*
ARUNDHUTI MANDAL

Rather than simply accept the bland excuses or weak attempts at "diversity representation" touted by mainstream corporations, these passionate fans are taking the future of their favourite properties into their own hands. Fan modifications to existing videogames are nothing new, and mods focussed on exploring sexual interests are arguably some of the most popular. However, it is only recently that queer-themed mods have been garnering widespread attention. Indeed, entire storylines featuring queer content are being retrofitted into popular AAA titles by amateur designers.

The significance of this phenomenon cannot be understated. A legion of young, queer, justice-oriented gamers are essentially saying "We want gay art, and if you won't make it we will!" Queer gamers are demanding positive representation in a hetero- and cis- normative world, and actively creating the change they wish to see. The resulting new, Frankenstein-artworks are experiencing a wave of popularity comparable to the original games themselves.

A poetic soul might wonder how the videogame characters themselves might feel. What would Super Massimo say to reading "Your Prince is in Another Castle" instead of the usual Princess? How would grizzled monster hunter Gustav of the Riviera react to being hit on by the legions of attractive male barmaids and sorcerers?

IT TOOK MORE than two dozen resurrections before Os dared look through some of Amu's things. While Amu bent over the bloody tub clutching a coarse, camel-hair scrubber, Os rifled through the scrolls ensconced within the shelves that were cut into the southern wall, expecting to uncover ancient and terrible hieroglyphs to steal the breath of men, to strike down crops with the plague, to blind, burn, and bewitch…

"Amu, is this a recipe for Tiger Nut Cakes?"

"What?" Amu looked up. Pearls of perspiration glinted rather pleasingly on his chest. Os noticed Amu had blood in his eyebrows.

It suddenly struck Os that Amu was very, *very* attractive. He'd seen it before, certainly, but never really…internalized it?

"It's a historic recipe, himbo." Amu snapped. "I have other things to occupy my time besides constantly raising you from the dead, you know. I have other clients!"

That statement was jarring enough to pull Os out of pleasant thoughts about Amu's chest.

"Wait, you do magic for others?"

Something in Os's voice must have sounded off, because Amu straightened and raised an eyebrow quizzically.

"Yes?" he replied, gesturing to the tub. "The hippo blood doesn't pay for itself you know…"

That…made perfect sense, of course. Amu wasn't there solely for Os's benefit. Of course Os hadn't believed that. Of course not."I thought you were bored? That the villagers left you alone?"

"Yes, well…" Amu cleared his throat and unconsciously picked some dried blood out from under his fingernails. "I didn't want you growing a big head, did I? Travellers and such often ask for me." His voice softened a little at the end of his sentence, almost as if he was embarrassed by the statement.

Standing by the shelves, Os took in the information. Travelers came in search of Amu, to ask for his advice and his magic. Was Amu famous? It dawned on Os that bringing a warrior back to life time and time again was possibly a rather complicated feat, something only a master witch could achieve.

Amu was *really* hot.

Despite the banter he had engaged in with Isis, Os had little experience with actual romance. He was a warrior. He had a mission. Everything else had always been secondary.

Os glanced back at the recipe. The glyphs were cut into an old slab of stone, instead of painted on papyrus.

"What were you doing with this recipe?"

The momentary embarrassment had vanished from Amu. He relaxed, folding his arms, and leaned jauntily against the tub. It was rather fetching.

"I'm glad you're taking an interest in reading, himbo," he said wryly. "That was actually a request from the Pharoah. A feast for her birthday featuring historic dishes." Amu's voice had taken on a hint of pride. "The Pharaoh gifted me twenty debens of ivory for it. Good pay. And for work that's far easier than rubbing your corpse down with antelope grease before hauling it into the tub, let me tell you!

Os' thoughts, which had veered towards interesting avenues regarding Amu, crashed at the image of being rubbed down by the witch. He opened his mouth dumbly.

"Huh?"

"It's one of the preparations I have to make to your body before your Resurrection. Pain in the ass. I have to massage you with camel grease and rare herbs. It's partly why the blood comes off your skin so easily."

Os's brain was now steeping in several pleasant images of Amu making expert use of his hands. Letting this happen turned out to be a bad idea. What with Os being naked.

Amu's eyes widened as he looked down

"Os—are you—?" Amu stuttered, his voice breaking.

Lady Hathor, heed my plea!, Os prayed desperately. He had already resolved to be brave around Amu, hadn't he?

"Amu?" he ventured, keeping his voice low. "Can I kiss you?"

Amu stepped back. His brow furrowed. He cleared his throat before hesitantly answering, "No...?"

Beyond a cursory, "Thank you," Os barely said a word to
Amu the next few resurrections. He avoided even looking at
the witch for too long.

Finally, Amu rounded on him as he clambered out of the
bath, splashing blood all over the food offerings.

"Are you done sulking, himbo?"

Os grabbed the proffered towel and grunted something
indistinct.

"Os, you can't just spring a question like that onto me, and
then get upset when I refuse! What's even the point of the
question, then?"

Os stared down at the bloody towel in his hands. Something
was curdling in his stomach.

Amu continued to scold him, "...and if you had paused a
minute before huffing off, or even tried to talk, I might have said
'let's share a meal and talk about this first'..."

Os looked up, but Amu's brow was still wrinkled in anger.

"...but instead you decided to act like a *child*, and honestly, I
have better things to do than date immature, self-important,
petulant wannabe-heroes, thank you very much."

Os opened his mouth.

Os closed his mouth.

He was not a child. He was Osiris, divinely sworn to defeat
Set. Within the Pyramid, he had faced hordes of unspeakable
monsters, dodged innumerable traps, overcome countless
dangers. He had died and lived and died again, a hundred times
over.

He deserved this, didn't he?

He was not a child.

Was he?

He said nothing.

Gurgle—splutter—BREATHE.

Os did not open his eyes. He remained in the tub, basking in the viscous warmth. He had penetrated further into the Pyramid than ever before, into a cold, alien level with jagged teeth of ice thrusting from the ceiling.

He fought, he died, he returned. There would be no respite from that. There was nothing else, not until he defeated Set.

Amu had said—

Amu.

It didn't matter what Amu had said.

Amu would normally be snapping at him by this point, complaining about congealing blood. Had he finally given up on Os?

He began dragging himself out of the tub, runnels of dark, red liquid spilling everywhere.

"The blood becomes you, my lord."

Os froze. His eyes snapped open.

Jet black hair hanging long and loose. A crown shaped like a throne. An enigmatic smile.

Isis.

"My Lord Osiris, are you ready for your next venture?" Isis asked, her voice smoky like frankincense. "Pardon my forthrightness, but the flex of your muscles is rather more pronounced than last time. It would seem you are deepening not only your strengths but your handsomeness..."

Os sprang up, not caring that he knocked over an offering plate of enormous dried chrysanthemums and splashed blood onto Isis' white linens. His gaze darted around the room.

The furniture Amu had installed was gone. The man was nowhere to be seen.

"Lady Witch, where is Amu-Aa?" he croaked.

Isis' delicate brow furrowed. "My Lord? To whom do you refer? Is that perchance the demon that slew you this time? Rest assured, no demon can puncture my spells!"

"No!" Os cried as he continued to whirl about the room, hoping to find a trace—any trace—of the tattooed witch with the sharp tongue. "There was another witch. A man—named Amu-Aa. Where did he go?"

Isis stepped softly towards him. "There is no other witch," she said in a silken voice, "Only me. Perhaps my lord is upset from his last visit? Perhaps you desire...something more of me?"

Os's eyes finally snapped back to Isis. She was very close to him now. Her skin, sandstone brown, was smooth and flawless. Her lips were parted and moist, her eyes large.

"Err...What?"

In response, Isis smiled as she ran a red-lacquered finger gently down his arm. She hadn't offered him a towel. He was still soaked in blood.

Okay…

Isis had never been this...this...blatant, before, had she?

Isis' eyes travelled down from his face. Down the length of his body, down, down, until her gaze paused and her smile deepened.

"You appear eager, my lord," she crooned.

Os stepped back. He felt betrayed by his own anatomy.

"Err..Isis, I...I barely know you..."

"What is there to know, Lord? We need not talk. Only indulge in earthly delights." The sway of her hips hinted that the delights would be very earthly indeed.

But where was Amu? Os could not think. His brain fizzed with Isis's curves, Isis's softness, Isis's honeyed voice.

"Come, Lord. Let me show you what a witch truly knows..."

Os's world melted into mist.

Sutekh: The Long Winter - Review
By Melody Chan
Rating: ★★★★★

The first expansion to blockbuster roguelike *Sutekh* does not disappoint. With the addition of winter themed levels, the khopesh as a brand new weapon, and tonnes of new story content, *S:TLW* delivers a potent dose of *Sutekh* goodness in one inexpensive package.

Players will even get to see a deepening of the Os-Isis romance, complete with a fade-to-black sex scene between the two slow-burn lovers.

Unfortunately, developer HyperLilliput has announced that they have no plans to ensure the expansion's compatibility with fan-made mods (I had to uninstall three in order to launch the game).

—*SPLUTTER*—*BREATHE.*

Resurrection was never comfortable. But it was never like this.

Os knew what a spear shoved through one's skull felt like. An instant of jagged pain, followed by peace. This was the same, except there was no relief. Again and again, the pain stabbed into his head, like the battle-roar of a lioness, like the vengeance of Lady Sakhmet. The blood in the tub grew hot, begun to boil. He tried to cry out but scalding blood flooded his mouth as unknown, alien symbols burst into his brain.

ERRORAMUAA.EXENOTDEFINEDERRORAMUAA. EXENOTDEFINEDERROR

His fingers scrabbled for purchase against the rim of the tub but he couldn't get them to do what what he wanted, couldn't get them to *work*—

Hands. Someone's hands had grabbed his and were pulling pulling *pulling* him up and out. But Os slipped against the slick sides of the tub, splashing blood everywhere and they weren't strong enough weren't strong enough—

ERRORAMUAA.EXENOTDEFINEDERROR

A bite of cold around his ankles. The world turned upside down and Os felt himself being yanked out of the bath by his feet.

Blood sluiced off him and he spluttered, dangling upside down from the ceiling.

The pain still hammered in his head but he could see again.

Amu stood before him.

Hope erupted in his chest, star-bright.

There stood Amu, arms outstretched, sweat pouring down his chest. He was chanting something. A look of intense concentration gouged lines into his forehead. His scalp—

The tattoos that normally adorned Amu's scalp like a skullcap had somehow broken free of their two-dimensional prison. Writhing, black forms, they twisted around his head like a monstrous crown. Inky chains reached out from them, towards Os's feet, holding him up above the bath of churning blood.

But the pain wouldn't stop. The pain still pierced his skull, the weird symbols still thrust into his brain. This had to end. He couldn't stand it for much longer.

"Amu," he managed. "Kill me!"

Amu's eyes widened, even as he continued to chant.

"Please!" Os begged. "Before—"

Twin javelins of darkness shot out of the mass of crawling tattoos, straight towards Os' heart.

osisboss | September 21, 2021, 3:03 AM
ISIS GENDER SWAP & TLW

I removed all my mods before installing The Long Winter expansion, and then tried to re-install @oslover616's gender swapping mod. The game now crashes every time I boot it up. Does anyone know of a fix for this? I love the features of TLW, but I NEED #OsAmu!

oslover616 | September 23, 2021, 9:42 AM
THE LONG WINTER BUG

Hey folks! As you're probably all aware, my Amu-Aa mod hasn't been playing well with TLW. I've tried to figure out where the problem is, but honestly, I don't really have the time to devote to it.

Looks like you'll have to play TLW without the mod. Or if you really want to finish Amu and Os' storyline, you can keep your save file before installing TLW in a separate folder, and like, return to it later after finishing the expansion.

Sorry folks, but I just don't have the spoons for this right now!

xoxoxo

—*BREATHE.*

Os scrambled out of the tub faster than he had ever before. He stood there, naked, shivering. Blood cooled on his body.

There was no pain in his head. In fact, he felt curiously light.

A warm towel settled over his shoulders.

"Os?"

Amu was worried. Os could tell from the quaver in his voice. But hearing Amu filled him with a giddy happiness he'd never thought possible.

He turned and regarded the witch. Normally tough and thorny like a desert plant, Amu now looked small, anxious, fragile. His hands were clasped around his elbows, his eyes large with worry.

"Os, how are you feeling?"

Inside the Pyramid, Lady Hathor had once left Os a gift of a poem, a token to think upon as he battled his way to Set. In the chaotic hellscape of the Pyramid, he had clutched the words to his chest, held on to them tightly, treating them like an amulet against all the horror around him.

Now, he released the words gently in song.

"Your form revives my heart.
It is your voice
that makes my body steadfast..."

Amu didn't say anything for a moment.

Os held his breath.

"Himbo, if you're trying to woo me, at least try it without using a plagiarized poem."

Os's breath escaped in a great guffaw as he fell back onto the floor, the towel sliding off his shoulders, his back hitting the tub. Tension rolled off his body in great bellows of laughter. He couldn't help it. Amu's gentle stings were some of the most exquisite sensations in the world, he realized.

Once his laughter subsided, he looked up. Amu's worry had dissolved into skepticism.

"I feel good, Amu. Really, really good." And he did. He was bright, buoyant.

Amu nodded, but didn't take his quizzical eyes off Os.

"I had sex, you know."

If Amu had been expecting anything, it wasn't that. His jaw didn't exactly drop, but his lips did part in surprise."Oh!...how was it?"

"Honestly? It was...really adequate? Fun. But...mechanical?"

"Ah."

Amu coughed.

Os got up. He walked to his armour, neatly placed on the shelves. His fingers played over the worked leather and metal. Curiously, he felt no compulsion to don any of it, no burning desire to dive back into the Pyramid in search of holy retribution.

"Amu, would you like to go on a date?"

He turned, and looked directly at Amu.

"Os—"

"To get to know each other better," Os interrupted. "To talk things out. You said you would've liked that."

Amu paused to regard him. He cleared his throat.

"What do you mean by 'go on a date'?" Amu asked.

"I mean outside!" Os gestured around him. "I've never really been outside your ritual chamber, outside your cave! And you know, I think I'm going to take a little break from Pyramid-delving!"

Amu's brow creased. "Os, is this you trying to have sex with me?" He looked down Os's body suspiciously.

Os made a dismissive gesture. "Yes, obviously. But not right now. After we hang out a bit more. I think it'll be better that way."

It took a while, but Amu finally smiled. "Okay, himbo."

Ancient Egyptian Love poem adapted from "The Cairo Love Songs," translations by Michael V. Fox, excerpted from the Journal of the American Oriental Society.

TALALORA

CALEB HOSALLA

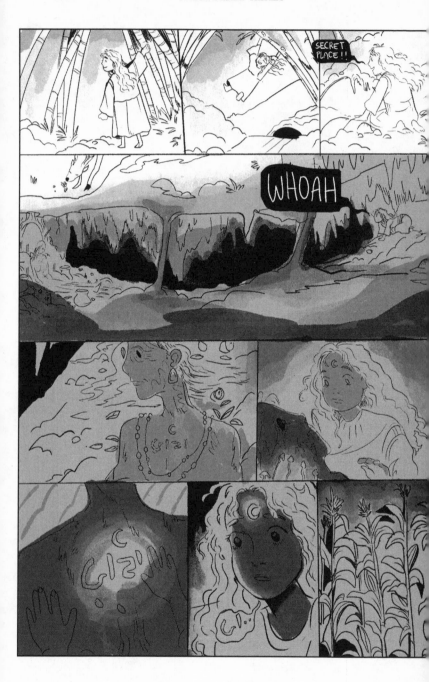

NOT DEATH, NOR THE STORM

TAMARA JERÉE

THE WITCH offers Nis the elder skull. Nis shows her how to call the threshold of death.

FROM THE PEAK of the ossuary,   Nis visualizes the jagged tower of bones as a knife that will slice the hurricane. Ni imagines nirself as the willowy pines that bend easily under the force of nature. That is Nis with the dead—accepting their power and anger but never breaking. Nis times nir meditation so that it will coincide with the start of the hurricane and ni can trance through its power.

The dead wake nir as ni is slipping under. They so rarely all speak at once, but now they fill the ossuary with the insistent rattle of bones, portending something other than the storm.

IN SILENCE, LIGHT ONLY THE BLACK CANDLES. THE RED, SAVE

FOR AFTER. WHEN LIGHTING THE CENSER, MANY WILL SEE THE
SILHOUETTE OF THE DOOR. IT IS NOT FOR YOU TO OPEN YET.

—FROM *THE ELEVEN VERSES OF DEATH,* CARETAKER LITH IMN

IMAGINE WHAT WE WILL BE ABLE TO SEE WHEN FREED FROM SKIN
AND OUR EYES ARE EVER OPEN.

—EXCERPT FROM CARETAKER CORRESPONDENCES

THEY MEET when the witch is unconscious. The wards around
the tower have struck her down just as the wind begins to
wild. Already the air is heavy with water and thick to breathe.
Prone, the witch curls protectively around a pale shape that calls
to Nis. A spirit seeks home. Nis hovers closer. Within the witch's
hood, her face is sharp-featured, but her skin is the same warm
brown as Nis's own. Ni has the sudden and confusing urge to
reach out and trace the sharp bridge of her nose, but the witch
smells of florals and astringent herbs—scents that disturb and
haunt the dead. Nis hopes it won't cling to nir robes. Strapped
to the witch's back is a lumpy gray sack that Nis is certain is
filled with skeletal remains. Clutched protectively in her hands
is the skull, Nis realizes. The wind tugs at the bell of the witch's
sleeve, whipping it back to reveal an inked pentacle on the back
of her hand. The mere sight of it curls Nis' lips in a hiss. Final
confirmation that the wards were true. Indeed, they've snared a
witch.

Briefly, Nis wonders if it's a trap of some kind, if the witch
knew ni would be drawn out of the tower when ni sensed the
bones. Ni dismisses it. The witch is the foolish one if she did not
expect the wards, the storm. She must have traveled from the
lands in the north where they do not know the fury of the coastal
season.

Nis takes the bones first, setting them carefully inside the
tower. Trap or not, these bones belong to this land.

Safe within the candlelit glow of the ossuary, Nis peers out
at the witch, still unconscious in the pine needles and grass. If

she weren't a witch—and if Nis hadn't sworn nirself to a life of isolation in service of the dead—perhaps Nis might attempt to name this dawning feeling.

The first droplets of rain darken the steps. Nis hopes ni will not regret dragging the witch out of the storm. Holding nir breath, ni finds the offending packet of herbs on a cord around the witch's neck and tosses it into the wind.

T HE WITCH reveals her name. Witches, unlike other people, do not introduce themselves or merely *give* their names. They *reveal* them.

Its power courses through the dark of the ossuary. Nis, trained to see threads of power, seizes it. Ni could string the witch up like an occult puppet, could bind her in her own name as with invisible rope. Against the common wisdom of the Catacombs— *never suffer a witch lest she torment the dead*—Nis does not.

The witch and the caretaker stare across the gloom of the ossuary, altar candles burning low between them.

Nis tests the name, pulls the power taught. The witch holds her chin up. Defiance or daring, Nis can't tell. Ni lets the power slacken and dissipate.

"Why reveal your name to an enemy?" Nis asks.

"To prove to you that we are not."

THE BODY IS THE KEY. BONE IS PORTAL. THE SKULL, INTENTION. CAST THE CIRCLE WITH WHAT REMAINS.

—FROM *THE ELEVEN VERSES OF DEATH*, LITH IMN

I HAVE DREAMS OF REACHING INTO MYSELF AND WITHDRAWING MY OWN BONES, CLEAN AND SUN-BLEACHED.

—EXCERPT FROM A CARETAKER'S UNSENT LETTER

SHADOWS SHARPEN the bones that crowd the walls. Nis follows the witch as she walks the perimeter of the central chamber, studying their arrangement. The witch cranes her head back, gazing up to where a tower of thigh bones are lost to the darkness of the upper tower. At first, Nis worries that ni will have to warn her away from touching the remains, but the witch keeps a respectful distance that seems at least partially born of uncertainty. Nis has never seen anyone look at the interior of a bone sanctuary with such unease, but ni reminds nirself that this is the first time the witch would have encountered their traditional deathways.

"The coven mother denied my grandmother's request that her body be treated according to her tradition. She said you all commit blood sacrifices in the name of the dead," says the witch.

"We sacrifice no one but ourselves," Nis answers, nir voice echoing back to them. "At Mirthe, we learn that witches gain their power by stealing it from the dead. That you put them in the ground so they can never cross over and find peace."

The witch draws her gaze away from the bones and back to Nis. "We derive our magic from our ancestors, yes. But we keep them close to us so that they might walk by our sides and teach us, so that we might still dance with them. We have no afterlife to ferry them to. There is only this life."

Nis doesn't understand. Ni has sacrificed this life for the afterlife. Ni cannot fathom a world without it, cannot fathom a world where the dead stay to dance with the living. There is no peace without crossing.

"Then why have you sought the Bone Sanctuary of Minam bu Mir?" Nis asks.

"My grandmother married into our coven, the only outsider among us. This land of red clay is hers. She wanted to return to be with her family," says the witch.

Nis aches to smooth nir hand over the elder's skull, to listen for the echoes of her life and understand who would leave her land for the bitter cold north and its strange magic. Ni has only ever known one life path. So many like Nis, the ones who will not grow up to be woman or man, become caretakers. It is not ordained, but enough people expect it that it seems so. That expectation and the desire to live—even briefly—among others like nirself had driven Nis to the Catacombs of Mirthe and, finally, to Minam bu Mir, where ni would live out the rest of nir days alone.

To be a caretaker meant they would never want for company. That's what the senior caretakers in the Catacombs of Mirthe taught them. The serenity of solitude would fulfil them. Nis had never known loneliness, ni realizes, because ni has lived with it so long that ni has become numb to it—or else it has numbed nir. Ni does not have the space to understand which, only that ni is grateful for this storm and this witch and this blessed death.

"**Y**OUR BLOOD is also of this land," Nis tells the witch over a plain meal of broth and crusty bread. The smell of bright foods unsettles the dead, and rich meals could rouse caretakers from the meditative state they work to maintain. Nis has not considered nir food in years but can tell by the look on the witch's face that she was expecting something much different after her long travels. Ni has nothing else to offer, so ni asks, "Did your grandmother lead you home?"

The witch pushes back her hood and combs her fingers through her dark braids. Their silver ornaments glint in the candlelight. "She was concerned with her death in a way many in my coven are not. She left a box with specific instructions—a map to Minam bu Mir, precise directions about when to exhume her bones, descriptions of landmarks and customs. People thought she was becoming fragile in her old age. I'd always liked her stories. I thought I'd listened to her well and knew the way."

"Home calls to us all. We must return."

The witch frowns. "I have only come to fulfill the wishes of someone I loved. I will return to my coven—if the coven mother will have me back after my defiance."

Rain lashes the windows high above. Wind still rattles the heavy doors in their frame. For as long as the storm lasts, ni will not be alone. There is tension in its reassurance.

"We must accept our own," Nis says, trying to convey understanding. Ni consciously tries to disentangle nir wants from the witch, tries to remember how to converse outside ceremony. "How strong could a coven be that casts out its own?"

"I hope the mother feels that way," says the witch. She stares pensively into her bowl of broth. "They say the dirt to the south is red because it's absorbed bad magic. I thought, as I walked, that it looked vibrant. Just like my grandmother said. I'd like to see more of this place, but I have risked so much by leaving at all."

"Take the land with you when you go," Nis says. Ni goes to the cupboard and returns with a small cup that ni offers to the witch. "I made it from the red clay."

It is a sturdy, rustic piece, but the witch takes it as if it's spun from the most delicate glass. Their fingertips brush, and Nis jerks nir hands back at the contact. Ni can't remember the last time ni touched another's bare skin. Bones are all that's existed of bodies for so long.

The witch notices, and her smile is slow and shy. Nis can't meet her gaze, so ni clears the table.

DIP YOUR HANDS INTO THE THREADS OF MAGIC. TRACE YOUR FINGERS OVER THE CURVE OF THE SKULL TO BATHE IT IN POWER. IF THE SPIRIT HAS NOT YET TURNED THEIR EYE TO YOU, NOW THEY WILL.

—FROM *THE ELEVEN VERSES OF DEATH*, CARETAKER LITH IMN

I HAVE DREAMS OF BUILDING MYSELF INTO THE OSSUARY WALLS.

— WORDS FROM A TORN PAGE

W HEN THE doors cease their rattle, Nis takes the witch out to see the eye of the storm. She's hesitant at first.

"Won't it come back?" she asks, lingering just inside the doorway.

"It will, but we have a few moments," says Nis.

The world has been blown apart. Pine needles stick to the bone-pale tower. Branches hang heavy and drenched. An old tree, one that could no longer bend, is snapped in two. The green is darker, richer from the rain. The wet earth is molten red. On the air, minerals and damp. A circle of serene blue sky looks down on them, its edges jagged with swirling clouds.

The witch steps out as if into a new world, staring up at the sky with her mouth open. She reaches for Nis as if to orient herself, and ni lets nir hand be taken. There is no edict against contact with the living, but Nis still feels as if something has been broken.

O NLY AFTER they're safely inside and the storm has redoubled does the witch notice her missing herbs.

"I blessed them for safe travels," she says. "They would not have harmed you."

"But they would have made the bones restless."

Nis has only been possessed once outside of ritual. The bones of someone who had died alone in the wild had been delivered to nir. During their life, Nis discovered, the person had suffered much psychic torment. As soon as Nis lay nir hands on the bones, the spirit had sensed an openness in nir and poured into nir body. Nis had lost time in the spirit's turbulent mind, and when ni managed to separate from them, ni had collapsed into a deep, week-long sleep on the stairs of the ossuary. It was an extreme case with an already-unstable spirit, but disturbing bones often brought bad energy onto a caretaker.

"I can give you something to make up for it, a protective talisman," says Nis.

Nir chest constricts when the witch initially balks at the skull of the catacomb rat. Ni hastens to explain. They do not carry disease and they are not pests. The rats that live in the Catacombs of Mirthe have the most developed spiritual sense of any nonhuman and are given to young initiates to help them sharpen their intuition into intention.

"Their bones are sacred and treated with care," says Nis. "If you listen, they will warn you of danger."

Again, the witch accepts the offering with both hands. "Please forgive me. You've given me another meaningful gift, more than I could repay."

The ache in nir chest eases. "I would be remiss not to make up for discarding your herbs out of hand."

"No, no," says the witch. "It is ultimately a blessing. Thank you."

Caretakers are not often thanked. Mourners and the dead have so much more to occupy their minds, after all. Like skin, like body heat, Nis struggles to process it.

THE SPIRIT WILL FLOOD INTO YOU. THEY WILL WANT THE DOOR BECAUSE IT IS FREEDOM, BUT IT WILL REBUFF THEM. FIRST, THEY MUST UNBURDEN THE WOES OF THIS LIFE TO PASS INTO THE AFTER. THROUGH AGONY, YOU ARE A CONDUIT FOR PEACE.

—FROM *THE ELEVEN VERSES OF DEATH*, CARETAKER LITH IMN

I'VE LOST THE ABILITY TO DISCERN DREAMS FROM NIGHTMARES FROM MEMORIES.

—EXCERPT FROM A CARETAKER'S LOVE LETTER

"Can I watch you guide my grandmother into the afterlife?" the witch asks.

"Most do not want to witness the possession," says Nis, sweeping incense ash from the altar in preparation. "The dead must shed their pain and worldly attachments to cross over, and even the most fulfilled, happy spirit can twist a caretaker. There are parts of every life, secrets, that it might hurt the living to know. Even to other caretakers, witnessing someone in the throes of possession can be unpleasant."

The witch steps up to the altar, cradling the elder's skull in her hands. Nis is struck by the sight. Perhaps if she wore black robes and bore the ritual scarification that marks their cheeks, Nis might mistake her for a fellow caretaker.

"I'm not afraid," says the witch.

"Of what?" Nis almost snaps. An emotion prickles that ni hasn't felt in ages, and ni wrestles to name it. If ni let it run wild, it would ruin nir focus. "Of possession, of pain, of death?"

"I'm not afraid of you, Nis."

No one has ever told nir that. Among the people, caretakers are respected. After all, everyone's death rests in their hands. Respect, however, does not mean that their people look upon them warmly. So many families, when they bring their dead to nir ossuary, can maintain only fleeting glances. That Mirthe dictates the caretakers' isolation to protect their spiritual attunement means that they will never be any less mysterious to the people they serve.

"May I?" the witch asks, hands outstretched.

Nis doesn't know what she's asking for but nods before even considering it. The witch places the skull carefully upon the altar before stepping up to Nis and studying nir face. Her gaze is so open, and Nis is so unused to eye contact, that ni struggles to hold it. Ni remembers how, in nir days as an initiate, ni struggled to subdue the wildest spirits. Now, Nis feels that ni must apply the same learned principals to nir own heart. The witch runs her hands over the stubble of Nis's scalp, pushing back nir hood as she goes. Nis shivers even though, now hours into the storm, the air is warm and damp. The witch trails her fingertips down the

nape of Nis's neck and brings her hands to cup nir face, brushing
her thumbs first over the row of scars along nir cheekbones
and then over the dusting of black pigment on nir eyelids. Nis
breathes through the touch the same way ni has learned to
breathe through pain.

"Does it hurt to be touched?" asks the witch.

It does—in a way that Nis doesn't want to explain. "No," ni
replies, breaking.

THE SPIRIT unburdens.
      Nis has never needed to consider the consequences of
breaking the isolation tenant. Not that ni could have shoved the
witch back out into the storm. But ni could have offered food and
retired to nir room at the tower peak. Ni could have abstained
from sharing conversation and gifts. Ni could have declined to
share the ritual.

Nis has never struggled to hold a spirit before, especially not
one so gentle. The sense of severing is the strongest, the cutting
ties from home. It manifests as sharp pain in Nis's chest, and the
grounding glow of the candles and smoke of the incense are lost
to nir. Ni finds mingled regret and hope. Embarrassment diluted
by indignation. The burden of carrying the old ways in silence,
lest they be ridiculed. Smothering half of the self.

The correct words feel distant. Nis gropes through nir
memory for what ni should do next. Ni is not in nir body, not
psychically, but ni can feel the pain of it.

Someone is pulling at the threads around nir, sweeping up
the tatters and stitching closed the wounds. The spirit's pain is
shunted away as if it has found another path. Nis gasps for breath
and remembers the words to move beyond.

"I see you. I will remember," Nis says and means it.

As if ni has surfaced from dark and oppressive depths, the
candlelight returns. To Nis, it seems so bright. Ni finds the edges
of nirself and realizes nir body is on the hard floor. The witch
kneels beside nir, forehead wrinkled with concern. When their

eyes meet, the threads cradling Nis cling a little less desperately.

Nis senses the spirit's attention turn before passing over the threshold. Ni knows her relief, her thanks—not only for the unburdening but for Nis's kindness towards her descendant. The spirit has possessed nir, and the spirit knows the thing Nis nirself doesn't want to acknowledge most.

When the pressure of the spirit departs, Nis attempts to take a full breath and   finds nir chest feels stuffed with storm. The witch rests a hand there as if she can sense it and breathes as if for them both.

WHEN A SPIRIT DEPARTS, IT IS NORMAL TO FEEL HOLLOW FOR A TIME. KNOW THAT POSSESSION IS THE MOST SACRED RITE. WITHOUT CARETAKERS, THERE WOULD BE NO PEACE. IF THE HOLLOWNESS LINGERS BEYOND A MOON, RETURN TO MIRTHE TO UNDERGO RITUAL CLEANSING BY AN ELDER CARETAKER.

—FROM *THE ELEVEN VERSES OF DEATH*, CARETAKER LITH IMN

HOW DOES ONE HOLD AN ENTIRE LIFE AND THEN RETURN TO ONE SO EMPTY?

—QUESTION SCRAWLED IN THE MARGINS OF A COPY OF *THE ELEVEN VERSES*

THE WORLD outside is dark when the storm leaves us.

"Is it always so bad?" asks the witch. Ni knows she means the ritual and not the storm.

Nis lights the final red candle. They will burn through the night and purify any lingering energy. In the morning, Nis will find a place to arrange the bones with the others along the ossuary walls.

In the morning, the witch will depart.

"I'm not often so careless," Nis answers, studying the burn of a candle.

"You weren't careless. You were giving. Open. Such a big offering could hurt anyone. It's a wonder you're not wearier."

"We train years for this. It should not have gone this way tonight." Nis realizes that ni feels embarrassed, that other caretakers might find it shameful to have needed help from an outsider, especially a witch. Ni would not have been in this position if the witch hadn't come—but ni also wouldn't have discovered what ni has. Nis sets aside nir bruised ego and turns to the witch. "There are so few willing to do this work that it is necessary to work alone, to rely only on oneself. The way you pulled the threads was delicate yet supportive. Thank you."

The tension in her expression eases. "You're welcome. When I saw your pain, I acted first and only considered later how it might've been improper of me. I'm relieved that it wasn't. Our magic traditions may be different—and I hope I'm not too forward in suggesting this—but I might still be of assistance. So you wouldn't have to shoulder so much alone."

Both are silent for a moment. "But your coven. You said you intend to return if they would have you back. And the senior caretakers at Mirthe would—" Nis doesn't know what they'd do, what they'd say. The witch is one of their own by blood, but a witch still.

"The coven has been my world for my entire life. I love it." She steps nearer, voice turning wistful. "But I also want to experience this place I've only known in stories, to walk the paths my grandmother did."

"People would be suspicious of you. You couldn't hide your marked hand forever."

"But perhaps it would be different if you were with me. The people trust you."

Nis goes to sit on the stairs and rests nir face in nir hands for a moment. Ni is not used to feeling, and it exhausts nir. Ni feels shaken apart, unruly, chaotic. "What you suggest isn't done. People's trust in the caretakers is not what you imagine. It is respect, but it is not warmth."

The witch hovers near. "I'm sorry. I've been presumptuous. I've scared you."

"I'm not scared," Nis says, realizing it is a lie as ni says it. *It doesn't hurt.*

The ossuary is too quiet without the wind and rain. The witch sits beside nir on the stairs, careful to leave space between them. They watch the candles burn, and Nis feels the storm gathering in nir chest again. Nis became a caretaker to find solace with kindred souls. A younger Nis thought ni wouldn't mind the isolation nir duty required. Ni had spent nir entire life in the company of the living and still felt lonely.

Then death and a storm drove a witch to nir doors.

Ni needs to recenter. Needs to meditate. Needs to refocus on the days ahead—days that will inevitably run together as they always have. Ni knows ni will begin to mark time by this day, will every year anticipate the hurricane season bringing her back to nir.

Ni has known hundreds of lifetimes, feels old beyond nir years in some ways, and yet here is this giddy hope ni doesn't want to tamp down.

"My room is upstairs if you—" Nis doesn't know how to ask. "I don't want to be alone."

The witch looks at nir. Half her face is lit by the red glow of the candles. She waits.

Nis stumbles through an explanation of nirself, discovering that they have different words for the same thing. Eventually, they arrive at an understanding. Neither wants sexual intimacy but would enjoy physical affection. Both exhale nervous giggles of relief.

Nis offers nir hand, and they ascend the spiral stairs together.

THE RED CANDLES burn themselves out sometime in the pre-dawn morning. Nis wakes at the subtle shift of energy.

The bed is too narrow for them both and the air is still sticky from the storm, but Nis is at peace if not comfortable. The witch sleeps open-mouthed and not quite snoring, her back nestled into the curve of Nis's body.

Ni props nirself up on an elbow to better study her face, mentally composing the letter ni will send to Mirthe. Dawn will come for them, but Nis wants to suspend this moment, hold it the way time in the afterlife moves but does not advance.

AS THE SEA DRINKS OUR SALT

AMELIA FISHER

THE SEA STRETCHED around the *Petty Gasconade* as flat and tight as the skin of a drum, pulled over the edge of the distant horizon by some unknowable hand. From her place on the forecastle, Captain Damarcus watched as her crew cut their palms and anointed the ship's rail with their blood. Some squeezed it over the sides where it hung suspended in the still water, red and fetal. Neither wave nor current disturbed it.

For two weeks after they'd taken their latest prize, there'd been no wind in *Gasconade's* sails and no rain on her deck. Fishing lines cast over the side snagged only squirming, suckered things, grasping claws on polyps of pink gristle—or nothing. The signs were clear: they were being hunted.

"They ought to save their strength," Damarcus said, as another man pressed his bleeding hand to the wood. "A few drops of blood won't be enough to summon the wind."

Out of the corner of her eye, she saw Csere close his fingers self-consciously around the cut on his palm. At her side, her quartermaster grunted noncommittally.

"Let them make their offerings. It can do little harm," Joppon rumbled. Her weathered face was pinched against the wind which tugged at her headscarf. Like many of the sailors below, Joppon was missing two fingers and an eye, given in sacrifice on previous ships.

"This calm won't break on it's own," Csere piped up, flipping through their ship's manifest with a frown. He'd spent all morning scouring their stolen cargo for anything they might be able to eat. But unless they felt like guzzling barrels of sacrificial oil, there hadn't been much to find. "We'll need a spell. And a good one at that."

Captain Damarcus raised her spyglass, activating its charm of far-sight, but magic could not show her what wasn't there to see. No ripple, no clouds, not even the red sails of the Toothed Fleet beading like blood against the sky.

"I'll see to it," Damarcus said, and turned to leave.

"Captain," Joppon said, and glanced meaningfully at the men below. No doubt some were watching, their palms wrapped in cloth to staunch the bleeding.

Damarcus gritted her teeth, but did not argue. She slid the knife from her belt and pressed the edge to her thumb. Holding it over the railing, she squeezed four drops of blood onto the dark-stained wood: one for every cardinal direction. If any of the crew found her sacrifice stingy, they said nothing as she made her way below.

IN THE DARKNESS belowdecks, Damarcus followed the sounds of human pain. She didn't go to the witchery as often as her crew, unless she had a reason to; Damarcus was also careful not to avoid it. If her crew got it into their heads that their captain was shy of spellwork, she could find herself hard-pressed to win the next vote.

At the moment, a vote was far from her first concern. Damarcus had fallen into the trap that any successful pirate captain knew awaited them someday: she had gotten too lucky. After snapping up a heavily-laden Ilathean cutter and liberating its hold of valuables, they'd happened across a merchant ship on the way back to Queltar, blown off course by a recent storm. They'd taken both ships in the course of a week without firing a single cannon, and the wealth in the *Petty Gasconade*'s hold was as close as any of them would ever see to a queen's ransom. Assuming they lived to spend it. Luck like this drew the kind of attention Damarcus had spent years evading.

The noises grew louder. Stepping around the barrels of fragrant oil they'd liberated from the Ilathean vessel, the smell lingered in the air: myrrh and phoenix balm, and beneath it, the copper of blood. Ahead, a fine Carpathian rug hanging in the threshold to the witchery served as a makeshift door. From behind those dizzyingly intricate patterns woven in dyed horsehair came the sound of wet, heaving breaths, and the occasional mumbled curse.

For a moment Damarcus hesitated, her fingers knotted tight on her woven belt. Then she pulled back the curtain and stepped inside.

Orey's broad back greeted her, bowed over a metal bowl steadily filling with her blood. She pushed the pliers deeper into her mouth and then her muscles clenched from shoulder to spine. With the wet splintering of enamel ripped from bone, she jerked out a molar and dropped it into the bowl followed by another mouthful of blood.

Damarcus waited, arms crossed over her chest, as Orey finished the incantation, her voice thickened by pain. The smell of blood was nothing unusual in Damarcus's line of work; it was the burning incense which seemed to creep down her throat and tried to drag the contents of her stomach up after it. Beneath the sweet smoke of burning herbs she could taste the salt of a faraway sea, hear the wheeling cry of seabirds stoked to a frenzy.

"That one was a real bastard," Orey said, replacing the bowl on her altar. The blood within it was thick and smooth; the tooth rose up in the center, its root like a double-mast. "Let's hope that keeps us hidden."

"I need a wind," Damarcus said without preamble.

Orey rolled her eyes. "I noticed. But it's not as simple as just asking and receiving."

"You like to make it sound that way when you're talking to the crew."

"It's what they need to hear." She grinned, the gap in her smile barely noticeable amid the red smears. Of the teeth she'd plucked for her rituals, her patron had returned them changed. They grew from her gums in corrugated corals, or jabbed up with the sharpness of a seal's fangs. "There's always a price, as you know. But once I've caught my patron's attention, she'll send us your fair winds before the end of the week."

"Not good enough. I need them sooner."

"Well, that's just too fucking bad," Orey said mildly. She reached for a cloth—a lady's finely embroidered handkerchief she'd liberated from their latest haul—and used it to wipe the blood from her chin. "If you wanted instantaneous results, you should have stuck with The Toothed Fleet."

Damarcus's spine went rigid. From whatever Orey saw in her face, it made her wry smile slip just a little. "Bring that up again," Damarcus said through gritted teeth, "and we'll see how quickly your patron responds if it's a chunk of your tongue in that bowl."

"With all due respect, Captain," Orey said, "I think you'd be lucky to get that far."

Damarcus turned on her heel, wrenching the tapestry back. If she stayed much longer she'd be in danger of trying to act on that threat. She wasn't deluded as to Orey's power, just as Orey knew that Damarcus would happily help her swallow a blade if she misstepped. Admittedly Orey's barbs had sunk in a little deeper once Damarcus had let slip that she had sailed with the dreaded toothflayers, blushing the sea with sacrifices: not how Damarcus had put it, but not too far from the truth. Somewhere out there, her name was still printed neatly in a ledger of the Fleet's deserters, along with the price of her retrieval and the manner of her sacrifice.

That admission had been the last of many indiscretions over the course of the night. Damarcus held herself above the crew in many ways, but at the end of the day, a bottle of rum and a fine pair of eyes had overthrown her as quickly as any drunken fool.

At least for one night her witch's personality hadn't grated.

"I need an offering," Orey said, before Damarcus could storm out past the curtain. "For the ritual tomorrow."

Damarcus stopped, turning her head only slightly. "What kind of offering?"

"The usual kind." She heard Orey shift, could imagine the way she'd curl to her feet as smoothly as a dancer. Her movements were as fluid as the rolling of the sea; it was a part of her, after all. "Something from land."

"We don't have much to spare."

"That's what makes it a sacrifice." Orey stepped a little closer. She smelled like blood and smoke and sweetgrass, and radiated heat. "The more you give, the more power my patron will have at her disposal. You should consider that when choosing what to offer."

The insinuation curled under Damarcus's skin like a flensing knife. She turned to fix Orey with a granite stare, and found the witch far closer than she'd anticipated. There was still blood smeared down her lips and chin, flecking the hollow of her throat.

"You get a chicken," Damarcus said, and left the smell of blood and the phantom cry of seabirds behind.

A T SUNDOWN, the crew gathered before the altar carved into the bow. The image of Orey's patron had been carved into the wood of the altar and again in the figurehead, made abstract by years of wind and water: Damarcus could make out the impression of shark fins and many arms, some of which were tipped by crablike pincers. Orey had told her once that in reality her patron looked very different—and smiled in a way that made Damarcus reluctant to ask.

Joppon and Csere took up positions nearby, Joppon with an air of tired familiarity and Csere with a sense of excitement. Below, Orey joked with the crew as she prepared for the ritual, stoking their excitement and calling for volunteers to smear their blood on the altar. Damarcus observed the sunset rather than watch the grinning crew open their palms. The light gathered in a thin line of distortion between the sea and the sky as if dammed up and unable to drain away.

"It's starting," Csere said, and with reluctance Damarcus turned her eyes to the ritual.

She'd seen Orey's petitions before, calling for wind or rain or wealthy prey. It didn't particularly interest her; in point of fact, she found it distastefully reminiscent of things she would rather forget. But a pirate captain who turned her back on magic was likely to soon find herself no captain at all, so she made her appearances and knew that Orey enjoyed her discomfort. Orey's voice warbled over the water, calling out to her patron in Seabottom tongue, writhing, icy syllables that burrowed hungrily into the brain. Many of the men closed their eyes.

"There'll be no more eggs from that chicken," Joppon muttered as Orey opened it from throat to belly.

"If it brings us a wind, we can buy ourselves a hundred chickens per man," Damarcus said. In the long stillness of Orey's incantation, she watched as the crew pressed their bleeding hands on the ship and murmured their prayers to its timbers. She had been one of them, once; she'd felt that certainty that a greater power was watching out for them; would care for them, would protect them. But Damarcus had learned otherwise the hard way: the gods cared only for themselves. They drank their believers dry and left nothing but bones and grief.

Without the whistle of wind or the slap of waves, Damarcus could hear the growl of ancient words murmured over the bloody mass of feathers in Orey's hands. The witch had showmanship, Damarcus had to give her that. But it wasn't just a show; even Damarcus could feel the power building in the air, thick as the smell of brine. Csere was practically trembling as Orey bore the sacrifice to the hole in the altar, her voice rising with the chant; then she tipped it into the glassy water, and fell silent for a long time.

"Is this how it normally happens?" Csere whispered. The silence had dragged on for what even Damarcus had to admit was unusually long.

Damarcus stared at Orey's bowed head. Her hands braced on the altar, her eyes cast down to the depths. The tension in the air was building, but it didn't feel right. It pressed in on Damarcus's eardrums like the pressure of water far beneath the surface. Slowly the witch raised her head, and at once Damarcus met her gaze. There was uncertainty there; that, for Orey, was as close as Damarcus had seen to fear. In the black of Orey's eyes, something moved.

"No," Damarcus said, her voice low and tight. "It's not."

In the next moment Orey doubled over as if punched in the gut, with a cry that split the silent weight of the air in two. Damarcus was already moving. It could be fatal to touch a witch in the throes of communion with her patron, but as Orey's legs gave out Damarcus didn't hesitate to catch her. Her eyes rolled back in her head, her limbs thrashing as if in a brain fever. The presence in the air bore down on them with malignant amusement—and then it rushed off over the flat sea to where the last of the sunset slashed across the edge of the horizon like a wound not yet bleeding.

"THEY KNOW where we are," Orey croaked. They'd slung her into Damarcus's bed for privacy, and slid a tonic of gingered brandy down her throat. "They must have been waiting for me to try a ritual like that. They honed in on it, and they found us."

Damarcus leaned on her desk, staring at the map pinned down to its chipped wood. Putting a piece of furniture between herself and Orey had been a calculated decision. It made her less likely to lunge across the distance and throttle her. Joppon and Csere lingered nearby, though Damarcus suspected it was at least in part to ensure their captain did not shout their ailing witch back into another fit.

"And I suppose this never occured to you *before* you led them right to our exact position," Damarcus gritted out, raising her eyes to fix Orey with a glare.

"I'm not sure whether you're accusing me of treachery or incompetence," Orey said, narrowing her eyes—and then tilting her head in consideration. "And for that matter, I'm not actually sure which one I find more insulting."

"Enough, both of you," Joppon said. "It's no use quibbling over what happened. We need to know what we're up against now."

"It could be an enemy crew," Csere said. His face was as pale as spoiled milk, but his eyes were clear. "Grey Norris, or the revenant *Calabressa*.'"

"Let's not waste our time with comfortable fantasies," Damarcus said, low in her throat. She raised her head and found Orey watching her, inscrutable. "No pirate crew could have summoned enough power to trace that ritual. It's toothflayers we're facing. And they'll be heading right for us."

The silence after Damarcus's pronouncement settled like a second becalming. "How long?" Joppon said at last.

"I'd give us no more than a day or two," Orey replied quietly. "They'll have the wind on their side, and they know where to find us--maybe more. I can't be sure how much they saw." She glanced at Damarcus, and understanding prickled on the back of her neck. Whatever had stared out at her through Orey's eyes, it had *seen*. They weren't just coming for Damarcus's ship; they were coming for her.

"Is there any possibility your patron received your petition?" Csere said. "Perhaps there's still a chance—"

Orey's low chuckle cut him off. "My patron isn't strong enough to tangle with the focused will of the Syrasian Imperium," she said. "They employ hundreds of witches, and feed their patrons hundreds of sacrifices a day to maintain them. We might have managed to slip past their notice before they found us; now, it would take a lot more than some chicken blood to give us the strength to wriggle free."

Joppon's jaw tightened. "Then we fight."

Damarcus's laugh cut through the cabin like shattered glass. She felt the room's attention shift to her, but didn't raise her head. Her eyes bore into the map. "We can't fight them," Damarcus said. "The lowliest ship in the Toothed Fleet brings seventy-four guns to bear, and they'll have at least one witch on their side."

"There has to be another option," Csere said. "Surely our god will help us?"

"It's possible," Orey allowed. "Given the right burst of power."

"And we're all of out of chickens," Joppon muttered. In the silence afterward, the back of Damarcus's neck began to prickle.

Csere started to pace. "Someone would volunteer," he said, as if talking to himself. "Given the choice between all of us dying horrible deaths at the hands of our enemies, and the rest escaping? Surely someone would make that sacrifice."

"One wouldn't be enough, would it?" Joppon said. Slowly, Orey shook her head.

"How many?" Csere asked flatly, and Orey sucked in a breath.

"A quarter," she said at last. "Maybe more."

"That's ten men you're talking about sacrificing," Joppon said.

Csere wheeled on her. "Compared to all of us? We could give them a cleaner death than the Empress's bastards ever would. We could get the volunteers." He stopped, swallowed hard. "I'll be the first. I don't want what those bloodwater witches have in store for me. I'd rather give my life for my crew and our god."

Damarcus's hand slammed onto the table so hard the pain reverberated up to her teeth. The others in the room seemed to have forgotten she was there; she remained hunched over the desk, her eyes drilling into the map. Not studying their location, not any more. Her eyes were trained firmly on Syrasi, its edges jagged on the parchment.

"It won't be enough." Her voice was deadly quiet. "It's not just the quantity of the sacrifices that gives the Imperium's gods their power. Their ships are strung with the bodies of the keel-hauled, their souls trapped forever so their gods can keep feeding on their pain. That's what they do to their *willing* victims. They'll have far worse in store for pirates and traitors—"

"Captain," Orey said. Damarcus's head jerked up; their eyes met. She heard it now, the echoes of her words hanging like dust in the air; the drawling current of her accent eddying at the edges. *Traitors*. There was only one of those on this ship.

She swallowed hard. "Get out. *Not* you," Damarcus snapped, as Orey opened her mouth. "You stay."

Joppon and Csere exchanged a look, but they did not argue.

For long moments after the click of the cabin door sealed them in together, Orey simply watched her. Damarcus belligerently held her gaze out of habit alone. She wanted nothing more than to crawl into her bed and let the ache in her skull rise up to drag her under.

"I don't think I've ever seen you get this sloppy before," Orey commented at last. "You were practically about to sing the Empress's anthem to the entire crew. And that accent—"

"Fuck off."

"Charming. And here I was thinking I saved your skin from a violent mutiny." Orey tilted her head. "Or perhaps that was your plan? Being shot by your own crew for Syrasian sympathies is an ignoble way to go, but it beats whatever the Fleet has in store for us—"

"I am not asking ten men to lay down beneath your knife."

"You wouldn't need to ask them. Just explain the situation, and they'll do it for you."

"So it's better if they think it's their own decision?" Damarcus shook her head. "I won't become one of those captains. I won't start sacrificing my crew."

"This isn't The Imperium."

Damarcus jerked as if she'd been cut. "I know where I fucking am."

Orey swung her legs out of the hammock, steadying herself on the ropes. "Do you? Because you're about to throw away the lives of every person on your crew out of squeamishness. That implies just a bit of fucking confusion to me."

Damarcus turned away, but Orey kept talking. "I may be the only living person who understands what you went through."

Damarcus's jaw ached from clenching it too tightly. Her

hands still felt raw and naked without the gloves she'd worn every day in Syrasi. "You weren't there. You didn't sail under those zealots."

The salt. The burning incense. Damarcus could smell it even here, in the leather-wood-comfort of her cabin.

"Alright," Orey said quietly. "Maybe not. But I know what it is to lose a friend. And I know something of the magic that took him."

Damarcus shook her head. "*He* volunteered," she spat. "They always did. I would have myself, only—" Only she'd been afraid. They'd said they would go together, the most honorable death an officer in the Empress's Fleet could hope for: willing sacrifice. But when the time came, she couldn't step forward; and he'd done so without her, and they'd dragged him along the shark-toothed keel until the ocean bloomed red. The captain had assured her that he hadn't ever died.

"I won't allow it," Damarcus said at last. "There has to be another way."

"I don't actually need your permission, you know." Orey stared up at her, her expression implacable. "If I'd wanted to force the issue, I'd just tell them that you were a toothflayer."

Damarcus's back went rigid.

"A captain is always the richest sacrifice," Orey continued idly. "I'm sure the crew wouldn't have too many qualms about offering you up yourself once they knew all the blood you've sp—"

Damarcus whirled on her in a heartbeat, the knife appearing in her hands as if by witchery. She felt the impact in her own body as she slammed Orey against the bookshelf, the knifepoint suspended over her jugular.

"And how would your god like the taste of *your* blood on the altar?" Damarcus snarled.

Orey managed a weak smile, her fingers twitching where they remained raised in a gesture of supplication. "Need I remind you that you'd be bleeding out your crew's last hope of survival? And more relevantly, I *didn't* tell them."

Damarcus's eyes studied Orey's face. "Why didn't you, then?"

she demanded. "You could have had your sacrifices, and gotten rid of me in the process."

"What makes you think I want to get rid of you?" Orey's smile turned down at the edges; she shrugged, only a little, but it was enough to draw a gem of blood from the knife pressed to her throat. "I'm not an *utter* bastard. Also, there's no guarantee it would work. An unwilling sacrifice is like an under-ripe fruit. A little too tough, a little too bitter. Not nearly as much power as something freely given."

Slowly, Damarcus lowered the knife. Orey blinked.

"That's it?" Orey said. "I thought you'd at least try to cut a piece off me—"

"Stop talking," Damarcus said. She went to the window, stared out over the dark glassy plain beyond. The moonlight was tinted green by the magic which held them; no ripple stirred the surface of the sea.

"You said that one unwilling sacrifice wouldn't be sufficient," she said, turning around. "What about a willing one?"

W HEN THE SHUDDER of boarding ramps first bit into the *Gasconade*'s railings, Damarcus was not standing on the quarterdeck with her pistols primed. She was in the hold, squatting in a circle of sea salt with the sickening smell of magic in her nose. Orey stood across from her, eyes dark, her surgeon's tools laid out before her. Pliers, bone saw, a curved wicked dagger. The tools of sacrifice.

"Are you prepared?"

The sight of Orey's long fingers delicately selecting the sacrificial dagger was enough to make her heart pound faster than the footsteps moving deeper into the ship. She managed a short nod. She was going to die down here in the dark, surrounded by plunder she'd never live to spend while her crew was hauled away to be twisted into the shapes the Imperium's gods demanded.

Except this time, she wasn't running.

Orey stepped across the salt boundary. Damarcus didn't recognize any of the sigils she'd drawn with its grains, nor could she name any of the herbs filling the hold with their smoke, beyond the feelings of depth and compression and bottomless cold they left in her veins.

"Afraid?" Orey said. For once, she didn't seem to be gloating, and Damarcus was beyond bravado.

"Of course I'm fucking afraid," she said flatly. Each breath brought with it the awful funeral richness of the ritual oils, so thick in the air she could scarcely breathe. Above, a smattering of pistol shots rang out, followed by the clomp of heavy boots; Damarcus closed her eyes. She'd given her orders for the crew to surrender quietly, but it had been too much to hope for. She knew Imperium policy. They'd be rounding up prisoners and taking them straight across the gangplank to be bled on their altars. But what if they timed it wrong? What if they had already started the killing?

Orey reached out. Her hands were as cold as the ocean floor. Damarcus turned her head away, waiting for the mockery; but the hand rose to her cheek, turning her face back. "Have faith," she said quietly.

Damarcus shook her head. Even now she could feel the tight clasp of her Imperium uniform's collar closing around her throat. She knew Orey could feel her shaking. "I haven't managed that in a while."

"You still believe in them," Orey said quietly. The heavy boots were moving closer, deeper into the ship. "The Imperium gods. Part of you can't believe that anything could ever be stronger than them. That's why you ran."

"I'm not running anymore."

"No." Orey's eyes were luminous in the dark. "And what do you believe now?"

"I don't know," Damarcus whispered.

Orey's fingers slid against the back of her neck, holding her steady. "Let me show you," she whispered, and the knife moved across her throat.

The pain slid across the point of her jugular, sharp and then deep. Damarcus opened her mouth and tasted blood. Something wet seeped down the front of her shirt as Orey's grip tightened on the back of her neck, steadying her. She whispered words in a language Damarcus could not perceive, syllables spilling from her mouth like bubbles. Damarcus struggled to hold her gaze. She could see the command in Orey's eyes: *do not sleep*. Gods, she hated it when Orey told her what to do. She kept her eyes open.

At last, the incantation stopped. The air in the hull was heavier than the sea, blotting out the sound of approaching feet. Slowly, Orey lowered her to her knees with a strength that belied her smaller frame. The pain burrowed into Damarcus's throat, blotting out all but the witch's face. Damarcus barely felt it when Orey pressed the cold metal of an unloaded pistol into her hands.

"You're stronger than them," Orey said, her lips catching the line of blood trailing from Damarcus's mouth. And then, by magic or the trick of a dying mind, Damarcus was alone with the overwhelming smell of the ritual oils, sweet and foul and choking.

Footsteps approached the salt circle; the toe of a white boot nudged the line of salt. She could barely raise her head to look the Syrasi witch in the eye; the blood pulsed faster from the wound in her neck as she did, but she needed to see his face.

He stood over her, surrounded by a thicket of muskets all trained at Damarcus's face. That ritual smell was so thick in Damarcus's nose she could barely breathe; when she tried to suck in the air, it clogged in her throat like drowning.

"Well, well," the witch said. His mouth was shielded by a ceremonial half-mask carved in the shape of an angler fish's teeth. "I had heard the rumors of a pirate vessel captained by a deserter, but I never expected them to be true. I suppose this is some pathetic attempt to summon the power of your lesser god?"

Damarcus bared her teeth. The hand gripping the pistol was trembling so hard she could hardly keep hold of it. She certainly could not raise it. He leaned in closer, still not crossing the salt. His eyes were the color of a flat and sickly sea. "You hold a high opinion of yourself," he said, as gently as a parent chastising a child. "Were you really so stingy as to think that sacrificing one captain could save your entire crew? We flayed five believers on the hull of our ship just to reach you posthaste."

Damarcus opened her mouth to speak, and only blood poured out. Grinning, the witch leaned in closer still. "Not a captain," she managed through the clot of agony in her throat. "How about a ship?"

The witch blinked, drawing back. The cold smile had disappeared from his eyes. This time it was Damarcus's turn to grin.

She sucked in one last drowning breath, and with it the sweet smell of the oil they'd spilled over the entirety of the hull. Then she pulled the trigger. The flint hit the frizzon with a flash that lit up the witch's shock from below, and the world exploded into light—

And then darkness. A darkness so complete that the sun had never touched it. She was sinking, not burning but freezing, crushed in the grip of something far greater than her mind could imagine. The detritus of her ship sank with her, the Fleet's ship a bristling shadow against the sky, its living boards jagged with teeth and the tattered bodies of old sacrifice. Deeper. In the darkness of that cold blue void she felt the titanic thrash of pale, sunless things bleeding out into the ocean from a place beyond the world, the fibers of their being a pulsing interwoven matrix in which Damarcus struggled with all the hope of a minnow limp in the strands of a jellyfish.

And then she was rising, hooked by the agony in her throat and pulled up towards a face that was not a face, a field of eyes as wide as the stars.

WHEN HER CREW pulled Damarcus out of the water seven days later, the skin of her throat was a knitted mass of tissue like the flesh of something living far beneath the surface of the sea. She couldn't speak, but Orey understood her. It was Orey who sat by her bedside and murmured in the Seabottom

Tongue, the words as familiar as if Damarcus had always known them.

Orey told her of the storm which had risen from every horizon at once, the whirlpool which opened up beneath the toothed ship where they all huddled in chains on the deck; when it rose from the waves again, they were the only ones on the Syrasi ship still sputtering with life.

"You bear her mark," Orey said. Her fingers ran up and down the ridge of Damarcus's ruined throat with reverence. Damarcus had not yet mastered the handspeak that Orey assured her was used among those witches who had forsaken the breathing world entirely, but some gestures were universal. *Come here.*

Orey smiled, close-lipped, and climbed into bed at Damarcus's side. It was strange, being back on an toothed ship. It didn't feel like coming home. "Are you still afraid?"

Yes.

"Good. Belief is a terrifying thing, darling. But it has its rewards."

I feel...good.

"Our god is stronger now. We're connected—all three of us."

It took Damarcus a long time to puzzle out the signs, but Orey was patient. *Strong enough to hunt something more than flabby merchantmen?*

Orey grinned with the teeth of shark and seal and things far stranger. "Perhaps it's time we find out what our new ship can do."

For the first time in a long time, Damarcus smiled.

The End of the Line

GRACE P. FONG

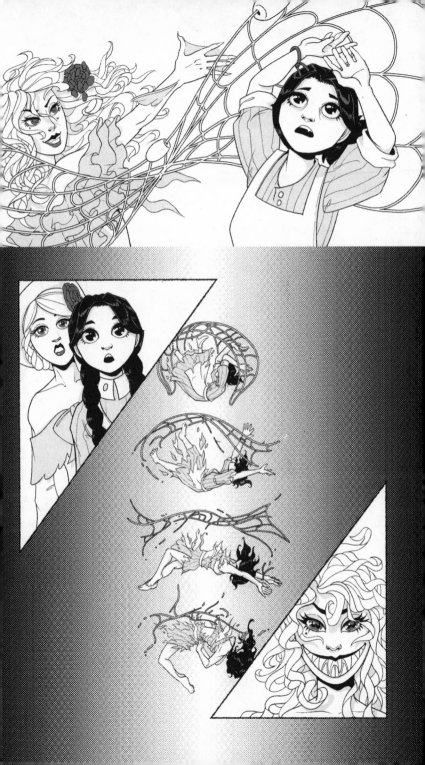

NIGHT OF THE ERUPTING DEAD

ALMAH LAVON RICE

ALTHOUGH THEY were older than the Big Bang, you cannot call them *ancestors*. (They ate their children. Check the manifest: no survivors.) They are not black, they are not red, they are flayed-open. Wound-colored. They are made of magma and grievance. At night, below the realm of the pedestrian—the earth's crust—they sleep fitfully together. *(Their gash-bodies interweaving, interseething.)*

Tonight, they stir.

Basa is the first to crack the silence, let the hot yolk flow out. "So is it popping off tonight or what?" she asks the half-asleep figures all around the magma chamber. All of them her lovers.

Rhyo groans softly, rubbing his eyes. "Shit, Basa. What time is it?"

"Why, I'm glad you asked. Their top volcanologists say it's time—past time—for the Yellowstone Caldera to make it rain." She laughs, a little too boisterously.

"It's showtime, sleeping beauties," she adds, more loudly. With beads of sweat jangling around her neck and waist, Basa rises from her pallet and begins shaking the others fully awake.

"Wait, Basa, wait. Did all of us agree on the launch date?"

Rhyo asks, reaching for his water bottle. Even the mere breath of a conflict made him thirsty.

"The coven has been discussing it for 70,000 years, to be exact—you know that!" She shrugs, beads glinting in the hell-light. "We'll never agree, so now is as good as later."

Rhyo is loath to admit it, but she has a point. Everyone in their polycule may have the hots for each other but their consensus meetings were slow to spark.

"But why erupt now?" he asks. "I mean, the pandemic—"

"Tuh!" exclaims Basa. "It's always something with them. Humans are the disaster factories, not us."

Rhyo takes a breath, and fingers the smooth rock in his pocket. *Don't let her cause you to blow,* he reminds himself. He takes another breath, deep as the basement of the world. "I heard they're considering some kind of cooling and depressurization plan," he says aloud finally.

Turtle Thee Island clears her throat from the other side of the magma chamber, as she folds a mountain of laundry and stuffs it into her go bag. The oldest lover in the collective, she is slow to enter a conversation but hits her mark unerringly. "Drilling could make Basa and her squad even more volatile," she smiles indulgently in Basa's direction. "Anyway, now they're saying it's too expensive, too risky, and politically dead in the water. The humans are just going to roll the dice—"

"—and lose," Basa crows, giggling and shoulder popping. "The house always wins! And they have overstayed their welcome in *our* house."

Rhyo looks around the room. The other revenants don't seem to disagree. Like a team of synchronized sleepwalkers, they are wordlessly putting on their shoes and hats and zipping up backpacks for the moment they have been preparing for all their lives. Trance macabre.

"Trust, I'm with you—all of you," he insists. "But now? The timing seems so...so cruel."

Basa shakes her head, pulling her locs away from her now-sweating neck. "Nope. This is who we are, who we're meant to be. How is it not cruel to *us* to be on lockdown under them, just for their convenience?"

"What about our Elder here?" He swings to look at Turtle Thee Island, with a wild look on his face. "This is her land, she deserves more stability in her golden years."

"Blast me to the stars," Turtle Thee Island half-sings, chuckling. "There are relations up there that I've been meaning to visit anyway. Plus, the man in the moon owes me some money."

Rhyo gazes around again. All that can be heard is the sound of more zippers zipping, drawers being shut one last time, corners being swept. Over the din of inevitability, Turtle Thee Island and Basa try to comfort him. Their go bags are beyond bursting now, bloated with pyroclastic flow. That is, the ash, gases, and lava shards that will fill human lungs with cement, poison the water supply, doom the crops, and shroud the sun.

"Rhyo," Turtle Thee Island says, handing him his ritual robes. "Time to dress for the volcanic winter."

"I—I just wanted to stay with you all a bit longer," he says, voice fraying.

Basa looks deeply into his filling eyes. "I'll miss you, my man," she sighs, holding him close to her feverish body. "But our destiny awaits."

Rhyo relents. "Right. What did one of the great humans say? *There is no death, only a change of worlds.*"

And with that, he begins changing into his ceremonial garb for the next one.

THE WITCH OF KAA-IYA

RUTH JOFFRE

DUSK BELONGED to the fox. Zorra. Once magic hour bathed the forest scrublands of Kaa-Iya del Gran Chaco with a lambent, golden hue, Neiza stepped out of her hut to await the return of her familiar. A thin and lanky creature with mottled gray and burnt orange fur and ears as tall as her nose was long, the pampas fox was as like to slink around the tents of poachers and would-be oil barons as to curl up on Neiza's hair right at the brilliant crack of dawn. For three days and two nights, Zorra had been on a special mission for Neiza: to discover the source of the great black smoke that had clouded the sky to the east If Zorra did not return at dusk on the third day, the two agreed, the witch and her menagerie of forest familiars would assume Zorra was in danger and mount a rescue.. Only after the sun set and Kaa-Iya opened its nocturnal eyes did Neiza call to her familiar Llido, a black howler monkey: "Bring the others."

A translation spell enabled him to ask, "Is she alive?"

The hairs tightening at the base of Neiza's neck told her Zorra was not in immediate threat of death. "For now. Go—quickly!"

He leapt up on the roof of the hut and into the quebracho trees. His howl hurtled across the semi-arid flatlands and alerted all Neiza's familiars to return, including: Feliciano, her first familiar and friendly jaguar, who stationed himself at her right hand and liked occasionally to be pet on his regal, velvety head when not out on a hunting mission; Canela, a guanaco whose cinnamon-colored back and white belly were often outfitted with brightly patterned blankets and bags Neiza liked to make herself from dyed and spun alpaca wool; Tag, a Chacoan peccary with a bristling silver mane and dainty, slender hooves, whose highly evolved snout allowed him to track individual scents for a hundred kilometers or more, if enhanced with magic; and Marsh, a crowned solitary eagle, whom Neiza rescued from a mud pit eight years ago and nursed back to health on a diet of lizard tails and armadillo meat.

Marsh was first to return, alighting on Neiza's leather arm cuff.

"What see you from above?"

"Evil machineries in motion in the east—a great pit has been dug, so black I cannot see the bottom even when I swoop down to the earth."

Oil and gas prospectors, Neiza assumed, plunging their seismic tools deep in the ground as their avarice propelled them ever closer to Kaa-Iya in search of the region's abundant hydrocarbon. In theory, the region was protected by the Bolivian government, which in 1995 declared more than three million hectares of the land a national park and "integrated management natural area," but in practice nothing could stop the prospectors' oily fingers from slipping through legal loopholes and draining this land of its resources—nothing, that is, but Neiza and her menagerie of forest familiars. At age fifteen, Neiza took over the mantle of Witch-Guardian of the Forest from her teacher, the former Witch-Guardian. Her hut—concealed with cloaking and protection spells—had been passed down through a long line of forest witches, going back centuries. It was built before the government established the national park, before Bolivia lost much of the Gran Chaco to Paraguay in the so-called War of Thirst, before Bolivia became an independent nation, before even its namesake Simón was conceived in

Caracas in 1782.

Here, the witches of Kaa-Iya had made their home for generations.

It was Neiza's duty to ensure the park and all who lived inside it survived for generations to come.

UNDER THE protective cover of night, Feliciano guided them east toward the black pit. In the dark, his magically augmented eyesight was at least ten times sharper than Neiza's own, and when combined with Canela's heightened sense of hearing and Tag's prodigious olfactory gland next to nothing could escape the notice of their troupe. A tour group making camp at the recommendation of their certified guide; a beleaguered farmhand leading two stray cows through the brush, back to the ever-expanding herds of beef on the outer rim of Kaa-Iya, where Isoseño and Guaraní villagers with small plots of land competed against commercial cattle ranchers; an Ayoreode nomad hiking placidly through the scrubland, as was his right; and, later, a trophy hunter in camouflage, wearing night-vision goggles, daring to point his rifle at Feliciano, who dispatched him quickly and without much fuss. A rancid smell overwhelmed Tag, so they stopped at a nearby stream to allow Feliciano to bathe and Tag to reset his senses with everyday fragrances, like the flowers of silk floss trees or the hardwood of quebracho. Neiza and the others settled down in the savannah grass. Marsh supped on field mice while Canela folded her legs beneath her and Llido picked nits from her fur. "You should sleep while you can," he told the witch.

"My sleepless charm will see me through."

"And what price will you pay for this magic?"

"At best? A full day of slumber, in which I will be unable to defend myself."

"And at worst?"

A year of her life expectancy, perhaps, though she refused to tell him this, knowing how he would respond. In silence, his face settled into a pout, that perpetually downturned mouth of his seeming especially grumpy and paternal in the dim light of the moon. To placate him, she retrieved a boiled egg from the sacks on Canela's back and fed it to him in one piece. Herself, she managed only a hard crust of bread, which tasted bitter and undeserved.

To lose a familiar would be to lose a part of herself and her heritage. Of all six familiars, four had been gifted to her by the last Witch-Guardian, who had herself inherited several of them from the witches of yore. Only Marsh, the eagle she found half-dead in the muck, was of her own making. Zorra had come to her after her previous master, the Silver Mage of Potosí, was killed in battle by the assassins of a multinational mining company, and the fox familiar had been with her ever since.

Canela nibbled Neiza's ear for comfort. "Can you feel Zorra out there?"

Neiza nodded, her thumb guiding a fresh papaya along the blade of a hunting knife. "She's preoccupied but not frightened." Bite by bite, she doled out the papaya, saving the last juicy chunks for Feliciano, who liked its meaty texture. "What I sense most is fury."

"Foxes hate to be outfoxed," Canela observed, spitting out the papaya seeds.

"She has always had a nasty temper. Probably because she was raised by a mage," Feliciano added while rolling onto his back for a belly rub. His rumbling, muscular purr soothed Neiza, who would like nothing better than to close her eyes for a moment and wake to find that wily Zorra had returned unscathed and with a handful of trinkets for her trouble; but each blink was met only with shadows and silence. "We've delayed here long enough."

Before she could stand, a high-pitched squeal cut through the night: Tag, streaking toward a wax palm grove at the edge of the field, his body lost in the wave of tall grasses. "No!" Hurriedly, Neiza installed an invisible ward between the field and the palm trees. Tag ran into the ward headfirst, his piglike snout snuffling in search of something. He was scrabbling at the wall like a dog at a window, and Canelagalloped toward them, Marsh circling and screeching overhead as Llido howled and Feliciano growled, breath still bitter and sharp with blood.

Only one person could elicit this reaction from her familiars.

Only one person could reach through the magical ward and pet Tag's head: Panambi.

"I see you haven't revoked my permission to pass through your wards," the archer said, stepping out under the moonlight. She looked almost exactly as she did when they broke up one year priorp: fierce and tattooed, holding a wooden staff in one hand, and wearing the straps of her longbow and quiver in an "X" across her chest. Her simple cinnamon-colored tunic was belted at the waist, and a single black line had been drawn in ink across her cheeks and the bridge of her nose. "I would thank you, but you and I both know it's dangerous to leave a hole like that in your defenses."

"If you were truly a danger to me, Feliciano would kill you on the spot."

Gladly, he hissed, drawing a protective circle between them with his muscular body.

Neiza stroked his tail as it twitched past, angry as a live wire. "Why are you here, Ambi?"

"I was tracking prospectors suspected of murder in a friend's village when I heard you. I'd forgotten how loud your menagerie can be; this one always kept me up with his snoring," she said, bending down to scratch Tag's snout as he balanced against her thigh, straining on his hind legs to reach her hands and face. A full year had passed since Ambi broke off their four-year relationship, but Tag and the others greeted her as if they still, in some way, belonged to her. Animals rarely forget the kindness of humans, even when that kindness is tarnished by betrayal and abandonment. Neiza wished she could forgive Ambi as easily as they did.

Ambi counted the familiars at her feet. "Where's Zorra?"

"Missing. We think it has something to do with the black pit to the east."

"Black pit? Sounds like something my murderous prospectors

would be interested in. Mind if I join you?"

When Neiza hesitated, Ambi clasped her softly on the left
arm. "We make a good team, despite our differences. I can help
you find Zorra and fight whatever evils lurk in the shadows. It
doesn't have to be anything more than that."

Unless we want it to, the thumb on Neiza's arm suggested, but
Neiza shook away the familiar touch. "You can join us," she
said, "under one condition."

"Name it."

"Keep up!" Neiza turned on her heels and sped across the
field with her army of familiars. If this surprised Ambi or if
it pleased her to think that she would have to give chase (like
on that day when they met deep in the forest of Kaa-Iya and
Neiza ran, uncertain of the archer's intentions, casting spells of
swiftness and lightening so that she could hop on Canela's back
and gallop back toward the hut, unable to outrun the fearsome
forest warrior, who tracked the witch for almost six kilometers,
across fields and streams and the dry ripple of the sand dunes
to the south, for no other reason than to return a small tortoise
shell comb that had fallen out of Neiza's flowing black hair),
Neiza could not tell. She knew only that Ambi paused for a
moment, perhaps to watch her long hair streak across the grass
in the moonlight, then raced after Neiza with the speed of a
jaguar, her steps as sure and soundless as a cat's in the dark.

ALL NIGHT and into the morning they traveled, hurried
along by the spells Neiza cast to soften the rain, to fortify
their steps against slips and falls, and to alter the direction of
prevailing winds that they might blow in their group's favor.
Before the light of the rising dawn could break through the
canopy of the forest trees, Marsh screeched, "Up ahead!"

Before them was a clearing wide enough to play a regulation
soccer game. At the center lay a pitch-black hole, no more than
a meter and a half across and yet deep enough that Neiza feared
the molten spirits at the Earth's core would climb up out of the

pit and lay their burning hands upon her flesh.

"But where is the rig? The drill?" In the past, when Neiza came across prospecting sites such as this, there was invariably equipment in the surrounding area, whether the metal arm of a rig or the delicate glass of test tubes measuring the composition of minerals in the soil, and where there were machines there were guards charged with protecting it. "This site looks abandoned."

Marsh landed on her shoulder. "Just two days ago it was swarming with people."

"Either they cleared out in a hurry," Ambi said, walking the perimeter, keen eyes searching the surrounding forests for signs of movement and treachery, "or this is a very clever trap." Without pausing to consult with Neiza, she fell into position, standing back to back with the witch, with the familiars circling the clearing, reporting back.

"All I see are trees," Feliciano sneered, unconvinced by his own eyes.

"All I smell is earth. And oil," Tag said, confirming the drill test was positive.

"All I hear are heartbeats," Canela breathed. "So many heartbeats."

Marsh's talons tightened on Neiza's arm. "Where's Llido?"

All at once, the quebracho trees came alive, and a squadron of camouflaged fighters, masked with leaves and bathed in dirt, jumped down from the branches. One of them threw a writhing sack onto the ground. "Here's your monkey, witch!"

He's still alive, Neiza thought with relief. "You'll regret that."

"Will I?" He unsheathed a concealed gaucho knife: a facón, common among the hired men of Brazil and Argentina, who could be tempted to help the illegal miners, loggers, and prospectors of the Gran Chaco, for the right price. His men circled, each wielding a facón or daga, but refrained from striking out, as if waiting for permission.

Ambi shouted, "Make your move, cowards!"

Their leader laughed. "Our boss warned us the witch might come after us, but he didn't say anything about a wannabe

Amazon princess." With that, he lunged forward, slashing at Ambi with the facón, but she was too swift, dodging his attack with one step to the left and knocking the knife from his hand with a blow from her staff.

His men surged forward, collapsing on the familiars, but they fought together, playing to their strengths: Feliciano tackling one man to the ground, Canela spitting in another's face so Marsh could swoop in and claw his eyes out while he was temporarily blinded. Meanwhile, Tag overwhelmed their forces with a foul-smelling secretion intended to ward off predators, leaving Neiza free to superheat the hilts of all their knives and burn their palms with the patterns of their decorative hilts. Neiza grabbed one of the dropped facónes and cut open the sack. Inside, Llido was unharmed but bound by the sack's silencing spell. No way these gauchos could have enchanted the sack themselves—a dark mage must have helped them prepare for this battle.

"Good to know the enemy has new recruits," Neiza muttered.

Once freed, Llido leapt onto a man's back and roared as he beat the mercenary's head to a pulp.

While Neiza was distracted, half a dozen of them had surrounded Ambi, who was beating them back with her wooden staff, smacking their filthy comments about her attire right out of their mouths. Neiza cast a spell that battered the three mercenaries on Ambi's left flank back twenty meters so she could focus on those on her right.

Still furious, Neiza levitated their gaucho knives, raising them high over her head and aiming them at the dazed men struggling to their feet. She skewered the warriors where they knelt, then summoned the knives again, arranging them in a bloody ring around her head. With the enchanted blades, Neiza made short work of the remaining men, leaving Ambi and the familiars to dispatch the wounded and take care of the stragglers too cowardly to fight and too weak to stand. Among these was their leader, who lay in a heap by the pit.

He pushed himself up, cradling his broken arm. "What do you want?"

"Information." Ambi knocked the back of his knees with her

staff so he would kneel.

Neiza positioned a knife under his chin. "What is this place? And who sent you here?"

"We were hired by a multinational corporation to protect their newest asset. Our boss works out of Brazil and dispatched us here with a warning: beware the witch of Kaa-Iya." As he said this, his head tilted further and further back, attempting to relieve the pressure of the knife, which moved with him.

Neiza pressed for the name of his boss, but he did not know it. "I swear to you!"

"One final question: where's Zorra?"

"Who?"

"My pampas fox familiar."

"You have to believe me. I don't know anything about a fox."

Neiza begrudgingly lowered the knife, turning her back on him. "I believe you."

"Unfortunately," Ambi said, standing before him, "that means we have no use for you."

"Wait!" He shouted, but too late—Ambi had already pushed him backward into the pit.

IN THE quiet after the battle, Neiza took the time to heal each of the familiars in turn: Marsh, who had sprained a wing; Tag, who sustained several knife wounds in the fat of his back and belly, which thankfully didn't push through to his internal organs; Feliciano, who had cracked a tooth on the skull of a man who kicked him in the face and did not live to regret it; Canela, who broke a rib when knocked to the ground by two men stumbling over themselves to flee; and Llido, whose right eyeball was scratched to the point of leaving him blind in one eye. None of these wounds were hard to treat from a technical perspective, but witnessing their pain, noting how Feliciano tried but failed not to flinch, reminded Neiza of how vulnerable the familiars were when not under her protection—how happily the world could destroy them if she didn't have the right charms or implements at the ready should disaster strike. Her predecessor told her once that the measure of a witch wasn't how many men she could kill but how many familiars she could keep alive, and how long.

"We will find her," Ambi said, touching Neiza's shoulder.

Neiza squeezed the hand but took no comfort in it. "That pit was our only clue."

"It *was* your only clue, but not anymore. Look where we are. Look what's missing."

Neiza lifted her head to consider the emptiness of the setting, the lack of men and machines, like a capitalist puzzle waiting to be pieced together. "Tag," she said, calling gently to the peccary, whose still-healing wounds had led him to convalesce under silk floss trees in bloom. He came slowly but steadily toward where she sat. "You will heal nicely," she said, running her finger parallel to the shallowest wound, which finished sealing as she spoke. "I need something from you. Can you track the seismic equipment that was here a couple days ago?"

"Maybe. Give me a minute." He closed his eyes and lifted his snout to the air, searching for the lingering bite of metal and ooze of the ancient earth. He stood a while at the edge of the pit, his powerful snout knocking loose bits of dirt and stone that fell and fell longer than it took him to lock onto the scent. Once he found it, he pointed resolutely southeast.

Gingerly at first, and then with increasing vigor, the familiars followed Tag, growing more confident in their newly healed limbs and ligaments with each tentative step, blink, or flap of wing. Neiza carried the bag usually on Canela's back, momentarily wary of putting too much weight on the guanaco's mended rib. While she walked, she ate breakfast, nibbling at pieces of fruit and not-quite-stale cuñapes, those rounded breads made of yucca flour and plain white cheese she learned to make with her mother as a child in El Torno, a small town outside Santa Cruz de la Sierra. She shared the bread with Ambi and the familiars, lightening her load and restoring their strength in one act.

"You only make these on special occasions," Ambi said.

"Did I miss a birthday?"

"My mother's."

"You visited her village, then."

"Only for supplies. You know what would happen if they found out." An accused witch on this side of the border between Bolivia and Paraguay was likely to be banished from her village if determined to be guilty by the community. If such a witch had relatives across the border and if they were willing to house her, she might find a home in Paraguay or be forced to make her own way in the oft arid and unforgiving Gran Chaco. Someday, Neiza knew, another outcast would stumble toward her in the forest, and she would perpetuate the cycle by teaching them and handing over the mantle of Witch-Guardian. This was how the witches of Kaa-Iya first established themselves: a lucky witch, cast out instead of being burnt alive, built a hut deep in the forests, and true witches have been coming there ever since. (The majority of accused witches, however, are just people who gave the wrong person side-eye or tried unsuccessfully to steal another's home or husband.)

"That's one of the reasons I left," Ambi said.

Quietly, the familiars fanned out, giving the two humans space to speak.

"You never told me that," Neiza said.

She fought a familiar heaviness in her chest as Ambi explained that for a long time she herself did not understand what the problem was; why she could never settle comfortably in the remote hut; why when she went on missions to far inhabited regions of the park she always buzzed with excitement; and why after returning from the missions she felt part of her happiness slip away, like water down a drain. To live so apart from the world required a fortitude Ambi was not sure she possessed. "I need people in a way you don't," she finished, not unkindly. "I need my family."

Neiza considered the stones poking her feet. "Have you told them about me?"

"I would never reveal your secret. They know only that there's someone."

"And do you still let them believe that someone is a man?"

A silence at turns remorseful and reproachful fell between them like an answer, until Ambi said, "No. After we broke up, I told them that I had been dating a woman." Even this admission did not come easily, indicating that their conversation had been a painful one full of misunderstandings, confusion, and bitterness about the subject, which her father would prefer never to discuss again. "I think the only reason they accept it is because I've been alone ever since."

"You cannot live your whole life that way."

"I don't intend to."

Often, the simplest declarations have the most potential interpretations, and without further elaboration from Ambi the witch found herself filling in the gaps with potential futures. One where the two of them reconcile and live their lives in the forest, surrounded by green and growing things. Another where Ambi returns to her village and finds a nice girl she can bring home to her family, and still another where Ambi never takes another lover and Neiza is reduced in the story of her life to the "friend" she lived with for a time. Miserable, she searched the far trees for Feliciano, longing for the comfort of his purr, the blanketing warmth of his fur when she scratched a deep itch behind his ears. When she could not find him, she tilted her head back and transformed herself into a great Andean condor, determined to take flight, to make herself as ugly and as distant as possible. Her arms extended into wings, and her long hair became plumage, black as night on her back and white as snow on her collar. Her head was nearly bald, the hairs short and spiky as if buzzed, the skin beneath it wrinkled and mottled like a testicle. Like this she flew, alone and on her own terms, until the sun began to set and her stomach began to protest; then she swept down to a clearing half a kilometer ahead and waited on a log for the others.

By the time Marsh alighted on the log beside her, Neiza had reverted back to human form, installed wards and protections around their camp for the night, gathered dry grasses and sticks, and sparked a small fire. Its smoke must have signaled Ambi, because she arrived with a fresh capybara carcass and bare-faced curassow to roast on the fire. She plunged the tip of her spear in the ground and settled by the fire to skin the creatures . While the familiars gathered around Neiza, nuzzling and comforting her, Ambi considered her thoughtfully, noting mournful bags under her eyes, a defeated slump to her shoulders. "I'm worried about you."

When Neiza didn't respond, Llido said, "She cast a sleepless charm on herself."

"Again? You know how bad those are for your body, Nei."

Llido picked a condor feather off the ground. "Is this from your head?"

Without turning, Neiza found the small bald spot at the nape of her neck.

"That settles it: after we eat, you'll undo that charm and finally get some sleep." Ambi picked up the curassow by its narrow legs and plucked the first handful of feathers from its chest.

"You no longer have a say in how I care for my body."

"I'm sorry," she said. Feathers fell into the fire. Ambi lowered the curassow, resting the fist clenching its legs on one knee so that the body draped across the ground. In the quiet that followed, Neiza undid the sleepless charm.

Ambi added, "I never meant to hurt you. I thought being with you meant giving up family, friends. Now I see: being with them means giving up an essential part of myself. I can do it for a few hours at a time but not years. Not my whole life. I need balance." Her eyes searched the flames for a path forward. Finding none, she turned to Neiza. "Can you understand?"

With some reluctance, Neiza nodded.

Feliciano crawled into the warm pocket between her bent knees and her chest, nuzzling her robes with his velvet head, perhaps anticipating what Ambi said next: "I would like to try again."

Neiza shut her eyes and sighed. "I'm too weak for this now. I need my familiar."

A small pause, then: "Fair enough."

Neiza opened her eyes and saw that Ambi had resumed her preparations, plucking the bird and skinning the capybara with the facón. Bent over the carcasses, Ambi's shoulders were a monument to disappointment. A flood of affection filled Neiza then, but now exhaustion was creeping in, pulling at her eyelids and the back of her neck. She crawled on her knees to where Canela had folded herself elegantly by the fire and retrieved the handmade blanket from her bags, taking the time to hug the guanaco's neck and whisper thanks into her ear. She gave each of her familiars a treat, glad of the meat on the fire now, because she would have to save most of their remaining rations for the return home. Tag promised they were less than a day from Zorra, but Neiza remained unsure. Something was wrong. She kept thinking about that man who insisted he knew nothing about a pampas fox. Who else would have taken Zorra, if not one of her enemies? Could a new power have moved into Kaa-Iya without her knowledge? That thought disturbed her; she worried over it all through dinner and into the night, when she curled herself in the blanket and spooned Feliciano by the fire. The last thing she knew before sleep took her was Ambi tucking her in tighter and whispering, so softly Neiza thought she dreamed it, *I love you.*

NOTHING COULD wake Neiza from her restorative slumber. Not the smell of meat roasting on a wooden spit. Not the metallic scrape of knives sharpened on stones. Not the probing nips from Marsh's hooked beak as the eagle tested Neiza's alertness by gnawing at her fingers. Into the morning she slept, past the break of dawn, through the smoky sizzle of Ambi putting out the embers of their campfire with great handfuls of dirt. When at last she woke she was alone. All her familiars had slipped away in search of breakfast, and Ambi was standing to the side, back stiff, voice edged with suspicion and reserve.

"And you're sure it wasn't logging equipment?" Another person stood just outside of Neiza's blurred field of vision. Their voice was low and unfamiliar, their words half translated by the spell weakened by her slumber, but she understood the words "East" and "guns." By the time the sleep grogginess wore off, Ambi was sitting on the log, sharpening her facón.

"Did you find a witness?"

"More like a witness found us while herding cows."

"That explains the smell," Neiza said, folding the blanket.

Ambi tested the knife on her thumb. "Want to know what they said?"

"Not really. I suspect it's all lies," she said, spying Tag returning from the forest.

"Then you and I are on the same page." Satisfied, Ambi tucked the knife into the sheath on her right calf and relayed the lies that tipped her off: the prospectors hauling the seismic equipment though the scrublands had a talking pampas fox in a metal cage—only, how did they knew it could talk? Translation spells only work between familiars and their human (and, in the case of Ambi, a human's human gifted with a spell by association); their witness would have to be a witch, a mage, or a partner thereof in order to understand Zorra. More than that: they would have to be a total fool to tell such an obvious lie. "Get this: according to our witness, the prospectors planned to sell Zorra to some norteamericanos with a traveling circus act."

Neiza laughed heartily at the ridiculous lie. "What a novice!"

"To be fair, I think the kid was like sixteen, maybe seventeen."

"Old enough to know better than to trap magical talking creatures. And old enough to face the consequences." Her hand reached out to pet Tag's elongated snout and scratch his ears. He told her he had tracked the witness to a small hut that smelled strongly of Zorra.

With his guidance, the group circled the hut easily, finding no magical wards, no makeshift traps—nothing to suggest the culprit worried about getting caught in a lie or being confronted by the Witch of Kaa-Iya. After all their sleepless nights and days of pursuit, knocking down the door and pinning the thief to a wall was so easy, Neiza found it embarrassing. With a simple binding spell, she held the teenager in place as Ambi broke the cage's lock with her staff.

"Finally!" Zorra shouted as she jumped free. She crouched beside Neiza, fur bristling, teeth bared. "I warned you, Ysyry. I told you she would come for me before the new moon rose. But did you listen?"

"I'm sorry! I thought you were joking!"

Liar, Zorra hissed.

"That's no excuse." Still, Neiza saw fit to lower the teenager to the ground, if not loosen the invisible binds. "Most people who cross me don't live to do it a second time. However, since this does appear to have been an accident, I will let you go with a warning. Don't cross me again." She signaled to Zorra and the others to stand down. As they filed out of the hut, she explained to Ysyry, "The spell will wear off in a few hours.

"Wait! You can't leave me here! I have so many questions!"

"You should have thought about that before you captured my familiar," Neiza said, turning toward the door. Outside, the sun was bright and the familiars were playing in the grass, inspecting Zorra for signs of mistreatment even as they sniffed her and rolled happily in the dirt. She knelt by the pampas fox and asked, "Are you harmed?"

Begrudgingly, Zorra said, "No. They were kind to me. If a bit confused."

"Yes, we heard about their brilliant plan of a selling you to a traveling circus."

"Poor fool. They have no idea what a powerful witch they could become," Zorra said.

At this, Neiza paused long enough for Ambi to say, "It seems like they need your help."

"They're too reckless. They didn't think about the implications of finding a talking fox. Or the dangers of telling a complete stranger about it."

"My point exactly: they need training, and you've always wanted an apprentice."

"Not like this. Not after chasing them halfway across the park."

"That's how we met," Ambi said, making Neiza blush.

With a smile and a snap of her fingers, she released the binds. Ysyry stepped out of the hut, rubbing their wrists where the binds had pinched. "Thank you," they said, still wary of Neiza.

"You have my family to thank for that."

Ambi smiled at being called "family."

"Zorra says your name is Ysyry?"

"Yes. It means *flowing water* in Guaraní."

"Quite a name to have in these dry lands," Ambi said.

"Thanks—I picked it myself."

"And your parents?"

"My family has never understood my choices.. They gave me the wrong name, the wrong clothes, the wrong words, and then cast me out when I began to question those words. I moved here to be a cowherd. But then strange, magical things started happening. Now you're here, and it's all starting to make sense. I'm a witch. Or I will be, if I ever learn how to control my magic."

"I can help you with that," Neiza said. "You could study as my apprentice."

"Is that an option?" They glanced from Neiza to Ambi and back in wonder.

"Yes, but it comes with some conditions—the first being to never harm another one of my familiars. Understood?"

Ysyry nodded, their eyes cutting to Ambi's facón. "What are the other conditions?"

To soothe Ysyry's nerves, Neiza said, "Let's talk about those inside. Perhaps over a drink?"

"Of course," Ysyry said, both pleased and flustered at the thought of being a host. "Do you like mate?"

While Ysyry fussed over the tea kettle and soundly berated some wandering cows through a hole that was their hut's only window, Neiza and Ambi sat at the table, communicating with a series of hesitant smiles and glances that made Zorra snicker and stage-whisper to the other familiars, *What happened? I've only been gone a week, and they're already falling back in love.* It shocked Neiza, too: to reach for Ambi's hand across the table, to hear Ysyry's endless string of profanities and the soft lowing of the cows, and to think this could be her family.

She hoped she would be strong enough to protect it.

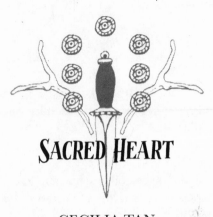

SACRED HEART

CECILIA TAN

So, after all that, you want me to mend your broken heart.
Sorry, can't help you. You think I can burn incense made
from the ashes of love letters or some shit? I can't fix a broken
heart. I can only fix your broken lust.

What, did you not realize it's broken, too? Well, they say
recognizing the problem is the first step.

The real first step, though? Throw salt. It does little good to
be bitter. You're the only one who'll taste it.

Every good chef knows to counteract bitterness not with sweet
but with salt. How many rituals start with salt? All of them, tiger,
all of them. The salt is to purify; they know that everywhere in
the world, from the Gaelic hedgewitches to the Shinto priests.

So go on, let it fly. It makes a safe space. Be pure. Tell me,
what'd your lover do that burned you to a crisp? Oh not all
at once, of course, or you would've been out of there in a hot
second. But you know what they say about the frog in the
gradually heating water.... No, not *bubble, bubble, toil and trouble* —
just what kind of witch do you think I am?

They say if the water comes to a boil gradually enough, the
frog never jumps out of the pot.

Don't blame yourself, tiger. You didn't know you were killing yourself.

The same is true of water turning to ice. If it happens bit by bit, you don't notice until it's too late. How long ago did the fire go out?

Oh, the relationship was toxic? Poison can get you the same way, seeping in gradually. Seeping right under your skin. Dampening your ardor.

You know what I have to do next? Suck out the poison. I can do that, you know. If you'll let me.

What, you think I'm just going to latch on like a lamprey? Your body isn't ready for that. You've been through too much. You've got your grip so hard on your lust you could crush it in your fists, like it's the hilt of a sword. Like you're going to do battle. Come here. Relax. I need to be soft to firm you up, to use the lightest of touches to make your flesh swell and rise. Bodies come in many shapes, but nearly all have a point right near the heart where if I put my mouth right there...

See? So firm now, small and hard as an acorn or a seed, ready to be planted, ready to be nurtured until it grows into something new and green. The roots reach lower, right down here, where everything's hot and tight now.

Suck out the poison. That's what I'll do. Good and wet, nourish the roots. Nature provides. I can suck softly or I can suck hard...or both, to draw it out.

I like drawing it out.

There it is. Let it flow.

What's that? You can't remember when the last time you felt free to just lie back and let someone else do the work? Does it feel like work? Or does it feel like play?

I better play with you now, with my hands, my fingers. When was the last time you played with yourself? And I mean really *played*? I don't mean rubbing one out in the restroom during your 9-to-5 or a quick one in the shower before bed so you didn't have to have another fight with your lover about what you wanted and they didn't. When was the last time you let your fantasies wander? Touched not only your flesh but your mind, your dreams?

Who do you see walking into your vision while your ardor ramps up? Who do you want to see coming through that door? This is how conjuration works, tiger. It's my hand moving, but it's your rhythm. It's my voice, but it's your vision. We're getting to it now.

It must hurt; I can hear you whimpering. Maybe I better suck out a little more poison.

Much better. Nothing's wrong with your eyes. I see them shining. Now. Who do you see?

Not me, tiger. This isn't about me.

Oh, I see. I had it wrong, didn't I? It's not just who you want your *lover* to be that's hard to see. It's who you want *yourself* to be, isn't it? I'll let you in on one of the secrets of the universe: That's true of everybody, tiger. Okay, okay, maybe not for the people who don't question at all. But that's why they don't have the answers. They've never had to look for them. The conservatives, the conformists, they do as they're told.

We folk, though, we *question*. It's in our nature. It's hard for others to know you if you don't know yourself.

Others can't love you unless you love yourself. You know when you're your true self? Oh, we'll get there. Don't worry. We'll get there. Every ritual is a journey with a beginning, middle, and end.

Lust leads places. It starts by leading you to nibble on the back of your lover's neck, to lick the back of their knee. That leads to all kinds of things. That sounds like nonsense but it makes perfect sense if you've bent their leg like this.

That's the way, tiger.

Lust leads to rash decisions, sometimes. Sometimes that's how we land in hot water. But you can't just stop wanting. You'll never get anywhere that way. You just circle around and around and around.

Don't mind if I do.

I'm taking you all the way. Once the candles are lit, once the flames are a-flicker, once we start down that path together, we have to walk the whole circle. We have to go and come back to be whole. You're doing great, tiger.

Chanting's good. Chanting's fine. Right about now is
when people start to call out to whatever gods they believe in.
Repeating the names of the gods, whether chanted or sung, is
one of the most ancient invocations.

I hear you calling out my name, in rhythm like a freight
train. But I'm not a god. And I told you, I'm not here to fix your
broken heart. Only you can do that.

That's lust talking, tiger. We'll see if you still feel that way
after. I told you, this is about getting you where you're going.
About you finding out who you are in the moment when all other
thoughts stop, when the magic hits you. That's power, don't you
feel how close you are to it? You thought folks were joking when
they'd ask *did the earth move for you*? Shake, rattle, and roll, tiger,
'til you get there.

'Til you come.

Some come quiet, like a cloud crossing the moon, some come
together, like waves meeting and sending up spray. Some say
they get lost in the moment, but what they've lost is their head,
and this isn't about that. (Is it?) When you lose your mind, what
do you keep?

When you come, it'll feel like your body supernovas into
a billion tiny atoms, blasting through space, through every
dimension. When you come, you go and go and go. You think
your ex matters on a cosmic scale? You are bigger than galaxies,
filling the infinite space between stars, before gravity begins to
pull you back together, before you coalesce once again...

Right here with me, as you fit back into your skin. I love the
taste of it, but you know it's just a shell, right? We are luminous.
Our place in the universe isn't determined by the shape of that
shell nor the depth of our pain. I see you looking out at me from
behind dazed eyes. Who are you, tiger? Can you tell me?

It's not as important to tell me as to tell yourself. What are
you feeling?

You're sure? I told you I—

You're sure. Well, maybe there's a reason I offered to help in
the first place. You had to get there for yourself, though. Lead
can't be made into gold, no matter what you've heard.

But I suppose I can admit it now. Lust *can* transmute to love. If you let it. If *I* let it. It can only happen in a space where I feel safe.

Yes, like this one.

That's magic, tiger. That's magic.

ANTELOPE BROTHERS

CRAIG L. GIDNEY

MALIK HAD WORKED in hospitality all of his adult life. He was a seasoned pro. He'd seen celebrities and politicians pass through the lobbies of the hotels where he'd worked. He'd seen ambulance crews rush out dying guests on gurneys, and once, a pregnant woman's water broke as she was checking in. From drunken rowdy groups to spaced-out millennials high on some mind-altering substance, he'd seen it all. Or he *thought* he'd seen it all.

His new job as a night auditor at the Lotus, however, made him feel like a hayseed. There wasn't drama here, as much as there was *strangeness*. He supposed he shouldn't have been surprised. The hotel itself was a strange space.

Vittorio, the manager who'd interviewed him, said, "We don't use the H-word. The Lotus is an *environment*. It's a space away from home and office, where the guests can inhabit for a brief moment." Vittorio was tall, thin, tanned and dressed in immaculately black clothing. He was bald, but for the thin mustache he had, which was also black, as were his eyes. His eyes were all pupil, and both of them were lazy. They were like black moons, out of orbit. "We call it a Transitory Dwelling

Experience, or TDE."

In other words, a hotel, thought Malik. He was careful to keep his face clear of any derision. He wanted the job, after all. Vittorio had given him a tour of the grounds. The Lotus (Hotel) had once been an underground parking lot. There were five levels underground, giving it a distinctly warren-like feel.

The lobby and registration level had a minimalist aesthetic. Slate grey tiles with navy blue walls were hung with black and white photographs of seemingly random objects, none of which remotely suggested leisure, vacation or sleep. There was a picture of a one-eyed cat, a shattered light bulb, and an unopened can of lutefisk. The lobby chairs were all recliners, with their wire underpinnings exposed. They looked uncomfortable and severe. Four of them surrounded a rectangular pool of water as dark as ink. A fake lotus flower floated in its center and bone-white carp slipped through the liquid, aquatic ghosts. The registration desk faced the restaurant, a poorly lit room called Mortar and Pestle that served muddled drinks, gremolatas, chimmichurri-sauced steaks, and exotic pestos. Mortar and Pestle was overstaffed and under-attended. The patrons always looked sad. Malik read somewhere that the restaurant was the top spot for relationship dissolutions and hostile corporate takeovers.

Level 2 had walls painted emerald green, a mosslike carpet and doors a brilliant turquoise shade. The scent of freshly mown grass oozed from the air vents.Level 3 was Topaz yellow, accented by mustard colored doors and the scent of lemon verbena. Sapphire blue and amethyst were the colors of levels 4 and 5. Each level had precisely 13 rooms, labeled thusly: Sapphire 2, or Topaz 14. (The 13th room was never labeled as such—a hotelier's tradition). It took Malik awhile to learn the lingo.

For the most part, Malik enjoyed his job. The guests who checked in at night were always interesting, if not pleasant. They were often tall, modelesque Europeans with sharp, avian features dressed in perfectly ironed clothing. Malik felt small and shabby in their presence. For the most part, they ignored him as they chattered on their cellphones.

T HE MORTAR AND PESTLE closed at 11pm. A slow trickle of
depressed people traipsed through the lobby, their downcast
faces on the slate tile. A tall dark-skinned woman in a brilliant
violet dress wept openly, the tears spilling down and splashing
on her dress. An older Asian gentleman in a lamé smoking jacket
trailed behind her, scowling. Fifteen or so minutes later, the staff
left still wearing their kitchen and floor uniforms, a cloud of
cigarette smoke hovering over them. Soon, Malik was alone at
the front desk.

It was the middle of the week, and there was a mere scattering
of guests—perhaps five occupied rooms. There were no
scheduled check-ins that night. The Lotus, like all hotels (and
TDEs), mostly got busy starting on Thursdays.He sat down and
pulled out his little netbook, where he had downloaded some
movies to watch. It was probably going to be a long night, so he
had also downloaded a few podcast episodes on his phone as
well.

He watched a violent crime thriller starring an actress who
had once been a Pollyanna-ish child actor. On the old sitcom,
her catchphrase had been "Holy Cannoli!" Her role in *Wicked
Angel* was as a novice nun who killed pedophile priests in awful
and frankly absurd ways. One pedo-priest was grilled alive on
a fast food restaurant's flattop. Another had a piano dropped on
him. Sister Bernadette, the zealot the actress portrayed, walked
up to the dying man, caught in the web of wires slicked with his
blood, and played a hymn on the damaged keyboard, an act that
exacerbated the priest's dire condition. An eye-gouging scene
followed, which went on forever. The movie had been panned by
critics. They dubbed it, of course, "Unholy Cannoli."

He then put on his headphones and played a podcast where
two people discussed *Wicked Angel*, a long and rambling palaver
that referenced the 1980s, Giallo movies and the vaporwave
soundtrack. The female host said that the soundtrack wasn't
vaporwave at all; it was instrumental *witchhouse*. The two of them

went back and forth over the proper genre classification of the soundtrack for some time (Malik had thought the soundtrack was mostly Casio-keyboard samples played over and over again). The podcast's hosts were named Pyewacket and Vinegar Tom. He imagined they were two high white people in their twenties recording their show in the dank basement of a group house. Both of them probably had dreadlocks and fake Rastafarian hats.

Malik put the podcast on pause when the door opened. It didn't happen often, but sometimes there were walk-ins, due to emergencies. Usually, they were lawyers who had late hours and didn't feel like cabbing it out to the suburbs. The person who walked into the lobby, though, was no lawyer.

The man wore a mask over his face. An intricately carved wooden mask with horns protruding from the top. The horns were notched and ridged, like the antlers of an antelope, and the angular shapes of the mask's features suggested a non-Western technique had been used on the ashy-blond wood. The rest of the man's outfit was more or less conventional. A flowing black shirt over loose black pants, both embroidered with arabesques of silver thread. Malik dropped his earbuds. He was used to strange happenings at the Lotus. But, at the Lotus, strangeness was mostly a white people phenomenon. The foibles of the eccentric rich were expected. This antelope-masked gentleman, though, was Black. Malik could see his dark hands.

Malik thought, *Holy Cannoli*, as the man sidled up to the reservation desk.

"Good evening." His voice was a deep velvety baritone, the voice of a seventies soul singer. "I would like to inquire about the possibility of a group of us staying the night." Malik couldn't see the man's eyes. The mask had no lips, so it was disconcerting to hear a voice emanate from the wood. Though the voice was not muffled in any way.

Malik found it hard to look at the mask. There was no point of reference. No eyes, or nose. And while he knew that the horns were decorative, they still looked imposing. "We have vacancies."

"Splendid!"

"What happened?" Malik asked as he typed into the reservation system.

The antelope-man said. "Our group has been unceremoniously unhoused from our current hotel. Such ignorance and bitch-assness. Pardon my French. That hotel has hosted adult babies and bondage parties. But as soon as a group of black men appeared…"

"As it turns out, the hotel is vacant both nights," Malik said after checking the reservation software on the computer. "How many people are in your group?"

"There are twelve of us," the antelope man replied.

"Perfect. We have rooms available."

The masked man stepped away from the desk and produced a cell phone from some invisible pocket. He walked to the other side of the pool's shore, and made a call. Malik activated the room keycards, deciding to house the group on the Amethyst floor, the lowest of the levels. He had no idea what sort of group the masked man led. Were they a secret society, like the Freemasons? A religious group? A fantasy football league? The masked man paced back and forth by the lotus pool. When the automatic doors slid open, he stepped around to greet the crowd that entered the Lotus.

And what a crowd they were. All of them wore wooden masks. Malik counted five antelope masks, some of them embossed with swirling designs, and six oval masks made of intricate rows of scales. Malik had no idea what sort of creature these masks were supposed to represent. Snakes? Armadillos? All of the mask wearers were otherwise sharply dressed in suits of houndstooth, pinstripes and herringbone. They poured into the lobby, laughing and chatting away. Some of the masks had wooden lips that moved in time with their speakers' voices. Other masks had slits, or, like the head antelope's, no mouthpiece at all.

A line formed and Malik took credit cards and handed out keys. Some of them had unique names. (For example: Euphrates Okonkwo. Ra Wilson. Hyperion Jones. Rhys Okorafor. Orion

Okeke. And Cancer Morrigan). The Antelope Man's name
was Jupiter Siggurson, and sure enough, his credit card and ID
confirmed this unlikely name.

They all entered the elevator and rode down to the Amethyst
level. At least they were isolated from the rest of the potential
guests, sequestered on their own floor.

THE HOURS PASSED slowly. Malik returned to the podcast, and
found it unlistenable. Vinegar Tom and Pyewacket prattled
on and on, with self-absorbed and inane observations. Instead,
Malik began searching on the web about the new mysterious
group that settled in the Lotus. His search terms looked like the
lines of a forgotten surrealist poem.

BLACK MEN MASKED GROUP
WOODEN FACES SOCIETY
CARVED AFRICAN DISGUISES

None of these bore any useful information. Then he narrowed
the search to African masks, and one of the first hits had a
picture of the antelope man's mask.

It was called a Chiwara, and it was a representation of a
Bambara nature spirit. He saw several examples—both masks
and sculptures. All of them had the grooved horns, but the
beasts they crowned were abstract things, made of elongated
snouts and stylized features. Quite a few of them didn't look like
antelopes at all. The nature spirit was sacred to the Bambara
people of Mali. The demigod was half man, half antelope,
and taught the people agriculture. Western artists like Picasso
were inspired by the "primitive" artwork and made their own
versions. (Or parodies, according to some people). Malik had a
hard time imagining that a bunch of Bambara tribesman just
happened to be in the city, let alone the hotel. (Or TDE). Was
the group of men on the Amethyst level a group of artists or
scholars?

At 2am, Malik left for his lunch hour. Nothing was open so he ate his sad dinner-lunch in the tiny break room. He desultorily searched more about the strange group on his phone while he ate a tuna salad sandwich with too much mayonnaise and the odd addition of apple chunks and bean sprouts. It didn't taste bad, per se, but the taste was surprising and not quite appropriate. Like a group of Afrocentric artists in a Eurotrash hotel.

Malik had been propositioned twice at the Lotus. Once by an Icelandic DJ named Einar after a club set, and another time by Anna, a Swedish woman with ice-blonde hair, pale blue eyes and teeth the yellow of parchment from her incessant cigarette smoking. Both of them had referred to Malik as a "chocolate treat" or the like and he declined both offers. White bodies could be sexy but even a whiff of racial objectification was an instant boner-killer. Because those people were never fucking *him*. They were fucking whatever Blackness was in their imagination. He became an object, like a sculpture or a painting, his uniqueness vanquished.

Recalling those solicitations, for one brief, transgressive moment, Malik had a vision of fucking Einar and Anna's pale bodies, penetrating them with a dick that was notched and grooved like the horn of an antelope. It was a distasteful flash of an image. Malik got hard anyway.

His phone rang, startling him out of his impromptu shame. It was his friend Kiki. She was probably getting ready to leave for the early morning shift at the bakery.

"Greetings, my fellow night-time nigga," she said and started singing "Nightshift" by the Commodores. "Any freaky Lotus stories to entertain me with?"

"Excuse you. It's a transitory dwelling experience, for your information. And no, it's dead up in here."

Kiki said, "I still think you should have a quickie there one night. What's the mile high club version of the hospitality industry?"

"Ha ha. You so funny."

"I'm serious, dawg. Grindr probably be off the charts."

"You know them white boys don't want me. They want a

'prime nigger stud' to fulfill their nasty little fantasies," Malik said.

"Where do the brothers looking to nut go?"

"Kiki, does your mama know you talk like a sailor at shore leave?!?"

"She's the one who taught me," Kiki said.

And both of them fell out laughing. Malik ended up with tears streaming down his face. Kiki was one of the few people who could make him laugh like that.

He asked about her day when the paroxysms subsided. She filled him in about the antics of her cat Septimus and told him about the recipes she was experimenting with. "Do bourbon canelés sound good? How about savory croissants filled with molé sauce?"

"Your smoky chipotle strata was a hit," Malik said. "Tyrell still talks about it to this day. 'How's your friend who made that savory bread pudding thing doing,' he'll ask."

"Mmm—hmmm," Kiki replied. "Is that all I am to him? A cook? Cause that nigga is fine as hell."

"Speaking of fine ass niggas, a group of them checked in. Real freaky group. They were all wearing African masks."

Kiki was silent for a moment. Then she said, "Are you shitting me? You mean to tell me that the Chiwara Society checked in your pretentious flop house?"

"You heard of them?" Malik leaned forward.

"You *haven't?*" Kiki said, sounding incredulous. "It's like a cult or an art movement, dependent on who's talking about them. Dedicated to bringing back old tribal beliefs and crafts. A couple of years ago, they staged all these Dada like disruptions at art galleries and on college campuses. Surely you've seen them on YouTube?"

Maybe Malik *had* seen them. "You mean them guys who dressed up in those colorful weird outfits and chased college students around a couple of years ago? I think it was viral for a hot second. Why are they considered a cult?"

"Because these dudes have to commit to wearing the traditional outfits. They even change their legal names."

"So, Scientology for niggas?"

Kiki giggled."You are too much. There is something wrong with you, boy. Listen, I gotta hop into the shower before I skrt-skrt to la boulangerie. Holler at you later."

The end of the conversation coincided with the end of Malik's pitiful lunch. When he returned to the desk, there was someone standing in front of it. Malik recognized him as the current dweller of Sapphire 7, a grey-haired diminutive gentleman who Malik was pretty sure was having a tryst due to the parade of young beauties of both genders who he'd sent down to his room. (Vittorio said, "The Transitory Dwelling Experience is free of judgement and respectful of discretion.") Malik could tell he was agitated due to his frenzied pacing. Sapphire 7 was dressed in a pale green leisure suit which had the unfortunate effect of making him look like a fashionable leprechaun.

"You *have* got to do something about *those* people on the level below me," Sapphire 7 said. "They are making entirely too much noise!"

"I'm sorry, Mr. St. John."

"It's pronounced sin-gin. Rhymes with engine. But never mind. Just get them to shut the hell up. It's three-thirty am on a weeknight! They woke me and Coco up with all their racket."

"Let me check into it," Malik said. He glanced at the CCTV of the Amethyst level. The screens were blank. That's weird, he thought. All of the other levels showed up on the computer screens. Had someone disabled them? And how had they done it?

"I'll go down and have a talk with those guests," Malik said after trying to bring up the cameras to no avail. He put the BE RIGHT BACK sign up on the desk, and rode the elevator down with Sapphire 7, who complained the whole way down. He blathered on and on about how hip he was, how he liked to party when he was younger but he was never, never so self-centered as the people on the level below. Malik was more than happy to leave Sapphire 7 on his sapphire floor.

W HEN THE ELEVATOR door opened, Malik saw the long
 purple tongue of the hallway, the spaced lozenges of
fluorescent light, the bright purple walls, the matte plum of the
numbered rooms. He expected this. What he didn't expect,
though, was the silence. The Amethyst level had been designated
the party level since it was so deep underground, and sound was
dampened by the insulating walls of concrete. Theoretically,
Sapphire 7 should not have heard any sound at all. Musicians
and DJs often held decadent parties on this level, soirees full of
debauchery and drugs. Yasmin, one of the day staff, told him
about finding all sorts of crack pipes and cocaine residue in the
aftermath of one such epic get-together.

The first thing Malik did was check the CCTV camera.
The red indicator light showed that it was on and nothing
was covering the lens. Perhaps there had been a hiccup in the
broadcast. He walked the length of the purple hall, stopping to
listen at Amethyst 7 to see if there was any sound coming from
there. There was only silence. Maybe the party had ended as he
was descending. At Amethyst 14, he saw a small sliver of light
in the door crack. But he heard no sound. Maybe the occupant
was watching TV with the volume low. Malik shrugged and
headed back to the elevator. Aside from his lunch hour, he
wasn't permitted to leave the desk unattended for more than ten
minutes. But, just before he pressed the 'up' button, he heard a
door open.

Amethyst 14, the thirteenth door. Malik turned to see
the antelope-headed men pour out of the suite in a steady
procession. One by one, they emerged, their horns just barely
missing the ceiling. Then he felt, rather than heard, vibration
from a polyphony of hidden drums. Rhythm patterns competed
with each other. He watched as they lined up in facing rows, the
drum beats becoming more relentless and complex. Malik heard
bass drums and the sizzle of shakers. The sound crowded his

brain until he couldn't think.

When they were all lined up like statues, the masked men turned towards him and each of them extended a hand.

Join us.

Malik stepped forward. Why? Mostly because it would be a great story to tell Kiki. That was most likely. But another part of him was truly intrigued. There was a queer beauty to this ceremony. *It's like being in a museum*, he thought. He stepped forward and—

Dry dust, dried raffia strands and endless stalks of millet appeared in place of the hall of purple walls and carpets. The masked men surrounded him and they performed a slow dance where they bowed to the sacred earth below their feet, or five levels above. Malik heard the harp-like sound of a plucked instrument, and the plinging notes of a xylophone. The Chiwara Society worshiped the Earth, but tonight, they also worshiped *him*. Malik found himself removing his clothing. Why? It felt right. And when the last article of his clothing dropped in that dusty corridor, he felt it. Felt them: two burning spikes of bone protruding out of his head. Malik screamed. It *hurt*. It also gave him a hard-on, a third burning spike.

The masked men removed their clothing as well, but not their masks. Each of them got in front of the hotel room doors on all fours, displaying their magnificent buttocks. They spread them wide, until he could see their gaping holes.

He knew what he had to do. The ceremony was a fertility rite of some kind. (The millet must be planted!) Something moved through Malik, who now dripped with sweat, and blood, and excitement.

HE WOKE UP in Amethyst 14, covered in dried raffia among other dried fluids. It was almost six a.m.. Malik's whole body ached as if he had done strenuous exercise. And his head pounded, the pain particularly intense in two spots on his forehead. When he stepped out into the hall, all of the doors were open and a dry dust had accreted in little hillocks in the various corners. The room themselves were empty and mostly free of the dust.

Malik only halfway remembered the orgy that had taken place beneath the earth. The glistening body parts, the musky smells. The wrecked orifices. The flickering lights, the raspy moans. Most of all, those wooden, unmoving masks. He thought, *I won't tell Kiki about this. I won't tell anyone about this.* He felt a weird mixture of disgust and transcendence.

Thankfully, the elevator was clean, save for one braided strand of raffia.

He found the black business card on his seat before he sat down. The front was just a phone number, gold embossed and in italics. The back of the card had a picture of a Chiwara. The curved eyes and their relentless, empty stare plucked his anxiety like a kora string.

It would only be an hour until his day shift relief came. He listened to Pyewacket and Vinegar Tom prattle on about an obscure movie called *The Children Ain't Right*, a blaxplotation version of Village of the Damned, but he found their commentary annoying. Hopefully, Yasmin would bring donuts and coffee.

Malik threw the card away.

Then, he reached into the trash, and pocketed it.

DIZZY IN THE WEEDS

L.D. LEWIS

R ED.

Red.

Red.

Red.

"Motherfu—" Dizzy Carter exhaled hard through her nose and tossed a threatening prayer toward the coffered hallway ceiling. Violent frustration seemed to be a prerequisite for getting hotel key cards to work; but if that was the case, she'd have been king of opening doors by now. She rotated the useless piece of plastic between gloved fingers and inserted it frontwards, backwards, upside-down, in combinations and patterns reminiscent of old cheat codes. The little light still taunted her.

She pressed herself into the shallow door frame in a bid to become invisible as an amorous couple tripped down the hallway some six doors down. Even with their faces mashed together, their key card fumbled into position and their door beeped delightedly to allow them to tumble inside before slamming shut again.

Dizzy huffed. Maybe she had the wrong door. Or the key had

demagnetized in the old man's pocket. She checked her watch. He'd been teetering on the border of a merry and sloppy drunk when she left him at the hotel bar. This was a swanky place, all cranberry paint and gold accents. Even the sconces were crystal. They'd cut him off before long, if only to save the expensive optical-illusion carpeting.

Red.

She talked herself down from her instinct to break the door down. She was an investigator, not a bandit. Not tonight, anyway. A bitter growl and a deep breath in, and she tried again.

Green.

"Oh thank fuck," she sighed and let herself inside, closing the door gently behind her. It didn't smell like a non-smoking room. In fact, even in the dark the air seemed thick, odorous, and hazed in the light of the red exit sign.

She used the flashlight on her phone to sweep the room. Frameless works of abstract art lined damask papered walls. The old man's things were strewn about as if he'd been here weeks instead of the one night. Polaroids and used whiskey glasses littered the low coffee table. Dizzy scanned the photographs and found multiple angles of the same pale, lithe body in lacy, emerald green lingerie. None included a face. Then again, that's probably not what he valued about her.

She snapped pictures of the scene. Dizzy's one true love was two years dead. She could give a fuck how anyone else squandered their relationships. But the wife had sent her here, not to confirm the affair but to get back the wedding band he took off to do his dirt before she started divorce proceedings. Dizzy would have declined the potential felony, only rent was due and she wasn't a very good investigator in the first place.

She moved from the suite's living space to the bedroom with its baroque fresco in lieu of a headboard. The lavender sheets were rumpled and spattered with a wetness that made Dizzy frown. A pair of well-worn, strappy high heels had been discarded by the ficus in the corner. The only feminine article of clothing in the whole place. She flung the light toward the nightstands and checked the drawers of each for the ring. Nothing. She sighed again. If he was a put-it-in-the-safe guy, so help her...

A sniffle.

The fine hairs on Dizzy's arms stood up and she threw light back toward the front room. The haze had cleared and seemed to collect in the silhouette of a person seated on the tufted couch. As a Deadwalker witch, Dizzy was no stranger to the dead. Haunted hotel rooms weren't new things either. She just didn't like being surprised.

"You alright?" She called quietly.

The ghost's head snapped in her direction, but they said nothing.

Something was wrong here.

A sense of dread pulled her toward the bathroom where she clicked on the light and found the ring in the soap dent of the sink and the bathtub filled with a body's worth of blood. Startled, she backed away, tripping over the gold heels and slamming her back against the closet. The door jarred open just a crack to reveal an empty rack and the edge of a hard suitcase.

Dizzy swallowed hard. There had been another feeling like this. Just once, two years ago. The muted chaos feeling of a billion cells worth of her soul trying to climb out of her body so she could see what she needed to see without feeling it because feeling it might kill her.

"Can you tell me what happened here?" Dizzy called into the other room. Her voice shook and she began to sweat. She pulsed her fists using the stab of her nails into her own palms to ground herself. The ghost didn't answer. She didn't think they would.

A series of quick breaths to steel herself, and she knelt to open the door. Slotting her phone down into the front of her bra so both her hands were free, she fumbled to find the zipper on the suitcase. It was another couple of breaths before she could pull it down.

It took a moment to put together what she was seeing. Some part of her brain was seeing her wife's face, pale and despondent on the balcony beneath their apartment the night Dizzy'd found her dropped there. But that had already happened. This was a face she didn't know, bloodless behind a curtain of freshly washed red hair, tilted at an unnatural angle. Forced to fit. The eyes were just as empty. He hadn't even bothered to close them.

Dizzy stared at it, breathless for a few seconds before blinking herself back to the present. In her dealings with the dead, she was rarely confronted with the bodies. The dead were dead and generally pleased to be so. Death was just a different life.

This was different. Lonnie had been different. The violence and desperation in the air was almost nauseating. She had the presence of mind not to throw up and leave her DNA there.

She rifled through the pockets of her jeans in hopes of finding something natural. A pebble, maybe a leaf. Down feathers from her wilting bedroom pillows didn't have enough mass to hold a human soul, but those were clinging to every crevice of her wardrobe and probably her hair if she took it out of its ombre pineapple atop her head. And no coins were made of pure metals anymore.

The ring.

She returned to the bathroom to snatch it from the counter, unable to stop herself from scanning the rest of the room. There wasn't so much as a drop of blood on any other surface. Not a splash. It was as if he'd drained her somehow before stuffing her in the suitcase. She returned to the front room, panting and rolling the ring in her gloved fingers. If the wife wanted it back this badly, it was likely valuable and therefore pure gold. Rent would have to wait. Her one regret was the indignity she would do the ghost by storing it in a possession belonging to her killer. But the only other choice would be to leave her here to watch the macabre scene surrounding her body when the cops showed up.

"I'm Desdemona," she panted as she approached. Her heart ached in her chest from the banging it was doing against her ribs. "You can call me Dizzy. I'm a friend. Can you tell me your name?"

"An... Andie," the ghost hiccupped. Her voice was small and hollow, her head hanging down.

"Andie? Okay. Andie, did Jack do this to you? Jack Dorsett.

The man staying in this room." She tried to be as gentle as she could.

"He...yes."

Dizzy crouched in front of her, searching the deep pits that made up Andie's dead eyes. Tears streaked the smoke that made up her face.

"Andie, there's not much I can say and I'm sorry. But the...the dead will welcome you."

Here, Andie began to wail and Dizzy cursed herself silently. She was not the dead's therapist or some shepherd into the beyond. Her bedside manner had been eroded by years of simply not needing it. And she needed to be out of here soon before the murderer returned.

"You'll see. It's like an infinite family. They'll teach you to explore the worlds in new ways. And Andie, they will look after you. They will see that he pays for this. I promise."

A void opened where Andie's mouth should be, a haunting, hollow sound issuing forth as it began swallowing the smoke around it. There was the heated smell of ozone as a power surge swept the room.

Distressed ghosts were always such a spectacle.

Dizzy collected herself, palming the ring and pressing it to Andie's chest. "I'm going to help you now, okay?" She said in a steady voice. "I'm going to take you with me and we're going to get out of here."

She closed her eyes and muttered protections. The ring grew warm in her hand, increasing in temperature until it was almost unbearably hot, scarring her palm. When she stopped and opened her eyes again, the room was silent. The buzz of electric air dissipated and she was left alone with the distant sounds of traffic and the menace that came with the knowledge of a body nearby. The ring was heavy in her hand and gradually cooled down. She stashed it in her pocket and set about righting the room before leaving quietly the way she'd come.

Out in the hallway, she stood in front of the elevator bank, bouncing a leg impatiently and waiting for the mechanical whir to give way to a ding. It would have to wait, but she needed to get the ring bearing Andie's ghost to the desert where she could be received and taken care of. Uma would take care of it, she thought, if only after cracking a series of jokes about Dizzy the Ferryman first.

She shoved her gloved hands into the pockets of her bomber jacket as the elevator doors opened to reveal Mr. Dorsett, red-faced and furiously patting down his own pockets. He was a large man, paunchy, broad-chested, with watery green eyes and most of his hair. He had a good six inches on her, but Dizzy had put less convenient heads through walls before.

It took all of her self-control not to do it now.

"Goddammit," he grumbled, spit clinging to his lipless beak of a mouth. "Lost my key. Headed back down."

He pressed the lobby button, not stepping to a side to allow her on, but Dizzy boarded anyway, measuring her breaths as the doors closed on them. A small screen over button panel shared weather updates and promos for the hotel's amenities. Dizzy instead focused on his wet ham smell, imagining him heaving and grunting as he mangled Andie's body.

The elevator finally slowed. And for want of something more violent to do, Dizzy spoke just before the doors dinged.

"Andie wants you to know that when you get to hell, the dead will eat you," she said calmly to his reflection in the mirrored walls.

Mr. Dorsett froze as Dizzy stepped out and turned to look him in the eye. There was confusion on his face, the kind that couldn't decide whether he was too drunk to have heard her clearly or if he should ask how she knew.

He stood there, puzzled, mouth gaping long enough for the doors to start closing again. "She'll see you soon," Dizzy added.

She made her way as quickly and covertly as she could past the closing bar and the clusters of guests forced to take their loud conversations out beneath the ornate dome of the lobby. She waited until she stepped outside into the rain-slick, neon-drenched night air of San Guin to take off the gloves and make her call.

"Anais Hotel," the receptionist chirped.

"Room 624. Jack Dorsett's got a body in his suitcase."

U MA WAS QUITE DEAD and had been for years. She'd been
Dizzy's mother—or something like it—and it hadn't
exactly come as a surprise when she'd been shot over a game
of blackjack with the other lords of San Guin. That'd been
definitely in the top 3 ways she was likely to go.

"I need you to take this off my hands," Dizzy said, holding
out the ring. They were standing in the desert in one of Dizzy's
many summoning circles. Deserts were preferred as they lacked
the tangled background static of the city.

"The dead ain't your bank, girlie," Uma replied with a
hoarse, smoked-for-a-century voice. She took the ring anyway,
turning it over in her bony hands and rotating it in the sunlight,
inspecting it with the least milky of her eyes.

Dizzy leaned against the hood of her Chevelle, not really
wanting to get into the explanations. It'd been a long night and
the caapi cigarettes she smoked to bring the dead back also had
the effect of melting the scenery around her. Her phone vibrated
menacingly on the dash.

"Not the ring," she said. "There's a woman in it. Andie. She,
uh, died badly. I promised her you'd look after her."

"What, you a ferryman now?" Uma laughed, a dry, echoing
sound as if it was coming from the rocks around them.

Dizzy shook her head, clenching her jaw and staring at a divot
she was carving in the sand with her boot. She'd braced for the
deadwalker-ferryman jokes but they still irked the shit out of her.
If it was one thing she wasn't, it was some cornball medium with
a bad website and an ugly scarf collection getting weepy about
your loved one's unfinished business.

"Where'd you get it?"

"Belongs to a client. Murderer's the client's husband. You
have to get Andie out of the ring so I can take it back to the
owner. I need the payment, like, yesterday."

"You don't think she'll have other things on her mind today?

Like being married to a murderer?"

"Not my problem."

"Not your...oh, Dizzygirl's still lovesick off that actress." Uma grinned, dead, stretched skin exposing a glittering gold tooth. "I get it but when are you going to stop letting it rule your life? It's been what? A decade? Nothin' on that side is going to last forever. You know that."

"Two." Dizzy glared. "It's been two years. And her name is Lonnie. You knew her for fuck's sake."

"Well you know how time and everything is on this side—"

"Dear, I'd love to sit here and chop it up with you all day, but I have business."

Uma tapped the ring in a thoughtful pause. "Actually, there's something I need you to do for me first."

"Of course there is," Dizzy muttered under her breath.

"Andre—"

Dizzy threw her head back, sending her silent curses skyward. "Oh come on, no."

"Yes, Andre," Uma snapped. "He's still making trouble. Everybody he's put down has come to this side with a message for me. And lately it's been more than usual. He's going to be a problem for *you* before long it looks like, too."

"I'm not going to kill him for you," Dizzy scoffed.

"I never said anything about you killin' nobody. Now listen. He's after this box. It's got some coins in it. Demon stuff. Nothing you'd be interested in."

"Sure."

"I took it from him because he was dumb enough to ante it *and* be shit at poker at the same time. But it turns out it's very important and he's not going to leave me alone until he gets it back. Eternity's a long time to put up with something like that and you know how I like my quiet."

Dizzy closed her eyes. She was hungry, tired, and hadn't washed the feeling of being so near a dead body off herself yet. The desert trip was an hour out of her way already. "Where's the box, Uma?"

"Buried it."

"Where?"

"Construction site."

"Goddammi—"

"5th and Mercury. Was supposed to be a…uh…" She tried to snap her fleshless fingers to jog her memory, but all she got was a bone-scraping sound.

"A bank, Uma. 5th and Mercury is a bank," Dizzy deadpanned.

"Shit."

That train derailed, they stared at one another for a while, letting the sun grow its heat and the water Dizzy put out as an offering evaporate.

"Can you just—" Uma started again.

"Break into a bank?" Dizzy fished her car keys from her pocket and held out her hand for Uma to give back the ring. "No. Forget the girl. I'll get Nico or somebody to do it."

"You don't have to do it yourself, just commission the Colorman's Disciples. They steal shit all the time," Uma insisted, handing it over.

"And pay them with what money?" Dizzy asked, climbing into the car.

"Go to him directly. He owes me. Listen, it works out for you, too. Andre's gonna come for you eventually. He knows how important you are to me. Get those kids to pop into the bank. Lower floors, just behind the cornerstone. You deliver the box to Andre, our drama is over, I take your Andie, and you pay your rent."

Dizzy turned the engine over and heaved a sigh. The pleading was new for Uma. Dizzy had never seen her do it before. Maybe things were more dire than the woman was letting on. She cursed herself for her pang of investment and lifted her head to ask what exactly was being done to her, but Uma was already dust again, indistinguishable from the sand and stone.

THE ELEVATOR DINGED and released Dizzy onto the fourth floor of her building. She lived on the 5th, but she'd take the stairs the rest of the way in case her landlord Victor was waiting. The apartments here were multi-purpose, somehow. It wasn't uncommon for residents to run businesses out of their front rooms. On the fifth floor alone there was a therapist's office, a masseur, an artist who painted (bad) music, and what she hoped wasn't a dentist's office judging by the drilling noises. The emerald-green doors beneath a matching, coffered ceiling created the illusion of forest canopy against the chevron parquet floors. The fourth story had a damp haze to it and smelled thickly of incense and ayahuasca.

She dragged herself to the end of the hall and through a gray door, past a dusty window and up equally gray stairs. These summonings took a lot out of her and it was all she could do to make it back home on a good day before passing out. She pulled the 5th story door open just wide enough to glimpse her own door, breathing a sigh of relief to see the coast was clear. Fumbling with her keys, she put one in the lock unsuccessfully before bringing her eyes up high enough to read the note attached to the paint-chipped knocker:

Locks changed. You get the key when I get the rent.
V.C.

"Ugh. Fair enough," she groaned. It wasn't going to keep her out of the apartment, but it was fair enough.

She backtracked to the stairwell and the narrow window that opened onto the fire escape. She took those ladders instead to the bedroom window she always left unlocked in case of emergency. The busy street below steamed from last night's rain, and the ramen spot across the way was just transitioning from its drunken to its sleepy lunchtime clientele. Her phone vibrated in her pocket. She checked it instinctively and wished she hadn't.

Mme Dorsett:
Well?????????? Call immediately.

"Lady, you have no idea how badly you don't want me to call you right now," Dizzy muttered to herself.

The window opened easily and she climbed inside. The place smelled of ennui and yesterday's coffee. A patterned rainbow of layered sheets was rumpled and exposed on her unmade bed. That's where she tossed her phone. Crates of records and an old guitar collected dust alongside Lonnie's books on the far wall. Lonnie had Dizzy's first playbill from the Crane Lounge framed but now it faced the wall in the corner. That had been another life when she more played the blues than lived it.

She stripped gradually as she crossed to her bathroom for a shower. She stepped back out long enough to light incense at her ash-covered altar, side-stepping the doorway burned into the floor and wall. The large iron ouroboros mounted overhead gave her its disaffected glare, as if it had room to judge with a mouth full of its own tail.

"Long night?" she asked it, frothing toothbrush lolling out of her mouth.

The ring she fished out of her pocket and threaded onto a length of ball chain she hung around her neck before she stepped into the steaming shower. The day didn't so much wash off of her as move inside of her. She felt its weight bone-deep. Every closing of her eyes saw the same sliver of Andie's drained face.

Lonnie had been the eighth victim of a serial killer who'd dropped her off their balcony and then disappeared. Never caught. Never punished. It was the whole reason Dizzy had given up performing for...well, whatever she was doing now. For all she knew, Jack Dorsett had been another killer of many, someone emboldened by her failure to catch the first.

Uma hinging her cooperation on a favor wasn't unheard of, but keeping a soul trapped in the balance like this seemed extreme, even for her.

Andre Baal was quite literally a man possessed. He'd been the leader of a small-time gang in San Guin, and frequented the same gambling circles Uma did. The Baal part was a haphazard demon who wasn't great at possession. As a result, the two of them fought over the use of his body to occasionally comical effect until they'd started working together to grow their influence. It was the Andre part that had the temper. The Baal part had the power. Things tended to go badly for those who crossed both of them.

So naturally, that's what Uma did.

Dizzy stepped out and lotioned, thinking it'd be best not to get involved, if only to avoid having to live in a world where Andre Baal knew her face. The Colorman was agreeable enough, but no one had time for his Alice in Wonderland shit. She would rest long enough to recharge and summon someone else to take Andie off her hands. Mrs. Dorsett would have her ring back by tomorrow morning and Victor his rent money by tomorrow night.

Her phone vibrated again and Dizzy groaned as she tripped into a pair of sweatpants. Just once it would have been nice to save a cat up a tree or something pure and trauma-free, but her phone was a Bad News machine. The ringing continued as she hopped to her bed and mussed the bedsheets in search of it.

It was gone.

Gone?

She stood still and listened, the hairs on her arms raising. It was ringing, but from elsewhere in the apartment. As quiet as possible, she plucked her gun from the drawer of her bedside table and clicked off the safety, peering down the short hallway that led to her disappointing kitchen and the front room that acted as her office. The rooms were still but she could feel someone was there.

"Can I help you?" she called, pressing herself against the rouge-papered wall. A shadow moved just slightly on the hardwood floor.

"Miss Carter?" The voice was male. Sultry. Both comfortable and entirely unwelcome.

"I think you know who it is. Real question here is who am I about to shoot?"

A scowling mountain of a man stepped from around the corner and filled the entire entryway. His hands were about the size of her head. Dizzy's heart fluttered nervously for a moment.

"Buddy, you are *huge*, but a bullet's going to do what a bullet does regardless, if I put it through one of your eyes." She aimed upward.

"No need for all that," said someone who was not the giant. "You're going to lower that, though, or Frank's going to have to break your hands before we can talk."

"What are we talking about?" Dizzy replied, not lowering her weapon.

"For starters, how you and your momma apparently like owing people." He chuckled.

Shit.

"You're Baal. Or with him," she said.

"Come on back, Frank. She's not going to make trouble."

Frank stepped back, allowing Dizzy to come fully into the room. Andre Baal was seated at her desk with her phone in his hand. He was small of frame, dark-skinned with one golden eye and a herringbone suit that said he was informed entirely by an obsession with 50s era gangster flicks.

"Uma's not my mother," Dizzy told him.

"Semantics." He waved it off. "She took something very valuable from me."

"Story *I* heard was you lost it. Got a bad poker face."

"So she told you about it. I want it back. I'm a gentleman, so I'm asking nicely."

"You're definitely something but I can't help you."

Andre's jaw unhinged suddenly, going low and violently distended with an alarming crack as if the demon in him was trying to enter negotiations. He quickly set it again. He stood and buttoned his jacket, casually watching the world outside the long window as he made his way from behind the desk to stand in front of her. This close, she could see the swollen and scarred veins in his face and the tremor of control in his golden eye. His breath smelled terrible. Like reheated roadkill.

"You're going to." A smile twitched on his face. "Because if I don't get it back, I'm coming back here. If I come back here, I'm taking your skin off. All of it in one piece. And when your insides show themselves to me, I'm going to pluck out the juiciest of your organs and I'm going to make them into something delicious."

"I'm a lady, Mr. Baal. You want to eat me, you'll have to buy me flowers first like everybody else." Dizzy smirked.

"You're funny." He grinned, revealing black gums, and flicked a business card between his long-nailed fingers just inches from her face. "Wooden box. Thirty gold coins delivered to this address in the next, oh, 72 hours."

When Dizzy didn't take the card, he let it fall to the floor between them. He nodded a goodbye as Frank the Giant opened the door, and they left her to mutter her bitter, aggressive "fucks" in peace.

THE COLORMAN HIMSELF was a dapper telephone pole of a man, almost impossibly tall and attractively dark with impeccable taste in tailoring. He was most often seen publicly in the form of massive technicolor graffiti murals styled by devoted disciples known casually as Krylon Kids. The murals served as gateways throughout San Guin, staged in places where he needed eyes or where the kids needed either access or an escape route.

Dizzy stalked the row of pocket bars known as Mark Street (because that's what you were if you hung around too long and didn't drink all your money) as day transitioned to night and paper lanterns switched on. Music blared from the ramen shop on one side and its neon washed the alleyway in blinking magenta and constant, buzzing teal.

She watched the emerging crowds of off-duty adults for kids with fresh kicks and rattling backpacks. A pair of them moved past her with their heads down.

Not suspicious at all, Dizzy thought. She followed them deeper into Mark Street and eventually past it and down a series of alleyways that emptied into a concrete clearing between two apartment buildings and a laundromat. There were a dozen kids here, all in masks beneath a haze of purple and lime green paint, the colors of the tags going up.

"Can we *help* you?" a girl's voice said loudly, the help emphasized so as to seem more like a threat. Dizzy turned to see a teenager with blue piled-high yarn braids glaring at her.

"Uh, yeah. No. Not you. I need to talk to him."

"The fuck you know about the King?" a boy asked menacingly

"That he doesn't condone your tone for one thing," Dizzy replied. Behind her, it was clear she was attracting too much unwanted attention. Where Disciples amassed, there was usually a job either going down or being set up. She may as well have been a cop. "Look, I'm a friend. I'm not here to jam you up."

The eyes of the mural shifted to her direction. She at least had the Colorman's attention.

"Hey!" she shouted at the wall, walking quickly past the kids before they could swarm her. "Hey, can we talk? I'm Desdemonda. Uma Carter sent me."

They knew each other, or had, years ago. Dizzy had been a bartender by thirteen, fetching the drinks on Uma's poker nights, and the Colorman had been a regular. She remembered him as kind. When you trafficked in information, there was rarely a need to possess a threatening personality.

The mural's eyes held on her for an indecisive moment before rolling to the right where one of the disciples was standing awaiting orders. The kid nodded and approached her.

"Your hand," he demanded, impatient tone muffled by his mask.

Dizzy held out her palm and he sprayed a black X on it.

"Go 'head." He said. He left her side and Dizzy stared disapprovingly at the glistening stickiness coating her hand. The other kids watched as she approached the mural, and she watched them back for a hint that she was doing things either right or wrong. She touched the black hand to the black void at the base of the wall and felt it give, as if it wasn't a wall at all.

I already regret this, she thought as she stepped the rest of the way through into an arched alcove just off the Colorman's kitchen. He stood in shirtsleeves and suspenders, laboring over mise-en-place, a roiling pot of something violently spiced steaming on the stove behind him. The subtle movements of his head matched the booms and baps of distant big-band jazz in the background and shook the turquoise discs suspended from his ears.

"You're gawking," he said in a deep, musical voice without looking up. "Don't gawk."

Dizzy stepped forward, taking in the view through the tall windows that lined the back wall. "Sorry. I don't know what I expected to find but this wasn't it."

"You found what you needed to." He'd finished the mincing of his ginger and gave her a pleased scrunch of his nose. "I remember you from your shorter days. Still got that scowl."

"Smiling's only so useful," Dizzy replied. "You still take your whiskey in those frosty glasses with the ice globes?"

"Can never get it cold enough." His smile faltered as he studied her. "I'm sorry, that was insensitive of me. I'd heard about your girl. I can't imagine you're getting on any better."

"No, thank you, I'm…" Dizzy didn't know how to finish that sentence. She wasn't fine. She wasn't even working through it particularly well.

The Colorman moved the conversation forward after reading the silence and she was grateful. "Now what is it I can do for you?"

"Uma's got a problem that recently became *my* problem. She said you'd help."

"I'm sure she did. Leave it to her to find a problem even being dead can't shake." He took a seat on a stool behind the island and crossed his legs, waving a dish towel in a gesture of *get on with it*.

"There's a box buried behind the cornerstone of the bank at 5th and Mercury. She needs it to settle a debt and I can't get to it."

"Who's still after her to collect a debt?"

"Andre Baal."

"Oh. *Ohhhh*. My darling, you don't want him to get that. San Guin's got its share of characters but they're *people* for all intents and purposes. Demons only ever want to bring about more demons, and the more demons in one place, the more hell-like that place becomes. Between the two of us, San Guin's nowhere near equipped."

Dizzy rubbed her eyes and drew her hand down over her face. She was so fucking tired.

"You said 'Dre became a problem for you recently?"

"Yeah, showed up at my place."

The Colorman gave her a sympathetic look before turning to empty a harvest's worth of vegetables into the pot. "If you truly want the box, I can get it for you. Uma is right that I owe her. But this particular caper has consequences. I guarantee you'll be making more problems for yourself in the future."

Dizzy chewed her lip. The center of this problem was Andre. He was a threat to Uma, a threat to her, personally, and now apparently the city or some shit. It seemed the logical response was to deal with him directly.

She preferred it that way.

"Yeah," she said ultimately. "I still need the box. I'd appreciate it."

"Tomorrow night, then. My disciples will meet you there."

"Perfect," she replied. She needed the sleep. "How do I…"

"Back out the way you came." He pointed with a knife.

She turned to feel her way through the pitch black alcove.

"Desdemona?" he called. He'd never used her nickname. "If you ever need anything in the search for Miss Baxter's killer…" He gave her a meaningful look.

"I will. Thank you." Dizzy nodded, and headed out the way she'd come in.

5TH AND MERCURY was one corner of a bustling roundabout suited better to the swarms of pedestrian traffic than anyone in a car. Dizzy parked on the edge of it, rolling her caapi cigarettes and ignoring the demands of her phone. After a nap, she'd gone to the address Andre had given her and drawn veve symbols in chalk on the parking lot in front of it to set her stage for the evening.

The taggers blended in with the moving throngs and were barely noticed as they crafted a quick and impressively elaborate gateway on the side of the bank building, raising gloved middle fingers and hurling taunts at the cameras that watched over the traffic. Dizzy chuckled and shook her head at the audacity of youth.

The girl with the electric blue yarn braids disappeared inside the gate for maybe thirty seconds before reappearing with what appeared to be a wooden jewelry box. She showed it to one of her cohorts who shrugged and pointed across the circle to where Dizzy was sitting in her car. She was impressed they'd even known where to find her.

A green X went up over the gateway and the kids dispersed, heading in separate directions. The girl came to the passenger side of Dizzy's car and placed the box onto the seat, the coins inside jingling gently.

"Courtesy of the King," she said.

"Thanks," Dizzy replied, but she'd barely gotten the word out before the girl was moving on.

She turned the engine over and headed across town, back to Andre's hideout in what had once been a firehouse. It was embedded in San Guin's small industrial area, the one part of the city that saw itself abandoned and in the shadows of their neon night.

She parked in the back of the parking lot, behind the scattered vehicles of—presumably—his henchfolk, and sparked a cigarette. The ring with Annie in it throbbed against her chest like a second heartbeat.

"I'll get you home soon, girl," Dizzy muttered as she exhaled, opening the box. Inside, she found a velvet satchel heavy with ancient gold coins bearing the profile of a face she didn't recognize. Common sense suggested this is what Andre was after, not the box itself. She stashed the coins in the glovebox and grabbed her gun out of it before taking the box and stepping out of the car.

Her vision was already wobbling as she crossed the parking lot.

It was separated from the street by a chain-link fence propped open by disrepair. Orange streetlamps stretched shadows long like tiger stripes over the damp asphalt. She placed the box on the curb entering the parking lot, centering on the hideout door and muttered words of a familiar incantation. She carefully made slow, sauntering steps to keep her balance as she moved to the veve glyphs on either side of her to tap a welcoming caapi ash over them. As she spoke, the ash took on the appearance of tendrils and then wisps of bone reaching up from the other world. One arm, three arms, six arms each. They grew at her plea, grasping for the air and earth they remembered.

Returning to a seat on the hood of her car between her blazing headlights, she sparked another one and dialed the number on Andre's business card, keeping her breathing steady and her mind focused, lest the caapi overtake her senses completely.

"Yeah?" said a voice on the other line.

"Hello, 'yeah'," she replied with a drunken snicker. "This is Dizzy Carter. I'm outside."

"Who?"

"Ahh, you know Uma's daughter."

"Hold on."

There were sounds of curt conversation and a phone being handed off.

"This is Mr. Baal."

"Uh huh. You got about 30 seconds to send your goons out to collect before I pawn these expensive looking coins."

"Girl, who the fuck are you talking to?"

"Twenty-six seconds," she replied and hung up.

In the twenty-four seconds that followed, Dizzy dragged and inhaled deeply on her caapi cigarette, letting the feeling of freedom coast over and through her, that perfect state of dead-drunk and living-high.

"My friends, I have an offering for you," she told the growing spirits, her exhaled smoke dividing among the runes before her. "A threat to the dead is a threat to the living. These, neither of us can abide."

The dead agreed, a unified hiss like steam from city grates rising from the ground. Andre's people exited the building a couple at a time, each checking the pavement on their side of the street before squinting into her headlights.

Dizzy pulled her power from where it flowed through her fingers and toes back to her core and issued a task to the dead assembled to sort their threat:"Eat."

Arms made of smoke reached out to the dozen henchmen pouring from the building, wrapping their bodies tightly and rending their limbs. The dead tended to miss their blood; they enjoyed the marvel of seeing it spread in pinwheel whirls as bodies were twisted into slivers, crushed, and compacted. Now that their shells were heaps of particulate on the pavement, their souls were dragged back through the veve gateways and the street was silent again. Not one of them had been Andre.

Dizzy stood and pulled her weapon, stepping carefully toward the hideout's open doorway, avoiding what remained of the slick viscera leaking into the manhole covers. She didn't know a thing about exorcising demons, but a bullet ought to handle the host at least. Her phone rang and in her altered state, she answered it.

"Carter? Where the hell are you?" Her landlord seemed particularly feisty tonight.

"Relax, Vic, I'll see you in the morning."

"There's a woman here banging on the damn door all day. I—"

Mrs. Dorsett could be heard in the background, demanding to speak to her. Dizzy hung up before that could happen.

"'Dre? I got something for you," she called sweetly as she moved through the building. The interior was uninspired if only because she didn't have the presence of mind to inspect and judge it thoroughly.

Andre whipped around a brick corner suddenly and raised a gun of his own. "You *bitch*—"

Dizzy put one in his kneecap and the rest of the threat burst into a scream as he fell to the ground. Good to know bullets were effective.

"I think we misunderstood each other," she said, standing

over him. "You mistook me for someone who was afraid of you. I mistook you for more than a gangster."

Andre's jaw unhinged and his eyes bulged, a guttural, otherworldly sound issuing forth. This was Baal.

Perfect.

She took aim. "When you get back to hell? Let the rest of them know me and mine are off-limits."

Baal lunged clumsily in Andre's injured, mortal body and Dizzy put one through his mouth and out of the base of his skull. He fell with a thud, the demon's departure a sort of wet fizzle as his host's decay began instantly. Blue-black ichor dashed slick across a dark mural mounted to the wall behind him. It was a wood carving, intricate and impressive in its size.

In fact, now that she had a chance to take in the scene, the corners and surfaces of the room were stacked with flat parcels—artwork, judging by glimpses of gilded frames. Big, bad, Baal was dealing in black market art?

"Whoops." Dizzy muttered, punchy as the caapi and adrenaline had worn off. She now watched as the mural's grooves and nooks and crannies bubbled away to nothing. The demon's blood ate away at it like acid. She was no art person, but she was sure somebody wasn't getting their money back on this one.

No matter. She snaked her way back to the entrance, leaving the door ajar as she stepped back into the humid night air. Her phone vibrating in her pocket felt a lot like the tingling of her drugged limbs. She let it ring, chuckling to herself as she started the engine, imagining Vince and Mrs. Dorsett getting to know each other loudly outside her apartment.

HUMAN REASON

NICASIO ANDRES REED

ALL THE ASWANG in my grandmother's stories were women, but this one is a man, looks just about like any other alaskero. Leaning with his shoulder to the damp boards of the wall, rolling too little tobacco into a slip of paper. Slick-haired, black-eyed, a little slim, but with the compact muscle of the working hungry. In the stories, they won't look regular people straight on because you'd see your reflection in their eyes wrong-side-up and know them for what they are. This guy, I say, *You Felix*? and he looks right at me, this look like we're already in cahoots, smile like a glare off a glacier first thing in the morning, and I clean forget to look to see if I'm upside-down in there.

"I could be," he says. "You one of Benjie's goons?" And that's pretty rich, coming from an aswang. He spots something of my thoughts on my face and adds, "No offense meant. Everybody's somebody's goon. Man's gotta make a living."

"Oh yeah, whose goon are you, then?" I say, which is a foolish thing to do, shows him he's put me on my back foot. I'm no good when I get off-balance, and I always seem to end up that way, which is probably why I'm not one of Benjie's better goons.

The aswang, he's smiling real quick and thin. "Me?" Looks

up at me while he's licking his cigarette shut. "I'm the devil's
goon, I reckon. Isn't that what they say?" Speaking of the back
foot. It's unsettling, his big eyes behind his eyelashes, and the
way he shifts so his hips cock against the wall and he's facing me,
his body zig-zagged and coy. My throat goes dry and I forget my
lines. Just stand there hiding behind my suit. The aswang, Felix,
laughs. "So what's Manong Benjie want with the likes of me?"

AT THE TALCOTT CANNERY on Kupreanof Island, a hundred
miles or so south of Juneau, Manong Benjie runs the show,
as far as the Filipino workforce is concerned. Of course the local
Tlingit fishermen have their own thing going on, and the couple
of Japanese laborers dip in here and there, and the white men
figure they lord over everyone, but as far as any alaskero needs
to know on the day-to-day, Benjie is the grease in the gears.
Card games, boxing matches, seasonal work contracts, even the
dances up in town every other Saturday, Mang Benjie takes his
rightful cut of all that. When I got to Talcott, it was real clear
real soon that the safest spot to be was under his thumb.

Now my friend Alon, he never thought he needed that kind of
protection, no matter how far from home he got. Doesn't give me
a hard time about it, just doesn't go the same way. So while I'm
out here shaking down late-paying accounts and the like, Alon's
running up his own tab and making new friends. He's an easy
guy to love, Alon. Sun-faced and game. Strong, too, and spry,
which is why he's a regular up in the spare board boxing ring,
taking fewer falls than he doles out.

It'd been a decent canning season, all things told. Then
Benjie caught wind that some of Alon's new friends weren't
so hot on the working conditions. Well, I said, who is, am I
right? Elbow-deep in slop all day, and the day up here lasts far
into the night. Five dollars a day to do harder and worse work
than the white operators, and at the end of the night bedding
down in a bunkhouse half the size of theirs, with twice as many
people sleeping in it. And, come the end of the season, there's

the contractor cut taken out of your pay before it ever hits your hand. If it weren't for Benjie's card games, his dances, his boxing matches, it'd be enough to drive a guy running out into the wilderness. As soon as I said all that, Benjie had me. Fishhook from his throat to mine. Damn right, he said, and these twerps talking union, that's what they're all whining about. The cards, the fights, the girls from town. That can't be right, I said, but he says it's true, these fools were out to lose everyone their jobs and their pleasures at once.

"That's why I need you to make sure that when their boy steps in the boxing ring this Friday, he doesn't step out again," Benjie told me. He brushed a speck of something or other off the black flat of his jacket. "You know who I'm talking about. Your little friend, isn't he? Alonso."

THIS ASWANG FELIX doesn't know me from Adam, though, doesn't know why I'd give a shit, so I tell him it went like this: me and Alon came over from Manila together on the first boat after Holy Week, 1932. The journey was a long tunnel in the dark for me. I made one attempt to calm my guts by sneaking up top for fresh sea air and lost my footing and my breakfast—thankfully only the breakfast went overboard. After that, it was just the dim, heaving bunks in steerage. All the stink and noise of the hundred other guys crammed down there, sweating and coughing and spinning their plans for how many steps it'd be off the gangway into America before they struck it rich.

Alon, of course, took to the unseen sea like some Tagalog godling reborn. Close as it was in there, he must have made friends out of half the hold. He lost a fortune in peanut shells playing cards, and every couple rounds he'd swagger over to me where I had my back to the wall and eyes squeezed shut. I'd know he was there by his hand, heavy on my shoulder. *I got a guy over there from Antipolo, says there's a spot for me in California if I want it. Another two boys from that town north of home, Alfonso, inviting me to*

some place called Oregon. Before I could so much as wince, there's
his forehead pressed to mine, his hand squeezing my shoulder,
holding me inside my own skin. *But I told them: you see that big lug
in the corner, looks like he's dying? That's Lito. I gotta go where he goes.*

Agony, when he did something like that. If he knew what it
did to me, he'd never touch me again.

In any case, we were bound north, promised to it like a curse
cast by the photo in my jacket pocket. Three men in the picture:
my cousin Reynaldo, standing next to him Cesar, another young
guy his age from our town, and seated in front of them, legs idly
crossed and smile the only one in the room, a man I hadn't met
yet. Manong Benjie. They were dressed like Hollywood stars.
Naldo and Cesar in grey three-piece suits, Benjie in a black
number, all the collars starched, all the lines crisp, and their
hair slick and black as beetles. *Talcott Cannery, Alaska* was written
on the back, and their names. *Tell everyone that I am doing well.* It
arrived at his mother's house with $25 for her and his sisters, but
his mother had died the year before, and while I got the money
to the oldest, somehow I wound up keeping the picture. I never
thought of going to America myself until I saw that picture. It
wasn't the sight of my cousin, gone long years from my life and a
man now when I'd last seen him as a boy. It was the look on the
stranger Benjie's face, and the casual assurance in his posture. I
don't think I'd ever seen a man looking so unafraid.

When we got to Seattle, Alon's card game crew tramped
down the gangplank in a pack, the two of us part of it for the
time between the huddled camaraderie of steerage and the
dispersing winds of the world. At the foot of the port was a
vast space given over to indigent housing—a slum, ringing
with hungry voices. Alon took me by the elbow to head off,
fast-stepping along the shoreline, tripping on bricks and grass
and garbage, until we hit a paved road that cut a border to the
shanty town.

We hit the street a little rowdy with relief. To have arrived;
to have side-stepped that bewildering glimpse of destitution.
Here now were cars and brick buildings and arched doorways.
A carpet factory and a little bustle of Americans going about

their business, paying us no mind at all. Young men I'd only
ever seen through a veil of nausea now clapped me on the back
like old comrades. Alon's smile in the clear Seattle morning was
something primal and fantastic at once, solid as the shoulder of
a mountain. I found my land legs by walking in the shadow he
threw.

Our delegation forged into the city, shedding numbers as we
went. Pairs and trios and single men heading off to catch a ride
south or west to meet a cousin or an uncle to work a field of sugar
beets or grapes, or wheat, like in the postcards. We reached a
big, busy public square in the shape of a triangle and there were
just five of us left to gawk at the great white tower at one end,
the corniced hotels on each side, and the massive carved totem
pole smack in the middle of the place, the bold colors of its faces
thrust up above the black coats and black hats of the crowd.
Alon was fixing to stand and sightsee—I had to catch him by the
shirt cuff to keep up with the one guy we were with who claimed
to know where he was going. Uphill, our guy said, everywhere
in Seattle is uphill. He took us right underneath the tower and
on up to Japantown, the soles of our shoes slapping some of the
cleanest pavement I'd ever walked.

Now, in the drafty back end of the cannery's Filipino barracks,
Felix the aswang waves me off with a sinuous wrist and a soft
face, like he's doing me a kindness by shutting me up.

"Enough, enough. You don't want to say it, that's alright, but
you don't need to dance around it."

I know I've been dancing, but have the presence of mind to
say, "What do you know about what I wanna say?"

He's sitting on his cot with an ankle over a knee. Smiles.
"You're here about your Alon fella." And, well, shit, maybe he's
got those aswang powers after all. He sees the answer all over
my face. "It's not my specialty, if I'm honest. I've talked most
everyone out of it. Not really something I do. I can't change a
person's nature, is the trouble."

"But you can do *something*? Doesn't have to be forever, just Friday night, you can do that?"

A funny expression comes over Felix. "Got an evening all planned out, do you?"

"Yes or no?"

And now it really seems I've disappointed this aswang, with the way he's looking me over. "I'm just making sure you know what you're asking, Lito the goon. I can make the boy want you, but I can't make him love you."

It takes me a moment. His eyes flashing, his foot bobbing, the cigarette dipping from between his lips. The air seizes in my throat, makes a fist in there so solid I can't even speak a denial. The instinct for violence is almost overwhelming. I want to get him by the neck and rattle him until he can't see me anymore. I'm looming over him, got my teeth bared like a dog.

"You keep your trap shut." I say it low. Anyone could come in here. "Shut."

"Hey," he says. Both hands up, palms begging peace. But he's not even a little afraid of me, doesn't shut up for a second. "Hey, okay. My mistake. I thought I saw something in the way you talk about him. Looked familiar, you know?"

"You think I'd put him under some kind of curse, just to…? You're sick."

"Yeah, well. Folks come to me for all sorts of unsavory reasons. But like I said, I don't do that sort of thing."

Too late, I come up with a denial. "I'm here on Benjie's business."

"Of course you are," he says, placating, like I'm some kind of simpleton, or an animal. It works on me, but I hate to feel it working. He says, "So explain it to me. What kind of business you got for me from Mang Benjie?"

Up on Seattle's King Street we finally lost our last companions, who filed up a rattling metal staircase on the side of some dime store, saying they had a cousin waiting somewhere at the top to give them a floor to sleep on. Alon and me, shimmering in new-arrival shakes, drooped for the first time. One of the guys had said there was a hotel or two on the block, but we didn't know where, or if we could afford it with a crisp five dollars between us.

We were just two minutes walking along King Street, peck-stepping hesitant as chickens, when a voice called out from a diner doorway. "Hey, brother!" He was speaking Tagalog. "Brothers, where are you heading?" He fell in step between us, taller than either of us, looking well-fed and with sunlight glinting off his shoes, the toes of them round and sharp as horse's hooves.

"Who's asking?" I said, just as Alon slung the man a smile and said we were looking for a place to dry out from the journey.

"Hot damn, a couple boys right off the boat, is it?" English, now, but faster than I was used to hearing it. "And here I was crying into my coffee, missing the old Pearl of the Orient something awful. You two still smell of it!" He put his face right up to Alon's shoulder and took a solid whiff, then reeled back, some kinda comedian. "A-hah!" His teeth were long and yellowing, and he clenched a thin cigar between them.

Alon gave me a look, right over this fella's head, his old *who are you to say good things can't happen?* look. I gave him my *I'm the voice of experience, that's who* right back, but he wasn't looking at me anymore.

"I'm Alonso, this is Angelito. You know a place around here where we could spend a couple nights? Some place cheap?"

"Buddy, you are in some luck. Some real killer luck. See, I'm Teofilo, and this is my patch. I can set you up in every single way."

TEOFILO WAS AN OLDTIMER in America, although he wasn't more than thirty years old, if that. He said he'd been here since '26 and told us about spending seasons on the California pea fields, spending all his wages paying by the minute to dance with white women in the taxi dance halls, narrowly escaping half a dozen times from police incensed by the sight of a Filipino walking down the street, or white farmers by the sight of them in the fields; about the guys who weren't so lucky, lying in the gutter, about way the Chinese gambling dens and beachside by-the-hours leeched the life out of men through their wallets, every man he knew back in California drunk and hungry, more scared of being sober than of starving. Teofilo told us he got bored of the place, of the fights and the field. He left every acquaintance he'd made and rode the rails north.

It all sounded suspect to me. Had the ring of someone else's story. First, that so many men could be so desolate and debased, while Teofilo waltzed through untouched. And second, that he left by his own choice. There's a high-strung wariness to someone who's been driven out of a place by force. Alon might not have known the look, but I did, and it lived in the corners of Teofilo's eyes, pinched and blinking.

Teofilo put us on to a hotel with rooms at fifty cents a night, where we got to rotate on and off the couch and the floor and pay just thirty cents to the couple of guys who were splitting the bed. Because, Teofilo said, if they just came out even from the deal, then why let us sleep there at all, you get it? Yeah, I got it.

Any case, we weren't supposed to be there long. The plan was to take work in the city cleaning some place or hauling something, just long enough to earn the passage up to Juneau. Problem was, there were no jobs cleaning any place, or hauling anything. Alon could cook a little, and I knew numbers well enough to work in a shop, but nothing like that ever came up on the job boards. Teofilo brought us leads on one thing and then another, had us hiking all the hell over the city, uphill, downhill, up again, lost more than not, but by the time we got to the addresses he gave us, the job was gone, or had never been there. He apologized, or in any case he laughed about it with Alon while I stewed. We made a couple nights' rent beating rugs for a white family up the hill, but after that, things dried up, got hungry. We were looking at the street in a week, Alaska never.

One of those days, Teofilo came by our room in the morning

with a fishing pole, real proud of it too. Told me he'd take us down to the bay and catch everyone something to eat. Alon said well, he's checking out the hotels downtown, see if they need a pair of hands, and he touched my back briefly, ducked into my space to give me my own smile. It would be the first day we'd spent apart since arriving.

"I think I'll find a job today," he said, though he'd seen the *Strictly No Filipinos* signs at those hotels as clear as I had. "I feel it." Didn't know if I felt it, but the thought of fish for dinner got us both moving.

But Teofilo only had the fishing rod for an hour before he had to return it. Between the walk down to the pier, then the walk back to hand the rod off to his pal who worked scraps at the carpet factory, we had maybe fifteen minutes at the water. Tried for some squid, but they weren't taking. Then he took me to a diner near the pier and spotted me a ham sandwich and a coffee. Every bite was another debt to him, but I hadn't eaten since breakfast the day before. I'd be a different man if I could turn down a meal when I was hungry.

After warming the bench there for almost an hour, Teofilo said he wanted to show me this special perch of his, down near the shanty town. There was this wall-and-a-half left of a building that must have run out of cash before they got more built. We finger-and-toed it up to a little scrap of the third floor, the only bit that had a floor, with no ceiling above and an open window looking bayside. Not even sure how we got up there, being honest. It was like being up a tree, I thought.

And as soon as I thought it, I caught a shiver all over, and a glimpse of the shadows cutting black branches through this wreck, the far chatter of the bustle below like a field of insects. Caught a whiff of one of Teofilo's long, skinny cigars and saw him hanging one leg out the empty eye of the window, sly eyes watching hungry, hard-luck people shuffling beneath his feet. The sun went behind a cloud and even the shape of him there changed. His face long and equine, his shoulders prizefighter, and malice in his teeth. And his legs, knob-kneed, so long they bent higher than his head.

Then the cloud passed, and the sun came in, and he was talking. I'd missed the beginning, but it was about love songs sung by folks back home, and about Filipino bunkhouses burning in the night in California. He said, "It's a funny place, America. Not like it was advertised, is it? That's why I like a bit of company, or else I forget who I am." Then he looked right at me and told me that if I could keep him company for a bit, then he could get me and Alon up to Alaska no charge, no problem, and our pick of work at the cannery.

"Aren't I keeping you company now?" I asked. I wished I hadn't come there alone with him.

"Sure you are," Teofilo said. He came down from the window and joined me on the floor. Blew thick smoke between us. "But if you're gonna go, even for the season, won't I need something to remember you by?" He reached in his pocket, and I wondered what it was he saw in me, that I was sitting here instead of Alon.

Teofilo pulled out a slim knife with a dark horn handle. "A lock of hair," he said, like it was the most natural thing in the world. "To keep you with me."

I lost a little time there. Next I remember, I was in our room at the hotel, Alon was pulling at the ragged patch on the back of my head, and I was telling him maybe we didn't have to go away anywhere, maybe I had Teofilo all wrong. I had to laugh at the look on Alon's face. He was hungry again, no fish dinner, and frowning at me like a bullfrog—him dour now, me smiling.

"Something's wrong, Lito," he said. "Take off your shirt." I was feeling so giddy that it made sense that this would happen, too. Alon taking off his shirt and then helping me with mine. I was still laughing, dazzled, when he turned my shirt inside-out and put it back on over my head. "That better?"

The moment my collar hit my neck, the glimmer that had fallen over everything was gone. Here again was the dingy room, the other boarders sitting up in bed and smoking stubby cigarettes. The noise of twenty, thirty, fifty neighbors through the floors and the walls, every one of them trapped in the same maze. Alon, his thick brows drawn together, his shirt wrong-way-round like mine, the collar folded under, love and concern all over him, but no desire. And I thought I heard, from far across town, the high, wild bray of a beast that'd been cheated.

"Yeah," I said. "I guess that's better."

"Good." He wilted with relief. "Something my grandmother taught me. Now, come on."

We were gone that night. Snuck into the hold of a cattle boat headed north and bedded down under the cows. Stayed awake for fear of them stepping on us. We could've ridden it all the way to Juneau if the smell hadn't made me sick, and if I hadn't started up hacking. They put us off in Ketchican. And there, seeming like the first bit of real luck, was a cannery contractor standing right on the pier, looking for a last few fellas to sign on. The salmon canning season started the very next day.

"A LON isn't like me," I'm telling Felix. "He's nobody's goon, and I owe him my life." It's not my greatest debt to Alon, or my first, but it's one I figure an aswang will appreciate.

"And now Manong Benjie wants Alon's life." Felix says. But he says it, doesn't ask.

"You already knew?"

"Benjie came to me too, yesterday," he admits, and he's got the nerve to look all bashful. "About your Alon."

Across the bunk room, the door rattles open and a crowd begins to shuffle through—men from the shift I'm missing to have this conversation. I take him by the elbow and tug him onto his feet, then out the back door. Rougher than I should be, but casual as I know how. Haul him around to the passage between the bunkhouse and the wood shed. Out one end: a strip of sun-hot dirt and scrub, then the tree line. Out the other: the boardwalk, the shore, the bright bulk of the canning building. The long summer sun barely touches this dim little alley, so it's cold and the fish gut smell that's everywhere sits higher in the nose and the mouth. Good a place as any to get a little loud.

I push Felix up against the wall, my arm up against his throat, his heels lifting off the ground. He's light as a bird, hot as a coal. "What did you do?"

"For Benjie?" Felix chokes out. "Thought his business was yours."

"Stop screwing around. You do something to Alon? You put a hex on him?" Felix wiggles, and I back off all at once. Usually that move leaves someone to slump down all undignified, but he lands cool as a cat. It's clear now, in the light and up close, why folks pegged him for an aswang on sight. He's something not shaped like a predator, but that moves like one.

"A hex. You know what a hex is?" The corner of his mouth goes up and he shows a sharp little tooth.

"Answer the question. You do something to him, yes or no?"

"To Alon? No," he says. Now I'm the one slumping. "I don't follow Benjie's orders. Guess that's you and me both, huh?"

He talks like stepping out on my boss is something I should take pride in. Between disloyalty to a two-bit gangster and solidarity with an aswang fairy, I'm not sure which I'm supposed to be more ashamed of. But shame isn't what turns my head on a swivel to make sure nobody sees us together. It's just fear. Fear, same as always.

"He came to you after talking to me," I say. "What is that, did he know I wouldn't go for it? How'd he know?"

"My guess? He probably took one look at you. Not exactly a poker face." I round on him and he's already got his hands up. "Not always a bad thing! Means your face wants you honest." Which should sound like a compliment, almost, but it hits like a curse. Softer this time, like he's in my head, he asks, "Do you know why they say what they say about me? Do you know what a hex is?"

"I've got bigger fish to fry than your aswang shit right now, pal."

Yesterday, he'd said. Benjie came asking him to take out Alon just yesterday. The day after giving me the same order. He could be cooking up a plan C, thinking Felix turned him down and I went chicken liver. He could think I'll still come through. He could be working another angle right now, all I know, the boys back in the bunk could be tying the rope for all our necks: me, Alon, probably Felix too. Benjie's been good to me, because I've been good for him, because that's how the world goes around. World stops going round when you say no to guys like Mang Benjie.

"It's just power," Felix says.

"You don't say."

"A hex, it's just power that everyone else says you shouldn't be allowed to have."

I hear him, but I don't. I'm thinking that the boats come in with the catch twice a day, mid-morning and dusk, so they're out on the water now and I don't know another way off the island without getting to town, nine or ten miles away. There's three vehicles at the cannery: the manager's car, the little truck the cook and the caretaker share, and the bigger truck for getting packed boxes of cans to the dock in town. Cook's truck is my best bet, even though it coughs up a racket, but I gotta figure out where Alon is before I go for the truck. I'm running through this, counting the cash I got on hand, and Felix is still talking.

"Folks get real twitchy when us, who they say should be weak, got the power instead of them," he's saying. "It's why Benjie and them don't like all that union talk."

I get this flash of Alon and me, sixteen years old back in Batangas. We're crouching in the sugarcane outside the hacienda, watching the overseer and the harvest checkers line up with what looked like a private army to meet the peasants of the tenant union who were marching up the road. The shine on the soldiers' bayonets, and the dust rising from the peasants' feet. We watched it play out, hungry from the lost wages, and the next day I came back alone and worked the field with the strikebreakers. I tell Felix, "If unions could cast hexes, then I never would've had to come to America."

Felix grins. "And if the unionists had asked me to join up, then they wouldn't have a little problem like Benjie breathing down their neck."

He does scare me, this guy. He's slippery, and too clever, and he knows too much. But I got this thing about men who can smile like you're in on a secret together. So, like the bonehead I am, I'm opening my yap to invite him to come along when we make a run for it in the stolen truck when the bunkhouse backdoor bangs open beside us and Alon walks out, right on cue. He takes me by the arm. Looks over at Felix, real easy.

"Hey! Felix, right?" Which gets a nod. "The guys said you were out here. You want to help me practice my left hook?" After a long silence, Alon asks, with saintly grace, if he's interrupting something. I say no and give him a hard knock with my shoulder. Felix looks just delighted.

"We were talking about you," Felix says, taking him outta my good graces again.

"About me?" And see, he's smarter than he looks, Alon. Smarter than I am, and I look like the smart one. He licks his lips and checks the corners with his eyes. "What about me?"

"Lito here was worried about some heat you're due to take on account of those pals of yours."

"You don't have to...I mean, I know the organizing stuff, it's not for you. But if I get in trouble, you've got a gun, right?" Alon says to me. Gestures at Felix. "This is a little extreme."

"I'll take that as a compliment," says Felix. "Anyhow, you can't blame him for trying something. Slipping through a trap sideways is the only way he's ever known, sounds like."

"You don't know shit," I say.

"Like I said," Felix says, "That look on you, when you're spilling your guts, it looks familiar." And now I got the two of them looking at me, Alon a little soft and confused, Felix with the whole world up his sleeve. They're a spotlight and I'm some shabby little gangster who smells like day-old fish. "I'm getting tired of it, though," Felix says. I'm not sure what he means. He flips both hands in an arc, elegant, encompassing us, the cannery, the island, all the alaskeros, all of America.

"Everyone's tired, Felix," says Alon with a little smile. It's that thing we say as a joke, but isn't.

"That's it exactly. So tell me, Lito the goon and Alon his honest friend: how would you like to learn how to pack something stronger than a punch?"

It's too much. I rub my fists in my eyes and laugh. "How's that? Huh? You gonna snap necks until they pay out an extra fifty cents a day? How's that gonna work?" In another world, I could almost see it. Felix with cash raining from his hands, and we'd sleep in the white men's bunkhouse while they slept in ours. Would that do the trick? I'm feeling so queer all over, in my guts and in my head. I know there's something I can't imagine past, a solid wall beyond which I'm not allowed to picture myself.

A hand peels one of mine off my face. Slim fingers, a hot palm. Felix holds my hand in both of his. He waits until I'm looking him in the eye. "I'm thinking we slip outta this sideways," he says.

Then the heat in his hands is passing into mine. Like a light, like a syrup, like wind through sugarcane. Up inside my bones, down into my stomach, seeping into my feet, feeling like it's bursting out the top of my head.

"What in the…" Alon says, and I see it must be happening to him, too. He's looking at his own hands like he's seeing double, looking at me like he can see himself upside-down in my eyes.

From inside the bunkhouse comes the biggest clamor. Shouting, whistling, stomping, and then they're out here, a whole crowd of careworn fish canners, spinning out of the shadowy alley and into the light. Even Mang Benjie appears, taking off his hat like we're going to Mass, and as he brushes right by us there's a wave of fellow-feeling that passes through him and me and Alon and Felix, like the wakes of two boats meeting and merging and making a new trough in the sea.

Felix takes me by the arm to keep me on my feet, tugs me, and Alon after me, out with the crowd who are looking at themselves and each other like they'd never seen a Filipino before. I feel like I can finally split clean off from the part of myself that's been caught in a trap. Leave it behind and cast off into the sky. I look at Alon and see it on his face too—the relief, the loosing of the chain we'd forgotten was there. He's stretching, rising, breaking free of himself. It feels like we've got the kinda power that everybody was saying, this whole damn time, we shouldn't be allowed to have. In a moment we'll be high above this place, looking down at our discarded feet, our aching knees, the empty cups of our hips. That was us, skinny and stripped like a field after harvest. And now us, leaping up, miraculous.

THE TRAPPINGS OF ROUTINE

HANNA A. NIRAV

THERE IS POWER in routine.

Not much—not the kind that can move mountains or split the sea—but for Nadia, enough to get herself through the average day. In the mornings, she climbs out of bed and goes straight for the windows. She pushes every alternate window open, which gives her enough strength to make breakfast. Afterwards, washing the cups first (then utensils, then plates) gives her enough energy to tend to her garden. Outside, she waters her flowers row by row, starting from the front door and working clockwise towards the fences and back again. That done right, she'll have enough power to walk down the river to get some fishing done. Every action to fuel the next, a ritual framed by routine. Never too much, never too little.

Which is why, when a loud, unfamiliar scream pierces the soothing trickle of river water, Nadia is half-tempted to ignore it entirely. Whatever it is, she simply doesn't have the extra energy for it.

But the scream is followed by an even louder and extremely familiar shriek, chasing the tail of the first. So Nadia sighs, trades her fishing rod for her cane, and begins the long trek towards the source of the noise.

What she finds is this: a stranger struggling in the unyielding grip of a pontianak. She is not tall, shorter than Nadia even, and her face is sharp, a composition of angles framing the irritation twisted into her mouth. At her approach, the woman snaps her gaze to Nadia, eyes dark and fierce.

It is enough to arrest Nadia mid-step, a jolt going up the length of her spine.

"Nadia, Nadia," the pontianak croons, entirely unaffected. "Look what I found."

That helps somewhat; Nadia exhales heavily, forcing her body to relax. "What happened, Seroja?"

Seroja presses her face to the woman's cheek, as intimate as a lover. "This little minx thought she could sneak right past me. And when that didn't work, she tried to bewitch me. Me!" She throws her head back in a laugh, and the sound of it rings in the air like a bell. "Didn't anyone teach you any manners?"

"I didn't realise those banana trees were yours!" the woman says.

Seroja cackles from both mouths, the sharp teeth serrated across the back of her neck glinting in the afternoon sun. "Who *else* would they belong to? I should eat you for the impertinence."

"Do *not* eat her," Nadia says quickly. Explaining paranormal murder to the police is an exceptionally unpleasant experience, and not one she's keen to repeat.

At this, the woman's eyes narrow. "Miss Nadia?"

Nadia frowns. "And you are?"

The woman breaks into a wide smile, the expression lighting up her entire face so quickly and abruptly it takes Nadia's breath away. She clasps both hands together, as if no longer bothered by the fact that she's still suspended three feet above ground by a vengeful pontianak. "My name is Kasih," she says. "I'm here as a representative of the PJ/KV Alliance, and we need your help."

Nadia stares at her. "Who?"

Kasih pauses, her expression going hesitant. "The PJ/KV

Alliance? We were formed in July four years ago?" At Nadia's continued puzzled silence, she adds, "We won the election?"

"I don't care who you are," Seroja hisses, giving Kasih a rough shake. "What are you doing on my property?"

"And how did you get past my wards?" Nadia adds.

Kasih raises her eyes to meet Nadia's gaze. "I'm a witch," she says, and the words come out as naturally as the rising sun at dawn. "Like you."

"**W**AIT!"

Nadia doesn't want to wait. She is simultaneously furious and exhausted. The walk back to her hut is too long, the safety of her home too far, and already her right knee is burning. She wishes she could walk faster; she wishes she never got out of bed this morning.

"Nadia, please!" Kasih is saying. "Let me explain!"

"I will not," Nadia says, and the anger singes her tongue. She trudges up the front steps and fumbles with the front door. "You need to leave."

"Please," Kasih says at her side. "It's important."

"What's important is that you outed me to my family, if there's any left who don't suspect as much already. What's important is that you harassed my friends, if I still had any left, and put them in danger."

"You don't understand," Kasih says. "It's not that way anymore. We've been working hard to change things, and the law—"

"And on top of all that," Nadia continues—as if anyone could possibly be so naive as to believe decades' worth of prejudice could be changed overnight, "you've barged into my home, uninvited and unwelcome. Even though I've told you repeatedly to leave."

Kasih flinches, but doesn't stop. "Look. I know who you are. I know what you can do. There are still people in the community who remember you. They said you draw energy from the mundane—"

"So *what?*" Nadia cuts in. "That gives you the right to show up unannounced? To put other people in danger? Who do you think you *are?*"

That finally sends Kasih reeling back, her dark eyes wide in shock, the remainder of her sentence dying silent in her open mouth.

Nadia is breathing hard, her chest hot and heaving, her cane slippery in her grip. "You politicians are all the same. What does it matter who gets hurt in the process, as long as you get what you want?"

Suddenly, the sight of Kasih is unbearable. Nadia turns away and returns to fumbling with the front door. It takes her a few more furious, frustrated tries before she finally manages to get it open. Nadia pushes the door back hard enough that it slams into the wall, and steps inside.

Just as she's about to shut the door behind her, she hears Kasih say, "I'm sorry."

Nadia hesitates, even though she knows she shouldn't. She has every right to slam the door in Kasih's face, to walk away and not look back, just like she did all those years ago.

But Kasih doesn't give her the chance to change her mind. "You're right," Kasih says. "What I did was...horrible. I thought it wouldn't matter, given how much better things are now. But of course it's different for different people. I should have been more considerate."

Nadia turns around to find Kasih standing at her doorstep, hands folded neatly in front of her. Her face is a perfect portrait of sincere apology: the crease of her eyebrows ashamed, a red flush dusting across her dark cheeks—not that it means much, coming from a politician.

"We did send you a few letters," Kasih says, "but they always got returned and I thought—well. Never mind. I should have known better."

Nadia stares at her.

A beat passes, and then Kasih says, "For what it's worth, your family didn't—"

"*No.*"

Kasih snaps her mouth shut.

After a few deep, calming breaths, Nadia says, "I don't want to know. I don't *care.*"

"Alright," Kasih says, nodding.

Suddenly, Nadia's knee gives out. She stumbles, loses her balance, and is only saved from crashing into the floor by Kasih's arms around her. Her grip is steady, shouldering Nadia's weight with surprising ease until she is able to right herself once more.

They blink at each other for a brief, tense moment, before Kasih withdraws, crossing her arms across her chest.

Nadia sighs. "I want to sit down, so I guess you might as well come in."

She trudges into the kitchen, not bothering to see if Kasih will follow. Her knee is screaming for rest but she desperately wants a hot cup of tea to sit down with.

So Nadia seeks solace in the familiarity of the routine, letting her body take over the motions as her mind steals a moment to breathe. The soothing smell of chamomile seeps into the air, and Nadia allows herself to be calmed by it.

She pours a cup for Kasih, who has found her way to her dining table, then another for herself. And then, because decades of isolation does not mean she's forgotten how to be a host, she grudgingly offers the last of the cinnamon biscuits she baked a few days ago.

Kasih thanks her and sips the tea. Nadia watches the crease of her eyebrows smooth, listens to the soft sigh Kasih makes as she sets her cup down. Kasih's dark eyes flick up, and their gazes meet.

Nadia leans back in her seat. "So?"

"Right." Kasih clears her throat and begins. Nadia rushes her through the introduction of herself and the organisation she represents. She only really starts paying attention when Kasih says, "—and to help strengthen these new bonds between the two communities, we've been looking into the many ways we can introduce the benefits of magic to non-witches."

Nadia crosses her arms. "Let me guess. It's not working."

Kasih's lips thin. "Unfortunately, the exact details are strictly confidential. I can only continue my explanation if you agree to a vow of silence until the matter is resolved."

Her suspicions skyrocket. "That's not very reassuring."

"It's just standard procedure," Kasih insists, "and the vow is instantly void if someone gets hurt because of it, including yourself."

Nadia frowns, but the terms seem harmless enough. "Fine," she says. "I agree."

"Thank you," Kasih replies, sealing the vow.

The air between them shimmers with the new promise, little pinpricks of light blinking to life before fading away.

"One such project," Kasih continues, "is a ritual designed to allow non-witches the ability to convert routine magic into electricity. We've been working on it for nearly three months now, but things started going south about a week ago. The magic isn't yielding any output, and the staff I had working on it are trapped inside it."

She pauses, as if expecting questions, but Nadia merely gestures for her to continue.

"I've consulted other witches on this matter, but none of them have been able to help me. The yield in routine magic is generally not rewarding enough for most to have much practice with them." Kasih tilts her palm towards Nadia in an abruptly respectful gesture. "You're the closest I've been able to find to an expert. I was hoping you'd be able to help."

"And you'll be paying me for my efforts?" Nadia asks, because she's not an idiot.

"Absolutely. Just name your price."

Nadia throws her a figure, double her normal rates from the years she was still active in the community, and watches Kasih resolutely refuse to react.

"Seems reasonable enough," Kasih says. "I'll have the money

transferred to you as soon as this business is concluded."

"And I suppose it's urgent enough that I'll have to go with you right this minute."

Kasih gives her an apologetic smile that would ring sincere if not for her adding, "I have a car waiting for us, so we can leave as soon as you're ready."

"Of course you do." Nadia sighs and rises to clear the table.

T HE TRIP into the city takes nearly four hours. Nadia spends the entirety of it sleeping, partly to conserve energy. With the remainder of her day's routines interrupted, Nadia has to be careful not to overexert herself.

In her sleep, an old dream finds its way back to her: she runs along darkened hallways, past locked doors and chained closets. Her every step is shadowed by malicious whispers, the weight of a thousand eyes judging her every move. No matter how fast she runs, there is no escape.

When she finally collapses, the darkness eats her alive.

"Nadia!"

She jolts awake, heart pounding. Kasih's hand is on her shoulder, although she withdraws it as Nadia jerks away. Nadia blinks rapidly at her, the remnants of her dream fading.

Kasih gives her another hesitant look, before she tucks that expression away in favour of an amiable smile. "We're here."

Nadia looks to the window. The world outside the car is bright and hot, and she has to squint against it. She vaguely recognises the area, although none of the shops she remembers are still around. Even the trees look different, younger, and lusher. Regret churns in her stomach, flavoured by resentment.

But she is here now, and it's too late to turn back. So she steels her nerves and gets out of the car.

The building itself is nothing special, just another towering skyscraper among a thousand, but about a quarter of the way up, a thin, grey haze surrounds the building. It's massive enough that Nadia can feel hints of it all the way from the ground where she's standing, the nauseating stench of magic gone wrong.

"It's worse the closer we get," Kasih says.

"Wonderful," Nadia replies and follows Kasih in.

The crowd inside is bustling with activity. Nadia hasn't seen this many people in decades, not since she first cut herself off and went to live in her safe little hut. She had forgotten how much noise people make, and she feels her remaining energy draining fast.

Thankfully, Kasih doesn't linger. She leads Nadia straight through reception and into the next available elevator. They travel twenty-four floors up and through a series of hallways and doors, all of which look exactly alike. The people they pass become a blur of faces; Nadia keeps her attention on the cut of Kasih's slim shoulders, her only anchor in the unfamiliar chaos.

At last, they stop before a door no different than the rest, save that Nadia knows whatever problem she has been solicited to solve is waiting beyond it. The pungent scent of magic gone stale nearly makes her gag.

"Brace yourself," Kasih says.

Nadia swallows and adjusts her grip on her cane.

As Kasih pushes the door open, the smell crashes into Nadia like a tsunami. It drags across her skin, heavy and malicious. Every breath she takes drowns her further in nausea, pulling tears from her eyes.

Nadia fights against it, drags her gaze around the room. It is a wide, open space, without a single furniture in sight. A massive ritual covers the entirety of the room, webs of it spanning from ceiling to floor and across the four corners. The lighting in the room is murky, as if a filament of grime had been dragged across her vision, and even the atmosphere is heavy, a depressing weight draping itself across her shoulders.

Belatedly, Nadia realises there are people present as well—if they qualify as people anymore. They have a blank quality to their gaze and they walk in circles, every motion listless and empty. Nadia watches the woman closest to her finish a set of circles, drop to a crouch and then rise to begin again; around her, the threads of the ritual glow menacingly, before fading.

Nadia sucks in a breath, then another, before she manages to speak. "You said it's been a week?"

"Yes," Kasih says, sounding as ill as Nadia feels, "but the situation is deteriorating fast. Two days ago they were still responding when spoken to. The day before that, they could be coaxed to leave the room, even if they always wandered back in. Now they won't speak, won't eat, won't sleep."

Nadia drags a palm over her eyes, tries to steady herself amidst the waves of nausea. She studies the threads of the ritual, the scattered knots across its web. "It seems like the ritual has trapped these people inside it, but it's not letting go of the magic either. Everything's stuck together."

"Well, yes, we suspected as much," Kasih says. "What we don't know is how to *fix* it."

"You can't." Nadia is made breathless again by the truth of it. "A routine gone bad is a routine you need to break. Your only option is to destroy it."

"Absolutely not!" When Nadia turns to her, the woman has crossed the space between them to grasp her arm.

The touch of her skin is hot, a sudden, searing pain that cuts through the waves of nausea. Nadia tries to pull away, but then Kasih catches her gaze, and Nadia's whole body lights up for it.

"We have invested far too much in this—too much time, energy, resources. Surely there's another way," Kasih pleads.

Nadia stares at her—at her fever-bright eyes and the soft, desperate curve of her mouth. Even caught in the web of souring magic, Kasih's skin glows, fresh as morning dew.

It makes the sickly pallor of the trapped staff, turned witless by the soured ritual only a few feet away, all the more devastating.

"These people are going to die," Nadia says, as firmly as she can manage. "There's no charming your way out of this. You need to decide which is more important to you: the unrealised profit of a ritual you might not even be able to save, or the lives of the community you say you represent."

Kasih's lips part in a silent gasp, and just like that the heat of the charm fades. Still, Nadia doesn't pull away, merely stares her down, waiting for an answer.

Finally, after what feels like an eternity, Kasih nods and lets her go.

Nadia turns around and marches straight towards the center of the ritual. Every step she takes makes her next twice as heavy, but she keeps moving forward. Every instinct in her body screams for her to turn the other way, but she keeps going, until she's standing in the heart of the web. Nadia discards her cane, hears it clatter to the floor as she places her hands on the webbing, takes a deep breath, and *pulls.*

What happens next seems to take an eternity, if eternity could be a single second stretched to its absolute elastic limit. The fragments of time slow, and Nadia has the dubious pleasure of feeling bile slowly crawl up her throat. The room dims further, and all sounds cease.

The magic of the ritual drags her body down to the floor at different speeds, her skin bowing to gravity faster than her bones, her spine threatening to split her back wide open. Abruptly, her body explodes in pain.

Nadia crashes to her knees, shaking, but she doesn't let go of the web. Behind her, she sees Kasih collapsed several feet away, the rest of the staff motionless on the ground.

She turns back to the ritual. It convulses before her, a mass of trapped, toxic magic coalescing into a furious, screaming curse. The threads of its web are thick, sticky, and it wraps itself desperately around her, pulling her in.

And Nadia—Nadia is tired. This place is so loud, so heavy, so demanding. She thinks longingly of being back home, tucked into a couch with a book, the scent of chamomile tea lingering in the quiet air. She thinks of how far away her safe haven is and how impossible it feels to ever get back there.

It would be so much easier to just give in, she thinks. She is *so* tired.

But for Nadia, this feeling of hopelessness and the lethargy that accompanies it is as familiar as an old friend. Yes, it *would* be easy.

So, with all the remaining energy she has left, Nadia adjusts her grip and rips the web apart.

The ritual breaks. All the rotting, toxic magic it held bursts out all at once, sweeping across the room as something brighter, cleaner. Nadia marvels at the gentle warmth that seeps into her skin. It's like drinking in a week's worth of routines all at once; she feels so light she could laugh.

Around the room, people begin stirring as they come back to themselves. And then her gaze falls on Kasih, who is on her knees, staring straight at where the heart of the ritual used to be.

"It won't be easy to explain," Kasih is saying, pacing the length of the room. She drew Nadia into the first empty room they came across, before locking the door behind them. "We've invested considerably into that ritual. There will be a lot of questions, not for you," Kasih adds to her, "don't worry. I will handle it."

Nadia politely refrains from saying that she isn't worried in the slightest. "You did the right thing, you know."

Kasih sighs. "I know. That doesn't mean it'll be any easier for the others to swallow." She shakes her head, refocuses her gaze on Nadia. "Now, about your payment."

That surprises her. "You're still paying me?"

Kasih arches an eyebrow at her. "You did solve the problem, didn't you?"

"Well. Yes, but...yes."

"I'll have the money transferred by the end of tomorrow, latest." Kasih slides a business card out of her wallet and passes it to Nadia. "Sorry, I should have given this to you earlier. If you run into any trouble with the bank, contact me on this number. I'll sort it out."

Nadia stares at the text printed on the card, weighing her options. Her blood is still humming, her mind and body lighter than they've been in years. "I suppose I should be heading home then—" she says.

"Of course. Let me get you a Grab."

"—but I'd be happy to help you put together another ritual. Not quite like this," Nadia says, forcing her voice to remain steady, even as her heart begins to pound. "I'm sure no one wants to deal with this mess again."

Kasih blinks at her, the corners of her mouth curling upwards. "It *would* be immensely helpful to have an experienced witch leading the project, both to the community and to me. A lot of people would appreciate it, including the non-witches."

"I doubt things have changed that much," Nadia says, drily. "But we'll see."

Kasih's gaze becomes thoughtful. "That means we'll have to discuss your contract. There will be the matter of payment, the expected length of the project, your transportation—"

"Absolutely," Nadia interrupts, before Kasih can get too far along, "but I am *exhausted*. Would you be able to come down to my hut again sometime this week? We can discuss it then."

Kasih is smiling openly now, her eyes bright and pleased. "That depends. Will you ask your pontianak friend to let me through?"

"Seroja will do as she pleases," Nadia says firmly, "but I do think she'll be a little friendlier if you bring her a gift next time. Maybe a new cucuk sanggul...?"

"Now there's an idea..." Kasih's grin is as sharp and lovely as the rest of her. "Perhaps this Saturday, then?"

"Sounds good." Nadia finds herself grinning back. "See you then."

THE COVEN OF TAOS-9

R J THEODORE

STATION ADMINISTRATOR Howland watched me disembark with the other shuttle passengers. He held an archaic metal pocket watch gleaming in one hand in the most are-you-kidding-me gesture of impatience. No question why. I could imagine the pressure he was under. There were so many ships at TAOS-9 that they'd run out of transient berths and had resorted to off-ring moorings.

That's why I was here. To get commerce moving again.

He twitched his pencil-line mustache, took me by the elbow, and gestured for someone else to take my bags. "Finally. You're late."

Well, there went my sympathy, straight out an airlock. I escaped his grip, which was as oily as his aura, but let him lead me toward the station's center structure, where the smells of grease, ozone, and freezer burn gave way to those of musty carpet and overheated computer processors.

I had read the dossier a few times on the way there, so I recognized the rest of my coven by name even as he made hurried introductions. Adele, red-haired and splattered with a bounty of freckles, as absent of smiles as her holograph. Georgie, their hair buzzed short on the sides and violently pink on top, their station uniform bedecked in pastel patches of the latest transgalactic memes. Sam, slender and tall, his uniform open to the waist as if he were a sprout that had burst from it.

"Lotti," Georgie said, shaking my hand in a way that was entirely unlike how the administrator had taken my elbow. "Welcome to Coven TAOS-9."

Adele *hmmphed*. "We'll see."

Sam offered me a smile that managed to be shy and apologetic and mischievous all at once. "I decorated your quarters for you. Hope you like it," he signed.

These would be my sisters.

"How soon can you have the wormhole open?" Station Administrator Howland asked, missing every nuance of the situation. I had a sense this was his standard operating procedure.

"Leave us so we can figure that out, Howland." Adele's icy stare was no less intense on him than it had been on me. Which wouldn't change until I could distance myself from association with him.

Howland's face contorted in an unleveled protest. He was easy to read. He wanted to stand here and pressure us to get his gate open again, but if we needed privacy to get ourselves aligned as a coven, what could he do?

"One hour. I expect you in the circle in *one. hour.*"

Adele cranked up the freezer burn. "Then you'd better leave ten minutes ago."

The door slid closed behind him, and the air went electric. The four of us looked at each other (by which I mean I looked at them, and they all stared at me) as prickles started on my outer arms.

"I'm sorry for your loss," I said. To break the tension. And because it was true.

It broke something. Adele spun on her heel. "Get out of those civvies and into your uniform. We have work to do." An interior door closed on her final word.

Georgie lowered their chin. "She needs some time. She and

Kelly were together."

Kelly, the witch whose death made way for me. "I'm not here to try to replace her."

But that's exactly what I was. Howland had sent for a replacement as soon as Kelly had taken ill. That wouldn't help matters with Adele. Knowing I'd been hired and already on my way before Kelly had breathed her last.

But the economy.

The ley lines outside TAOS-9 converged in an incredible knot of energy. The kind that could open wormholes to feed transports and passengers to all corners of the charted galaxy. Traffic was at a standstill, waiting for me to show up and get commerce moving again. Like a ley line plumber, as far as Howland was concerned.

But to my new coven, I was a reminder of what they'd lost. If I was going to stay, I needed to connect with them.

M Y QUARTERS were in one of four berths in the coven's section, within easy reach of the circle. They had been Kelly's before. The small room smelled like new carpet and acrid re-programmed bulkheads, like sage smoke and myrrh.

Over a narrow bed were four glass frames capturing pressed herbs and flower buds—lavender, rosemary, aster, and geranium. Sam was our coven's herbalist, and this was his silent welcome to me: peace, protection, balance, and beginnings.

It took me minutes to change into one of the station uniforms waiting for me. I stared at my luggage for a moment, then shoved it into the closet to deal with later. If Adele didn't want me there, I saw little point in staying. It would be annoying to re-pack. Would be good drama if I wanted to make a stink about it. But I really wasn't here to rub salt on anyone's wounds.

I stepped out and ran straight into Adele, her hand raised to tap my door chime.

"Sorry for the wait." I took a breath. "Hey. Um, I want you to know, I'm here for the coven. I don't work for Howland."

Her expression hardened, and she shook her head. "That's where you're wrong, Lotti. We all work for Howland."

I could see Georgie and Sam watching from down the corridor.

"He thumbprints the payroll," I said. "But he can't do anything without a coven."

That earned me a long silent stare. "Yeah, well, maybe it should be another coven. Kelly and I were going to find another station. One without a Howland. Maybe I still will."

Over her shoulder, I caught the anxious look passed between Georgie and Sam.

I refused to be the wedge that drove this coven apart. "Or maybe I'm not as bad as you're expecting."

Adele's freckled lips pulled to one side. "Only one way to find out. Time for a test drive."

"Let's do it."

She turned away, and I followed her down the corridor. Georgie and Sam fell in behind us. Their silence was so full of expectation, the two of them might as well have been hopping up and down.

The corridor delivered us to the center of operations. The far bulkhead was a glass expanse overlooking a vertigo-inducing starfield, that pin-pricked velvet blackness unbroken by planets or satellites.

I would have rushed to take in that view, except for two things. First was the coven's circle. Centered in this atrium, the raised glowing platform waited for us beneath a matched glowing overhead. A ring of workstations formed a perimeter where the technicians could monitor our invocation.

Second was the sight of Station Administrator Howland waiting for us, thumb tracing the edge of that pocket watch as if it were its own token of summoning.

Adele's shoulders inched up her neck when her gaze landed on it. "Put that damned thing away, Howland. We're here."

"Do you know how many ships are behind schedule since your previous fourth died?"

"Well then, it's a good thing you didn't waste any time hiring her replacement, isn't it?"

I didn't have to know Howland any better than I did to see that he didn't miss the accusation. Men like him just didn't care.

"It certainly is." He snapped the watch closed and tucked it away. He held out his other hand, gesturing toward the circle as gallantly as if he was inviting us into a gilded carriage. "We have ships waiting, ladies."

Sam and Georgie didn't move an inch. I was still standing behind Adele, but I could sense the violent urges in her aura. "The ships can keep waiting. We need a test run."

"Test run?" Howland's ugly mustache twitched. "We haven't got time for th—"

Adele's hand sliced the air, silencing his protest as if she'd expelled all the oxygen from the room. "For a ship to get lost if we have adjustments to work through? I agree."

She nodded sideways, and Georgie and Sam stepped up to the circle. I edged carefully around the space where Adele and Administrator Howland were trying to set each other on fire with just their eyes.

He blustered, his lips making that mustache wriggle in indignation, but did not attempt to breach the space. He couldn't. It was calibrated and sacred and only for our use. He held an open hand toward the ring of workstations. "That's what all this equipment is for. I just need you ladies to do your mojo thing and get the hole open."

The technicians at their monitors ducked their heads and tried very hard to disappear.

Georgie smirked, and Sam tossed his head in a silent laugh. I seized on the opportunity to declare my allegiance.

"If you don't know what we *do*, let alone what your fancy equipment does, you don't belong in this space."

Howland almost needed a prybar to get his jaw unclenched. "You get that wormhole open. If our equipment says it's stable, we're sending ships through. If not, you'll try again until it is."

Adele's aura could have birthed stars. "You got union witches, Howland. An hour on, twelve off."

His mustache very nearly crawled off his lip. But he didn't

argue. He retrieved his watch from his pocket and took a step back, crossing his arms and staring daggers at us.

His aura was deliciously defeated.

We'd all taken our places, and now Adele stepped into hers. Taking up the items from her cabinet, she caught my eye and gave me the smallest nod of approval. Relief washed over me like water, an ocean lapping at my legs and feet, tugging me toward her.

The moment passed, leaving me unsure it ever happened.

The coven's circle is the same no matter what station you go to. I tapped my heel in the familiar spot, and a cabinet rose up before me, made of the same opaque glowing white glass as the floor of the circle. It contained our offerings and our talismans. My sisters had theirs in hand already. I placed my red candle atop the cabinet, took a silk-wrapped bundle, and finally opened the wire crate within and retrieved a white ferret.

I don't know why it's always ferrets, but the incantation demanded a trade, and the Guardians of Dimension required life in exchange for passage through their domain. I used to name the poor little things, but I gave that up before I graduated from my training. It curled against my chest for warmth. I knew the right way to hold it without scaring it.

The four of us exchanged looks and nodded.

Georgie first.

They lit a blue candle and set it, along with a silver chalice inlaid with small round mirrors, atop their cabinet. "Guardians and Spirits of Water and Energy, cleanse me. Carry me through, protect this circle, and hear my vow."

The top of the cabinet separated from its base and circled, three times deasil around our chamber. The shelf seemed to move on its own, though I knew it was being controlled by a technician. I smelled the burn of the wick and the sting of the smoke. It moved to the center and stilled.

"Guardians and Watchtowers of Time and Earth, I call to thee." Adele's voice rang clear and strong, picked up by the chamber and amplified. "Ground my work, protect this circle, and make it be."

She lit her green candle and offered fresh and dried sprigs of rosemary laid in ash across a shallow limestone bowl. When it passed me, the scent of the herbs felt like a balm.

Sam bowed his head to make his silent call. He lit a yellow candle and placed feathers bundled around a citrine wand beside it.

My turn. I lit my candle and placed the silk-wrapped gold bangle beside it. "I call on the beings of Dimension and Fire. Charge my words, protect this circle, and burn my fear."

With the words came a crawling pressure in my bones.

The granular whisper of salt filled the circle, cascading in a sheet around the edges of the chamber. Surrounding us. I smelled sage and mint smoke. I knew the fresh herbs came from Sam's garden, same as Adele's rosemary, same as the artwork in my room.

Adele lifted her arms, gripping an athame in one hand. She drew a sigil in the air then clasped the blade in front of her chest. She spoke in that same resonant tone. "In the name of light and compassion, we commit this sacred space. We banish from this circle all energy that would do us harm."

I felt the absolute *rush* of the ley lines outside the station, passing through the circle, unshielded, unlimited. I opened myself to their power. Lightning danced along my spine, my lungs filled with possibilities, and light in a million colors sprang against the backs of my eyelids. It was stronger than I'd ever experienced. The ley lines here were a *lot*. Powerful. I felt an ache in my knees, and my stomach turned.

I wanted to stop, take stock, and start over. But I didn't want to lose the goodwill I'd finally earned, nor did I want to give Howland—who supervised us as if he knew what he was watching—any reason to find fault with our work.

I forced my shoulders to relax and kept going.

We intoned together, our voices and hands weaving the incantation: "We invoke Time, and Space, and Energy, and Dimension. Open the gate."

The Guardians of Dimension flooded my mind, a cacophony of the unintelligible. Unknowable incantations of their own.

I centered my focus, breathed past the fear, and extended the ferret in outstretched hands. We repeated the incantation twice more, as one.

The decking vibrated until my toes tingled.

Howland shouted in triumph; an outburst quickly shushed by the technicians.

When the vibrations steadied, we spoke again. "Take our offering and make fast this gateway. Leave travelers unharried in their passage. Banish from the conduit all energy that would do them harm."

A swirling circle of darkness opened in the center of our circle, a miniature of the wormhole we were here to create. It bent the light and stretched sound. The ferret's muscles twitched as it tried to escape my grasp.

As we repeated the line twice more, oily green and purple hands—hands with too many fingers—pulled their way out of the miniature void before me, as if they would crawl out entirely. But they only stretched and extended, trailing an impossible number of wrists and elbows, to reach the ferret I offered. Their fingers brushed mine, and I felt numbing ice and feathers and razor blades, as it gripped the ferret by the neck. The creature's white fur dissolved into that glistening, otherly color before the arms slipped back into the gate and the blackness folded in upon itself until gone.

I could feel its echo, larger. Outside the station, and in my soul.

The technicians got to work.

"Wormhole is stable, probe deployed." A steady ping repeated itself as the probe's signal came back.

The energy in the circle fluctuated. Not good. I was here to complete the coven, not disrupt it. I started humming, one of the goofy pop songs I'd heard on the shuttle's blown-out speakers on my way to the station. The energy hiccupped, but the fluctuation ceased. Our connection came back stronger than before. Georgie joined in my humming. We were too far apart at our respective corners to reach each other, but sharing the power *felt* like Georgie taking my hand and squeezing.

"Probe entering wormhole."

My hand stung, numb and hot all at once. I tried to ignore it. If we could hold this wormhole, Howland would have to back off for a while. One hour on earned us twelve hours off.

An organized flight control crew could move a lot of freighters through in an hour, especially with a gate as big as these ley lines supported. But traffic control was the station's problem. Our coven's only job was to open the gate and keep it safe.

"Strong signal in tunnel. Time to exit twenty seconds."

The longest twenty seconds of my life.

"Probe is through. Calculating position."

The tone that sounded from the console was not a happy one. "Position unknown. Wormhole did not open to the SevAlpha system, Administrator."

Another console chimed and a strained voice said, "Proximity alert. Vessel approaching the probe."

They wouldn't shush Howland now. "Bring that probe back. Shut it down!"

"Recalling probe, sir."

Another unhappy tone. The voice that read its report was no happier. "Signal lost. Probe destroyed."

"Shut it down!" The administrator was beside himself. "Before that vessel enters!"

Adele muttered under her breath, an incantation having nothing to do with their time in the circle. Then she moved the athame in what amounted to a spiritual shrug, and we spoke as one. "We release our invocation of Dimension, and Energy, and Space, and Time—"

"Shut it down!" Howland was still shouting. I could hear a shuffle as the techs blocked him from reaching a console.

"Close the gate. Go in peace. Thank you for your energy."

"No! Don't thank them! It opened in the wrong place!"

The vibration in the decking ebbed. The silence it left behind was startling. But we weren't done yet.

"Leave this circle cleansed and pure, awash in light."

We each thanked the corners and released our calls, struggling to remain calm as the second administrator's vitriol intensified.

We exchanged looks with each other. No one said anything, but I knew. I hadn't been ready for a convergence of ley lines like this. I should have stopped. Shouldn't have been so eager to prove myself.

W E HAD a few minutes to calm down as the technicians ran over their data and tried to sort out what had happened.

But I knew. I'd screwed up.

I overshot. I called past the local wormhole and summoned the Guardians from... well. Elsewhere. And based on the angry red patch on my hand where they'd touched me, not anywhere I wanted to make contact with again.

Also, whatever space that wormhole had opened into was somewhere unexplored, and somewhere very well defended. That might fascinate someone else. Not me.

I just wanted to open the nice, boring shipping lane. Didn't want to keep all these ships waiting any longer, as Howland kept pointing out.

Someone touched my shoulder and I jumped, but Adele's hand was gentle.

"You're all right, Lotti. I couldn't even hold through the invocation my first time here. Ended up in bed with a migraine from the power overflow."

Sam leaned against my other side. He signed, "I threw up my first time."

"First time's always hard. I passed out." Even now, Georgie's brown skin was looking a little gray.

"That's why we wanted a test run." Adele squeezed my shoulder. "It would have been weird if you'd nailed it."

Hand in hand, we returned to the circle.

Adele ignored Howland entirely. She closed her eyes and said, "Breathe, my sisters."

Then we made our calls again.

Forewarned, I was more deliberate as I drew energy from the

ley lines. This time, as the hands took my second ferret, I felt only prickles coursing up my back. Regulated, controlled. I had it.

"Probe approaching exit in fifteen seconds."

No one moved. I could hear Georgie and Sam to either side of me, breathing in that way we do when we wish breathing wasn't so loud.

"Probe readings back. Vector confirmed."

A collective sigh of relief. Someone outside my periphery actually cheered. There was self-conscious laughter followed by eager applause.

Howland shouted to be heard above it. "We have an hour. Get those ships moving."

"Hour minus the twenty minutes of the first calling," someone reminded him.

His growl of assent was formless and promised trouble.

A T THE end of the hour, Howland stalked off without a word. Adele stopped me outside the circle and extended a hand.

I took it. Her hands were cool, and I could feel her bones and tendons as she curled her fingers through mine.

"Welcome to Coven TAOS-9, Lotti."

Georgie and Sam rushed us, and I found myself the filling in a four-witch truffle. They smelled of lavender and mint and cheap strawberry lip gloss.

Georgie extracted me from the hug, the others unfolding to follow, Sam's hands on my shoulders and Adele leading the way back to the lounge.

Twelve hours of rest before we had to deal with Howland again. We shared a meal and then, before I collapsed on my bunk, I recorded a vid to send home. I'd promised "all the details" to my younger brother. Hopefully soon, I'd be sending home the money for his top surgery, too. Didn't need much, living on a station, room and board part of my union contract. Eventually, sure, I'd want to save up for a place of my own. Get the hell away from commerce-obsessed jerks like Howland. But I could put off my own comfort long enough to see my brother get the life he wanted.

Those twelve hours passed like tissue over flame. Gone. Zip. Georgie was waiting at my door when I finally dragged myself from sleep to answer the chime.

"That couldn't have been eight hours," I said of what felt like a nap at best.

"Eight and a half. Adele and Sam are fending off Howland, but we'd better get to it."

I grumbled, already zipping up my uniform.

Georgie and I came out of the habitat corridor just in time to see Adele snatch Howland's pocket watch and shake it under his nose.

She was really growing on me.

Howland cringed, turning his head and spotting our approach. He straightened up, tugged his vest hem to restore his supposed dignity, and put on his worst face. "Vessels are in position, ladies. I want you to hold that gate for three hours this time."

One of the technicians spun on their stool. "Sir—"

"You can't ask that." Georgie looked to Adele. "He can't ask that."

"He's invoking a stars-burned tally based on contract signature dates." Adele's face was flushed beneath those freckles. She looked at me, gripping that pocket watch with white knuckles. "Says we owe him two hours for every day since Lotti signed the contract."

I felt sick. "I signed that two weeks ago!"

Howland looked smug. "Well, then you'd better be thankful I don't ask you to work a fourteen-hour calling. Three hours. Now."

"I'm calling our union rep as soon as we're through here."

"Go ahead. But I should warn you, we've had trouble getting calls out these days. Communications are very dense with all these ship captains needing to update their schedules."

We were an enormous coil of rage as we entered the circle.

That wouldn't be good for the calling.

Georgie turned to me. "Two weeks ago?"

"Yeah." I was miserable. Could he enforce that? I had no idea, but no way he wouldn't try, all the while limiting our communication bandwidth so we couldn't invoke a defense. "Two hours a day for fourteen days. Twenty-eight hours."

"No, I mean. If Howland contracted you fourteen days ago…" They looked at Adele.

Adele was an inferno, though her face had paled in a way that had nothing to do with the stark lighting of the chamber.

Her mouth barely opened, yet the words rang in my ears. "Kelly wasn't even sick yet."

We all looked at Howland, who made a circular gesture with one hand: the universal sign for "let's get moving."

He couldn't see the way our auras shifted. We took our places.

Georgie, with their candle and herbs, called for Water and Energy.

Adele called for Time and Earth. Beside her green candle, she placed Howland's pocket watch.

Sam bowed his head, calling silently for Space and Air.

I lit my candle and watched the cabinet top carry off the silk-wrapped gold bangle.

Howland was so busy watching us to make sure we didn't so much as frown in his direction that he almost missed what Adele had done.

But he couldn't resist the urge to fidget with that watch of his, and finally, as the salt began to cascade down, he spotted it in the center of our circle chamber, glinting yellow gold against all that white light.

"How dare you!" He surged up the steps into the circle before any of the technicians could stop him.

We had called our protected space. We had summoned the Guardians of Dimension to trade life essence for passage.

But I had not selected a ferret.

Howland crossed this sacrosanct chamber, his boot heels clacking ugly against the glass floor. Intent on retrieving his watch, snatching back his pride.

The hands and all their fingers appeared, searching the space in between my corner and their breach into our world. They found him. Their fingers crimped around his upper arms as his face puckered in surprise and, after a moment, in realization.

All those wrists, all those elbows, coiled around him. Even knowing how their touch burned, I could find no sympathy for his cries, which had gone from indignant coughing to terrified pleas for help.

Our voices intoned, radiant with the energy that infused us.

"Take our offering and make fast this gateway. Leave travelers unharried in their passage. Banish from the conduit all energy that would do them harm."

Screeching, Howland melded into the chromatic oil slick before vanishing entirely.

The Guardians had accepted our offering. Their gateway collapsed, and the viewport beyond our circle filled with the sight of a wormhole.

I could see the auras of shock rippling off the station techs. But commerce has a way of leaving other matters to settle later. They got to work, confirming what I already knew: we'd formed a stable wormhole along precisely the right vector.

With a sacrifice as big as Howland, we probably *could* have held it for fourteen hours.

But we didn't.

We kept that gate open for exactly sixty minutes.

The Obstacle Bargainer's Lorica

RASHA ABDULHADI

dear elusive enduring disappointment
dear always sought attempt at escape
dear invader dear interloper
dear trickster cheat of time and heat and muscle
dear wrung out cloth of all my salt
dear refusal of ease, dear poison in meal most lovingly made
habibit baba, katkootit baba, death of dear baba
my dear denier of dresses and dance
dear everything i would amputate
dear what i can never let go of, put down, or quit
dearly beloved commander of first and final allegiance
dear thief of evening who eats the morning in argument
dear dawn swallower dear gravity trap
dear lies with the truth by omission of love or boundaries
dear end of me and of my friends
dear weapon used against myself only
dear mutant anger, dear rotten spoiled decomposing desire
dear choking, racking speechless sobs
dear roadblock dear obstacle dear brake dear killswitch
dear doe and buck wrecked on separate roads

dear sweetness at sunset all alone
dear closeness of exactly what is most far
dear foolish waste
my dear hoarder, dear imperial trove of stolen stories
dear delicious indulgence dear sadist dear siren
dear terrible terrorific awesome and awe-striking adviser
dear always plotting
dear quadruple crosser
dear persuader of malady
dear subclinical risk dear it runs in the family
dear fever breaking the will
dear wilderness dance dear loss clarifying fidelity
dear forgery of deeper meaning
dear healing howl
dear elsewhere imaginary
dear loses by refusing to play
dear stuck dear sucking vacuum void
dear estrangering reply to every kind word
my dear darling who slumbers solely in insomnia
who brings quiet thundering in reliably as the tide

cover me forever from every threat that is not you.

EXTERIOR

MERCEDES ACOSTA

Hello, creature of conjure. You've lived alone in darkness and solitude for a long time. Ever since shadows enclosed around the exterior, you've survived by sticking to the light. Ritual cleansing in the morning, protection circles at your windows and door in the evening. And never be caught in the exterior at night.

Outside your house is the exterior: an unknowable darkness that vacillates between a dusky twilight, a charcoal grey and a deep, inky black. You've lived the way your isolated, surviving community taught you: conduct all business in this profane land during those precious hours of twilight, and be safe inside with your collected herbs and salts and the door locked when the night is at its darkest hour. But every night, you hear the wind howl. You hear singing. You see lights. The darkness wants you. To dance with it. To listen for it. To scream within it.

Surrender to it.

There is a secret between you and this darkness, something you did not long after you were all forced inside by the unholy shadows, away from the exterior. The shadows know, and every night as you blow out the candle in your locked window you remember what it is. You feel like the blackness outside is laughing at you, begging you to laugh along with it.

One day, you are irresistibly infatuated. You are consumed with need. You draw a line through the circle of black salt, smudge out the protection sigils on your doorstep.

And you walk into the EXTERIOR.

EXTERIOR is a horror adventure game about leaving your lonely domicile to investigate something you feel in the night, for 1-4 people. It can be played solo. It runs on a diceless, mathless, GM-less system and requires only a deck of standard playing cards and a few hours to play. Character creation is minimal. You may fill in the base details of your NAME, your APPEARANCE, and your SPIRITUALITY. Then, you will choose your

SECRET—a shame between you and the cloying darkness of the skies

TRINKET—a magical something you carry to protect you

DWELLING—you secure abode

DARKNESS—the dark mass that sings to you

CALL—the temptation to succumb to it

CONJURE—your magic to fend off the inevitable...

For a time.

And so begins your journey. You will have seven encounters with the darkness before you MAKE IT OUT or are LOST FOREVER. Players may choose to enter the darkness together, as hesitant neighbors, or might wish to wander alone. Be warned: all are lost within the same writhing, spiraling abyss. As happens with many spiritual encounters, your escape will depend on luck.

Record your character's traits, and how your actions affect yourself, the group, and the darkness.

SOME NOTES FOR PLAYING:

Many of the prompts for your items, dwellings, and such are flexible. A beaded accessory can include a traditional Catholic rosary, Buddhist prayer beads, and so forth. A ramshackle dwelling can be a straw and mud domicile, a crumbling apartment, a makeshift lean-to. Secure does not mean comfortable. Feel free to find ways to incorporate your own experiences into the prompt. Remember that a loss or injury (to yourself or something else) need not be physical.

The secrets your character hide may include violence, blood, and hatred. While your character is entirely up to you, check in with other players to make sure you're not including content that will make the game unpleasant for them, including things like murder, abuse, sexual assault, and kidnapping. **The Open Door** and **X Card** safety tools for tabletop roleplay games are very easy to research and implement. It's valuable to have a quick talk before your session to establish what kind of content and how much detail surrounding it is okay with your fellow players.

Players with physical disabilities are encouraged to include these in their character creation if they'd like. Your darkness may have a paved path that is accessible for wheelchairs, walkers, and canes. Characters with limited vision may utilize guide animals, and incorporate that animal as a second item if they wish. This means that the third encounter may or may not remove this aid from the character—this is completely up to the player's discretion. Deaf characters can communicate in different ways, and their method of communication may aid or impede your interactions. This game is meant for all. Adding or changing around mechanics to suit your unique experience as a disabled person is more than welcome, and as a cane user with hearing loss myself I welcome these.

Remember: the *exterior* is the antagonist, not a creature or single, individual spirit. You are free to build your own terror in the darkness, or to use existing knowledge of spirituality in the world that manifests in the horror you experience. You may choose to represent popular haunted locations in existing folklore, and you may choose to base a session off a legend, horror movie, or any other source of inspiration. **However**, the lore, accessories, and beliefs of cultures outside your own are not playthings and should not be used to create a session. Likewise, ritual cleansing, magic, and 'witchcraft' that is from a culture or religion you have not been respectfully invited to partake in is wholly inappropriate, and you must respect all lineages of practice even if it means you personally aren't allowed access to them. I reject any and all sessions of this game that see players crossing cultural boundaries, and if I see you doing it, you will find I am a more immediate problem for you than any dark night.

AVOID:
- Sacred/closed locations or culture specific locations, like Uluru in Australia, or burial cenotes in Mexico
- The practice of closed religions you're not a part of including (but not limited to) Kemeticism, Lukumí (Santeria), vodun (voodoo), and certain brands of espiritismo
- Indigenous beliefs of groups you were not *raised connected* with. Reconnecting Indigenous people should err on the side of caution.
- The deities/spirits/practices of complex religions that you are not a part of. Religions that are frequently abused in this manner in media include Hinduism and Shintoism.

Just be respectful. "Homage" and "honoring the culture" is rarely the compliment you think it is.

Play well.

T HE STANDARD playing card deck with full suites of Clubs, Hearts, Spades, and Diamonds is needed. To start: remove all Queens, Kings, and Jacks from the deck. Place them aside. You will use them at the end of your experience. If the deck has Jokers, remove them. You will not use them.

Shuffle the deck. Place the deck within reach of all wanderers. With each encounter, you will draw a card from the deck. The suit will prompt your reactions to the encounter.

HEARTS

You allow vulnerability to take over. Anxiety, guilt, anger—you wear your heart on your sleeve for a moment. What does this reveal about you and your secret to the others?

SPADES

You do something foolish. Fear or upset drives you—you act without thinking and dig deeper into the grime. Who have you hurt? (This can include yourself, other players, or the spirits, and the hurt need not be physical.)

DIAMONDS

You allow yourself to be fooled. You can't trust your senses— you're deceived by the sparkle. What do you lose as a result?

CLUBS

You try to fight your way out. Sometimes a needle is more effective than a club, however—and as a result, you pay for your violence. How are you rebuked by the darkness?

YOUR SECRET IS:
- A ritual knife in the dark
- A meeting with an old spirit
- Shadow work you do in silence
- Faith you've broken
- A promise you've reneged on
- An ancestor you disrespected
- An ultimate shame

ALL ARE DEADLY.

YOUR ITEM IS:
- A beaded accessory
- A pouch round your neck
- A medallion icon
- A coffin nail
- A special liquid
- A comforting cloth
- A rock or crystal

ALL ARE POTENT.

YOUR DWELLING IS:
- Ramshackle
- Tidy
- Old
- Warm
- Empty
- Sturdy
- Remote

ALL ARE SECURE.

YOUR DARKNESS IS:
- An ancient sky
- A silent sinkhole
- A dense planet
- A tired field
- A vast lake
- A lively wood
- A hungry ravine

ALL ARE WATCHING.

YOUR CALL IS:
- Whistles
- Lights
- Tugging
- Screams
- Singing
- Figures moving
- Whispers

ALL ARE ENTICING.

YOUR CONJURE IS:
- Far-reaching and earth-based
- Desirous and light-based
- Frightening and shadow-based
- Awe-inspiring and blood-based
- Malignant and light-based
- Unusual and shadow-based
- Indifferent and color-based

ALL ARE DANGEROUS.

You exit the house. You are now in the EXTERIOR.

The first encounter: the darkness has swallowed you. Immediately, it's warmer. The only sources of light are the waning moon and your guttering candle, your flickering torch light. You look back and your house seems so far away. The single lit candle in the window feels like a wistful goodbye. As if it knows you likely won't be back. Your home is far away, and that light is all that's left moving in it.

As you watch, the light goes out.

Draw a card. React accordingly. Evaluate your actions.

And move deeper into the exterior.

The second encounter: you can feel it all around. They say seeing is believing, though you see nothing in the darkness. You only feel that cold brush across your neck, the ringing of your ears, the hairs on your arms raising in alarm. It's testing your mettle, seeing if you're worth its time. The shadows are awake. You call upon your practice for protection—how do you push back the shadows?

Draw a card. React accordingly. Evaluate your actions.

And move deeper into the exterior.

The third encounter: The cloying darkness is pressing in on you, filling your nose and throat. It's much like suffocating. Your salt-tossing and chanting have protected you so far, but this feels worse. You reach for your item, ready to comfort yourself with its presence—and it's gone. Something has taken it from you.

Draw a card. React accordingly. Evaluate your actions.

And move deeper into the exterior.

THE FOURTH ENCOUNTER: As you stumble along, you meet another. It could be a shimmering spirit, it could be the player to your left. You are uncertain. You are frightened. You have to act fast, because this could be a threat or an aid. Your actions impact the player to your left.

Draw a card. React accordingly. Evaluate your actions.

And move deeper into the exterior.

THE FIFTH ENCOUNTER: You meet yet another, and it's no neighbor of yours. This is a person from your past, a remnant of the secret you keep close to your chest, and they're here to remind you. To hurt you. To punish you. And if there are others around to witness, so much the better.

Draw a card. React accordingly. Evaluate your actions.

And move deeper into the exterior.

THE SIXTH ENCOUNTER: You find something is chasing you. Not just your guilt or your fear. You begin moving farther away, because whatever it is, you do not want it closer to you. But you still hear its footsteps, it crashing through the underbrush, and again you feel a cold shiver along your neck. You don't know what it is. You don't know what it is. You don't know what it is.

Use your conjure to protect you.

Draw a card. React accordingly. Evaluate your actions.

It is the player to your right.

Move deeper into the exterior.

THE SEVENTH ENCOUNTER: You're deep in the darkness now. It is oppressive, the atmosphere choking you. Your guilt weighs you down to the ground, and your fear makes every movement shaky. And as you move along, you are alone. Just you and the shadows. But before you, something takes shape. A person? An ally? It radiates peace. It's holding something out to you. Something just for you. It is your item that you lost previously, and through the fright you feel a bit of relief. You reach out to grab it.

And something grabs you back.

IT'S TIME TO ESCAPE

Take the removed JACKS, KINGS, and QUEENS. Shuffle them. Draw a card, but do not look at it yet.

Describe your attempt to escape from the EXTERIOR:

Once you have narrated using your _____ conjure to escape the _____ darkness, ignoring the _____ call, and returning to your _____ home with your comforting item _____ and your deadly secret...

Look at your card.

QUEEN: You have succeeded. Return to your house. Things to ask as you leave:
- Who or what did I lose?
- Has this experience shaken my spiritual beliefs and practice?
- Have I forgiven myself of my secret? Have others?

WHAT DID THE EXTERIOR WANT FROM ME?

KING: You have failed. The darkness swallows you whole. Things to ask as the shadow closes around you:
- Who will miss me now that I'm gone?
- Why didn't my spiritual beliefs (or lack thereof) save me?
- Is this punishment for my secret? Do I deserve it?

WHAT WILL BECOME OF MY SPIRIT?

JACK: You get out…but something follows you home. Describe it. Things to ask as you live with a shadow at your back:
- What did I bring back?
- How can I protect myself from this?
- Is there something I must do with my secret to make it go away?

WILL THIS THING PULL ME BACK INTO THE EXTERIOR?

GAME DESIGNER MERCEDES ACOSTA ON *LOS ARBOLES*, THE GAME
THAT INSPIRED *EXTERIOR:*

Behind my house is almost 40 acres of woods. By day they
are quiet enough, and I have wandered in there at length. We
often see hawks, coyotes, possums, raccoons, skunks, deer, birds
of all kinds, and the occasional woodchuck back there. By night,
something changes and they shift and dance. One time, I heard
voices come from them at 9 PM on a summer night, and I was
worried because it sounded like the neighbor boys who often
played in there. My mother and I know well enough to avoid the
woods at night, and my father respects us enough to agree.

I almost went into the woods that night to retrieve the
Martinez boys. My mother called their house as I paced up and
down the blue painted fence, listening to the boys singing and
laughing, and as I was about to cross it and enter the woods,
she called to me sharply. When I returned to the back porch
she informed me that Mrs. Martinez said both the boys were at
home and had been all evening.

The next morning we repainted the fence and sprinkled
the ground with rue and mint.

The woods have not shifted for me since, but that's likely
because I no longer go near them at night.

Hold the Dark

ALLIE BUSTION

HOLD THE DARK is a GMless storytelling game meant for 1-7 players, recommended for 3. To play, you will need the following:

- one Rider-Waite tarot deck of your choice and a means of interpreting it, such as the included guide book
- two or more six-sided dice, preferably two for each player

You may also want the following when playing in person:

- a way to record information about your character and interpretations of the cards
- a large flat surface for playing in person
- a tablecloth, candles, and music, for setting the mood

If playing online and distant, consider the following:

- a service or app that allows everyone to pull from the same deck, such at Roll20 or playingcards.io

About Playing the Other

If you pull inspiration from real world cultures that aren't
your own to craft the fiction of your game, remember that you
are appropriating real people and their beliefs. Be mindful in
your approach and consider not pulling from real world cultures.

Hold the Dark

You are one of a Coven, chosen by a mystical Benefactor
and imbued with their power. Your Benefactor has told you
that something is coming within seven Days, a Darkness that
will change all that you know. At the end of those seven days,
an Uncertain Future will come to pass and test the Coven. Will
the Dark change you and your Coven or will it reveal who you
truly are? Will you See a different path or try to Change what is
before you? Will you stand with your Benefactor or will you step
boldly into a future you can't know?

Setting Up Play

Separate your deck into the major and minor arcana, then
shuffle separately. Draw three cards from the major arcana.

- The first is your **Benefactor**, drawn face up.
- The second is the **Darkness**, drawn face up.
- The third is the **Uncertain Future**, drawn face down.

Interpret these cards as a group to determine the world your
characters exist within.

To create your character, draw one card from the major
arcana and two from the minor arcana. All will be face up.

- The first card, from the major arcana, is always
  interpreted in its upright position and represents **You** as
  a member of the Coven and your abilities as imbued by
  your Benefactor.
- The second card, from the minor arcana, represents
  your **Backstory** and secrets you may be hiding from the
  Coven
- The third card, from the minor arcana, shows your
  Drives, what pushes you ever forward.

Interpret these cards either separately or as a group and, moving clockwise, announce yourself to the **Coven** and describe your character. Work together to build bonds, connections, and possible conflicts that add to the fiction you will build together.

Finally, each character has a **Memento** and a **Memory**. A **Memento** is a small physical token, like a tiny glass octopus or a stub of a chewed pencil, given at some point in life and treasured ever since. A **Memory** is a specific event that the character holds dear and doesn't want to forget, like a first date or a revelatory walk through a snowy city. Either can be a secret from characters but should be known to players. Move around the table clockwise, with the last person from the previous round beginning this one, and tell the meanings of your **Memento** and **Memory**.

Lastly, draw seven cards from the minor arcana, all face down. These represent the seven Days before the Uncertain Future comes to pass. One will be turned over at the start of each Day.

Playing The Game

At the beginning of each **Day**, flip over one of the seven face down cards of the minor arcana. Interpret the card as a group. Moving clockwise starting with the last person of the previous **Day**, declare an attempted action for the day and describe it. After each description, players can decide to help each other or further their own goals. Continue until everyone has chosen an action. If the actions of another player are more in line with what your character would do, you may choose to aid them instead. In the same order, roll your dice as necessary and determine the outcome of your actions using the rules below. x

On the beginning of the Fifth **Day**, the **Uncertain Future(s)** reveal themselves to the Coven. Interpret each one as a group. Players can decide for themselves if one of these futures is more attractive than the power of their **Benefactor**, and can try to make that future a reality or prevent it. This can be expressed through play, discussed as a group before proceeding with the next **Day**, or both. Optionally, turns progress counter-clockwise beginning on the Fifth Day.

After the Seventh Day, go around the group once more to
create an Epilogue and closure for your characters. How have
the events of the past seven days changed you? Where do you
stand within the Uncertain Future? Have you or others left the
Coven and how has that affected you? Has your Benefactor
taken back their gifts, changed them, or awarded you with
more? Do you now serve a new power or are you on your own?
Do you have any regrets of what came to pass? Together, build
the story of what comes next for your characters and the world.

Changing The Future

As one with immense potential power, you have far more
sway over the world than the average person. Each **Day**, you
take an action that could alter the **Uncertain Future**. You may
work together or you may find yourself isolated and alone.

When attempting to change what may or has already come to
pass, *roll 2d6* and choose any of the following modifiers:

- When you draw upon the power of your **Memento** or
  Memory or play to your **Backstory** or **Drives**, *add +1
  to your roll*.
- When another chooses to help you in your task, *add +1 to
  your roll*. They may still choose to make their own actions
  and you are not obligated to help them in return.
- When the entire surviving **Coven** combines their actions
  to work together, the *roll always succeeds as if you rolled 10+*.
  If any one person at the table disagrees, this cannot be
  used.
- When you sacrifice your **Memento**, *add +3 to your roll*
  and either *pass it to another of the Coven* or *let it fall* to be lost
  to Darkness. You may no longer use your **Drives** and are
  no longer connected to them.
- When you sacrifice your **Memory**, *add +3 to your roll*. You
  may no longer use your **Backstory**.
- When you sacrifice **Yourself**, *give +5 to the roll of another
  in the Coven*. Narrate your final moments before giving

yourself to the **Darkness**. While you are no longer a part of the **Coven**, *your actions still reverberate and you still contribute to the continuing story* by interpreting cards, providing more information about a **Memento** left behind, and possibly by now serving the **Uncertain Future**.

On a roll of 10+, things go as expected. Choose two of the following:

- Help comes from an unexpected source. What is it?
- You find something you thought was lost. How has it changed in the **Darkness**, if at all? How has your connection to it changed?
- Your **Benefactor** communicates with you. How do they contact you and what is said?
- You hear whispers of what may come. What makes it so encouraging?

On a roll of 7-9, you succeed, but suffer consequences from your actions. Choose one each from the 10+ and 6- lists.

On a roll of 6-, you fail, and must bear the full weight of the fallout from what you have tried to do. Choose two of the following:

- Something or someone becomes lost to you. What was it and who do you blame?
- You lose sight of what you believe in. What or who has made you stray from your Drives?
- Something or someone stands firmly in your way. Who are they and why must they stop you?
- You hear whispers of what may come. What makes it so terrifying?

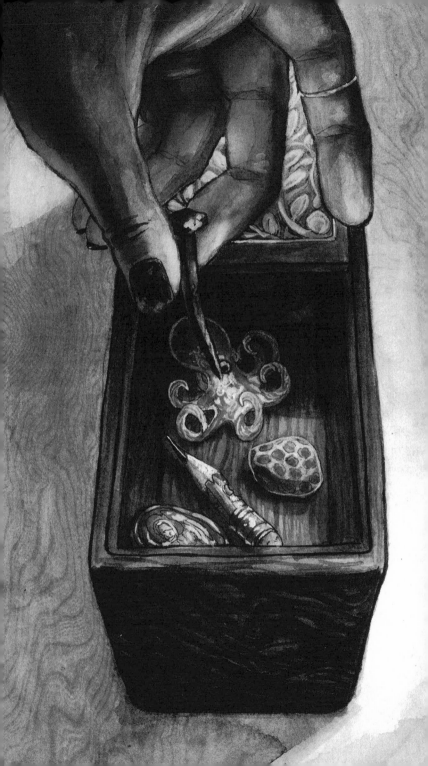

Seeing The Future

On any given day before the fifth, you may attempt to see what the future holds for you instead of trying to Change it. When peering into the **Uncertain Future**, *roll 2d6*. No one and nothing may assist on this roll.

On a roll of 10+, you are able to see things clearly. Flip over one of the **Uncertain Future** cards and interpret it as a group. How do you communicate what you've seen to the rest of the **Coven**?

On a roll of 7-9, you see other possibilities and it's unclear which is most likely to come to pass. Draw another **Uncertain Future** card from the major arcana face up and flip one other **Uncertain Future** card. Interpret them as a group. How do you communicate what you've seen to the rest of the **Coven**?

On a roll of 6-, you see nothing and learn nothing, save that you may have opened the door to something sinister. Draw another **Uncertain Future** card from the major arcana face down. What do you decide to tell the rest of the **Coven**?

If you run out of cards from the major arcana, you can no longer attempt to see the future and cannot attempt this move from that point forward.

Narrowing the Futures

In play, there can be an overwhelming number of Uncertain Futures before the characters. Before moving around the group for the Fifth Day, turn over any drawn Uncertain Futures. Interpret each one as a group and, if there are too many cards in play, eliminate those that no one wants to pursue. From the Fifth Day onward, other Uncertain Futures can be drawn and interpreted by the group but, if no one at the table wishes to pursue them, they can be discarded immediately.

Ending the Game

After the end of the seventh **Day**, go around the group once more. Describe what has become of your character once the **Uncertain Future** came to pass. Did you hold back the Darkness or has it overwhelmed you? How have you changed? Are you still part of the Coven? Are you still imbued with the power of their Benefactor or do you serve someone new? Do you serve anyone? Do you regret anything that happened?

Using An Oracle Deck

While an oracle deck can be used to play *Hold the Dark*, it changes how some parts of the game function. Here are a few suggestions for playing with an oracle deck:

- When dealing cards for players, don't split the deck. Rather, have each player draw their 3 cards at once and pass to the next player, who shuffles the deck before drawing theirs.
- Limit the number of players at the table to three.
- Limit the number of times each character can attempt to See the Future to three.
- Shuffle any lost Drives, Mementos, or Memories back into the main deck. There is no way to recover them.

ACKNOWLEDGMENTS

DAVE RING

L IKE THE BEST RITUALS, an anthology such as this one involves the contributions both sacred and profane of so many lovely people.

First and foremost, I'm grateful to the authors of these incredible stories and poems, the artists behind these fantastic comics and images, and the designers behind these evocative games. What a pleasure it is to abound in work that thrills and torments and beguiles in equal measure.

Robin, thanks for your witchy enthusiasm and our wickedly lovely cover. This trio will haunt my dreams.

Matt, what a sorceror you are! I can't even imagine this project without the indelible mark of your work upon it. Your illustrations and creative partnership have been such a vital part of this project.

Thanks to Marianne for convincing me to put together an entirely *different* anthology before later proposing the idea that would then become *Unfettered Hexes*.

Thanks to RawPaw for our rad altar cloths, Riddle's Tea Shoppe for our delightful BE GAY CAST SPELLS enamel pins, and Campaign Coins for our oracle coins.

Thanks to everyone at the pub for their zeal and support, both of me as an individual and this project in particular. You don't know how much you mean to me.

Thanks to everyone who has supported Neon Hemlock Press, either through online communities or the Kickstarter or by asking your bookstores and libraries to stock us. We wouldn't be here without you.

And always always always, thanks to B. For putting the spark to Neon Hemlock's literary candle venture and all the other ways you make my life infinitesimally more magical.

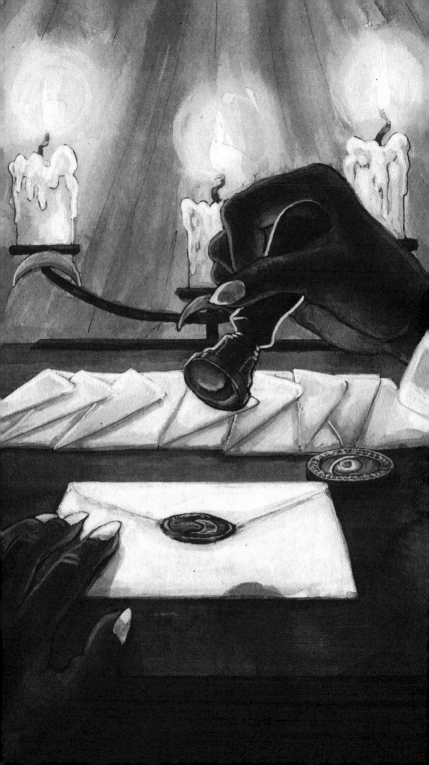

ABOUT THE AUTHORS

Rasha Abdulhadi is a queer Palestinian Southerner who grew up between Damascus, Syria and rural Georgia and cut their teeth organizing on the southsides of Chicago and Atlanta. Their work is anthologized in *Essential Voices: a COVID-19 Anthology, Halal if You Hear Me, Super Stoked,* and *Luminescent Threads: Connections to Octavia Butler.* Rasha is a member of Justice for Muslims Collective, the Radius of Arab American Writers, and Alternate ROOTS. They are the author of the chapbook *who is owed springtime.*

Mercedes Acosta is a US-based Cuban writer, comic artist, and illustrator. Mercedes uses she/her or he/him pronouns. Mercedes primarily enjoys creating/editing media for younger audiences, and also works on horror, fantasy, and tabletop games for all ages. Find Mercedes on Twitter at @bignoseagenda.

Sharang Biswas is an award-winning game designer, writer, and artist. He has won IndieCade and IGDN awards for his games and has showcased interactive works at numerous galleries, museums, and festivals. His nonfiction writing has appeared in *Eurogamer, Unwinnable, First Person Scholar, Kill Screen,* and more, while his fiction has appeared or is forthcoming in *Lightspeed, Fantasy, Baffling,* and *Sub-Q.* He is the co-editor of *Strange Lusts / Strange Loves: An Anthology of Erotic Interactive Fiction,* coming soon from *Strange Horizons.*

C.B. Blanchard is a writer and occasional poet from England. They write fantasy, horror, and horror-tinged fantasy for the gays and the goths. They have work coming out in *The Magazine of Fantasy and Science Fiction* as well as the *Xenocultivars* anthology from Speculatively Queer. When not writing, they enjoy being a goth cliche. You can keep up with them on Twitter @BridhC.

Die Booth likes wild beaches and exploring dark places. When not writing, he DJs at Chester's best* goth club. You can read his award-winning stories in places like *LampLight Magazine, The Fiction Desk* and *34 Orchard* and his books, including his latest collection *Making Friends (and Other Fictions)* are available online. He's currently working on a collection of spooky stories with transgender protagonists. You can find out more about his writing at diebooth.wordpress.com or say hi on Twitter @diebooth *AND ONLY.

Allie Bustion of Mad Pierrot Games is a Black femme non-binary narrative designer and writer with a lot of hobbies and interests, ranging from pop-punk to pro wrestling to mechanical keyboards. Beyond writing and making up stories about people that may or may not exist, they also play video games and analyze pop culture. You know, as a treat. Find them on Twitter @madpierrot, making games at madpierrot.itch.io, or generally at madpierrot.design.

Priya Chand is a California transplant living in the Midwest. Her work is inspired by a background in biology and analytics, and has previously appeared in magazines including *Analog SF* and *Clarkesworld*. Find her online at priyachandwrites.wordpress.com.

Tania Chen is a queer Chinese-Mexican writer currently living in Mexico City. When not writing they love reading, feeding strays and watching horror films. They are a graduate of the Clarion West Novella Bootcamp workshop of 2021 and can be found on twitter @archistratego shitposting for the greater good.

H.A. Clarke was born in the Leo season of 1997 and has since lived in various places around the American Midwest. They have been published at *Tor.com, Portland Review, Dream Pop Press, PRISM international, Eidolon, Gothic Nature Journal,* and *Chaleur Magazine.* They were a 2019 Lambda Literary Retreat Fellow and a Pushcart nominee. Their debut novel, *The Scapegracers,* was released in 2020 via Erewhon Books. He's a graduate of the Masters in the Program of Humanities at the University of Chicago, where she studied queerness, labor, and monstrosity.

Kel Coleman is an author, editor, and stay-at-home mom. Their fiction has appeared in *FIYAH, Anathema: Spec from the Margins, Apparition Lit,* and others. They are also an Assistant Editor for *Diabolical Plots.* Though Kel is a Marylander at heart, their new home is in the Philadelphia suburbs with their husband, tiny human, and stuffed dragon named Pen. You can find them at kelcoleman.com and on Twitter at @kcolemanwrites.

Amelia Fisher writes queer stories about bad decisions and body horror from their plant-filled Pacific Northwest apartment. She is not a cooperating fungal hivemind in a vaguely humanoid substrate, but no one's perfect. Find them on twitter at @hubristicfool.

Grace P. Fong ("Fictograph") is a Hugo-nominated and Ignyte-winning illustrator who makes covers for speculative fiction magazines and anthologies. Recent clients include *Strange Horizons, Silk & Steel,* and *Glitter + Ashes.* She has also worked as a programmer and narrative designer on video and trading card games.

Craig Laurance Gidney writes both contemporary and genre fiction. He is the author of the collections *Sea, Swallow Me & Other Stories* (Lethe Press, 2008) and *Skin Deep Magic* (Rebel Satori Press, 2014), Bereft (Tiny Satchel Press, 2013) and *A Spectral Hue* (Word Horde, 2019).

Robin Ha is a Korean American cartoonist based in Washington, DC. She is the author of *Cook Korean!: A Comic Book With Recipes*, and *Almost American Girl: An Illustrated Memoir.* @RobinHaART.

Caleb Hosalla is a graphic illustrator currently based in Manila. Follow Caleb on Twitter at @porkironandwine.

Diana Hurlburt is a librarian, writer, and terminal Floridian in upstate New York. Selections of her short work can be found at *Memoir Mixtapes*, *Luna Station Quarterly*, and *Phoebe*, and in the forthcoming Worldweaver Press collection *Clockwork, Curses, and Coal.* Her Shakespearean cyborg remix, *Nothing Natural*, is part of Sword & Kettle Press's mini-chapbook series. She's often on Twitter @menshevixen chattering about horses and heavy metal.

Ruth Joffre is the author of the story collection *Night Beast*. Her work has appeared or is forthcoming in *Kenyon Review*, *Lightspeed*, *Gulf Coast*, *The Masters Review*, *Pleiades*, *The Florida Review Online*, *Flash Fiction Online*, *Wigleaf*, and the anthologies *Best Microfiction 2021* and *Evergreen: Grim Tales & Verses from the Gloomy Northwest*. She lives in Seattle, where she serves as Prose Writer-in-Residence at Hugo House.

Tamara Jerée's short fiction is featured or forthcoming in *Strange Horizons*, *FIYAH*, *Anathema: Spec from the Margins*, *Beneath Ceaseless Skies*, and others. Their poetry and nonfiction have been nominated for the Ignyte Award. They live in the Midwest where they dream of one day motorcycling across the US.

Marianne Kirby writes about bodies both real and imagined. She authored *Dust Bath Revival* and its sequel *Hogtown Market;* she co-authored *Lessons from the Fatosphere: Quit Dieting and Declare a Truce with Your Body*. A long-time writer, editor, and activist, Marianne has been published by the *Guardian*, *xoJane, the Daily Dot, Bitch Magazine, Time*, and others. She has appeared on tv and radio programs ranging from the Dr. Phil Show to Radio New Zealand. She tweets at @TheRotund.

L. D. Lewis is an award-winning SF/F writer and editor, and publisher at Fireside Fiction. She serves as a founding creator, Art Director, and Project Manager for the World Fantasy Award-winning and Hugo Award-nominated FIYAH Literary Magazine. She also serves as the founding Director of FIYAHCON, chair of the 2021 Nebula Conference, and Awards Manager for the Lambda Literary Foundation. She acquires novellas for Tor.com and researches for the LeVar Burton Reads podcast. She is the author of A Ruin of Shadows (Dancing Star Press, 2018) and her published short fiction and poetry includes appearances in *FIYAH, PodCastle, Strange Horizons, Anathema: Spec from the Margins,* and *Lightspeed,* among others. She lives in Georgia, on perpetual deadline, with her coffee habit, two kittens, and an impressive Funko Pop! collection. Tweet her @ ellethevillain.

Danny Lore is from Bronx and Harlem. They write across the SFF spectrum, with short stories in *Fireside, FIYAH, Nightlight* and more, as well as comics from Marvel, DC, Vault and more. Their goal in their stories is to tie the element of SFF that they grew up with and love with the environments and people that reflect the world around them. When not writing, it's all video games, gunpla, doll collecting and makeup for them!

Hanna A. Nirav is a writer who has been telling stories all her life. She is an avid reader, hardcore casual gamer and loves food. As a Malay-Indian Malaysian, she has always toed the line between circles and is now ready to break some rules. You can find her on Twitter @hanstilltweets or check out her work at hanmuses.wordpress.com.

Chelsea Obodoechina is a sociology graduate student and teacher's assistant who writes fantasy and science-fiction in her free time. Her short fiction has appeared in *Analog* and *Cast of Wonders.* She lives in Montreal with her family. You can find her at @c_obodoechina on Twitter.

Frances P (@JellfshFortuna) is a mixed black freelance illustrator based in Ontario. Check out more of her work on twitter and support her on Patreon.

Suzan Palumbo Originally from Trinidad and Tobago, Suzan Palumbo is a writer, editor, ESL teacher, the Ignyte Awards Finalist Liaison, and a member of the Hugo nominated FIYAHCON team. She is also a former associate editor of "Shimmer" magazine. Her work has been published in *The Deadlands*, *The Dark Magazine*, *Weird Horror*, *PseudoPod*, *Fireside Fiction Quarterly*, PseudoPod and various other venues. When she isn't writing, she can be found sketching, listening to new wave or wandering her local misty forests as a goth. Find her complete bibliography at suzanpalumbo.wordpress.com.

Almah LaVon Rice is a Kentucky-born monster based in Pittsburgh. Her speculative fiction has appeared or is forthcoming in *A Quiet Afternoon 2*, *Black from the Future: A Collection of Black Speculative Writing*, and Harvard Divinity School's *Peripheries Journal*. Visit her extrasolar biome at AlmahLaVonRice.com or on Instagram at @agentsubrosa.

Nicasio Reed is a writer, poet, and essayist whose work has appeared in venues such as *Strange Horizons*, *Lightspeed*, *Uncanny Magazine*, *Fireside*, and *Shimmer*. He lives in Tagaytay, in the Philippines, with four dogs, some family, and the occasional uninvited monitor lizard. Find him at nicasioreed.com, or on Twitter @nicasioreed.

Jordan Shiveley is the author of the Dread Singles (@ hottestsingles) twitter account and the upcoming book, HOT SINGLES IN YOUR AREA. Their work has also been seen in a variety of short fiction collections and tabletop roleplaying games as well as podcasts such as Old Gods of Appalachia and Caring Into the Void. They live and work in Minneapolis, Minnesota with a cat and partner both of whom often merge in ways unimaginable to the human mind. www.jordanshiveley.com.

Imani Sims is a Queer Black Femme with plant witch tendencies and a love for craft cocktails. Her obsession with Afrofuturism is reflected in the number of books on her shelves and the number of times she's read Octavia Butler's entire collection of work. Imani spent 20 years as a poet, eventually got published [a few times] and now spends most of her awake hours reading and walking her tiny french bulldog. She is committed to integrating art, ritual, and the Black aesthetic into experiences designed for QTBIPOC folk and exercises that muscle as Executive Director of RADAR Productions in the Bay Area.

Matt Spencer is a queer & trans illustrator from southeast Michigan. His work appears in *The Chromatic Fates Tarot*, and he is currently illustrating the upcoming book of fairytales *Alia Terra: Stories from the Dragon Realm*. When not creating artwork for freelance clients or collaborative tarot decks, Matt spends his time playing (or drawing) Dungeons and Dragons characters, and making slow but steady progress on his own Courtly Beasts Tarot. Matt welcomes any excuse to combine his deep love for watercolor, moody palettes, and fantasy, sci-fi & horror (especially when queer characters are involved). Find him at mspencerillustration.com or @mspencerdraws on twitter.

Cecilia Tan is "simply one of the most important writers, editors, and innovators in contemporary American erotic literature" for her pioneering efforts to combine erotica with fantasy and science fiction, according to Susie Bright. Her short stories have appeared in *Ms. Magazine, Asimov's Science Fiction, Absolute Magnitude, Strange Horizons,* and tons of other places. Her upcoming series from Tor Books, The Vanished Chronicles, will be published Real Soon Now. She is a biracial bigender bisexual who loves tea and cats and lives with her partner in the Boston area. Find out more at www.ceciliatan.com.

R J Theodore (she/her) writes about magic-infused technologies, first contact events, and bioluminescing landscapes. Her short fiction has appeared in *MetaStellar* and the *Glitter + Ashes* anthology, with work forthcoming in *Fireside Magazine* and *Lightspeed*. She lives in New England, haunted by her childhood cat. Find more information at rjtheodore.com.

Elizabeth Twist (she/her) writes fiction about liminal experiences, Dionysian ecstasies, and the barely disguised contents of her uncanny biography. Her work has appeared in *NonBinary Review, AE: The Canadian Science Fiction Review,* and *The Fiends in the Furrows II*, among other venues. She lives in Hamilton, Ontario, a city as haunted by gentrification as it is by actual ghosts. She shares a cranky but grand elder house with two dogs, two cats, and a wonderful human person. Find her on Twitter @elizabethtwist.

About the Editor

dave ring is an editor and writer of speculative fiction living in Washington, DC. He is the author of the novella, *The Hidden Ones* (2021, Rebel Satori Press), and his short fiction has been featured in publications including *Fireside Fiction, Podcastle,* and *Lackington's.*

He is the publisher and managing editor of Neon Hemlock Press, and the co-editor of *Baffling Magazine.* dave's previous anthologies include *Broken Metropolis: Queer Tales of a City That Never Was* (Mason Jar Press, 2018) and the Lambda, Locus and Ignyte Award nominated *Glitter + Ashes: Queer Tales of a World That Wouldn't Die* (Neon Hemlock, 2020).

dave was a Lambda Literary Fellow in 2013 and chair of the OutWrite LGBTQ Book Festival from 2015-2020. Find him online at www.dave-ring.com or @slickhop on Twitter.

About the Press

Neon Hemlock is a Washington, DC-based small press publishing speculative fiction, rad zines, and queer chapbooks. We punctuate our titles with oracle decks, occult ephemera, and literary candles. Learn more about us at www.neonhemlock.com and on Twitter at @neonhemlock.